A VOYAGE TOWARD VENGEANCE

BY

JULE A. MILLER

This is a work of fiction. The characters and events in this story are inventions of the author and do not depict any real persons or events. Any resemblance to actual people or incidents is entirely coincidental. Any similarity between the fictional island of St. James and any of the Leeward Islands is stricly coincidental.

Cover Design by Rob Johnson. www.robjohnsondesigns.com
Book Design and Editing by Linda Scantlebury, www.we-edit.com

Printed in the United States of America
First Edition

ISBN 0-939837-61-7

Published by Paradise Cay Publications
P. O. Box 29
Arcata, CA 95518-0029
800-736-4509
707-822-9163 Fax
paracay@humboldt1.com
www.paracay.com

For Heide
and for the daughters:
Robin and Gail and Christianna

ABOUT THE AUTHOR

Jule Miller grew up in Milford, Connecticut, was educated and worked as an engineer, and sailed for many years on Long Island Sound. In 1991 he moved to Nevis, where with his wife Heide he lives, writes, and sails on the Caribbean Sea.

ACKNOWLEDGMENTS

There are many people I would like to thank for their contributions to this book. First, I would like to thank Linda Scantlebury, my editor—although it would be more accurate to call me her author—for all her support in bringing this book to finished form. I also want to thank Matt Morehouse for his help and support and Lin Pardey for reviewing the manuscript and making several very useful suggestions.

I would like to acknowledge the contributions of all the people with whom I sailed, raced, and simply messed about in boats over the years. In particular, I must mention my father and his friend Walt Thomas, who let a small boy steer his 38-foot cruiser and taught him how to tie a bowline. I must also mention that elite group of offshore racers, the Sea Oal Crew.

My wife Heide deserves special thanks for all those years of help and support with my writing career, as in all else. And finally, I would like to thank Robin I. Miller for proofreading the original manuscript, and for teaching me everything I know about the relationships between fathers and daughters.

As long as greed, lust, and island-sprinkled seas exist,
there will be piracy.

PROLOGUE

As **Caribbean squalls go, it was nothing much:** just a bubble of rain blown across the sea by the trade winds. Other than a few fickle puffs on the leading edge, it contained no winds of its own, just the fresh force-five breeze that pushed it along. It had been born as Antigua cooled in the night and in turn had cooled the moisture-laden wind that blew in from the Atlantic. If the squall had not overtaken the yacht as it entered the narrows between St. Kitts and Nevis at three-thirty that morning, no one ever would have known of its short existence. There are few things more secret, or more useless, than rain that falls into the sea at night.

It caught the 38-foot sloop at precisely the worst time. A half-hour earlier and this small blob of rain scurrying across the sea in the otherwise clear night would have been past by the time the boat reached tiny Booby Island in the entrance to the narrows; a half-hour later and she would have been safely through before the squall overtook her.

Like most tropical squalls, it had a prelude, a line of scattered oversize drops followed by a short ominous silence before the main downpour arrived with a roar. It instantly drenched the blue polo shirt, red Breton fisherman's shorts, and leather deck shoes worn by the man at the wheel, but he ignored the discomfort, switched off the autopilot, and took over the steering. Running with a squall is usually a mistake unless one wants to stay in it for as long as possible, but in these confined waters, he had no other choice but to hold his course until it had passed. It shouldn't be very long. He had been through a great many squalls, most of them worse than this one.

He was a pleasant-looking man, with sunbleached brown hair and a cowlick, now plastered against his head by the rain, and an unremarkable face that was still freckled and boyish in his thirties. He had the powerful body and sloping shoulders of a weight lifter; the only fault in his appearance was that his long, narrow head belonged on a much taller, more willowy body. Perched on his muscular neck, it gave him the somewhat ridiculous look of an inverted funnel when seen from the back. But when seen from the front, especially now as he ignored the chill of his wet clothes and concentrated on steering, there was nothing ridiculous about him at all.

Booby Island had been just forward of the port bow and about a quarter mile off when the squall hit. As long as he held this course, he should easily clear it and the Cow Rocks that just broke the surface a mile farther down the center of the channel. He turned his head to the left, trying to see the high, loaf-shaped islet through the wall of rain, but the 20-knot wind blew his eyes full of water so he could now see nothing at all. He turned away from the wind, wiping his eyes with the fingertips of one hand while steering with the other, and peered to starboard, hoping for a glimpse of the lights on St. Kitts. But all he could see was wet blackness.

Booby was shaped like a miniature Gibraltar, and if it weren't for this damned rain, he would be able to see the white of the breakers on its seaward side and its loom against the lights of Nevis. It must be abeam by now. He held his left wrist close to his face, squinted at his stainless and gold Rolex, and noted the time. He would hold this course for another twenty minutes. By then they should be safely past the Cow Rocks and he could harden up toward Charlestown, the capital of Nevis. Hopefully the squall would have passed by then. They were making almost seven knots and should certainly do a mile every twenty minutes or so. He wasn't very good at numbers, but he knew it.

From long practice he kept the boat sailing at a constant angle to the wind as he searched for something to confirm his mental estimate of his position. But the featureless black wall of rain that surrounded the boat disoriented him enough so he did not notice the wind backing to the north as it funneled through the narrow channel between the mountainous islands. He glanced down at the red-lit compass in the wheel pedestal once or twice as he steered by the feel of the boat and of the wind on his neck, but the combination of the rain in his eyes and the water running over its dome obscured it enough so its message made no impression on him.

The pounding of the rain on the deck above her head woke the woman in the tiny aft cabin that the yacht's designer had squeezed in beside the engine compartment and the cockpit foot well. It contained only a narrow bunk with four built-in drawers beneath it, a shelf above, and a small hanging locker at its foot. There was just enough room to stand beside the bunk and open the door that separated the cabin from the galley at the after end of the salon. It wasn't much bigger than a couple of phone booths and was made even more confining by being finished in dark, rubbed teak. But she wasn't claustrophobic—just the opposite. She loved this tiny, luxurious den that she told herself was the same size as the captain's cabin in the sloop of war that had been Nelson's first command. Then too, it may have appealed subconsciously to her nesting urge, one of the few feminine instincts she possessed.

She listened to the roar of the rain for a few seconds before she turned on the reading lamp over the bunk and checked her watch. It, too, was a man's Rolex and it read twenty to four. They must be almost to Nevis by now. She might as well get up. She hated making landfall in the mid watch, but it couldn't be helped. They had been late leaving Antigua, and then they'd had to sail halfway to Barbuda. On top of it, he had dragged out his part of the business so it had taken much longer than it should have.

She climbed out of the bunk, pulled on Bermuda shorts and a polo shirt with the Royal Jamaica Yacht Club's logo on the pocket, stepped into her salt-stained deck shoes, and went forward into the galley, craving a cup of coffee from the thermos that stood in a rack over the sink. But she knew that if she drank it, she wouldn't be able to get back to sleep.

A passport, a stack of traveler's checks, a red velvet jewelry box, and four credit cards lay on the chart table opposite the galley. She picked up the passport and studied the photo for a moment, then looked at her watch again. She wanted to be ashore when the banks opened, so there wouldn't be all that much time to sleep, anyway.

The drumming of the rain on the deck seemed to be letting up, so she decided to have her mug of coffee and stand in the hatch, under the dodger, sipping it until the squall passed. As she poured, there was a loud crash from somewhere beneath her feet and the boat suddenly stopped, throwing her forward so her back hit the waist-high bulkhead that separated the galley from the salon. Before she could recover, the boat swerved violently to port as it rolled steeply to starboard; she fell across the cabin, to land against the base of the navigator's desk, her shirt soaked with coffee. If it had been hot she would have been scalded, but it only felt warm and sticky as she sat on the cabin sole recovering from the shock of the collision and waiting for the pain in her back to subside. Then, with a series of awful grinding noises, the boat began to move again, and she yelled, "What the hell did you hit?"

At that instant the squall passed as abruptly as it had arrived. "I think we hit the edge of those rocks in the middle of the channel. The Cow Rocks. We're over them now, though. We're moving." He didn't have to tell her that. The boat had come upright again and the expensive-sounding noises under her feet had stopped. "How is it down there?"

"Let me check." She lifted the hatch in the cabin sole. Water was pouring into the bilge sump from somewhere forward, and, as she watched, it came over the edge of the varnished teak and holly sole in a gin-clear sheet. "We're sinking, that's how it is down here. You must have torn the keel loose."

"Oh shit. What should I do?"

She forgot both the clammy shirt and the pain in her back as she pulled herself to her feet at the nav station and studied the chart taped to the desk. "Steer about two sixty. There's deep water off Horse Shoe Point. It's less

than two miles to where it drops off. Keep her going as long as you can."
The jewelry box, passport, traveler's checks, and credit cards had slid against
the instrument panel at the side of the desk. She swept everything but the
jewelry box into a plastic garbage bag and added a rock from a locker under
the sink as she called, "What's the depth-sounder say?"

"Twenty-six feet. She feels logy."

"She ought to. The water's over my shoes already." She squeezed the
air out of the bag, knotted it, then splashed into the head and pulled a
hidden catch so the medicine chest swung out of the bulkhead as a unit.
From the space behind it, she took a yellow plastic scram bag and sloshed
back into the main cabin carrying it. The water seemed to be climbing
more slowly, but she knew that was only because it now had a bigger area to
fill. They were sinking, all right. Time to get her stuff and get out of here.

The water was almost to her knees by the time she waded out of the aft
cabin with her purse and the canvas tote bag in which she kept her knitting.
She stuffed the jewelry box, her purse, and the scram bag into the knitting
tote and zipped it closed, then stood at the bottom of the ladder and glanced
around the cabin one last time before carrying it and the garbage bag up
into the cockpit.

Now he was steering with his eyes glued to the compass. "She needs
more sail if we're going to make it. What about the engine?"

"The batteries must be just about under." She unfurled the jib all the
way, then trimmed the mainsail. The digital depth-sounder read thirty-two
feet, then thirty-six, then fifty-eight, finally jumping to ninety-two feet before going blank at the same instant the lights in the other instruments
went out. She studied the angle of the lights on Nevis and the dark loom of
Horse Shoe Point at the tip of St. Kitts before saying, "I think we made it. It
drops off to seventeen fathoms right along here." She slung the plastic bag
with the rock overboard ahead of the boat and, carrying her knitting bag,
went forward to inflate the life raft. "Keep her going as long as you can."

"Jesus, Alice, I'm sorry."

"That's all right. It was time for a trip to the States and a new boat,
anyway."

CHAPTER ONE

It began for **William Tecumseh Stroud** on the Tuesday after Columbus Day, even though he was sure that nothing would ever begin for him again. For over a year now, he had felt like one of those spring-driven toys that slows as its spring unwinds, until, with one or two last jerks, everything stops in midmotion. That morning his main spring tension seemed very close to zero.

His father had hung the name on him. It was certainly not one you wanted to sign, even today, on a motel registration card in a small town in Georgia. But Stroud lived in a town on the coast of Connecticut and never went to Georgia—or anyplace else, for that matter. The old man had been a nineteenth-century history buff who admired Sherman, because, as he often said, "That bastard really knew how to get the job done." Getting the job done, in its broadest sense, had been the most important thing in life to the older Stroud, and he had blessed his son with the same compulsion. But now there was nothing important, and certainly nothing of interest, for his son to do, so the blessing had become a curse.

Bill Stroud washed, dressed, made his bed, and went downstairs to the kitchen, where he prepared a simple breakfast of orange juice, an English muffin, and a cup of the instant coffee he found barely palatable; then he placed the single aspirin he took every morning beside his plate. If he were to just put the pill bottle on the table, he would be about halfway through the meal when he'd begin to wonder if he had already taken one or not. He had the same problem with the Lanoxin pill he took every evening, which was also for the atrial fibrillation that ran in his family and had been diagnosed in him a few months before. His father had started on the same medication to slow and smooth his heart rate at about the same age Bill Stroud had. Somewhere in the family's DNA there was a timer that made their heart-rate controllers crap out when they reached their early sixties, much like the timers that make Detroit cars need expensive repairs as soon as the warrantee expires.

He wondered why he even bothered to take the damn pills.

Well, it would all stop with him, the last of the Strouds. The old man was dead now, and so were Stroud's mother and wife and son and daughter and son-in-law, most of them buried in the family plot his father had bought when his mother died.

Yet even with death all around him, Bill Stroud still clung to life and took his damn pills. Again he asked himself why. "Because you have to get the job done, shithead. Besides, you don't have anything better to do." He said it aloud. That was one of the few good things about living alone: You could talk to yourself out loud, and there was no one around to know just how far gone you were. Unless, of course, you slipped up and did it in public, something he caught himself doing more and more often. "Old age is a bitch."

Every morning he made himself do something, some routine task, because he felt guilty if he sat around all day and read or dozed in front of the TV. No matter what he did, he felt useless, and he knew that he would never have the opportunity to do anything of any real value again. But even if they were just the repetitive tasks that life required and were of absolutely no value to anyone or anything other than himself, he felt compelled to accomplish something each day. He might go to the bank or the post office, or shop for groceries, or wash or service his car. But he always did something. His pension check and Social Security were both directly deposited to his savings account, and the bank had a service that would have allowed him to pay his bills by phone, but he didn't use it. First, because it cost fifteen bucks a month, and second, because if he used the service, he would have even fewer places to go and things to do. This feeling of total uselessness was the very worst part of growing old.

On Saturday mornings he had what he called a G.I. party. He vacuumed the house, dusted the furniture, and cleaned the upstairs bathroom and the downstairs lavatory while he ran his laundry through the washer and dryer. It wasn't a very big house, just six rooms and a screen porch that now needed to be closed in for the winter. With a reasonably neat single man living alone, it didn't get very dirty.

When he had finished his breakfast and washed the dishes, he went upstairs and sat at his wife's desk to balance the checkbook and pay the bills. Liz had always taken care of their finances and had kept all the accounts on her computer, but he didn't use it. Every time he turned it on he felt lousy for a week. Everything that appeared on the monitor was a small part of a detailed picture of exactly how his wife's mind had worked: the neatness, precision, and occasional wry humor of it.

He studied the balance in his savings account and decided he had accumulated enough to pay for what was probably the last project he would ever do. He'd go to the post office and mail his bills, then go to the bank and transfer the money into his checking account. It wouldn't leave a whole lot in savings, but that was all right—he didn't have anything else to save for, anyway.

He was filing the bill stubs when the phone rang. "Hello Mr. Stroud. This is Nancy Newton at the Boat Works. I have some people here who are seriously interested in buying your boat. They're coming back this afternoon, and they'd like to see the sails and the outboard and the other gear."

He had owned the Ranger 26 since Dwight was fourteen and Nell eleven, but it hadn't been in the water for two years, ever since Liz got sick. They had cruised and raced it as a family and it was too loaded down with memories for him to ever sail it again.

"It's stored in my basement and it's all in pretty good shape. When are they coming?"

"After lunch. Can you make it by then?"

"Sure thing."

He made a list in his mind of where he must go that morning and shuffled the items into the most efficient order: post office, bank, Boat Works, and then the cemetery. His whole family, except his daughter Nell, were buried together, each under a similar simple stone set flush with the ground bearing their names and the dates of their births and deaths. But Liz, who had died almost a year before, had no stone yet, and Nell, who had been gone over three years now, had neither a stone nor a grave.

He went into the bathroom to shave. He only shaved every second or third day now, when it started to itch. But it didn't seem right to go to the cemetery without shaving.

When he was done he walked into his bedroom and stood studying the photos on his bed table for a minute. Propped against the studio photo of Dwight in his dress blues was a snapshot of Liz, Steve, and Nell he had found on the last roll of film in Liz's camera. It had been taken on a dock in Morehead City, North Carolina the day before Nell and Steve had sailed out into the Atlantic and disappeared. Stroud had left the negative at a camera shop to be enlarged, but he wouldn't pick it up today. If he did too much today, he wouldn't have anything to do to-morrow.

Alice Holbrook reached up through the hatch and put a cup of coffee and a pair of 7x50 binoculars on the bridge deck, then climbed into the cockpit carrying her knitting bag. Another perfect day in paradise. *Cinderella* and a half dozen other boats were at anchor in the little bay on the lee side of the high, lushly green, volcanic island. Alice loved the colors of the Caribbean: the dark green of the islands; the intense blue of the sea, accented by whitecaps and constantly changing in tone as cloud shadows blew across it; and the lighter, but equally intense, blue of the sky. Blue was her favorite color. Whenever she was con-sciously aware of blue, it reminded her of her father. He was the finest man she had ever known, and had always seemed like a huge blue cliff until he reached down, swung her up into his arms, and asked, "And how is the Princess Alice today? Are all of your royal subjects behaving as you wish them to? I guess they'd better."

Gordon was forward, preparing to varnish the teak grating that covered the glass of the forehatch. This was the only time of day he could work on teak in the Caribbean: after the dew had dried, but before the sun became so hot that the varnish hardened without adhering to the coats beneath it. Most people didn't varnish teak; they just let it weather and smoothed the surface with fine sandpaper every year or so. Only gold-platers with paid crews had varnished teak that required continual maintenance. Well, *Cinderella* was a gold-plater all right, and she had a paid crew. When Gordon finished with the teak, he could clean and wax the deckhouse. It was important to keep him busy.

She used the binoculars to study each of the other boats in the anchorage in turn. Two of the monohulls and a catamaran were charter boats, so she eliminated them immediately. The other cat was a sixty-footer that appeared to have at least eight people aboard. That left two monohulls about thirty-eight feet long. Both had their dinghies inflated and in the water, although the forward air chamber of one of them was flat, giving it the appearance of being half inserted into the transom of its old, gray, Morgan Out Island mother ship.

As she watched, a man climbed aft from the Morgan's center cockpit, looked over the transom, and called to someone. A deeply tanned woman wearing a string bikini came and joined him in conversation for a moment, then the two of them dragged the inflatable up onto the afterdeck and the man went below as the woman lifted the flaccid forward section, obviously trying to find the latest leak in the dozens of patches that covered it. Alice studied the woman through the glasses. There ought to be strictly enforced rules about who was permitted to wear string bikinis. The woman's body looked as worn out and flaccid as her dink. Dirtbaggers—nautical hobos bumming around the islands in a beat-up old boat.

The other boat might have potential, though. It was much newer, better cared for, and far better equipped. Two men were having breakfast under the sun awning in the cockpit; Alice put down the glasses, took a sip of coffee, and then began to knit as she watched them. If there were any women aboard, they must be sleeping late this morning. When the men finished their breakfast, one of them leaned over and kissed the other on the lips before they both disappeared from sight behind the cockpit coaming. She decided there were probably no women aboard.

Her knitting needles clicked as she decided that once Gordon's varnish was dry, they'd get under way. It was only a couple of hours to the next island. They were in no hurry. There were hundreds of anchorages and thousands of boats.

It was almost two when Stroud came up the stairs from the base-ment garage and put an unsealed business envelope on the kitchen counter under a mahogany sign that read, "Never, but never, ques-tion the captain's judgment." The people who had worked for him had given it to him at his retirement party. He was a manufacturing engineer and good at it, but nobody in Connecticut wanted any-thing to do with manufacturing or manufacturing engineers any more.

He warmed a can of clam chowder, toasted two slices of white bread, poured himself a glass of milk, and sat down to eat lunch and reread the two contracts he had signed that morning. The first was for a granite headstone with a bronze plaque similar to those on his parents' and son's graves. It would be inscribed with Liz's name and the dates of her birth and death. Beside it they would put his name—William T., not William Tecumseh—and the date of his birth. He wondered who would have the other date inscribed when the time came. He supposed he had a military funeral coming. The local VFW or American Legion would probably take care of that, although he belonged to neither. He had done his two years of active duty and four in the reserves, too late for Korea and too early for Viet Nam, but he had done them and had been honorably discharged.

He really ought to make a new will, though, if only so whoever came in here and found him would have some idea what to do. There wasn't a great deal of money, but the house was free and clear, and if he didn't have a will, some Connecticut probate judge would steal it all, if that bastard Browne didn't get to it first.

Steve had been a fine man, more of a son than a son-in-law to the Strouds, but he had detested his own parents and had been estranged from them for years. He had never said what caused the break, but although his father was a wealthy lawyer, Steve had worked his way through to a Ph.D. in biochemistry. At Liz's insistence, he had invited his parents to the wedding, where they had made it very obvious that their son was marrying far beneath them. Everything was beneath them: people who majored in science, Nell and her parents—everything except grabbing money any way they could and waving it in people's faces. The only time Steve had discussed them had been on the test sail of the Far Horizons 38 that he and Nell were going to take south for his sabbatical year. Steve had said, "You've met them, Dad. I don't think my mother has ever really heard a single word anyone has said to her in her whole life, and what is worse, she doesn't even have the decency to pretend she's listening. My father—well, my father's like an Apache; he thinks everyone else on earth is a trespasser, only here to steal property that belongs to him by divine right. There are two things you have to remember about my parents, Dad. The first is that they live in a world where the only things that exist are money and the hollow status that money buys. The other is that they are absolutely hopeless."

The elder Brownes had been particularly incensed that their son and daughter-in-law had made the Strouds the executors of their wills and even more incensed to discover that the wills had been drawn by the Yale Law School's most eminent expert on such matters, who was their son's next-door neighbor and good friend. Even Steve's father, a lawyer so crooked his own son didn't trust him, could not find a way to break it. "Fucking lawyers."

Nell and Steve had had $50,000 policies on each other with double-indemnity clauses and had made the Strouds the alternate beneficiaries without telling them. Browne had harassed and threatened them for three years while the insurance company waited for the kids to be declared legally dead. Those years with Liz dying of cancer weren't bad enough. There had to be a steady stream of registered letters from that asshole. Three months before, on the day the insurance company had finally paid off, Stroud had thought about going over there and burning the whole two hundred thousand bucks on the bastard's front lawn. But he hadn't. He stuck it in two savings accounts in two different banks. Why would anyone want blood money for a son who detested him? To get his mind off Browne, Bill went back to reading the cemetery contracts. The second was for a similar stone that would have "Steven B. Browne" and "Eleanor S. Browne" on it. It would give the dates of their births and the month and year of their deaths. No one knew the exact date they had died. Centered beneath the dates would be "Lost at Sea." The cemetery had no objection to the stone being placed on the empty graves.

When he had finished his lunch, he washed, dried, and put away the dishes. He really ought to do something this afternoon. The leaves were just about all off the trees; he should rake and bag them or hire someone to do it. It had rained all the week before, so the leaves were starting to rot into a sodden mess on the lawn and in the driveway. And the porch needed the screens replaced with the storm windows for the winter. There was plenty to do.

But, as he did most afternoons, he sat down in the recliner in the living room and alternately read and flipped through the channels on the TV. He was reading a new library book on the Battle of Savo Island, but nothing held his interest for very long. This afternoon he was lucky and dozed off for a while. At five-thirty he went into the kitchen and made himself an oversize bourbon old-fashioned in a water glass. If you only allowed yourself one drink a day, it might as well be a good one. He carried it and a plate of cheese and crackers back into the living room and sipped while he watched the news. The only time he felt any interest at all was when they showed a street in some Middle Eastern city filled with towel-heads screaming their hatred of the United States. Then he wished that someone would come in low and drop napalm on the whole damned bunch of them. When someone keeps screaming for a holy war, the charitable thing to do is give it to him—in spades. Lance Corporal Dwight Stroud, U.S.M.C., had been killed in an embassy bombing eighteen years before.

After Bill finished his drink and snacks, he went out on the front porch and brought in the newspaper. Then he made supper: a salad and a precooked entree he took out of the freezer and put into the microwave. He only looked at the label to read the oven settings. Everything tasted alike, anyway. He read the paper as he ate, and when he was done, he filled a bowl with ice cream, made a cup of tea, and finished his meal.

It was hard to believe that he had once been a bear for exercise. The year after Dwight was killed, he had run and finished the Boston Marathon. In those days his answer to stress or anxiety had been hard exercise; now it was ice cream. Back then he had thought that he could tough himself through anything. But he had discovered that even if he could tough his way through anything, he could not tough himself through everything. Eventually there was just too much.

He had weighed about 190 when he was running. Now he was about thirty pounds heavier, although he was so large-framed that other than a slight paunch, it hardly showed. He told himself he couldn't run because of his heart. This made him remember his Lanoxin pill and he took one, noting it on the pad he kept next to the bottle. If he didn't, before the evening was over he'd be trying to remember if he had taken the damn thing or not.

He had started to get the discomfort in his upper chest right after Liz got sick. It was caused by one chamber of his heart going into rapid, irregular contractions. He had silently ignored it until she was gone. It was a feeling of breathlessness combined with a large, trapped burp—

not painful, but unbelievably uncomfortable. The night the doctor had given them the worst possible news, he had tried to run seven miles and the atrial fibrillation—although he didn't know what it was then—had been very bad. Not like a heart attack or angina, not painful at all. It was just very unpleasant and very frightening, like being trapped in an airless box that was being carted off to some strange place. He was used to it now and understood it, and he was no longer frightened of the place where it might eventually take him, but it was still very uncomfortable. He imagined drowning was like that: not painful, just brutally uncomfortable.

"Oh, Nell . . ."

He could have walked. The doctor said he could walk as much as he wanted and even run, if he took it easy and didn't punish himself the way serious runners always do. But what was the point?

He knew he should do something. So he watched a John Wayne Western on the Classic Movie Channel, had a glass of milk and half a dozen cookies, then went to bed thinking that tomorrow would be just like today.

It began with another ending. He was eating breakfast when the Boat Works called to say they had a firm offer for his Ranger 26 and if it was acceptable he should come by and sign some papers. It wasn't as much as he had hoped, but it was close, and the storage bill he had been paying every month would finally end. Besides, just like everything, the gravestones had cost more than he had been originally quoted and had made a pretty big dent in his savings account. He had an IRA at a brokerage house into which he had rolled his 401K when he retired, but he hated to touch it and every time he did, he had to pay taxes on it. Selling the boat was a very good thing, but a very sad thing. It was just a different kind of funeral.

When Stroud came up from the garage at noon, he no longer owned a boat. He had owned boats since his parents had given him a sailing dinghy for his ninth birthday, and except while he was in college and the army and during the first few financially strapped years of marriage, he had always owned boats. The broker was holding the deposit; they would close on Friday, but his last boat now belonged to a young couple with twin girls about ten years old. Those kids had been just as happy and just as excited as his kids had been on the day he bought it. He wondered if a good boat somehow sensed the joy it brought to people.

They were even going to keep her name, *Terrible Twosome*, which he suspected had been what had attracted them to her in the first place.

As he put the bag of groceries and his camera shop purchases on the counter, he thought about getting another boat in the spring: something small and inexpensive that he could sail by himself—a Cape Dory Typhoon, perhaps. Or maybe a small powerboat for fishing. Something he could haul home on a trailer and store in the back yard. He still owned a mooring in the Ansantawae River that he had loaned to a friend. It would be a shame to give it up. He'd never get another one—the waiting list was years long now. Boats were a lot of work, but he had always loved the work. Maybe he should build another sailing dory like the one he had built with the kids when they were small. It would give him something to do, but it would probably bring back too many memories.

After lunch, he mounted the enlargements of that last photo of Liz, Nell, and Steve standing on a finger pier next to *Brownian Movement* in the frames he had bought that morning. He put one copy on the mantle in the living room and the other at the bottom of the stairs to take up on his next trip. Liz had driven down to North Carolina alone to see The Kids off—something he had always regretted—because he had been on some supposedly urgent business trip that he could not even remember now. Urgent. Six months later the company decided it had no more use for him or a dozen other older managers the bean-counters thought made too much money. By threatening to eliminate their retirement medical benefits, they had forced them to retire early. It had reduced the pension he would have received at sixty-five by 40 percent.

"*Brownian Movement.*" He said it aloud. He had never liked the name The Kids had chosen for their boat; he had teased Nell that it sounded too much like Bowel Movement. But she was a microbiologist and Steve was a professor of biochemistry and their name was Browne and they thought it was clever. Stroud didn't think puns wore well as boat names. But maybe he had liked it, after all. It had given him something to tease Nell about, and he had always enjoyed teasing Nell from the time she was a very beautiful and very serious little girl.

The Kids—he and Liz had always called them The Kids. "The Kids called, they want us for dinner on Sunday." Or, "Are The Kids going to crew for you in the Invitational next week?" The Kids had once been Nell and Dwight. Then the phrase had lain unused in their vocabularies until Nell met Steve and they became The Kids, although they were both in their thirties when they married.

He stood looking at the other photos on the mantle for a long time without saying, or even thinking, anything, then went out and brought in the mail. The box was stuffed with a couple of day's accumulation—he must have forgotten to bring it in again. On top of the heap was a registered mail notice for another threatening letter from Old Man Browne. He'd pick it up the next time he went by the post office and toss it, unopened, into the file with the others. He would have dearly loved to write "Go fuck yourself" across it and send it back, but Steve's lawyer friend had told him to ignore Browne and file and forget his letters. The bastard had no case and he knew it, but like most lawyers without a case, he expected to be paid handsomely just for being a pain in the ass.

Stroud certainly didn't want the insurance money or the rest of The Kid's estate and could not believe that anyone, even Steve's asshole father, could want that kind of money. He would probably leave everything to the Hospice where Liz had spent her last days. Or maybe split it between Hospice and the Yale School of Medicine where The Kids had worked. He really had to get a new will, though.

There were a couple of bills, the usual stack of third-class mail, and catalogs—*Ocean Navigator* and *Wooden Boat*. Between the two magazines there was a postcard from Fred and Doris Parker. Fred had worked with him for years and Doris had been Liz' best friend. "Hi. Just about to depart for a cruise on this beautiful windjammer. Bill, you ought to think about something like this. We'll get together and give you all the details when we get back. And don't forget Thanksgiving and Christmas. See you soon."

They always invited him to spend holidays with them, but he seldom accepted. He had always been opinionated, too opinionated. But now, when he could go weeks without any conversation except passing words with strangers, his opinions and the bitter anger behind many of them seemed to keep building within him. He was never very long with friends before something would come boiling out, some comment on the president, or the government, or some acquaintance, that, while it might be perfectly true, was so vehemently stated that it embarrassed everyone, and no one more than Bill Stroud himself. Then, for weeks afterwards, whenever he thought of it, he would dislike himself even more intensely than usual.

But Doris and Fred were good friends. After all the others had given up on him, they still kept trying. This would be the first in a stream of notes and cards Doris would send.

It was one of those oversized six-by-eight-inch postcards, and after he had read the message, he turned it over and looked at the photo. It showed a windjammer tied to the end of a dock at what the caption said was the Ginger Bay Marina in St. Thomas, U.S. Virgin Islands. Yachts ranging from thirty to fifty feet were tied in slips in the foreground. It was a very good photo taken on a very clear Caribbean day.

He warmed his soup and made his toast and while he ate, he studied the Ginger Bay Marina with the eye of someone who had been given his first boat for his ninth birthday. He knew he ought to close in the porch, or rake the leaves, or get in touch with the lawyer about a new will this afternoon, but he had accomplished a lot this morning. When the dishes were washed and put away, he sat down in front of the TV and while his eyes followed the parade of images across the screen, his mind remembered all the boats he had sailed on, worked on, raced, and owned.

He dozed off for a while and then woke with a start, not knowing if he had dreamed it, imagined it, or actually seen it.

He went into the kitchen and put the postcard from the Parkers on the counter directly under a fluorescent light and peered at it. Then he ran, he actually ran, up the stairs and searched through Liz's desk for the magnifying glass he knew was there.

A few minutes later he set the magnifier down next to the picture and slumped into a chair while he tried to catch his breath. His heart was fibrillating badly. Unless he was completely mistaken, the postcard showed the *Brownian Movement* tied up in a slip at the Ginger Bay Marina.

It took almost half an hour for his heart to begin to recover. When it did, he went outside and paced slowly back and forth in the fresh air of the screen porch for another half hour. Then he went back into the kitchen and again studied the photo with the magnifier.

Half an hour after that, he hurried into the camera shop again, put the postcard on the counter, and asked the man who waited on him, "How big can you blow this up?"

"The biggest paper I've got on hand is seventeen by twenty-two. I can order special stuff, but it will take a couple of days. If you go much bigger, it will start to get fuzzy." Then he pushed the postcard back toward Stroud. "I can't copy this, though. It's copyrighted."

"After I look at the blow-up you can destroy it. I just want to see something that I can't quite make out."

"I'm sorry, but I can't do it. These new copyright laws have penalties you wouldn't believe. Murderers don't get as much time."

"Jesus Christ, this goddamned country. I need to see the name on the transom of this boat, and this bracket here on the afterrail. I'm not going to sell the pictures to anyone."

"Doesn't matter. We could both be in big trouble if I copy it."

Stroud thought about it for a moment, then asked, "Okay, what do I need to do it myself?"

"Well, you'd need an enlarger, of course, and a developing setup. You're serious about buying a set-up just to enlarge one photo?"

"You bet."

"Well, I guess you could talk to them in Blinns; that's the computer place down the street. They do restorations of old photos and stuff like that. Maybe they can help you."

Blinns helped him. It seemed you could do things with a computer that were illegal with a camera. When he came home, Stroud had an enhanced computer printout that showed a Far Horizons 38 with *Cinderella, Monterey* CA, carved into a varnished teak trailboard mounted on the transom. Above it, the radio, LORAN and GPS antennae, the radar mast, and a wind-powered generator were supported by a stainless steel frame welded to the sternrail. He could not be absolutely sure it was the same one he had designed and had made for Steve—there could have been others like it—but it looked identical. *Brownian Movement's* bow had been toward the camera in the picture of Nell and Steve and Liz taken in Morehead City and they had obscured the sternrail, so he was working from a four-year-old memory of what it had looked like. Then he remembered the sketch he had drawn for the welding shop that made it.

He went upstairs and searched through his fat folder of things about boats that he thought he might need someday. There were specifications and sail plans of boats that had at one time or another interested him. There was an article on the mathematics of sailboat design written years before by a designer whose work Stroud admired. There was the owner's manual for a 1962 Evinrude outboard, an article about longships, a set of plans for the sailing dory, and all sorts of other things. But there was no sketch of *Brownian Movement's* sternrail bracket.

He spent the evening searching the house for other photos, finding several. Like most pictures of boats taken by those who sail in them, they were taken from either too close or too far away. But one of them showed Nell steering, and the part of the rail visible behind her appeared to be identical with the one in the blown-up postcard photo. The only other picture that might help, showed the boom with the mainsail hoisted. It reminded him that he had reworked the boom, rigging all the sail control lines inside the aluminum extrusion exactly as he had rigged *Terrible Twosome*'s. Nell had asked him to do it because she said it was the best setup she had ever seen. The cover was on the boom in the postcard photo, but if he could find the boat and get a look at the boom . . . .

This whole thing was nuts, the logical result of letting himself slide downhill, living like a hermit and refusing invitations from friends until they stopped calling. Crazy. He went out on the porch and paced for almost an hour. Totally nuts.

Eventually he went to bed and lay awake for most of what remained of the night, still wondering if he was losing his mind. It couldn't be Nell's boat. *Brownian Movement* had sailed out into the Atlantic almost four years before and had never been heard from again. *Cinderella* was just a sister ship.

But he couldn't let it go. Early the next morning he called the printing company in San Juan whose name was in the corner of the card. They weren't much help. When he finally reached someone who spoke English, he learned only that they used photos supplied by commercial photographers, and although the card he described had been part of a batch printed last summer, the photo could have been taken any time. If there was a record of who had taken it, the person he talked to was not about to look it up for him.

Over breakfast, he slowly studied all the pictures one more time, then turned to a new page of the pad where he kept his shopping list and recorded his medication, and drew a vertical line down its center. At the top of one column, after thinking about it for a moment, he wrote, "Nuts?" At the head of the other column he wrote, "Not nuts?"

He sipped his coffee while he studied the otherwise blank page. He needed more information; he could think of only one place to get it, and that was in a place he did not want to look. But there was no way out of it, so he finally went upstairs, lit up Liz's computer, and searched the program manager until he found a directory called *Brnmvmt* and read all of the files it contained. Besides the letters Liz had written to the company that had carried the hull insurance on *Brownian Movement*, there were also letters to the marina in Morehead City and to the city clerk. These asked if there was any record of an address for John and Alice Perkins, the couple Steve and Nell had met somewhere along the way south from Connecticut and with whom they had sailed out into the Atlantic. The only other letter in the file was, judging by the mail-merge list of over a hundred addresses, written to everyone named Perkins in coastal Delaware, Virginia, and North Carolina asking if they were related to, or knew, John and Alice. In the file cabinet, he found the folder where Liz had put the replies. The few she had received were all negative. She had never found out who the Perkins were.

He remembered talking about it. Liz only knew that they were a nice young couple who had previously sailed in the Caribbean and then come north and worked for a while. But they had missed the sailing life and were heading south again hoping to get jobs in the charter business. It had made sense to take a couple of experienced sailors along on the 1600-mile offshore leg from North Carolina to St. Thomas. They appeared to have been drifters though decent people, but they too had no graves and no markers. He considered putting a small stone with their names on it in the Stroud family plot. Decent people shouldn't just disappear as if they had never existed.

He focused on the monitor again and called up the directory where Liz had stored everything about probating The Kid's wills and closing their other affairs. There was a large subdirectory as well as a paper file of correspondence about the Coast Guard inquiry, but neither provided any evidence that this whole snipe hunt wasn't just a grief-driven hallucination.

In a half dozen other subdirectories designed by Liz's logical mind were stored all the other information about the whole mess. He read it all and then called up the spreadsheet file labeled Ledger in which she had kept a record of all of the financial transactions. He stared at the meticulously laid out spreadsheet and thought, *If it is a grief-driven hallucination, this is only making it worse.* Right now Liz was here in the room with him, talking to him through the records in her computer, but he dreaded the feeling of loneliness he knew would crash down on him when he turned it off.

When he had gone line by line through all the financial transactions, he sat back, clasped his hands behind his head, and stared at the empty wall above the monitor. It was all just like Liz—complete unto itself with not a single loose end.

Yet there had been a loose end, some dog that hadn't barked in the night, but damned if he could think what it was. He had to skim all the files twice more and then go through the ledger line by line again before he found it.

Liz had written a letter to American Express just before a routine chest x-ray had found the spot on her lung and she had been sucked down that whirlpool of biopsies, operations, chemotherapy, radiation, and experimental treatments that had ended at the Hospice.

Dear Sirs:

Enclosed are certified copies of receipts for one hundred (100) fifty dollar ($50 U.S.) traveler's checks issued by your company. These were sold to my daughter, Eleanor S. Browne, and my son-in-law Steven G. Browne on the date shown prior to their departure in the yacht Brownian Movement from Morehead City, South Carolina. Also enclosed are certified copies of their Death Certificates and documents from the U.S. Coast Guard Court of Inquiry that concluded their vessel is overdue and presumed lost.

I am the executrix of their estate. Please inform me of what steps are necessary to obtain a refund.

But there was no record of a refund anywhere. It would have taken more than terminal cancer to make Liz fail to enter a five-thousand-dollar check in her ledger.

He found the reason in a letter from American Express in a folder labeled Action. Dated about the time they had started the final, hopeless
round of experimental chemo, it said the checks in question had been cashed
in Charleston, South Carolina eight days after *Brownian Movement* left
Morehead City and six weeks before the yacht had been reported overdue. The writer apologized for taking so long to reply, giving the standard corporate excuse that they were converting their computer system.

Nell would never have landed in Charleston without calling them.
And why would she buy traveler's checks in Morehead City, give her
mother the receipts, and then cash them all in Charleston two weeks
later?

He walked around the house for a while, picking up things and
putting them down, until he finally went into the bedroom and
changed into a pair of running shoes and an old gray sweatsuit he
hadn't worn in years. He had to think, and he'd never been able to
think, really think, while sitting still. That was why he now spent so
much time sitting still.

He walked almost six miles. When he came home he showered
and then, starting with the photos, reviewed everything he had found.
Should he take it to the Coast Guard? If he did, he was sure they
wouldn't take it seriously. No one took seriously anything that was
said by any private citizen over sixty years old any more. Besides, he
was not sure that he took it seriously himself.

He should just forget it. He had neither the money nor the cred-
ibility, even with himself, to chase this wild goose. It was just a Far
Horizons 38 that looked like Nell's boat. Hell, they had probably
built a lot of them. He checked the photo that showed Nell's boat
with its mainsail up. The number on the sail below the logo was 21,
so they had built at least twenty-one of them, perhaps many more.

But the order in which the wind-powered generator, the radar,
and the other antennae were mounted on *Cinderella's* sternrail was
exactly as he remembered mounting *Brownian Movement's*. And there
were the traveler's checks. They made no sense at all, unless The

Kids had had a problem that required expensive repairs and had put back into Charleston. But then they would surely have called.

Maybe they had. Maybe he had been away at the time; perhaps Liz hadn't told him or he had forgotten. He went back upstairs and pulled a cardboard carton filled with trip reports and expense accounts from the bottom of Dwight's closet. He had kept them because he half expected some bean-counter to come after him claiming he still owed the company money. He checked the dates of his travel records against the date the checks had been cashed: He had been home. If Nell had called with a problem, he would have talked to her and would certainly remember it. Even if he hadn't, Liz would have and wouldn't have tried for a refund.

He stared for a long time at the blow-up of the postcard, then went back to the original. The sail cover and dodger were both blue—a lighter blue than he remembered *Brownian Movement*'s being, but after over three years in the tropics, they would certainly have faded. He didn't have much of a memory for colors, anyway.

He had to stop this. There was nothing he could do. He certainly couldn't afford to just run off to St. Thomas, and if he did, the boat would probably be long gone. He had no idea when the picture had been taken. He was old and lonely, and he had to admit, bitter about how his life had turned out. This whole boat thing was just something his mind had generated because it couldn't deal with the idea that after a lifetime of postponing and looking forward, everything good was behind him, and he had been too stupid to recognize the best moments of his life while he was living them.

But Bill Stroud also sensed that somehow his life had profoundly changed. For the first time in a very long time, there was something he wanted. He wanted a close look at a Far Horizons 38 called *Cinderella*.

CHAPTER TWO

Alice Holbrook crouched in *Cinderella's* varnished mahogany aft cabin—her cabin—with the engine manual on her knees. They had removed the panel that separated it from the cramped engine space under the cockpit and Gordon lay on the opposite side between the turn of the bilge and the diesel. She reached across the engine, handed him a flashlight, and said, "The book says it has to be lack of fuel and to start with the filters. Here. Shine this through the filter glass. What does it look like?" The engine had lost power the afternoon before as they motored around from the island's capital to the cove where they were now anchored. This morning it had been hard to start and then had stalled when put into gear. He did as she ordered, but had hardly finished when she asked, "Well?"

"It looks shitty. I'll have to change it."

"I told you that an hour ago."

An hour later, when he had changed the filter and bled the air out of the fuel system, the engine ran a little better for a few minutes. They let it wheeze along to charge the batteries, hoping it would clear itself, but it didn't. In half an hour the filter was plugged again. They had obviously been sold a load of very bad fuel the day before on the government dock. While he again cleaned the filter and then dismantled and cleaned the rest of the injection system, she went ashore in the dink and bought two Jerry cans of fresh diesel fuel at a service station. They drained the main tank into three other cans, dumped in some clean fuel and sloshed it around by running back and forth across the boat, then drained that, too. That evening as they left the cove with the engine now running fine, she dumped all of the contaminated fuel over the sternrail just off the beach in front of the island's biggest hotel. Nobody could pull that kind of crap on her and expect to get away with it.

Bill Stroud alternately looked out of the plane window at the incredibly blue sea and studied the map of the Caribbean inside the cover of the cruising guide he had bought the day before. For a body of water renowned for its islands, the Caribbean seemed amazingly empty. A chain of thirty major islands and hundreds of minor ones curved from Cuba down to Trinidad, separating the Caribbean from the Gulf of Mexico and the Atlantic. But only a few of those islands were actually located in it: Jamaica, the Caymans, and those along the northern coast of South America on the old Spanish Main. A rough measurement with his thumb showed it to be fifteen hundred miles from Martinique to the Yucatán and almost six hundred from Colombia to Jamaica. In all those nine hundred thousand square miles, there was nothing but salt water and those making their way across it.

Lydia Polizzi sat in her corner office at the Midwestern First National Bank in Columbus, Ohio studying the letter she had received that morning from the financial services company for which the bank was an agent. It didn't make any sense, but letters from that company usually didn't make any sense. It was one of those outfits that had been in a buying frenzy for years, gobbling up one competitor after another while its quality of service dropped precipitously with each new acquisition. But Wall Street loved it and kept providing the funds it needed to support its buying binge. She supposed it wouldn't be too long before they, or some outfit like them, grabbed the good old Midwestern First National and her job as VP of Human Resources would disappear, along with any chance of getting a rational answer from anyone about anything ever again.

She picked up her phone, called them, and started through the menu maze, although she knew the chances of getting any useful information, even if she eventually found her way to a human being, were just about nil. The person in charge of whatever you were calling about wouldn't be available at the moment, and the computer system would be down. Nobody with any brains was ever available, and their computer system was always down. The letter she held in her hand was typical. Their reason for refusing a refund of her niece's traveler's checks made no sense at all.

But Wall Street loved them.

Stroud had expected it to be warm in St. Thomas, but he was still surprised when he stepped out of the airport into the sun. He should have left his overcoat in the car at the airport in Hartford; he certainly wouldn't need it here. He didn't need his blue blazer, either. Under it, the sweat started to run down his back almost instantly. He took it off as he looked around for the cabstand, when a man speaking what sounded like an unknown foreign language snatched his bag and overcoat from where he had set them by his feet. Stroud chased him across the parking lot to a van which one of the other tourists explained would take them to their hotels. During the circuitous trip the driver kept up a running monologue, of which Stroud understood perhaps five isolated words.

Once he had checked in, he showered and changed into a pair of the new khaki shorts he bought the day before when he had discovered that none of those he owned, still fit him. The polo shirt from Lands End and the Timberland deck shoes without socks that had been his summer sailing uniform for years felt strange on a day that had started before dawn with a drive through a cold, raw rain to the airport.

At the desk, he asked for directions to the Ginger Bay Marina and was told it was almost two miles and he should take a cab. "That's okay. I need a walk after sitting in planes all day."

"If you want. Go out to the road and turn right. It's up over the hill past the powerhouse." He had not gone far before his shirt was soaked with sweat and he realized that the first things he had better buy were a hat and sun lotion. Even in October, the tropical sun packed more punch than the July sun of Connecticut.

The smell of diesel exhaust told him he was approaching the pow-erhouse; the building itself told him that he wasn't in Connecticut any longer. A large, square structure made of rusted corrugated steel, it stood in an unpaved and rutted yard littered with parts and pieces of machinery that ranged from twisted coils of electrical wire to the rusted carcass of a huge old diesel engine. There was an even more ancient connecting rod and flywheel that had probably come from a steam engine.

By the time he reached the marina he was very thirsty and was tempted to get something to drink in the open-air bar and restaurant at the head of the docks. But after taking a moment to orient him-self, he walked past the restaurant and the marine supply store that shared the building with it, and went up the hill toward the marina office and the spot from which the postcard photo had been taken. A fifty-foot motor yacht now occupied *Cinderella*'s slip, and although he could look down on most of the marina from here, he couldn't see any boat that even resembled her.

Rather than continue up the hill to the office, he walked back to the restaurant, sat down at a table under the red and white striped awning, ordered a glass of ice water and a beer, and then took a Xerox copy of the postcard from his wallet, unfolded it, and, as he told him-self, contemplated his next miscalculation. What the hell was he doing here? He didn't even have the courage to walk down the docks and verify there wasn't a Far Horizons 38 with a custom stainless steel frame welded to its sternrail in one of the slips he couldn't see from the hill.

What was he more afraid of—finding it, or not finding it? He was an old, overweight engineer with a heart problem chasing a hal-lucination born of grief and loneliness, and he didn't even know if he was more afraid of losing his hallucination or of having to deal with the consequences if it wasn't a hallucination after all. The wait-ress brought his order; he drank the water first, then sipped the beer. What the hell was he doing here? Was he any less lonely, was he any less fucked up than he had been in Connecticut? If there was an afterlife, would he ever be able to explain this crazy wild-goose chase to Liz? Always rational, always practical Liz.

He finished his beer, paid for it, and then walked slowly up and down the docks, studying the boats—nice boats, hundreds of them, most in superb condition. Tied on either side of a pier at the far end of the marina were two motor yachts over a hundred feet long. There was even a small submarine with thick electric cables running down its hatch to charge its batteries. A sign said it left every day at ten on a tour of the reefs.

But there was no Far Horizons 38.

He climbed back up the hill to the marina office building and found it closed. A sign in the corner of the front window said, "Office Hours, 8 to 5." His watch said it was only four-twenty, but a wall clock visible through the window said it was twenty past five. Then he remembered they were an hour ahead of East Coast time. He had meant to change his watch, a cheap, accurate, and complicated digital alarm chronograph, but he needed the instructions that had come with the watch to do it. He shook his head at his own sad, fat image in the window. He had come down here to unravel some great mystery but he couldn't even set his watch to the correct local time.

He ate dinner in the restaurant at the head of the dock and listened to the conversations at the tables around him. It could have been any yacht club or marina restaurant in the States. No one noticed him. He had been in places like this since he was a child.

The next morning he was waiting when an attractive woman in his same uniform of Bermuda shorts, polo shirt, and Timberlands came up the hill and opened the office. It looked a lot better on her than it did on him. They introduced themselves—her name was Ruth Connelly— and after she had gone around behind the counter and put away her purse, she asked, "Now. How can I help you, Mr. Stroud?"

"I'm looking for a boat."

"There are several for sale; the brokerage office next door handles them. They should be opening any minute."

"Not to buy." He finally decided which of the dozen different approaches he had been rehearsing for two days he would try. "It belongs to the daughter and son-in-law of an old friend who asked me to look them up. It's a Far Horizons 38, and its name is *Cinderella*, but for the life of me I can't remember her married name—my friend's daughter, not Cinderella. *Her* married name was Mrs. Charming, wasn't it? It's hell to get old, believe me."

She smiled and said, "I don't believe they're here now, but I think I remember them. Let me look. Sometimes when I'm out of the office, my boss or one of the guys checks someone in and forgets to tell me." She powered up her desktop computer, pulled up a list, and said, "No. They're not here now."

"When were they here? Do you expect them back?"

She called up another file and scrolled through it. "Holbrook. Gordon and Alice Holbrook. They were here from the twenty-fourth of May to the twelfth of June."

"Do you expect them back? I mean, do people make reservations months ahead like they do for Cuttyhunk?" She looked at him quizzically, so he explained, "It's an island off Massachusetts. I've never sailed down here. I don't know your drill."

"I've heard the name, just didn't know where it was. And you have to make reservations months ahead?"

"If you want a slip in the marina."

"Must be a gold mine."

"Well, not really. The season is about six weeks long and it's socked in with fog for four or five of them."

"I'm originally from Pensacola. Never sailed in fog. I guess it's scary." Then she continued, "We usually have a few slips open except when the Caribbean Rally comes down from the States in November. At most, someone might call a week ahead just to make sure something's open."

"I have to be honest with you, my friend and his daughter had a falling out and haven't spoken in over a year. When I told him I was coming down here, he asked if I'd locate her and talk to her for him, see if I could get her to call him."

She tweaked the computer again and wondered if the friend existed. But if the man in front of her was looking for his own daughter, he would have known her married name, wouldn't he? But who could tell? There was something about him, a look of exhaustion perhaps, or of sadness, that told her he might very well be a man looking for a lost daughter. "They didn't leave any forwarding address, but a lot of the boats go south in the late spring to spend the hurricane season below the paths the storms normally follow."

He thought for moment and then asked, "Have they been here before last spring? Do they come back periodically?"

When she looked up from the computer this time, she said, "They were here last year, for ten days in January. That's as far back as the records go."

He debated giving her his name and phone number and asking her to have them call him if they returned. But it might not be for years and if they did call, what then? "Well, thanks a lot for your help."

"You know who might know something? The Frankfurts. They were in A-12 last spring, next to the slip the Holbrooks were in. They're in B-16 now. She went back to the States to have a baby, but the husband, Stanley Frankfurt, is living aboard. He might know where the Holbrooks went or what their plans were."

"B-16?"

"That's right. It's a Hallberg-Rassy 29."

"I'll talk to him. And thanks again."

"Any time. Sorry I couldn't be more help."

Stroud was vaguely familiar with Hallberg and Rassy. The Christmas before she died, Liz had given him a coffee-table book called *The World's Best Sailboats*. It had devoted a chapter to them. All he could recall about them now was that they were built in Sweden to Lloyd's Specifications, and had windshields, blue cove stripes, and the most beautifully laid teak decks of any of the boats in the book.

The decks of the boat in slip B-16 were a work of art in desperate need of attention. They were badly weathered and discolored. He suspected it came from the power plant exhaust, because the top of the mainsail cover and the dodger appeared to be stained the same way.

But beneath the layer of grime she was one hell of a boat. Hallbergs were serious cruising boats that the Swedes built like trucks, but this boat didn't look anything like a truck. Her lines gave her the appearance of a spearhead. Not the freaky, light displacement wedge of some modern racers, but the long, curving, lethal look of the real thing. A large part of this impression, he saw, came from the fact that she was on the narrow side for her length, had a very low and streamlined deck house, and the designer had gotten the curves of her shear and bow overhang just right. There was something imperious about the bow.

A voice behind him asked, "Like her?"

Stroud turned toward the voice and said, "I think I'm in love."

"She's seriously for sale." He was a very slight young man with a scraggly beard and long black hair tied in a ponytail. His tee shirt and cut-off dungaree shorts, although clean, were sunbleached and frayed, but Stroud knew this didn't mean much when assessing the net worth of someone on a dock. But the old running shoes mended with duct tape told the story. He knew from having once made a similar emergency repair at sea, that there are few things more slippery on a wet deck than shoe soles mended with duct tape. "Are you interested? Let me show you around. My name's Stan Frankfurt. Like the city in Germany."

Stroud introduced himself, then Frankfurt led him down the finger pier as he said, "She's a Hallberg-Rassy, the smallest one they make—that's why she doesn't have a windshield like all the others—a 1985. Hop aboard." Before Stroud could respond, Frankfurt stepped up over the teak caprail and, straddling the lifelines, held out his hand to help the older man.

Stroud ignored the hand and climbed over the lifelines, hoping that he didn't look so old and feeble that he needed the help of this ninety-eight-pound weakling to do it. Frankfurt explained everything as if Stroud were blind and could not see it for himself.

She was steered with a tiller that was now folded up against the backstay out of the way. It was a good thing, because the cockpit was small and a wheel would have cluttered it badly. The sheet winches were oversize and self-tailing. There were large scuppers and a high and substantial bridge deck at the forward end of the cockpit. Stroud liked that. Bridge decks and lifelines were alike: If you were too feeble to climb over them, you shouldn't be on a sailboat in the first place. It would take a hell of a sea coming up behind this boat to put any water below.

As Frankfurt climbed through the companionway, he said, "The cabin's beautiful. Come look."

She was also unbelievably hot. The only ventilation was through a couple of stainless steel blister vents, the narrow companionway from the cockpit, and the deck hatch into the forecabin that for some reason was closed. None of the cabin windows opened, and with the tropical sun beating on her she was an oven—a gorgeous oven, though. Ignoring the clothes strewn about, the dirty dishes that filled the sink, and the miscellany piled on chart table opposite the galley, Stroud saw only a simple interior layout of beautifully crafted, rubbed mahogany. Forward of the galley and the stand-up navigation station, there was a sofa on either side of the main cabin with an elegantly designed and built folding table between them. When Frankfurt saw him looking at the table, he lifted the solid mahogany lid off the center pedestal to which the leaves were hinged and said, "There's a bottle rack in here, would you believe. A wine cellar. Clever, huh?"

A full-width head forward of the salon separated it from the forecabin. When Stroud looked into the head, he saw there was no shower but that a stainless steel cabin heater was bolted to the bulkhead. He turned back to the young man. "Nice boat, but she needs work. If you're really serious about selling her, you ought to clean her up."

"I could let her go very reasonably."

"I'm not really in the market. I just sold a boat in Connecticut. That's where I live. I'm just visiting down here. Have you had breakfast yet? I was just going to eat. Why don't you join me?" He had to get out of this furnace. The sweat was pouring off him, the air was too stifling to breathe, and his heart was starting to fibrillate.

"Sounds good. You ought to look around the deck before you make up your mind, though. The rig is really elegant. The spinnaker pole stows vertically on the front of the mast and all the hardware is 316 stainless; there's not a spot of rust on any of it."

"Some other time. Let's get something to eat. My treat."

Frankfurt kept up his desperate sales pitch as they walked up to the restaurant, only pausing to order a breakfast that weighed almost as much as he did. When the waitress had taken their order, Stroud said, "I really didn't come down here to buy a boat. I'm looking for some people I think you know: the Holbrooks, Gordon and Alice. The lady in the office said you might know where they went."

"Was it a Niagara 35? No, but it was like one—a big boat for its length, as they always say about tubs. A Far Horizons 38?" Stroud nodded and Frankfurt continued, "They were in the slip next to us last spring. Seemed like nice people. Kept to themselves, though. Jennifer, she's my wife, she was here then, and she's a really sociable person. She kept inviting them over for a drink and so on, but they never responded. She's up north with her mother now. We're going to have a baby. That's why I need to sell *Lullaby*.

"We were going to go around the world, stopping to work whenever we ran out of money, but it doesn't seem to work that way, what with work permits and all. Jenny's up north pregnant and working—she's a nurse; we met in the Peace Corps—and I'm down here minding the boat and living on what she can send me. She can only work for another month or so."

Frankfurt had to be the worst negotiator Stroud had ever met. Could anyone actually have so little business sense? Then he smiled to himself as he silently added, *Without an MBA.*

The waitress brought their food. Like the women in the marina office, the clerks at his hotel, and several of the women he had seen on the docks, she was beautiful. The Caribbean, like California, seemed to be one of those places that attracted more than its share of beautiful women. Was it the weather or the money? Probably both.

The food gave him a chance to talk as Frankfurt tore into it. "What do you do, Stanley? It is Stanley, isn't it?"

"Yup, Stanley or Stan. I have a degree in physical ed. That's what I was doing in the Peace Corps when I met Jennifer."

If he had said he was a Sumo wrestler, Stroud couldn't have been more surprised. He looked about as athletic as Stroud usually felt. "What does a gym teacher do in the Peace Corps?"

Frankfurt explained between bites. "Oh, teach the locals to play cricket and soccer and set up leagues for them and all. It's a lot of work. We should have stayed in. It's a pretty good life. We were on a British island. Then Jenny's father died—her mother and father were divorced years ago—and he left us this boat and a few bucks and we thought we had it made.

"But living on a boat down here isn't like you'd think from weekend cruising on Barnegat Bay. Jenny was seasick whenever it got rough and it seemed like it was rough all the time. And there's no shower or bathtub in the boat, and so when we got here we just sort of stayed until she got pregnant and, I'll be honest with you, our money ran out. I'd really like to sell that damned boat."

Stroud thought, *Teach the locals on a British island to play cricket. Your tax dollars in action.* But he said, "The Holbrooks. Let's get back to them for a second. They didn't say where they were going, did they?"

"Nope. I took Jennifer to the States on the fifth of June, and when I came back three weeks later, they were gone."

"Do you remember anything about their boat? How was the boom rigged?"

"Hmmm. Now that you mention it, I do remember something about it. Gordon had the cover off one day to replace the reef lines—you spend a lot of time reefed down here—and I remember thinking it was the only setup I'd ever seen that was as elegant as the one on the Hallberg. Everything was internal and all the lines came out on the starboard side of the boom next to labeled cleats, all set at the same angle." He sat back, wiped his mouth, and took a sip of coffee, "Boy, that was great. Beats eating my own cooking. I sure want to thank you."

Then the contented expression disappeared from his face as someone came up to the table. He was a tall, handsome, and athletic looking man, everything that Stanley Frankfurt wasn't, even if he did have a degree in physical education. The newcomer wore an expensive-looking sport shirt and slacks; his leather deck shoes were polished to a high shine. "Hello, Stanley. Found a potential buyer for your boat, have you?"

Frankfurt seemed to be completely intimidated by him. "No, Mr. Stroud isn't in the market for a boat. We were—Mr. Stroud, this is Granville Evans– just having breakfast together."

Evans held out his hand and gave Stroud a firm, practiced handshake and a gleaming smile filled with perfect teeth. Stroud half-rose from the table, shook the hand, and said, "Bill Stroud," as he sat back down. He had already begun to dislike this guy.

Then Evans told Frankfurt, "You seem to have finished your meal, Stanley. Why don't you go and clean your teak or something. I'd like to talk to Bill, here, alone."

Frankfurt dutifully stood up. Stroud was hoping that he would tell Evans to screw off, but instead he shook Stroud's hand and thanked him for breakfast, then walked down the dock as Evans dropped into a chair, waved at the waitress and told her, "Just coffee, Marilyn, my love. For the moment, just coffee." Then he turned to Stroud. "Bill, I run the yacht brokerage here, and *we* have a contract with Frankfurt. Believe me, if *we* could sell that damn boat and not have him cluttering up the landscape *we'd* do it in a minute." It was obviously the imperial *we* .

Stroud thought, *But not so gladly as you're pretending, Mister. You don't want to be rid of Stanley. It's too much fun kicking him around.* But he didn't say anything. He really had no desire to play mine-is-bigger-than-yours with this minor-league twerp. He had spent the last few years of his professional career playing that game with world-class twerps.

When Stroud didn't respond, Evans went on, "You look like a man who has wrung a bit of salt water out of his socks upon occasion."

Stroud picked up the last piece of toast from his plate, took a bite, and said, "Upon occasion," as he studied Evans over the rim of his sunglasses.

"First off, you and I both know how Frankfurt's kind of people are. I'll bet he was telling you what a great deal he'd give you if you helped him beat us out of our commission."

"We didn't talk deals. As I said, I'm not in the market for a boat. Actually, we were discussing mutual friends, although I don't know what business that is of yours. And just what kind of people are you talking about, Granville? What kind of people would try to beat you out of your commission? Be specific."

That stopped him. He hesitated for a second, then said, "Well, if you decide to look for a boat, come see us. We've got better listings than that beat-up Hallberg. Nice to have met you." He got up and walked away, ignoring Marilyn, who was just bringing his coffee.

Stroud walked up over the hill past the power plant in the noonday heat and noticed none of it. Alice Holbrook and Alice Perkins—a coincidence? A bracket on a sternrail and a boom with the cleats neatly placed and the lines neatly led—coincidence? And some traveler's checks that were cashed where and when they shouldn't have been cashed. It certainly wasn't enough to go to the authorities with. Then he asked himself, *What authorities?*

When he got to the hotel, he showered, changed, and after making a list of the commercial photographers in Charlotte Amalie—there were only four of them—took a cab into town. Maybe his luck had finally begun to change, because the first one he tried had taken the postcard picture. The photographer was a very large, very black man who looked like a pro football player. "Oh yes. Dat is my work. Notice how de lighting is handled. It is not easy to take a picture with all de shiny white boats set against de sparkling water and get de lighting just right so de other colors, dey all be true."

"When was it taken?"

"Why would you want to know that, Mon?"

"I might want to buy copies of any other photos you took at the same time."

"My work, she's not inexpensive."

"And you probably sell very little of it by this method. Tell me when this was taken, show me what else was taken at the same time, and then we'll talk money."

"Now is de information age, Mon. Why would I give out de word on only de promise of de stranger to pay?"

"Okay. A deposit." Stroud put a twenty-dollar bill on the counter. It disappeared instantly in the blur of a black hand.

"Come back in two hours, Mon, after lunch, and I'll have it all ready for you."

"No. If I walk out that door, my money and I are gone for good. Now, tell me when it was taken, show me the others, and I'll give you another twenty bucks. Take it or leave it."

"Forty."

"Twenty. Fifty percent of something is a hell of a lot more than a hundred percent of nothing."

There was only one other picture that showed any part of *Cinderella*. It had been taken straight down the dock and showed her bow and foredeck in a line of bows and foredecks. He was sure it was hers because it was next to *Lullaby's*, and that bow he could recognize anywhere. The Far Horizons 38 had a large glass hatch in the center of the foredeck that became a skating rink when it was wet. The best deck shoes could slip on it. That was why Stroud and his son-in-law had made a teak grating to fit over it. The hatch in the photo had such a grating, but the picture showed it at such an acute angle that there was no way he could tell if it was the same one. But there was no way he could tell it was not the same one, either.

The pictures had been taken the beginning of June.

After Stroud got back to the hotel, he went for a long, slow swim off the beach—twenty strokes of left sidestroke, then twenty on his right side, then twenty on his back. He should have been able to do any one of them indefinitely, but he couldn't. Stroud had been on the swim team in college and had worked as a lifeguard and sailing instructor in the summers, but he knew that if he tried the crawl stroke now, his heart wouldn't stand for it. But he found he was still capable of the Water Safety Instructor's way of swimming long distances while, if necessary, towing someone. The swimming was easier than he expected because the high salinity of the water and, he had to admit, his own greatly increased displacement eliminated any problem keeping afloat. But he couldn't think about anything else while he swam. That was the big difference between swimming and running. Once, he could run miles without being aware of it while his mind ground away at some problem or other. But no more. The water was perfect, though: crystal clear and precisely the right temperature.

As he walked back to the hotel, he admired the women sunning themselves on the beach. He was old, but not that old, and, he told himself, although his heart had problems, it was still beating. He wondered if he swam every day would he, after a while, be able to think about other things while he swam? It made him pause. He was scheduled to fly back to Connecticut in three days, and the only swimming he could do there in the next six months would be in a pool at a Y. At that moment he felt better than he had in years, but he knew that if he went back to Connecticut, it would be back to the chair in front of the TV and irreversible decline.

He stood under the shower for a very long time, thinking so intently that he was unaware of where he was. He dried himself without realizing it and then walked into the bedroom naked and took the computer blow-up of the postcard out of the large brown envelope in his suitcase. Of course!

How could he have missed it? He looked at his watch. Ten past four. That meant it was ten past five here and ten past one in California.

It took him a few minutes to get through the phone system and find the number of the U.S. Coast Guard Station at Monterey.

As he was dialing, it dawned on him that they might not just give out information to anyone who called. He hung up the phone and paced around the room for a while, concocting a story to explain his questions. There had been a time when he would never have lied to a representative of the U.S. Government about anything; but that seemed almost funny now. When he finally placed the call, he was told that vessel documentation was handled by an office in San Francisco and was given its number.

"Hello, U.S. Coast Guard Documentation Office. Ms. Yakuri. How can I help you?" She had a very pleasant voice and no trace of an accent, which, Stroud admitted to himself, shouldn't be surprising since her family had probably been in the United States longer than his had. He visualized her as a pretty Oriental woman and felt vaguely uncomfortable lying to her. He supposed it dated him, but he would get over it. He would make himself get over it. If he could have gotten over it while he was working in the midst of that pack of professional liars, perhaps he would have gotten his entire pension.

"Ms. Yakuri, my name is Bill Stroud and I'm calling from St. Thomas in the Virgin Islands."

"How's the weather there today, Mr. Stroud? It's gray, cold, and foggy here."

"Perfect, of course. Sunny and in the eighties."

"It sounds lovely. I could use some of that." Then the wistfulness went out of her voice. "How can I help you?"

"I'm thinking about buying a boat from some people down here. A Far Horizons 38. Their name is Holbrook, and they claim they can't find their certificate of documentation and have applied for a duplicate. The boat's name is *Cinderella* and its home port is Monterey, California.

To tell the truth, I'm in love with the boat, but the people seem a little, I don't know, hinky is as good a word as any. I have a limited time down here and I don't want to waste it dealing with them if they can't produce a clean title." It was probably a bit too long and complicated for a good lie, but he wasn't much practiced and it was the best he could do.

"Let me look. Hold on, please."

After a couple of minutes she came back and asked, "You don't have the document number, do you? It's supposed to be carved into the mainframe of the vessel, but since most boats don't have a wooden mainframe any more, it's usually on a plaque or something that's supposed to be permanently attached to the vessel's structure."

"Hold on." He fished through his papers until he found *Brownian Movement's* number and read it to her. Then he said, "I think this is it, but I wrote it down from memory. I could be wrong."

Again he waited, and then she said, "We have seven *Cinderellas* in Northern California, but none of them has Monterey as a home port, and none of them has applied to this office for a replacement document, either. You're sure they were talking about U.S. Coast Guard documentation and not California state registration?"

"If it was a state registration, the boat would have a CF number on the bow, wouldn't it? Hold on, please." He did not trust his own memory, so he dug out the photo of the line of bows at the dock. "No. No number. I have a photo and I just wanted to be sure."

She thought for a minute and then said, "I guess it was a good thing you listened to your instincts. It seems like hinky might be exactly the right word. You know, people still try to use documentation as a dodge to avoid paying state sales and property taxes on their boats, even though it doesn't work as well as it once did. Most of the loopholes have been plugged. But I suppose if someone were sailing around the Caribbean from one foreign country to the next . . . " Her voice trailed off. Then she said, "Hold on." A minute later she said, "That can't be the right registration number, either. That's an East Coast number and it's inactive. I just checked."

"I'm sure glad I called you, Ms. Yakuri. I can see how making a deal with these people could have been the beginning of a never-ending mess."

"Where is this boat now, Mr. Stroud? In St. Thomas? That's the U.S. Virgin Islands, isn't it?"

He could see where that might lead. "They left here heading south down the island chain. They're supposed to call me from wherever they wind up. But now I really don't care if they do."

"Well, if you hear from them, would you let the nearest U.S. Coast Guard station know? If they come back into U.S. jurisdiction, someone might want to talk to them."

"Oh, I certainly will, although I certainly don't want to talk to them again."

After he had thanked her and hung up he thought, *And that was a lie, too. Now I want to talk to the bastards more than ever.*

The next morning he rented a car and drove to the marina. At the marine supply store he bought a detailed map of the island, a chart book for the Virgin Islands, two more cruising guides and a pair of inexpensive binoculars. He hated to do it because he had a perfectly good pair of 7x50s at home.

As he ate breakfast he marked up the map, and when he had finished eating, he started a counterclockwise circuit of the island's anchorages. By ten o'clock he was pretty sure it was not going to work. By noon he was completely sure. The other marinas were easy to get to and search, but only a small percentage of the boats were in the marinas. Many were in anchorages that were inaccessible or even invisible from the road, and there were anchorages on dozens of surrounding islets that were unreachable except by boat. And that did not take into account the dozens of boats, any one of which could be *Cinderella*, that he could see sailing offshore.

He abandoned his original idea of flying from island to island and searching from the land. If he wanted to conduct any sort of a serious, methodical search, it would have to be from the air. He drove out to the airport.

The charter company had no planes available, but they did have a tour flight of the Virgin Islands scheduled for the next morning. He booked a seat.

The eight-passenger Bristol Islander had two engines and an interior that looked like the Brits had salvaged it from a junked bus originally built in an Iron Curtain country. The other passengers were three tourist couples, so it was easy for Stroud, the odd man, to grab the seat next to the pilot. They were only about fifteen minutes into the flight when he began to suspect that Plan B, while not hopeless, would probably bankrupt him very quickly. In the Virgin Islands alone, there were hundreds of anchorages and thousands of boats. An air search for a particular one could involve months of flying, much of it at low level—he wondered what the regulations were about that—and God only knew how much per hour a plane and pilot would cost.

He was back at the hotel in time for lunch but decided to skip it and swim instead. He still couldn't think about anything except counting the strokes as he swam, but maybe it cleared his head. Afterwards, he again stood in the shower, lost in thought. There had to be some way to conduct a systematic search through the Antilles for *Cinderella*. It could take years, and it would take spectacularly good luck to succeed. But he had had such spectacularly bad luck for so long, that if it ever turned...

What would Nell say? A large part of it was her money. His pension and savings wouldn't support the effort for very long, but he just didn't feel right about touching The Kids' estate.

He dried himself and walked into the bedroom where the last photo of Nell, Liz, and Steve stood on the bed table and asked it aloud: "Well, Miss Priss, what do you want your Daddy to do?" Although he had studied the photo minutely many times, he had never before really noticed what his daughter had been wearing. It was a white tee shirt with lettering on the front too small to read in the photo. But that didn't matter because he knew what it said. *Carpe Diem*. Steve had given it to her and had kidded her that it was her personal motto and meant, "Complain Daily." But that wasn't what it meant. Not at all.

He ate an early supper, took a long walk on the beach, and then went to bed, where he lay awake for a long time. There had to be some way to narrow the search. Some bit of intelligence that would at least give him an idea where to start.

He spent the next two days visiting every place boaties might frequent—chandleries, sailmakers, boatyards, and the restaurants and bars within walking distance of the marinas—but no one had ever heard of the Holbrooks or of *Cinderella.* That afternoon he had another long, slow swim and ate dinner in the hotel. It was a lot more expensive and not any better than the restaurant at the Ginger Bay Marina, and it had only the beach and the sea for a view, no boats. He liked the view, but he liked to look at boats more.

That was probably the true basis of his problem—no boat. He had watched all these people playing with his very favorite kind of toy and he didn't have one. Maybe that's all this was, an excuse to buy a boat. In all the long history of bizarre ways to justify buying a boat, this had to be one of the weirdest.

He sipped his second cup of tea looking out over the darkened sea while he decided, quite rationally, to go home on schedule. His mind was made up when he went to bed, but he couldn't sleep, so he turned on the light and tried to read one of his three cruising guides to the Caribbean, but he couldn't do that, either. He could not stop his mind from working on the problem of what sort of boat would be best for the job, if he were to attempt it. But of course he wasn't going to attempt it. He was going to go home. His mind was made up.

It was after midnight when he finally admitted that his mind was made up, all right. *What the hell.* He didn't have anything better to do and he had been without a boat for almost a week now—that was as long as he had been boatless in thirty years.

He also knew, although he did not verbalize it in his mind, that if he went back into the Connecticut winter and his Connecticut lifestyle, he probably would not live to see the spring. He took the pad and pen the hotel had placed on the bed table, and as he started to make notes he said aloud, "Carpe diem, Miss Priss. Carpe diem."

Cinderella ghosted into Deshaies Bay on the northwest tip of Guadeloupe late on a night so brightly lit by a full moon that one could read by it. Gordon was steering, and Alice was helping him spot the thin bamboo poles the locals used to mark their fish traps. He snaked the boat through them and between the half dozen yachts sleeping at anchor. A couple of them might have potential. One in particular caught her eye: a dark blue custom cutter about forty-two feet long with twin steering wheels so one could walk between them onto the steps in the transom that led down to the teak inlaid swim platform. It had oversized electric winches and every power sail furling and handling device available. Just the deck hardware alone must have cost a fortune. A large Canadian flag permanently attached to the backstay lifted and fluttered occasionally in the light, puffy breeze here in the lee of the island.

They anchored a couple of hundred yards off. In the morning Alice would investigate further. Perhaps their luck had finally changed.

But it hadn't. When she came on deck right after dawn, the 42-footer had already sailed.

When the brokerage office at the marina opened in the morning, Stroud was waiting, armed with the hotel pad filled with the notes he had made during the night. Every time he had been about to doze off he had thought of something else, turned on the light, and jotted it down.

Evans immediately began trying to make sure Stroud knew that he was the scion of some old and fabulously wealthy family with a great hereditary knowledge of yachting. "So you're looking for a boat after all, Bill. Just what sort of boat are you looking for? Even though you may only have the vaguest idea of what you want, if you share it with me, I'm sure I can flesh it out for you. My family has been messing about with boats forever."

Being patronized and called by his first name by someone half his age whom he didn't know and didn't want to know, irritated Stroud mightily. He had come here hoping to talk to another broker, but now he realized that Evans' "we" truly was the lonely, imperial We. "A power boat, Mr. Evans." He emphasized the word Mister. "A small trawler, maybe twenty-eight or thirty feet, suitable for one person to live aboard down here for an extended period. Diesel powered, of course. Doesn't have to be fast; ten or twelve knots is fine as long as she's a decent sea boat and has substantial tankage. I actually like lobster yachts more than trawlers, but I know that most of them in the size I'm interested in don't have enough accommodation for a long-term live-aboard. And let me explain, Mr. Evans," again the emphasis on Mister, "I've owned boats all my life, and I'm not interested in anything less than first quality."

"Let me see what I've got. Give me just a second, will you, Bill?"

Stroud was very close to just walking out, but Evans pulled a folder from his file and handed Stroud a listing from it. "This sounds exactly like the boat you want. She's lying at Virgin Gorda."

"A thirty-eighty-footer. That's a bit bigger than I had in mind."

"You don't want anything smaller down here where you have to plow into substantial head seas so much of the time. And she's a steal. They're asking two dollars and twenty cents, but I think you could get her for a buck ninety-five." That was boat talk for a hundred and ninety-five thousand dollars.

"That's a lot more than I want to spend."

Evans gave him a look that said, *I expected as much,* went back into his files, and pulled out another listing. "This boat is down here in slip, ah, E-14." It was a 26-foot sport fisherman with a large cockpit and a small trunk cabin powered by two big outboards. "This is close to the lobster type you mentioned. They're only asking eighty cents for her and it would cost well over a buck to replace her. The engines alone cost almost a quarter apiece."

"Outboards? How much do they burn, a barrel an hour?"

"She cruises at over twenty knots. The gallons per hour may seem a little high, but the miles per gallon aren't all that bad. And you're new to the Caribbean. Let me explain something to you. Down here, diesel fuel can be a real problem. Contamination, you know. All the moisture and heat make the microbes that live in the stuff grow like you wouldn't believe. Gasoline doesn't have that problem. I know you're probably afraid of the explosion hazard, but . . . "

Stroud thought, *Enough*, so he interrupted him. "My father had gasoline-powered boats for forty years and never blew himself up, not even once. I know how to deal with gasoline. That's not the problem." He studied the listing. This was a boat for day trips, not a home for months or maybe years. "I'll look at it. But I don't think so."

"Here's another that you might want to look at: a thirty-five-foot Bertram. It's in F-4. A really first-quality boat with twin GMC Diesels."

"What year?"

"A seventy-three, but that doesn't matter. A boat of that quality literally lasts forever."

"How about the engines? Are they two- or four-cycle?" From the look on Evans' face, it was obvious his great knowledge of yachts and yachting ended at the engine-room door. When he didn't answer, Stroud asked, "Okay, does it say if the engines are original or newer?"

He did not hand Stroud the listing but scanned it just a little too long to be believable. "Gee, it doesn't say that either. But I know they're in great condition. I've seen them and they look new. You could get this boat at a steal, Bill. Only about a buck ten."

A buck ten for a boat that probably needed a couple of engines and God only knew what else. "The Bertram is in F-4 and the other one is in what slip again?"

"E-14."

"I'll go look at them."

"I can't get away right now. I'm expecting some people any minute. But you take a look at them, and if you want to know more about either, come on back. I'll tell you what I'll do: I have a pretty good idea of what you want. As soon as I get a chance, I'll get on the blower and see what I can find. Give me a couple of days, then give me a call."

It was very obvious to Stroud that Evans did not think him a genuine prospect and was going out of his way to let him know it. He swallowed the urge to tell him what he thought of his sales technique and instead asked, "Oh, by the way. You don't know the Holbrooks, do you? *Cinderella*, a Far Horizons 38? They were here last spring."

"Noooo. I don't think so. Doesn't ring a bell."

"Well, thanks anyway."

"Keep in touch in case I find something for you, Bill."

Stroud did not say, "Noooo, I don't think so," although he was tempted.

He walked down the docks, looking not only at the boats in E-14 and F-4, but also at all the other powerboats that filled the slips on both sides of those docks. His father had had a powerboat. The old wooden raised-deck cruiser had been the center of his and the old man's life while he was growing up; his father had only sold it when the maintenance had become too much for him while Stroud was overseas in the army. Years later he had come across her rotting in the back of a boatyard in Norwalk, too far gone for even her most ardent admirer to attempt a restoration. She was the only powerboat Bill Stroud had ever wanted, and he knew it wasn't the boat but his own childhood that he really craved.

There was a great selection of powerboats along E and F docks, but none he could afford that was suitable for the job.

He wandered around the docks for a while, then walked over to B-dock and tapped on *Lullaby*'s coaming. When Stanley Frankfurt's head appeared through the hatch, Bill said, "Come on. I'll buy you another breakfast. We have to talk."

When they were settled at a table—Frankfurt had ordered another hundred pounds of food while Stroud had ordered raisin bran, juice, and coffee—Stroud said, "This is how I'd like to do this. You tell me how much you really want right now. Then I'll give you a couple of hours to get your crap straightened up in the cabin before I go through the boat. If she seems all right, we'll take her out and sail her. If I want her, and depending on what I find, I'll either say okay or I'll make a counter-offer. If we get a tentative deal, I'll pay to have her hauled so I can look at the bottom, rudder, shaft, and so on. While she's out I'll pay for a hotel room for you. If, after all that, I still want her, and we agree on a price, I'll pay in cash or certified check or have the money transferred directly into your account within five business days, whatever you want. Okay?"

"What if, after she's out, you decide you don't want her?"

"I'll pay to have her put back in."

"Evans the broker has the listing. Shouldn't we talk to him?"

"You'll have to pay him whatever percentage of the price was in the contract you signed. I won't be a party to cheating him, but that's between you and him. But I really don't have any need to put up with Evans and his bullshit, and I don't think you do either." He paused for a moment. "I'll tell you what. After I go through the boat this afternoon, if it looks like we might have a deal, we'll both go up and tell him what's going on." He didn't want Frankfurt going up there alone. Evans would surely intimidate him into some stupidity just to prove whose was bigger than whose. He didn't want Evans to handle the paperwork and screw up his title, either. He was sure Evans was incompetent. People who behaved that way generally were. "Do we have the framework for a deal?"

Frankfurt thought about it for just a moment, then said, "I guess we do."

"How much do you want?"

"I've got her listed for fifty, but I'd take forty-two."

"In the ball park. Let's see what she's like."

While Frankfurt leaped about the boat packing clothes, washing dishes, and straightening out the forecabin he had been using for a catchall, Stroud went shopping. At a supermarket across the road from the marina he bought a loose-leaf binder, a package of paper, a roll of cellophane tape, a ruler, and a package of pens. Then he sat down at one of the tables in front of the restaurant, ordered a cup of coffee, and used the tape to reinforce the holes of each of the sheets of paper. It was maddening to have loose-leaf sheets tear out of a binder and those gummed reinforcement things were useless in the damp atmosphere of a boat. On the first page he wrote, *Lullaby, Maintenance Log,* and at the top of the second, *Initial Survey* and the date. When he was finished, he browsed in the chandlery until Frankfurt came looking for him.

He started in the anchor locker at the very bow. Beneath the stained teak of the beautifully made hatch that he longed to clean, the locker was an even worse mess. There was a dangerously rusted propane tank with an equally corroded regulator and solenoid valve. The insulation on the wires casually swinging between the solenoid and the collision bulkhead was badly cracked. This wasn't surprising, since whoever had installed the thing had used household lamp cord. Stroud had spent his career designing, building, and running manufacturing equipment; he knew that under the best of conditions, electrical solenoid valves are among the least dependable of devices. Here, where it was periodically drenched with salt water when *Lullaby* stuck her nose into a steep head sea, the thing didn't have a chance. If he couldn't walk to the bow and turn off the gas when he was through with the stove, he was too feeble to be on a boat. He made a note to get rid of the solenoid; get a new, corrosion-resistant gas bottle; and make a red streamer to hang on the hatch cover when the gas valve was turned on.

Frankfurt, standing behind him, said, "That electric valve sticks sometimes. You have to come up here and rap it with something when it does."

In the same locker, though, were a 35-pound CQR plow anchor, a 12-pound Danforth high tensile to serve as a lunch hook, and two anchor rodes. Both were two hundred feet of high quality nylon line in good condition. The one on the lunch hook had about fifteen feet of galvanized chain, and the working anchor had four times as much. "Are there any other anchors?"

"No. There was a big old fisherman's anchor down in the bilge that must have weighed a hundred pounds. We never used it. It was all I could do to lift it, so I sold it."

That was the way it went through the whole boat: excellent design, quality, and equipment overlaid with dirt and what he came to think of as Peace Corps engineering.

There were a few problems, of course. Most of the sails had obviously been delivered with the boat. The roller furling 130 percent jib that was the boat's Number One would have to be replaced. The roller furler would have to go, too. He would no more allow a roller furler on a boat than he would allow a maniac with a brace and bit. He'd also need a new mainsail and a replacement for the worn-out working jib. Because the jibs would be attached to the head stay with bronze piston hanks and wouldn't be wrapped around the head stay except by accident, he'd also need a new Number Three jib. It would be a little larger than the working jib and would be designed and built for the heavy air of the Caribbean. He knew exactly what he wanted.

But *Lullaby's* storm jib and trysail looked as if they had never been out of the bag, and there was a beautiful three-quarter-ounce tri-radial spinnaker that looked just as new. There was a line of Zs across its center, each a little smaller than the one to its left. *Lullaby.* He would keep the name. After all, the purpose of the whole project was to allow him to sleep at night.

He found a small stress-corrosion crack in the bottom swage fitting of a shroud and decided all the standing rigging needed replacement. She had a fractional rig with set back spreaders, so there was no redundancy at all. If one wire went, everything would be over the side instantly.

But the biggest problem was the engine. It was an eighteen-horsepower Volvo diesel, and although it looked as neglected and dirty as the rest of the boat, it started and ran fine. There was one raw-water connection that showed corrosion where it had obviously been leaking a little, but that was no big deal. What was a big deal was that it was a sail drive: the engine was connected to something that looked like the lower unit of an outboard motor and protruded through the bottom of the boat via a hole sealed by a thick rubber doughnut. Frankfurt had no idea when, or even if, the doughnut had ever been replaced, and by peering down at it with a flashlight, Stroud discovered that it was criss-crossed with the small cracks that appear on rubber when it gets old.

As Stroud went through the boat, Frankfurt, who had started out explaining every item in great detail, became quieter and quieter as page after page of the notebook filled with comments. Just as Frankfurt thought Stroud had been through every nook and cranny, Stroud pulled out the boatswain's chair he had found at the bottom of a cockpit locker and asked, "Are there a couple of beefy guys around here who will help you haul me aloft?"

"Is that a good idea?"

Stroud knew that what he meant was, "Aren't you too old and fat for that?" After he had crouched on the deck to study the lower terminals of the rigging, he had had to sit for a few minutes before he could get his breath. It had happened twice more when he bent over to inspect something. Stroud had passed it off by saying, "I can do anything I could at twenty-five as long as it doesn't involve bending over," but it had obviously scared Frankfurt a little.

"Just to the spreaders. I want to look at the roots." The spreader roots and tips were heavily wrapped with vinyl tape, the ends of which streamed in the breeze. If the mast was corroded under all that tape, it would be a deal stopper. It would cost big bucks and take forever to replace it.

Frankfurt went down the dock and returned with Horst and Sven. Horst was big and beefy, Sven was wiry, and they both knew what they were doing. The mast, once Stroud had dug through the layers of tape, was fine.

When he was on deck again and Horst and Sven had been thanked and had left, Stroud opened the plastic life-raft container that sat on the cabin top between the mast and the dodger. Printed in large letters on its sides was a brand name Stroud did not recognize. The four-man life raft was in a sealed bag. Attached to the bag was an inspection tag (a year overdue), an inventory list, and an inflation lanyard. When Frankfurt saw Stroud was studying the tag, he said, "I've been meaning to get that checked. I bought it because everyone said you shouldn't go offshore without one. It cost me fifteen hundred bucks."

Before Frankfurt could stop him, Stroud pulled the lanyard. There was a feeble little hiss that stopped before the raft had even finished unrolling out of the bag. "Just be thankful you never needed it." Stroud pointed at a seam that had split for almost its entire length.

Next he pulled out a plastic bag labeled "Emergency Equipment." Most of the items listed on the inventory were missing—there was no food and only two cheap plastic quart bottles of water—and what equipment there was, was junk. The fishing equipment consisted of one rusty spinner, two hooks, thirty tangled feet of twine, and a dime store paring knife also covered with rust. None of the signaling equipment—flares, flare gun, smoke bombs, or dye markers—was present.

"What did you do with the rest of this stuff, Stanley?"

"Nothing. The instructions that came with it said not to open it unless you needed it, and if you did, it would have to be inspected again. What sort of people would sell you something like that?"

"Why, the graduates of the finest business schools in the country, of course. They learn it in a course called Cost Reduction and Profit Maximization."

"What should I do with it?"

"Toss it on the dock. I'll throw it in the dumpster when I go up. Save the box, though. That's the only serviceable part of it. I'll paint it and use it to store my inflatable dink at sea."

"They told me a dinghy isn't suitable as a life raft. That's why Debby and I bought this one."

"And this thing is? I prefer to put my money into making sure I never need a life raft."

Again Frankfurt asked, "What sort of people would sell something like that?"

Stroud ignored him. "Okay. Let's go sailing."

Frankfurt had obviously been worrying about it. "I don't think she'll sail too well. The bottom's pretty foul. I've been meaning to get it scrubbed, but . . . ." A thick line of grass was growing along the water-line; God only knew what was living farther down.

"Who does it?"

"A guy who works on the submarine—he's a diver." The submarine had just tied up and was letting off its load of tourists from the afternoon cruise.

"Go hire him and have him do it tonight. We'll take her out in the morning." Stroud noticed Frankfurt's face. "I'll pay. While you do that, I'll go talk to Evans. I won't pay his commission, though. That comes out of your money."

He walked into Evans' office and greeted him by saying, "Frankfurt and I are close to making a deal for *Lullaby*— the Hallberg-Rassy 29."

Suddenly Stroud became a real prospect. Amazing. "We've got much better listings, Bill, but if that's the sort of boat you want. I thought you were looking for a powerboat."

"*Lullaby* will do fine."

"Well, okay. Let me tell my girl in the office next door where I'm going, and I'll take you down and explain her to you."

"That won't be necessary. She already explained herself to me. She needs some work, but if the bottom is all right and the test sail is okay, I'll buy her. We're going to take her out in the morning and then go around to the yard in Frenchtown to have her hauled."

"Well, I don't think it will be that easy, Bill. The marina won't let him move her without paying the bill."

"Okay. I'll pay it. Now, let's talk about your commission. What's the rate?"

"Ten percent."

"You know that Frankfurt has neither pot nor window and his wife is about to have a baby—at Christmas time, yet. It sounds like an O. Henry story, doesn't it? I don't suppose you could see your way to picking up some of that slip rental out of your commission? Whatever he gets out of this deal is all they'll have to start over."

"Oh no, I couldn't do that. Ten percent is marina policy, and I'm only an employee of the marina, after all. What are you going to give him—forty cents?"

"About that."

"Suppose the paperwork said twenty-eight. It's a desperation sale. Everyone knows that and would believe it. Then he and I could split the difference between a commission of twenty-eight hundred and one of four grand down the middle. Your sales tax would be that much less, too. Everybody wins."

Good God, he kept talking like a hundred thousand dollars meant nothing to him, but he was ready to cheat his employer for a lousy six hundred bucks. But Stroud only said, "Let me think about it. In the meantime, I'll go next door and pay his marina bill so we can take her out in the morning."

"I'll go out with you. What time?"

As Stroud walked out he said, "That will not be necessary."

Frankfurt's bill came to over three thousand dollars; Stroud wasn't surprised that the marina didn't want him to move the boat until he paid it. He asked Ruth Connelly if the manager was around.

"Let me check." She dialed a three-digit number on the phone and said, "Sam, there's a Mr. Stroud here who'd like to talk to you. He wants to pay Stanley Frankfurt's bill. I'll send him right up."

Twenty minutes later, when Stroud came down, the marina had agreed to deduct twenty-five percent of the bill from their commission on the sale, and fifteen minutes after that, Granville Evans was unemployed.

When Bill Stroud got back to the hotel that evening, he was truly exhausted and truly convinced he was nuts. The just-bought-a-boat guilt was upon him. He had started out that morning telling himself he was only going to do some preliminary shopping for a powerboat that he probably wouldn't buy. Ten hours later he had practically bought a sailboat he couldn't afford.

He sat down at the small desk in the corner of his hotel room and added up estimates of what *Lullaby* would cost by the time she was ready for sea: at least a half a buck, as the unlamented Mr. Evans would have said. That was, even with the money from *Terrible Twosome* thrown in, almost half the total value of his savings and the stock portfolio in his IRA. The Kid's money was his only in theory. In his mind, it still belonged to them, and he felt like a thief because he was going to have to dip into it sooner or later. He tried to rationalize it by saying he would pay The Kids back when he sold the boat, but it didn't work. That was one of the worst things about just-bought-a-boat guilt: Before you bought the damned thing, any rationalization kept it at bay, but afterwards, nothing could dispel it.

Then he told himself neither of The Kids would blame him for buying *Lullaby*—she was one hell of a boat. That was true, but it didn't work either.

He remembered that he had felt this same intense guilt the night they bought *Twosome*. Now he had only an approximate memory of what she had cost, but he had wonderful memories of all that had happened in her. He had the vague feeling of breathlessness that came at the beginning of fibrillation and was fairly sure he hadn't taken his medication last night or the night before. He took a Lanoxin tablet, kicked off his deck shoes and lay down on the bed, trying to decide, between intense attacks of guilt, the best way to get *Lullaby*'s teak, dodger, and sail cover clean.

Only three other boats had been in the anchorage when they sailed in the night before, but there were five when Alice came on deck that morning. The pair of identical CYC 44s must have arrived late. Gordon was kneeling on the cockpit seat with the binoculars propped on the cabin top, studying one of them through the window of the dodger. "How does it look, Gordo?"

"I like this one a lot."

She took the glasses from him, looked over at the boat, and thought, *I'll just bet you do.* Two young women were standing nude on the steps built into the transom, taking turns spraying each other with a shower nozzle. "Forget it. It's a charter boat."

"Look, Alice . . ."

"Forget it. It's probably sailing in company with the other one. And even if it isn't, how many times do I have to tell you that charter boats have to be someplace at a set time, and that time is usually only a week or so away. We'll find something soon, don't worry. Take a swim. Better yet, scrub the bottom. You haven't done it in almost a month." She scanned the other boats as he got his brush, mask, snorkel, and plumber's helper out of a seat locker, pulled off his clothes, and climbed down the stern ladder. The other three boats were charters, too. "And don't take all day. I want to be under way by noon, and I think you do, too."

It was a brutal job, working under the boat, scrubbing with one hand and holding onto a sink plunger stuck to the bottom with the other, while holding his breath. But she wouldn't let him use his SCUBA gear, saying they had to save the tanks for an emergency.

She went below, hung the binoculars in the rack over the chart table, and changed into a very conservatively cut one-piece bathing suit: an old lady's bathing suit. Then she put on her mask and snorkel and, holding the faceplate, stepped backwards off the transom. For the next two hours she floated on the surface watching him work and pointing out spots he had not scrubbed to her satisfaction. She nagged him until every square inch of the bottom had been scrubbed at least twice and was perfectly clean. It was important to keep him exhausted at times like this.

CHAPTER THREE

Lullaby sailed, if anything, even better than Stroud had hoped, particularly when he factored in the worn-out sails and his suspicions that
the rig wasn't set up correctly. He wasn't absolutely sure, because *Twosome* had been a masthead rig, but he had crewed on a few fractionally
rigged boats, and this one just didn't feel right. When he got back to
Connecticut, he would pump the sailmaker and some other people about
the nuances of this rig.

That afternoon they hauled her. After he had checked the gel coat
for blistering and the through-hull fittings for corrosion, he offered Frankfurt forty thousand and Frankfurt jumped at it.

While Stanley phoned his wife, Stroud arranged for the yard to prop
Lullaby up and pull her mast so he could work on her. Then he walked
slowly around the boat as she hung in the travel lift, studying the lines
of her underbody.

She was just under thirty feet overall—on the small side for an offshore cruiser, but he wasn't as young as he once had been and would be
sailing her alone. He didn't plan to have a lot of guests or haul a lot of
luxuries, either. Her bilges were fairly slack, and she had a moderately
long—but not too long—fin keel that was a part of her underbody, not
just an appendage hung onto it. Her rudder was mounted on a skeg set
far aft. It was precisely the underbody he had always thought was the
best combination for both sea keeping and speed.

Of course she could not stay with modern skimming-dish racing
boats, which were just large, ultralight copies of the Flying Dutchman or

nineteenth century sandbaggers that needed a dozen guys hanging on
the weather rail to stay upright. But he was sure she would step out with
the offshore cruising types even five to ten feet longer, because she would
not be hauling several thousand pounds of supposedly necessary conve-
niences that complicate and encumber so many modern boats. No
shower with hot and cold running water; he'd shower in the cockpit
under a solar-heated water bag hung on the boom. No refrigeration
system; he'd get along on ice when he could get it and plan his meals
assuming he would not be able to get it. She would carry none of the
110-volt accessories that made hundreds of pounds of auxiliary genera-
tors and inverters and battery banks necessary. Just twelve-volt lights,
radios, a depthsounder, and a global positioning system receiver; all of
which would run for several days on *Lullaby*'s two modest-size house
batteries before it would be necessary to use the third battery to start the
engine to recharge them. This also reduced the amount of fuel he would
have to carry—more weight saved.

When you cut through all the bullshit, what makes any machine go
fast is a big engine mounted on a light structure. Her rig was certainly
big enough, and it was up to him to make sure the structure stayed light.

He ran his hand over the bottom; it felt like a solidified shag rug.
He knew how to fix that, too. He stood rubbing the roughness and said
very quietly, "Oh yeah, girl, we're going to get along."

Frankfurt came running across the yard and called, "It's all settled.
If we can get flights up tomorrow, my wife and I will meet you at our
attorney's office in Toms River, New Jersey on Wednesday. He was her
father's lawyer. How does nine o'clock sound to you?"

"Too early. I have to go to the bank, and then it's about a five-hour
drive from Connecticut. Make it three in the afternoon. I'll bring two
checks: one made out to your wife, since the boat's in her name, and one
to the marina for their commission. You can mail it from right there. I
don't want to have any trouble with them when I get back here."

"Oh. I'll have to call her back and tell her to change the appointment."

"Did you get a reservation on a flight yet?"

"No. Not yet."

"Maybe we better do that before she makes the appointment."

"Gee, I didn't think of that."

When it was all settled and Frankfurt had a thousand-dollar cash down payment in his pocket, he said, "Tonight I'm buying you dinner, Bill."

While they were eating, he said, "Oh, and Bill, I told Jennifer how you and I met— about your asking about the Holbrooks and all—and she reminded me of something. I think I told you that they always kept to themselves. Well, that wasn't completely true. They got to be quite chummy with an older couple off a big Grand Banks trawler yacht that was in a slip over on the other side of the marina. I'd forgotten about them. Italian name, Parisi, or something like that. I should have re-membered it. You don't see powerboaters and sailors hanging around together all that much."

"Are they still here? The Parisis, I mean. "

"No. At least I haven't seen them around."

The next morning, before he caught the plane, Stroud went into the marina office and asked about them. Ruth Connelly twiddled her com-puter and said, "Not Parisi, Polizzi. A Grand Banks 42. They left on the eleventh of June and, oh my . . . Now I remember them. How could I have forgotten? They went missing in the Anegada Passage a few weeks after they left here. It was big news at the time. Nice older couple, just retired. They had the boat shipped down from someplace in the Midwest. Tropical Shipping put it in the water and towed it around here, and we got it ready– cleaned up the shipping dirt, filled the tanks, started the engines, checked everything out. It was a brand new boat, a real gold-plater. Nice people. It was just so sad. To work your whole life and then when you're ready to begin living your dream . . . Are you all right, Mr. Stroud?"

Stroud sat down on the rattan sofa and said, "I'm fine. I just get these spells once in a while. It's atrial fibrillation; it comes and goes without reason."

"My father has that. Can I get you a glass of water or something?"

"No. But thanks. I'm better already. It comes and goes." He sat still for a few minutes and then said, "If I walk slowly, that sometimes helps. I'll be back in a bit."

He paced on the porch for a while, then came back in and said, "*Lullaby* is hauled out over at Frenchtown in the yard you recommended. I'll be in Connecticut for about ten days, and it'll take me a couple of weeks after that to get back in the water. Any trouble getting a slip? It'll just be for a week or so, then I'll head out."

"No problem. We should have plenty of space."

"I talked to Sam about how we're going to handle the commission payment."

"He told me."

"I'll see you in a couple of weeks."

"Have a good trip. And take it easy, Mr. Stroud."

He was back in ten days after ordering sails, spending a fortune at West Marine, and dropping another fortune in excess baggage fees for the duffel bags filled with clothes, gear, tools, a new inflatable dinghy, and an old 1973 Evinrude outboard to power it. He even had a proper certificate of documentation that showed him to be the owner of the yacht *Lullaby*. The house was closed, the leaves were raked, and a neighbor had agreed to watch the place and collect his mail. The only surprise of the whole trip was that the Bermuda shorts that hadn't fit him at all three weeks before could now be zipped up, even if they were still too tight to wear comfortably. When he tried them on, he realized that even if this turned out to be a wild goose chase, it had given him back something that had started to slip away when Dwight died. Now he had two of the three things he needed for a complete life: a collection of short-term obstacles to be overcome and a long-term problem to be solved. The other thing he needed, he knew he would never have again.

There were plenty of short-term obstacles—the second most daunting was *Lullaby's* bottom. He unpacked the old Porter Cable body grinder he had used on boat bottoms for years, stuck on a coarse grit disk, pulled on goggles and a respirator, and started down through about six kinds of bottom paint, most of which appeared to have been applied with a trowel. The top layers were so hard that they dulled the paper almost instantly; the coats just below them were so soft that they plugged the grit almost as fast, leaving the sandpaper as shiny and smooth as tile. He had brought four dozen 60-grit disks and twenty-four 120s, thinking it would be enough to remove all the old paint. By eleven o'clock on the first morning, he was only about six feet from the bow on one side and knew he would need a lot more sandpaper and a lot more time than he had thought.

And he was already exhausted. He wore an old pair of trousers and a long-sleeved shirt, and from his head to his ankles he was soaked with sweat and bright red with paint dust. He wiped his hands and face with an old towel, also bright red—everything within twenty feet of him was bright red—and took a swig of Gatorade. At that moment, *Lullaby*'s bottom appeared to be about the size of *Enterprise*'s.

Then a voice behind him asked, "Are you Bill Shroud?"

"Stroud. Bill Stroud." She was, of all things, about the last he needed at that moment: a large woman with lots of gray streaked black hair tied back in a knot and strong legs that ended in big feet stuck in leather sandals. She wore an expensive silk blouse and a khaki skirt, and no one would ever call her beautiful or even pretty. Her features were too large for her face and her hairline was too close to her heavy, black eyebrows. In some lights and depending on her mood and the mood of the observer, at best she might be considered handsome, but she would as often be seen as downright ugly.

Right now she was ugly. "I want to know why you've been asking questions about the Polizzi family and their boat. How were you involved with them?" She obviously was not much impressed by the bright red man standing before her.

Stroud considered telling her to go pound sand or worse, but he just didn't have the energy to waste on an argument with someone who so obviously wanted an argument. He picked up the grinder and went back to work. She came up in back of him and pulled the plug out of the extension cord, but not before she had gotten some of the dust on herself. "I'm talking to you."

"No, you aren't. You're shouting at me, and I'm beginning to get a little pissed off about it." He plugged the grinder back in, then said, "Now unless you want to get completely covered by this red shit, I suggest you either moderate your tone or get the hell out of here and leave me alone."

She moderated her tone, but just barely. Her voice wasn't shrill, but there was an intensity about her which, with the way she wagged those oversized eyebrows when she talked, made it seem shrill. "My name is Lydia Polizzi, and I'm the daughter of the people you're so nosy about. I think I have a perfect right to ask why."

He knew the type. A big broad with brass balls, probably either a lawyer or an MBA, who thought she could get anything she wanted either by intimidation or manipulation because she had always gotten everything she wanted by intimidation or manipulation. Toward the end, the company where he had worked had been crawling with them. Because she obviously took him to be a peon who couldn't afford to pay someone to do this filthy job, she hadn't even tried manipulation. Yeah, either a law degree or an MBA. Everybody in her generation was an aging hippy, a lawyer, or an MBA. Because she hadn't offered him a joint, or threatened to sue him, she was probably a goddamned beanie. "Lady, what I do is none of your business. Now, unless you want to wind up looking like Pocahontas, I suggest you get the hell out of here and let me get back to work."

She looked at her watch. "I have to catch a plane, but this isn't finished, believe me."

As she walked away and he started to sand again, he thought, *Why a plane? Is your broom in for repairs?* It was one of those thoughts that always come just too late.

He knew he should have talked to her. She might know something useful. But if she did, she would be the first barracuda he had ever met who did. Beneath the carefully selected clothes, the carefully exercised bodies, and the carefully practiced demeanor, there was always ignorance of whatever it was they were supposed to be doing. Sooner or later she would ask him to "fill her in" on the details. They always needed to be filled in on the details—like which way was up, and why do engineers insist that every electrical device have two wires connected to it when obviously one should be quite enough. Tough stuff like that that no one had bothered to explain to them in six or seven years of expensive and useless higher education.

During his last years at work, worried sick about his wife and his medical benefits, he had tried to placate them, to do everything they wanted, even when he knew those things were based on either ignorance or downright stupidity. But it hadn't helped him. They tossed him out just as quickly as those who had not gone along with them: those who had argued with them and tried to talk sense to them.

She came back five days later—again at precisely the wrong time. *Lullaby*'s bottom was sanded and ready for the first coat of paint, but first he needed to change the thick rubber doughnut that kept the sea from flowing up through the aperture in the hull from which the engine's lower drive unit protruded. The entire engine had to be lifted clear before the old doughnut could be removed and the new one installed. The yard had seemed to have neither the equipment nor any interest in the job, so he tackled it himself. Besides, he really didn't trust the yard to do it. If it wasn't done right, it could sink the boat in about two minutes, and the lackadaisical, no-problem-Mon, West Indian approach to any job had begun to grate on his Connecticut Yankee engineer's mentality.

First he fashioned a frame of 4x4 timbers, from which he hung a chain fall. Then he disconnected the exhaust, the water and fuel lines, and the electrical harnesses before unbolting the engine mounts and the doughnut's inner diameter from the lower unit. When everything was free, he lifted the engine up through the hatch in the cockpit sole

and left it hanging there while he cut, fitted, and bolted in place another timber to support it if the hoist slipped. Then he crawled under
the engine and started to unbolt the ring that held the doughnut's outer
diameter to the hull. He lay on his stomach in the engine space with
four hundred pounds of machinery hanging over his head and discovered that turning the bolt heads did no good because the nuts turned
with them. They were not, as he had assumed, welded to the lower
retaining ring. He slithered back into the main cabin and climbed up
through the companionway, hoping that someone from the delegation
that had watched him work and made useless suggestions all morning
was still hanging around. Now, of course, the yard was deserted.

He crawled back onto the bed of nails of the protruding motor mounts
and reached down through the center of the doughnut with one hand to
hold a nut with a box wrench, while with the other he used a socket
drive to back out the bolt. He could just reach three of the eight nuts
this way and dropped the wrench while trying to fit it by feel onto the
fourth.

He said, "Oh shit," and as he crawled back out and stood up in the
companionway, the Polizzi woman appeared on the ladder that leaned
against the hull.

"Do you need this?" She waved the wrench at him.

"Only if there's someone holding onto the end of it."

"What are you trying to do?

"Back out the bolts."

"Could I help?"

He wasn't about to look a gift wrench-holder in the mouth, and
besides, whether he liked her or not, he needed to talk to her. He hoisted
himself out of the hatch. "I'll show you." She was dressed in another
expensive-looking silk blouse, this time with a contrasting navy blue
skirt. "Be careful of your clothes, though. The nuts and everything
around them are soaked with Mystery Oil." He followed her down the
ladder and then knelt on one knee under the hull and pointed up into
the aperture. "Those."

She crouched beside him, pushed her sunglasses up into her thick gray and black hair, squinted upward, and said, "I see them. The, um, five left on that ring thing, right?"

He climbed back up in the boat and in about five minutes had the ring and the old doughnut out.

While he was scraping the dried sealant off the sealing face, she came up the ladder again and looked down through the hatch in the cockpit sole at where he worked under the hanging engine. "I've got the nuts and lower ring. Where do you want them?"

He couldn't twist around enough to see her, but he said, "Put them on that plastic sheet on the seat: there with the others. Thanks. I'm glad you came along."

"I'll bet you never thought you'd say that."

"I guess not."

"You want me to stick around and help you tighten them? I imagine you want to get that engine back down. That looks like about the worst place to work I've ever seen."

"Can't be helped. As long as you're here, could you hand me that sealant gun and the new doughnut? I should have put them where I could reach them before I crawled in here." She climbed aboard and reached down past the engine to hand them to him as he thought, *Intimidation didn't work, so now we'll try manipulation through charm.* He might as well take advantage of it. She'd probably make him pay for it later.

By late afternoon, the engine was back in place, with all the pipes and wires again connected, and she was sitting on the cabin top with her legs hanging in the cockpit where she had spent most of the afternoon watching him. He had to admit, she had a rare skill for a woman watching a man work at a difficult mechanical task: sense enough to shut up and not interrupt his train of thought. Her elegant outfit had suffered. There was an oil spot on one shoulder of her blouse and a streak of sealant on the hem of her skirt.

He gave her a clean rag and a bottle of solvent, and as she wiped the sealer—she seemed to be spreading it around rather than removing it—

he said, "Okay, Miss Polizzi. Even though I want to thank you, I don't think you came over here to help me change the engine doughnut."

She gave up on the skirt. "Maybe a dry cleaner will have more luck." She did not seem hopeful. "No, I didn't. We have to talk. We have something in common, don't we?"

"Do we?"

"My parents and niece disappeared at sea sometime last June."

"I'm sorry. I didn't know your niece was with them. But . . . ."

"Mr. Stroud, let's not jerk each other around. I'm senior vice-president of human resources for the Midwestern First National Bank of Ohio, and I looked into your background. I know about your daughter and son-in-law."

He knew she was right. They shouldn't jerk each other around. But the intensity of her expression, those eyebrows jumping up and down like a couple of spastic caterpillars, and the idea that because she was a VP she had the right to check him out, more than just irritated him. So he said, "No one is safe from senior vice-presidents in the information age, are they?" He didn't care about the edge in his voice.

"I have to know what's going on. Just what do you think you're doing?"

He kept silent for several minutes as he cleaned and sorted the sockets into their individual pockets in the toolbox. He really wanted to tell her where to go and what to do when she got there, but she was right, they did have something in common. A socket was missing and he looked all over the cockpit for it while she stared at him, awaiting a reply. He was afraid that he had left it in some cranny under the engine where it would bounce into the very worst place at the very worst time. He was about to start disconnecting things again, when he found it on the chart table. It didn't help his attitude.

As he closed the toolbox, she asked, "Well?"

"Tell me, Miss Polizzi, who's managing all the human resources of the Midwestern First National of Ohio while you're down here? They aren't just wandering around behaving like human beings instead of human resources, are they? I can't imagine you'd permit that." He knew he ought to talk to her, but he was exhausted, his chest was a mass of scratches and contusions from crawling in and out over those damned engine mounts, and those eyebrows and the self-assured, patronizing tone of her "Well?" just pissed him off.

She realized it and tried to make amends, although she obviously disliked him as much as he disliked her. "Look. I know we got off on the wrong foot last week, and I've been trying to make up for it all afternoon. We have to talk."

He sighed and accepted the olive branch. She didn't look like a woman who handed out many of them. "Okay, you're right. We have to talk, but right now I'm too dirty and too tired." He checked his watch. "It's four-fifteen. I eat most of my meals at the restaurant at the Ginger Bay Marina. Six-thirty okay?"

As he expected, she was a few minutes late, and when they were settled with drinks—she ordered white wine, of course; it had to be either that or mineral water—he asked, "Okay. How much did your spies find out about me and my family?"

"That your daughter, son-in-law, and another couple disappeared in the Atlantic on their way to the Caribbean three and a half years ago. I also know about your wife and your son. I want to tell you how sorry I am."

"Thank you. Now tell me about your people."

"My father, Vincent Polizzi, owned one of the biggest construction companies in the Midwest, and last year he retired. My brothers run it now. Pop always had boats—powerboats on the lake—and he always wanted to take a leisurely cruise through the islands when he retired. He and Mom came down for a vacation years ago, but he had to cut it short because of some crisis in the business. They never tried it again. But I think he always carried that memory of the Caribbean around with him. He'd mention it once in a while. Then we finally got him to retire, and my brothers knew that if they didn't get him to go away, he'd hang around and drive everyone nuts. So we all worked on him to buy a new and bigger boat, ship it down here, and let us ship him down here, too. It was the worst mistake we ever made."

"What about your mother? What did she think about it?"

"Mom was the standard, mark one, Italian wife. If that's what he wanted, that's what they'd do. But, like a lot of lake sailors, no matter how much they tell themselves that the Great Lakes are among the most dangerous bodies of water on earth, she was in awe of, and afraid of, salt water. So was Pop, but of course he'd never admit it. It was a good thing. At least we thought it was.

"He bought one hell of a boat, and he prepared it and himself just as well as humanly possible. I know that you ragboaters don't think stinkpotters have the foggiest idea what real seamanship is, but I'll tell you, my old man knew what he was doing. The boat had every electronic gadget available, and he not only knew how to use them, he knew how to fix most of them. You don't build the kind of business my father built without being pretty smart and a pretty good mechanic. He wasn't one of those power boaters who go out on Sunday afternoon and if anything goes wrong scream for the Coast Guard to come save them.

"He spent almost a year getting ready for this. He went to the school the engine manufacturer runs for mechanics—not the two-day course for owners, the three-week one for mechanics—and he even took a course in celestial navigation so he'd have a back-up for all those electronics."

"What happened?"

"Just like your daughter. No one really knows. My niece was a junior at Ohio State; she came down as soon as school was out and joined them. They left here on the eleventh of June and spent three weeks cruising in the Virgins. Every day or two, one of them would call someone back home to say what a great time they were having. Lydi was a great girl. Lydia. Same name as mine."

She looked out over the marina for a moment before continuing, "They were going across the Anegada Passage to cruise the northeastern islands and then haul out for the hurricane season either in St. Martin or Antigua. Probably Antigua. They left Virgin Gorda on the third of July and were never heard from again. They call it overdue and presumed lost. The theory is that they hit a drifting container and went down before they could get off a Mayday. Either that or some freighter ran them down in the dark and never even noticed."

"Oh yes. The ubiquitous drifting container or the inattentive freighter. They think that's what happened to Nell and Steve, too. Did they ever find anything?"

"Just a couple of floating deck chairs and cushions."

"Did they have an EPIRB?"

"The very latest kind was mounted on the fly bridge where it should have floated off and started to broadcast a Mayday and an identification number as soon as it got wet. Nobody ever heard a peep. I cannot imagine that Pop would have turned it off."

"Just the three of them were aboard?"

"We guess so. As I said, Mom was scared of salt water, and everyone is scared of the Anegada Passage: it has a fearsome reputation. It was pretty quiescent at the time they went missing, though. Anyway, they had lined up a man who was going to make the crossing with them, but he obviously crapped out at the last minute."

"How do you know?"

"If he had gone with them, we would have heard from his wife by now, I'm sure."

He was silent for a moment and then asked, "Are you hungry yet?"

"No. This isn't a topic that helps my appetite."

He tossed some money on the table and said, "Let's take a walk."

As they strolled down the dock he asked, "So what is this all about, Miss Polizzi? Why are you prowling around asking questions? It all seems straightforward. Tragic, but straightforward."

They walked in silence to the end of A-dock and then turned around, looking like any other couple admiring the yachts. Halfway back, she made a decision and said, "It isn't completely straightforward. They left Virgin Gorda on the third of July and were never heard from again. Ten

days later, on the thirteenth, two folding deck chairs and a cushion from
the seats on the flying bridge were found floating in the Anegada Passage up toward Sombrero Island. I can show you where on a chart. But
on the seventh, Lidy cashed twenty-five hundred dollars worth of
traveler's checks in St. Martin. Why would they cross the Anegada, go
into St. Martin, then go right back out into the Anegada for their appointment with the drifting container or the inattentive freighter? It
doesn't make any sense."

"How did you find out she cashed them?"

"I work in a bank, remember. And I bought them for her so she'd
have some walking-around money of her own. My brother is a skinflint.
A month or so ago I remembered them. No, that's not true. I've thought
of them once in a while in the last five months, but I couldn't bring
myself to try for a refund until a couple of weeks ago."

They walked two more docks in silence before he said, "Nell cashed
all of her traveler's checks in Charleston a week after they sailed from
Morehead City. I can't believe she would have made port again and not
called us."

"Lidy was in love with a young man at college. She never called
him from St. Martin. She was nineteen; she might not have called her
parents or me, but she certainly would have called him."

"I found out about Nell's checks last month when I finally went
through my wife's files. She died in January."

"I know. I'm sorry. You certainly haven't had much luck lately,
have you?"

They strolled on in silence until she finally said, "Last week I flew
over to Tortola, where they cleared into the British Virgins, and then
went to Virgin Gorda, where they cleared out. Nobody could tell me
anything. In St. Martin it was the same story, except the manager of the
bank where the checks were cashed said they have a strict policy of
always checking the person's passport, and for large sums, anything over
a thousand dollars, not only the teller but also a supervisor has to check
it. It had to have been Lidy. But it doesn't feel right. Maybe I'm just

looking for something because I can't deal with this. Ever since it happened, I've been a mess. I encouraged my parents to come down here, and I gave Lidy the plane ticket and the money." She fumbled a handkerchief out of her purse, blew her nose loudly, and then wiped her eyes.

Stroud didn't know whether to touch her or not. He was not the sort who hugged acquaintances, and even if he were, she wasn't the sort of person one hugged.

Then she continued, "I've spent the last three months in intense counseling, but it hasn't helped a bit. All I want is to find some closure, some way to put this behind me so I can get on with my life."

Stroud stopped thinking about hugging her and started thinking about hitting her. "You sound like a spokesperson for Bill and Hillary Clinton, for Christ's sake. The first steps in dealing with this kind of thing, Miss Polizzi—and I've had a lot of experience at it—is to stop kidding yourself and stop thinking in adolescent platitudes. And forget about closure. There are things in life for which there will never be any closure, and which only a sociopath can put behind him. When you grow up, you'll know that all you can do is live with those things and the pain they cause—if you ever grow up, that is. But, believe me, no matter how many shrinks you try to unburden yourself to, the pain will always be yours, and you can never offload it on someone else or get it behind you, wherever the hell that is." He turned and walked away from her.

She caught his arm. "You think you're the only person on earth who hurts, don't you? And that no one else's pain is real?"

He turned and faced her, thought about it for a moment, and said, "That's right. I don't think your pain is real. If it were, you'd be able to talk about it in your own words and not the clichés from television talk shows. Right now I doubt if you're capable of feeling real pain, or real sorrow, or real anything else. I think you know you're supposed to feel those things, but you don't know how, so you mouth all the platitudes your generation says you should mouth to fool yourself and everybody else into thinking you have genuine feelings. I'll bet when you lay some-

one off at the Midwestern Bank, you have the same look of phony concern you have now, with the waving eyebrows and all, while you tell the
poor bastard just how saddened you are to have to do it. And all the
while, inside, you're smiling a mean, dirty little secret smile, and enjoying the sense of power it gives you. Now you're the one whose life has
been torn up, and you don't think that's fair. Tough."

"That's the rottenest thing anyone ever said to me."

"Good. Think how pleased all the poor bastards you've ever shafted
would be to hear it."

"You really hate me, don't you?"

"Sure. But don't let it go to your head. I hate lots of people."

"Why? What did I ever do to you, other than look into your background? I had a perfect right to find out everything I could about you."

He stopped and faced her. "You don't know anything about me."

"Oh no? What don't I know?"

"For one thing, you don't know that I know the name of the guy
who was supposed to sail across the Anegada with your folks. It was
Gordon Holbrook, wasn't it? Your spies didn't find that out about me,
did they? And his wife's name is Alice, and they have a boat called
Cinderella, and I'll tell you one more of the infinite number of things
you don't know, lady; I'll bet the son-of-a-bitch did sail with your parents, because I'm almost sure he and his wife sailed with my daughter
and son-in-law, too."

She stopped and stared at him. "My God."

This time when he walked away she did not follow him. He was just
like her father. She had never won an argument with her father either,
because he always knew something she didn't know. Pop had been short
and stocky with a full head of black hair turned silver gray. Stroud was big,
and what hair he had left had probably once been light, but they were the
same. Her father had always patronized her, treated her like a twelve-year-
old who constantly needed to be told to grow up. She really hadn't liked
her father; the analyst had finally gotten her to admit it because he was sure
it was a large part of her problem. She liked this guy Stroud even less.

But if what he said about the Holbrooks was true . . . But it couldn't be true. Things like that didn't happen . . . "Oh God."

The next morning, Stroud carefully masked Lullaby's waterline and put the first coat of paint on the bottom. As he worked, he thought of Lydia Polizzi. Just another baby boomer who had stayed a baby: an entire generation of permanent children. They lived in a world where the proper platitudes and a smug certainty of their own moral superiority were all they needed to prevail over everyone and everything   And God help anyone who did not accept their moral superiority as a given and talked about ugly and irrelevant things like reality. Well, she might learn about reality now, but he damn well didn't have the time or the energy to teach her.

While his paint dried, he drove along the waterfront to a cinder block and corrugated iron building. It had never seen paint except for a barely legible sign that said, "Wes Lundy Enterprises—Good Boat Stuff Bought and Sold" in a front window made opaque by years of accumulated dirt and salt spray from the harbor across the street.

The inside was as dingy as the window; some good boat stuff and a lot of bad boat junk was stacked, hung, and heaped on and around a collection of counters and old showcases so that it was just barely possible to squeeze through the aisles that wove like a maze through it all. At the back of the store, a skinny old white man sat at an ancient soda fountain posting entries in a ledger that looked like Bob Cratchit's. The place must have been a drugstore once. He ignored Stroud so completely when he called to him that he was sure he was deaf. When Stroud finally found his way to the soda fountain, he closed the ledger and asked, "How can I help you?" in a lower-class British accent. "I" was pronounced "Oy."

"You could have told me how to get back here to begin with."

"No, I couldn't. That would be against the rules of modern marketing. If you go into one of your Yank supermarkets to get a quart of milk, they have it arranged so you have to go through the whole store to get to the milk cabinet, don't they? Same idea. Did you see anything you want in your travels?"

"I'm looking for a storm anchor. I just bought a boat, and the guy I bought it from said he sold you a fisherman's. By the size of the chocks in the bilge, I'd guess it was about seventy-five pounds."

"I have several. Shall we look?" He slid off the stool and led Stroud up one aisle and down another until they had crossed the store to a wall where two rusty steel cabinets stood. In a heap between them were about two dozen anchors. He lifted the top one from the pile—it was a badly bent Danforth—and handed it to Stroud. "Give us a hand, mate. Put this one over there, will you?"

Stroud had no idea where over there was, but he found an empty space between two piles of moldy, cork-filled life jackets that looked as if they had come from *Titanic*. He dumped the Danforth and the next four anchors he was handed there.

"I think this is what you're looking for." It was a Paul Luke version of the original Herreshoff, the best fisherman's anchor ever made.

"How much?"

Thus began a ten-minute haggle that ended with Stroud sure he was paying double what Frankfurt had gotten for the anchor, but still less than half of what a new one would cost.

"Now, what else can I get you? Maybe some loyfe jackets. Can't ever 'ave too many loyfe jackets." He pointed at *Titanic's*.

"I think that's about it for now." He would have liked to browse through the place, but it would take at least a week.

"Going cruising through the islands, are you? What about a bit of firepower? There are sharks and other things down here we don't have on the Solent, you know." He unlocked one of the steel cabinets. "Do you have a shotgun? Crazy to go out there without one, as anyone who has ever read *Jaws* should know." The cabinet was stuffed with long guns ranging from a short-stocked, bolt-action .22 caliber child's rifle, to what appeared to be an eight-gauge double-barreled goose gun that must have been at least five feet long and a hundred years old. Lundy reached into the cabinet and pulled out one gun and then caught the three others that fell out with it. All of them were covered with rust. "Here's what you need."

It was a bolt-action Mossberg twelve gauge. Stroud reflexively pulled open the action and checked to be sure it was not loaded, as he said, "From what I've heard, a gun is more trouble than it's worth when you're going from one jurisdiction to the next in the islands."

"Only if you declare it. Few people do. Surely if you take a gun ashore, and particularly if you went onto an island packing a pistol and got caught, you'd have plenty of trouble. But nobody ever comes out and searches the boat. As long as you're discreet, there's no problem."

Stroud handed the shotgun back as he thought about it. Then he saw something standing in the back corner of the cabinet that caught his attention. "What's that back there?" He pointed at a muzzle with a gas cylinder and bayonet stud attached to it.

"Where?"

Stroud reached past him and, trying to keep the rest of the arsenal from falling out of the cabinet, slowly maneuvered an old rifle out as the proprietor steadied the other weapons. "Oh, that. Oy've had it forever. Bit of an antique."

It was a battered old M-1 rifle. When Stroud tried to open the bolt it was frozen, so he dropped the butt to the floor, put his heel on the operating rod handle, and forced the action open. It was unloaded, so he put his thumbnail into the action to reflect the light of the dirty overhead bulb as he swung it up and looked into the muzzle. The barrel was plugged, but whether it was with grease, rust, dirt, or all of the above, he couldn't tell. As he lowered the butt to the floor, he rubbed the head of the bolt with the pad of his thumb and then smelled it. Grease.

"Oy get the impression this ain't the first time you've ever seen one of those."

Stroud turned it muzzle-down and opened the door in the butt plate. The cleaning kit was still there in its oilcloth case. He closed the butt and then hooked the side of his right hand in front of the operating handle as his thumb pushed the magazine follower down. Then he rolled his hand so his thumb came clear of the bolt as it closed. It was a skill he and millions of other young Americans had once learned, often at the cost of a painful case of M-1 thumb if the bolt caught it. There was no chance of that now, because the action only closed about halfway and he had to whack it shut with the heel of his hand.

He stood looking at the old rifle, thinking about it. On the back of the receiver, above the serial number, was the *Winchester* logo. Then he asked, "Do you have any ammunition for this thing?"

"Let's look. What does it shoot?" He unlocked the other cabinet. It had shelves from top to bottom. On the top ones were stacked mildewed boxes of shotgun shells and other types of ammunition. The others held Very pistols and all sorts of flares. Stroud decided that he wouldn't want to be within 500 yards of this place if it ever caught fire.

"It shoots .30-06,"—he pronounced it *thirty ought six*—"in eight-shot spring clips."

The proprietor pushed some boxes aside and pulled out three boxes of cartridges that had obviously been badly soaked at some time or other. The printing was barely legible, so Stroud opened one box and checked. "Yup. Not much use without the clips, though."

Without another word, Lundy went down the aisle and returned carrying an old kitchen ladder speckled with paint. He stood it in front of the cabinet, mounted it, and reaching in between the other boxes, pulled out an old, olive-drab bandolier of the sort Stroud hadn't seen in forty years. In each of its ten pouches were eight rounds of ammunition held in a spring clip. Stroud popped the shells out of one clip and looked closely at it. Although it was covered by decades of dirt and mildew, it wasn't rusted or pitted and seemed to be structurally okay. The black protective coating put on God-only-knew how long ago had done its job. Then he noticed that the bullet heads were painted black, too. Armour piercing. He wondered how on earth they had ever gotten here. "How much for the whole mess? Lock, stock, barrel, and all the bullets."

"That's one 'ell of a weapon. That will stop anything you might run into down 'ere. And it's a lot of ammunition. How does three hundred U.S. sound?"

"It sounds nuts. When I clean it, I may find that I don't want to shoot it unless I tie it in a tree and pull the trigger with a very long string. I'll give you fifty bucks, and if I have to drop the whole mess over the side, I won't bother you. If I give you any more than that and find out it's not serviceable, I'll want my money back."

"A hundred."

"Fifty. Take it or leave it."

"Seventy-five, take it or leave it "

"Okay. What kind of paperwork do they require down here to transfer a firearm?"

Lundy wrapped the rifle and ammunition in a dark green plastic garbage bag and never bothered to answer his question. Probably because there didn't seem to be any paperwork required at all.

"I think they're going to go ashore." She sat in the cockpit knitting and watching the custom 42-footer anchored next to them, a hundred yards away. Gordon was in the galley, making her a sundowner. "He just came on deck wearing long pants, and he's pulling their dink around to the ladder. I think he's waiting for . . . Yup. Here comes the young one, all dolled up." Alice stuffed her knitting into its bag, climbed down the companionway, and as she opened the door to the after cabin, said, "Forget the drinks, Gordon. We're going to dine ashore tonight. Get changed. Hurry up. Long pants and a good shirt." He stood with her half-made drink and the open bottle of light beer that was all she allowed him, trying to decide what to do first. He wasn't very flexible in some ways, but in others he was infinitely flexible. "Just leave them in the sink and get changed."

As he scurried into the forecabin where he lived, she selected a dress from the hanging locker, laid it on her bunk, and thought, *Finally. Some action.*

CHAPTER FOUR

In the age of sail, the ability to work to windward was absolutely essential for survival. To sail a few degrees closer to the wind and a few tenths of a knot faster could be the difference between a successful voyage and death on a lee shore or at the hands of an enemy. But working to weather is even more than that; when done well, it is the essence of sailing. The greatest delight in the sport is the feel of a boat heeled down precisely on her lines and carrying exactly the right amount of perfectly trimmed sail for the wind and sea conditions, as she drives as fast and as close to the wind as possible.

But no one on either of the two boats in the impromptu race across the Caribbean that afternoon was experiencing any delight at all, because neither boat was worth a damn upwind. As always happens when two sailboats heading toward a common destination encounter each other, a race ensued. In this case, it was a race between the tortoise and the turtle.

Both were sloops of supposedly moderate displacement loaded down with all the extra gear that accumulates on a cruising boat unless the discipline of a William Bligh is enforced. Nor was their performance improved by the other faults common to their type. To avoid the feeling that one was living in a sewer pipe, and to provide more space below, they were both excessively wide for their lengths; therefore, their sails could not easily push them through the steep chop that the southwest wind was building atop the old swell from the northeast. It did not help that those sails were no longer new or that their original design had been an unhappy compromise between performance, particularly to weather, and ease of handling by a short-handed crew. Working to weather is not normally a problem for the crews of such boats. When the wind comes from ahead, they either change their plans and go someplace else, or they roll up their baggy jibs and, depending on their personalities, either stow the mainsail or leave it up and flopping as they motor. But it is 1200 miles from Martinique to Colon on the Atlantic side of the Panama Canal, a long way to motor in a boat too wide to easily cut through the chop and under-fueled for such a trip, even with a half dozen Jerry cans tied to its rail.

The trade winds are supposed to blow relentlessly from the northeast in the Caribbean, making it an easy eight- to ten-day reach down to the Canal. It is not supposed to blow from the southwest, and when it does, everyone gets edgy.

If Charles and Missy hadn't been in such beastly moods, and if they had been making better progress, Charmaine Bissette could have enjoyed such a beautiful day with such a perfect Force-4 sailing breeze— even if it was blowing from exactly the wrong direction. But one or the other of them had to be on the wheel all the time because the autopilot did not anticipate the seas and therefore could not snake the boat through the chop. And steering wasn't easy. The helmsman's choice was to point as close to the wind as possible and have the short, steep seas pound *Colibrei* almost to a stop. Or he could sail well off the wind, headed approximately toward Puerto Rico on one tack or Caracas on the other. Poor *Colibrei* was like a fat lady trying to get back into a theater when everyone else was leaving.

By midafternoon they had only made good about thirty kilometers toward the Canal since leaving Fort de France at six that morning, and Missy was being even more difficult than normal. It was a terrible thing to say about your own sixteen-year-old daughter, but Charmaine would be glad when they were through the canal and could put her on a plane to Montreal. They had let her take the term off from school because Charles had said the trip would be an educational experience for her.

So now, instead of just waiting out this wind in Martinique, no matter how long it took, Charles was steering the boat close-hauled across the Caribbean and Missy was sulking because Charmaine had sent her below to work on the studies she had promised to do every day. A Catholic girl's school was the best place for Missy, anyway. In the last year or so she had blossomed so she could wear Charmaine's clothes and fill them almost as well, and she had become excessively body-proud, as her mother thought of it. Every time she went ashore in her skimpy bikini top and cut-off shorts, she brought back men—not nice boys her own age, but older men of all sizes, shapes, and colors. Instead of Melissa they should have named her Missalina.

A half-mile astern, the boat that had been gaining on them all afternoon was crossing their track on the other tack. It looked like that nice American couple they had had dinner with the other night in that marvelous restaurant. Both dinghies had arrived at the dock in Fort de France at the same time, and as they had walked together into town they had chatted and discovered they were heading for the same restaurant, so they had shared a table. The Holbrooks. They were on their way to the Pacific, too. But they were under no time compulsion to get through the canal by a certain date. She wondered why they hadn't waited out the wind in Martinique.

Lullaby was back in her slip at the Ginger Bay Marina. Her teak had been scrubbed and sanded, her gel coat gleamed through two coats of wax, and all her standing rigging and most of her halyards had been replaced with new. Her engine, with all its fluids changed, was spotless in its new coat of enamel so that the slightest leak would be instantly visible. It stood in an equally spotless engine compartment.

Stroud finished bending on the new mainsail, installed the battens, and then hoisted it to be sure the sailmaker hadn't cut the roach so large that it caught on the backstay, as had happened to the last mainsail he had bought for *Terrible Twosome*. It was fine. He dropped it, rigged the reef lines, then carefully folded it on the boom and put on the cover. He hadn't been able to get the sail cover or the dodger completely clean, but the material was fine. They would have to serve. Enough was enough. Tomorrow he would move aboard.

He looked at his watch. Two-twenty. The hell he would. He'd check out of the hotel and move aboard this afternoon.

Cinderella crossed tacks with Colibrei twice more as the afternoon wore on and Charles and Charmaine took turns steering. Each time they were closer. Just before sunset, Charmaine went below to mix drinks and tell Missy she could stop staring at her books, but the girl was asleep in the aft cabin. It was just as well; it would be a long night, and if the wind didn't free up, it could be the first of several.

She had no idea just how long that night was to be.

As Stroud stowed the last of his things aboard, he noticed that the cabin temperature was almost bearable, thanks to the three small electric fans he had installed to keep the air moving through the boat. It was starting to get dark when he finished. He stood looking out the companionway for a moment and decided it was too early for dinner, so he turned on the light over the table in the center of the cabin, opened the table's leaves, and covered the surface with newspapers. He lifted the back of the sofa and from under the bedding stored there, took out the old rifle, still wrapped in the green plastic garbage bag in which he had brought it aboard, and placed it on the table. He had just finished unwrapping it and, by snapping out the trigger assembly, had broken it into its three major pieces, when he heard someone say, "Permission to come aboard," as the boat rocked.

He just had time to cover the table with the plastic bag before Lydia Polizzi's head appeared in the hatch. "Mr. Stroud, we really have to talk. Have you eaten yet?"

"No, not yet."

"Well, aren't you going to invite me below for a drink, at least? The boat looks gorgeous. You've done wonders." She didn't wait for an answer but turned around, hiked up her skirt, and climbed down the ladder.

There wasn't much else he could do, so as she sat down on the settee opposite him he said, "Why certainly, Ms. Polizzi. Please come aboard. And would you like a drink? Rum or beer—that's all there is."

"Rum with ginger ale or Coke, if you have it. And I'm hoping we can keep this civil. I'm willing to try."

"Ginger ale. I don't have any Coke. But I have to warn you, it's Virgin Island rum and tastes like jet fuel."

"What are you having?"

"Twenty-seven years in the airplane engine business, I like the taste of jet fuel."

"Yes, I know the company. I had a plane with one of your engines once."

"A recip? I worked for the jet engine division. Defunct now. The MBAs ran it into the ground and then peddled the pieces." He fished a handful of cubes through the tiny icebox hatch in the counter top and made the drinks, then handed her one and asked, "What now? I guess we do have to talk. Let's talk."

"I just got back from Columbus yesterday. I am now unemployed. Well, on indefinite leave of absence, which is really the same thing."

"And?"

"And I have to find out what really happened to my people just as much as you do."

"How do you propose to do that?"

"I have a pilot's license. Had it for years. Twin engine, instrument rated. I chartered a Twin Beach in San Juan for a month and flew it over. If that's not long enough, I'll extend."

"Won't work. Too many boats that all look alike from the air."

"Sailboats that all look alike. But there can't be that many Grand Banks 42s."

"What makes you think it's still afloat?"

"You think your daughter's boat is still afloat, don't you?"

"Yes. But I have reason to think it."

She looked at him intently before asking, "Are you going to tell me what those reasons are and how you knew Gordon Holbrook was supposed to sail with my parents, or aren't you?" Her eyebrows for once were still while she asked it.

He opened a drawer under the chart table, brought out his brown manila envelope, then sat down next to her and showed her the photos.

When he had finished she said, "That's not very conclusive, is it? You bought this boat and got it ready for sea based on that?"

"I'm pretty sure my son-in-law and I made that sternrail bracket and the grate on the forward hatch. One could be a coincidence, but not both. And Frankfurt described the boom to me: that's three. And there's Nell's traveler's checks, and the phony documentation of the boat the Holbrooks must be using as they go from one country to another. And there's your niece's traveler's checks, and the relationship between the Holbrooks and your folks, although I had already decided to look for them before I knew about your family."

"Do you have any idea how many islands and anchorages there are? Just between here and San Juan I saw dozens, and they all had from one to a hundred sailboats in them. And there are hundreds more boats scurrying from one harbor to the next on any given day. You could sail around the Caribbean for a hundred years and never find them."

"I don't have anything better to do. Until this came along, I was sitting in front of a television set waiting for an angel to yell, 'Next.' And I'll find them. I am not the richest or the smartest or the nicest person you will ever meet, lady, but I guarantee you, I am the most relentless. I'll find them."

"I could increase your chances by narrowing your search area down for you. If I flew over an anchorage and it was empty, or the only boats couldn't possibly be the ones we're looking for, it could save you miles of sailing and years of looking. I could check out the ones at sea, too." He was silent while he thought about it. After a while she asked, "What do you intend to do when and if you find them?"

"That depends on where I find them and what their story is. But right now, if it's my daughter's boat, I can only think of one explanation, and it's so ghastly that I don't want to think about it. You want another drink?"

"Please." As he stood, he brushed the plastic and it slid off the table. "What's that?"

"The U.S. Rifle, M-1, Caliber .30, semiautomatic, clip-fed, gas-operated. Sometimes called the Garand, after its inventor."

"I don't believe in guns." Her eyebrows bounced when she said it.

"Is that like not believing in Santa Claus or the Easter Bunny?"

"Guns bring nothing but human pain and suffering. I hate them."

"Sometimes they alleviate human pain and suffering. A number of rifles just like this one had a lot to do with ending the Holocaust and the Nazi reign of terror, as I recall." He put the plastic back. Just the sight of it had upset her. But it was phony upset, as though she was upset because she believed she was supposed to be upset. For a few minutes there, before she had seen the rifle, she had behaved genuinely. Too bad it hadn't lasted.

"I won't have anything to do with anything that involves guns. If you expect my help, you'll have to get rid of it."

"In the first place, I don't expect your help. You offered it, but I don't remember accepting it. And the last time I got helped by the likes of you, lady, I wound up out of a job with my pension cut in half. But tell me, I'm curious, what do you intend to do if you find the Holbrooks and it turns out our worst fears are true? Drop leaflets on them asking them to repent?"

"I believe in the rule of law. If I find them, and if there is credible evidence that they did something wrong, I'll turn them in to the proper authorities. What are you going to do? Use that thing?" She pointed at the plastic as though it concealed an angry rattlesnake.

"If they sailed in here right now, I'd give their boat a careful look over, and if it was *Brownian Movement*, I'd run right down to the Coast Guard Station and the cop shop and scream like hell. But if I run into them someplace else? I don't know. The Caribbean is a hodgepodge of colonies, protectorates, and independent countries, most of them smaller than my little hometown in Connecticut. I have no idea who the proper authorities might be in most of them, let alone once I'm outside their three-mile, or twelve-mile, or whatever their limits are.

"Your folks left this U.S. possession and went to Virgin Gorda, a British colony. From there they headed for St. Martin, an island about six miles in diameter, one half of which is a Department of European France and the other half of which is a Dutch colony. If they didn't go there, they planned to go to Antigua, an independent country in the British Commonwealth. To get there, they would have passed about a half dozen other islands, all of them independent countries or colonies or suzerainties of one sort or another. About the only things missing are a Dukedom in the Holy Roman Empire and an Arab Emirate. So please tell me who the proper authorities are if we find them in one of those places, let alone out at sea?"

"All of our relatives were U.S. citizens. If we go to a U.S. Consulate with evidence that crimes may have been committed against Americans, they'll have to do something."

"God, I'm getting tired of telling you to grow up. Look. Do you really think that bunch in Washington will give a damn about five people lost at sea under mysterious circumstances? Who the proper authorities are, and what they can do about whatever I find, will depend on what I find and where I find it. And if the worst is true, the Holbrooks might not be too anxious to have me go running to any authorities about it." He pointed at the chart table. "But I'm an Eagle Scout, lady. I believe in being prepared. And I'd be grateful if you didn't tell anyone about my antique."

"So you admit that it's illegal to have that thing. That doesn't make you any better than you suspect the Holbrooks are."

"If you can't distinguish between discreetly owning a firearm for self-protection and what we suspect the Holbrooks did, you aren't immature. I take that back. You're an idiot."

"A gun will only make this whole terrible situation worse."

"A gun is just a machine for throwing balls––that's Oliver Winchester's definition—and, in the immortal words of Shane, it's no better and no worse than the man who uses it, Joey."

"I know: guns don't kill people, people kill people. That's just a meaningless slogan."

"Well, since you seem to be the expert on meaningless slogans, I'll defer to you on that. You know, I've known guys who owned handguns, had permits for them, and carried them around, being dug in the back and getting oil all over their clothes, while they secretly hoped that someone would give them a really good reason to shoot them. They thought that a gun was more than it actually was, and that it would make them more than they actually were. I have also known people like you, who think all guns possess some intrinsic evil which it is their duty to sweep from the face of the earth so they can show the world just how righteous and morally superior they are. They, too, think that guns can make them more than they really are. Well, in my opinion, one group is as crazy as the other. A gun is a machine for throwing balls, that's all: just a tool that cannot make anyone more than he actually is. If everyone understood that, guns wouldn't be a problem."

"So you won't get rid of it, even if it means losing my help."

"Nope. Besides, that particular rifle intrigues me. It may have gone up a beach in Normandy or at Tarawa, for all I know. How it got here, to lie on this table, in this boat, in this island . . . . Do you know what my middle name is? Did your spies find that out for you?" She shook her head, no. "Tecumseh. William Tecumseh Stroud. My father was a history buff. He'd never forgive me if I got rid of a historical artifact like that." Then he changed his tone. "But believe me, Miss Polizzi. I'm not some gun nut who's looking for an excuse to shoot someone, any more than I own a hammer because I'm looking for some excuse to drive nails into something."

She sipped her drink while she thought for a moment, then she said, "Okay. Since you're a man who obviously values candor, that's all bullshit, and we both know it. I don't believe what you just said, and deep down, I don't think you do, either. You keep telling me I'm a naive adolescent who ought to grow up. Well, I think you're at exactly the opposite end of the spectrum—a bitter, hate-filled old man with plenty of reasons to be bitter and plenty of people to hate, who's just hoping for an excuse to open up on someone with that thing.

"If we find out that the worst happened, I'll go all the way—to the courts and the Congress and the press and anyplace else I have to go in order to get justice. I'll only work through the proper authorities any way I have to, but I won't become part of some vigilante posse." She held out her glass. "Could I have another drink?"

He didn't seem to hear her or see the glass. "Those bastards in Washington that you think will help you, they stuck my son Dwight and his buddies out on the very end of the limb in that little shithole of a country for no purpose whatsoever except that some overeducated moron from Georgetown thought it might help his career at the State Department. Then, after the towel-heads blew the limb off, they never did a damn thing about it, just closed the embassy and never opened it again and sent this poor Marine captain to officiate at the funeral and give us a flag, a Purple Heart, and a nice form letter from the idiot who was soiling the White House at the time. I came close to dumping the flag, the medal, and the letter in a trash barrel right there in front of the cameras from the local TV station, but Liz and Nell stopped me.

"The proper authorities. There are no proper authorities in this fucking country any more, lady. There are only self-serving opportunists on the make, who don't give a damn about you or me or our families or anyone else. Who only care about advancing their own pathetic careers, or hanging onto jobs they don't have any idea how to do, because they know they're the best jobs they can ever hope to get. The proper authorities, my ass. You want to know who the proper authorities are? We, you and me and the U.S. Rifle, M-1, we're the proper authorities by default."

She held out her glass again but he still didn't seem to see it, although he was looking right at it, so after a moment she jiggled the ice cubes at him. It brought him back from wherever it was he had gone, and he said, "Oh. Oh, sure." This time as he got up, he was very careful not to move the plastic. He made her another rum and ginger in silence, and after he handed it to her, turned back to the galley and filled his own glass with the remains from the can of the ginger ale. More than one or two drinks were usually all he could handle without bringing on the fibs.

She took a long pull and then broke the silence by asking, "What's your plan?" As soon as she said it she realized how dumb it sounded, so she rephrased it. "I mean, when are you leaving and which way are you headed?"

He changed his mind and poured a large belt of rum into the remaining ginger ale in his glass. Then he said, "And I'll tell you something else about these Holbrooks whose rights you're so worried I might violate. It was three years between the time my people disappeared and your people disappeared. How many others disappeared in those three years that your proper authorities didn't notice or do anything about? You think I'm a bitter old man? Well, that's about the only thing you've gotten right since I met you." He slumped onto the sofa across from her, took a long pull of his drink, and then said, "*In vino veritas.* But I promise you, I won't do anything that doesn't need to be done."

"Get rid of the gun, Bill. It will only make whatever is going to happen that much worse."

He didn't want to argue about it or anything else anymore. Everything she had said was probably right and everything he had said was probably right. Except for those arguments where both sides were dead wrong, it was the most useless kind.

"A long time ago I wore a green suit, believed in a lot of things I don't believe in any more, and lugged one of those around for a living. A long time ago. I don't know if I want to try to shoot it except by pulling a string tied to the trigger while I hide behind a stone wall. It has to be at least forty-five years old, and it shows every one of them. It's probably not a weapon at all anymore, just a relic of my wasted youth. Maybe I'll send it home to hang over the mantle."

She sipped the last of her drink as they silently agreed to drop the matter there. "When are you leaving and which way are you headed?"

"I've got a few odd jobs to do tomorrow. Then on Wednesday I'm going out on a shakedown cruise, and if everything works okay, I'll load provisions and leave on Saturday, heading east and south to search through the Virgins. If I don't find anything, I'll cross the Anegada Passage and keep looking. It's a trail long cold, but it's the only trail I've got."

"Why not leave on Friday?"

"No one starts a voyage that needs as much luck as this one does on a Friday."

"So you do believe in luck, then."

"If you'd had my luck, lady, wouldn't you believe in luck?"

Gordon Holbrook was steering as the boats once more converged. The engine had been running all day, and it gave them the edge they needed to catch the custom-built forty-two-foot sloop with the Canadian flag permanently attached to its backstay. He asked down the hatch, "How is it, Alice? We're just about there."

She climbed up into the cockpit as she replied, "All clear. Nothing on the radio or the radar." Then she looked over at the other boat. "I'll take her. You get ready."

For the next twenty minutes she worked toward the other boat, carefully estimating and calculating angles and speeds. They were on port tack, the Bissettes were on starboard, and she did not want to get far enough ahead to cross their bow. If they couldn't, the Canucks would expect them to change course and duck close under *Colibrei's* stern at the last moment. Boats working to windward never willingly gave up an inch of the distance they were fighting to gain. The boat on starboard tack had right of way, and when their paths crossed, the port tack boat always ducked around the other boat's stern as close as possible.

Soon now. Gordon was standing out of sight at the bottom of the hatch. "We're just about there. I'll say when. Turn on the radios and the tape player." The microphones of the VHF and single side-band radios were held back-to-back by a couple of thick rubber bands that also held down both talk buttons. The earphones of a cheap tape player were clamped to them so that when the radios were tuned to their hailing and emergency frequencies, and the reggae tape was playing, it blotted out any other radio that might try to broadcast.

She stood up behind the wheel so she could see over the bow and smiled and waved to the man steering the other boat. Perfect.

Just as they crossed his transom she said, "Now," and luffed up as Gordon stood up in the hatch and shot Charles Bissette in the head with a short, ugly, and complicated-looking machine pistol. He did it and she witnessed it with no more compunction than they felt about the deaths of the flying fish that landed on deck. With its wheel freed, the Canadian boat swung head to wind as *Cinderella* came alongside and Gordon jumped across, the weapon in one hand and a white plastic bag in the other. As he dropped down the hatch, Alice bore off across the wind and switched on the autopilot, then she rolled up the jib and rigged fenders. It was too rough to raft the boats; he'd have to jump back and forth. God, how she loved this. This was what it was like to be really alive.

It took only a few minutes before Gordon reappeared in the cockpit, gave her the thumbs-up sign, and tossed the plastic bag over to land at her feet in the cockpit. She checked the course, then carried the bag below and left it on the chart table while she turned off the jammer and the radios before she hurried topside again. Gordon rolled up *Colibrei's* jib, double-reefed the main, engaged the autopilot, and put the Canadian boat on a slow reach across the wind. Alice did the same with *Cinderella*, except that she left some of the jib exposed and put the boat on a close reach so she would work out to windward of the other boat. She preferred not to hear any of the sounds that might escape from its cabin.

When they were perhaps a quarter of a mile apart, she put *Cinderella* on a parallel course, played with the sail trim until she was moving at about the same speed, then went below. She picked up a hand-held VHF radio identical to the one he had taken with him and said, "Zip" into it.

In a few seconds the answer came back "Zip. Zip."

It seemed a bit too loud and clear, so she said, "Check W." The radios had one-watt and five-watt output settings, and at one watt, with their built-in antennae so close to the water, there was no chance of anyone else picking up their transmissions. But Gordon was not good with numbers, and at times like these he tended to ignore details, so she had to check on him constantly.

"W checked one."

"Lights." Through the cabin window she saw the running lights come on in the short tropical twilight, so she signed off and left him to his pleasures. "Zip. Zip."

She dumped the plastic bag out on the chart table. It contained their wallets and passports, $1700 Canadian, $8400 U.S., a stack of traveler's checks redeemable by either Charles or Charmaine Bissette, and a small, satin zipper bag containing the three-carat emerald ring the wife had worn to dinner the other night. There was also a diamond ring with a stone almost as large, a couple of tennis bracelets, three sets of diamond earrings, a spectacular string of pearls, several expensive watches, and a tangle of gold chain bracelets and necklaces. She dug through the wallets, adding the cash to the piles on the table, and then slipped the woman's credit cards into her passport and the girl's credit cards into hers, along with a studio photo of the two of them from the man's wallet. She scooped the man's passport and all the wallets back into the plastic bag, along with a rock she took from the garbage locker under the sink, and then stepped up into the companionway and threw the bag overboard, disposing of Charles Bissette forever. Charmaine and Melissa Bissette's identity would outlive them by a few days.

Charmaine and Missy. God, how she hated women with dachshund names like Missy and Mitzi and Buffy and Ali—although Charmaine was more suitable for a poodle—who got diamond earrings for their dear, sweet, little birthdays from their dearest daddy, and diamonds and emeralds from their drooling husbands and boyfriends. She hated them almost as much as Gordon hated little cockteasers like Missy and big cockteasers like her mother. The girl had come on to him with little looks and gestures through dinner, and then, none too subtlety, told him how she'd love to take a walk on the beach if she could only find someone who would go with her and then drop her off at the boat afterwards. Well, she had wanted a quick affair with Gordon and she was getting it now, but strictly on his terms. Both of them were. A mother-daughter doubleheader. Gordon had never had one of those before.

Bitches.

Rich, self-assured bitches. She hoped they were enjoying the evening as much as Gordon was, but she doubted it. It was only fair. Their enjoyment always came first and fuck everyone else. Well, not tonight, ladies. Tonight, for once, you is de fuckees instead of the de fuckors.

She turned on the radar and watched the display until she was sure it was still clear, then took a pair of 7x70 night glasses from a rack and went forward onto the foredeck with them. She stared into the darkness to let her eyes adjust before she carefully searched all around with the glasses. Radar sometimes missed small boats.

When she had finished her scan, she went back into the cockpit and set a kitchen timer she had brought on deck along with the binoculars. Then she settled down in the corner of the cockpit to knit and occasionally enjoy the sparkle of the emerald ring she wore in the faint light coming up through the hatch. It was a shame she couldn't keep it . . . but then, maybe she could.

When the timer went off after thirty minutes, she went forward again to search with the glasses, then went below and checked the radar before returning to the deck and her knitting while the autopilot steered *Cinderella* parallel to the course of the Canadian boat.

Alice was a very medium woman: medium height, medium build, perhaps thirty, and quite attractive when she wanted to be. She had perfected the art of looking like almost anyone she wanted to look like. With a little padding, a blond wig, and too much makeup, she could convincingly imitate an overblown, fifty-year-old floozy off a motor yacht. With no padding, the right makeup, and a baggy and unstylish dress, she could look like Anne Frank.

"Zip."
   "Zip, zip."
   "Dawn soon."
   "Coming."
   "Zip."

She didn't think he understood his own double entendre. Gordon's mind worked rather strangely. He could appear to be charming in a quiet, unassuming, "aw, shucks" sort of way that completely put people off their guard. He also seemed to be adequately intelligent to someone who did not know him. But he wasn't. What others mistook for intelligence was really a highly developed animal cunning. She was convinced that he did not think with the same parts of his brain most people used. But he functioned very well with the lower, more instinctive parts that he did use. He was a superb sail trimmer and helmsman, but he could not learn to navigate at all. Charts and courses, anything mathematical or logical, was quite beyond him. Reading a compass was right at the edge of his intelligence: sometimes he could and sometimes he couldn't.

He lived only for the times like right now when he could stop pretending to be human and be whatever it was that he really was. The pretending was heavy work for him; when they had not scored for a while, she could see it weighing him down. She felt nothing for him—she felt nothing for anyone—but she knew that like some starving wolfhound turning on its master, one day, if she let him get hungry enough, he might try to devour her.

But Alice was supremely confident of her own ability to know when that day had come. He always treated her with the businesslike respect of a happy subordinate. When he turned that sociopath's charm on her, she would not hesitate. She would put a bullet or the sharpened knitting needle she kept at the bottom of her bag into him, or set him up and let the authorities put another kind of needle into him.

The radio beside her on the bridge deck said, "Zip."

"Zip. Zip."

"Done."

"Zip."

The other boat was already beginning to settle when she came alongside and picked him up. It was a shame—it was worth a fortune. But it was too unique, and anyway, they hadn't had time to set up a sale. She stood on the cockpit seat and looked into the other boat to make sure he had dumped the man's body and anything else that might float down the hatch before closing it. Then he jumped back aboard and she bore off again.

"What's the course, Alice? Where we headed?" He started to unroll the jib. "Let's get some sail on her and go someplace."

Wasn't sex supposed to make men mellow? At the moment, he was still hyper. But it would pass, and then he would be as lethargic as a digesting snake. Until he started to get hungry again. "Dominica. I want to cash their traveler's checks and hit their credit cards hard. I'll lay out a course."

She went below as he jumped around the boat shaking out the reef and mumbling excitedly to himself. When she came on deck a few minutes later, the Canadian boat's mast had settled out of sight, the sun was coming up, and Gordon had begun to calm down and enter his digestive phase.

When Lydia Polizzi came down the dock on Thursday morning, Stroud was on the foredeck clipping a jib to the headstay. "Hi. Don't you have one of those roller things? Every boat I've ever sailed on except the very smallest had one."

"It's called a geriatric jib, and I'm not old enough to have one yet." He tied the jib to the pulpit with lengths of quarter-inch line. The sail was stiff and dazzling white in the sunlight. "Besides, one-size-fits-all may work for nylon socks, but jib size, weight, and cut can only be optimized for a limited range of wind and sea conditions. I like to be able to change jibs easily. Even if I usually pick the wrong one. I didn't know you were a sailor."

"Just an occasional passenger. Most of my experience has been on powerboats."

"Well, do you want to go sailing?"

"Sure. I brought you a cell phone." She had been surprised when he suggested a complicated schedule for them to communicate by VHF radio, as though he had never heard of cell phones. "From what I was told, it will work on all but a few of the French islands and generally about eight or ten miles offshore. That ought to be fine, because we'll usually be within eight or ten miles of some island or other. It works just like a regular phone most of the time. My number, and the number of a message machine I rented at one of those business address places in Charlotte Amalie, are in memory and also taped to the back, in case the battery dies. This way we should be able to reach each other most of the time."

"Most of the time?"

"There are dead spots, just like everywhere else. But if we can't reach each other directly, we can go through the message machine. The pin number to retrieve messages is taped to the back, too."

He tied the sheets into the jib with bowlines, then moved aft as she walked down the finger pier beside him and reached across to hand him the phone. "Here. Can you put this someplace? When we get out to sea we can try calling the machine. I tried it last night, and it worked fine from here on the island. Where do you want me?"

"You might as well stay on the dock to free up the lines once I get the engine going. You can take in the springs now."

Alice Holbrook sat facing aft on the forward seat of the inflatable dingy as Gordon steered across Prince Rupert Bay on the northwest corner of Dominica. The wind had finally come around into the northeast where it belonged and, as they moved out into the bay, spray came over the round bow of the dink and made her cringe when it hit her bare back above her tank top. Over the sound of the outboard, she yelled, "Slow down. I'm getting drenched." He slowed the engine, and the motion moderated so she no longer had to hold onto the seat with one hand and the braided rope that ran around the side of the boat with the other. Without thinking about it, she pulled her knitting out of the cloth tote bag that lay at her feet among the sacks of groceries and started to pull apart whatever it was she had been making. She never actually made anything. Knitting relaxed her, and besides, no one ever suspected a woman who knitted of anything worse than gossiping.

She wore a wig and was made up to look enough like Charmaine Bissette's passport photo so there had been no problems in the three banks where she had cashed the traveler's checks or the fourth where she had drawn the maximum in cash out of each of Charmaine's credit cards.

Cinderella was at anchor among a group of charter boats at the north end of the bay, as inconspicuous as a single blossom on a bougainvillea bush. While Alice had gone from bank to bank, Gordon bought a few groceries and then hung around the Customs house in Portsmouth as though he were waiting for her to join him before they cleared in. They hadn't cleared, of course. As soon as the dink was aboard and the anchor was up, they would be gone.

She looked over the stern to make sure no one was following them, then studied Gordon while her hands pulled apart the stitches and rewound the yarn with no help from her conscious mind. Two days after his date with the Bissette women he was back to his quiet, affable, harmless-appearing self: a boa constrictor digesting. And like a boa constrictor digesting, his indolence wouldn't last. In a while the tension would start to build in him, just as a different kind of tension would build in her, and they would have to hunt again.

She would miss the hunt. But there was almost enough money, so it was almost time to stop. She had heard that people were nosing around asking questions about the Holbrooks and *Cinderella*—not that they could find anything; but just the fact that they were nosing around was a sign that it was time for the Holbrooks and *Cinderella* to evaporate. She would sell this boat and perhaps one more and, with luck, make a few more scores as good as this one; then she would stop. Not stopping in time was the ultimate mistake. But, as she had learned in the business courses in secretarial school, one should set reasonable goals, work like hell to meet them, then take stock, set new goals, and move on. After Gordon had wrecked their last boat on the Cow Rocks, they had gone ashore on Nevis and been taken in by some of the expatriates who had homes there. With a home like theirs and enough money to support the lifestyle such a home demanded, she could live the life she was supposed to live, the life her father had intended her to live.

If he hadn't died tragically and her uncle hadn't stolen her inheritance . . . Over the years she had convinced herself that her parents had been killed in the crash of their private jet and her aunt and uncle had taken her in and looted her trust fund. Like all fiction, there was some truth at its core.

Prince Rupert Bay was a very long way from the little house in Royal Oak, Michigan, but she had long since chosen to forget that house. She had not been an abused child: quite the opposite. If anyone had so much as touched her, her father would have killed him.

Her father was the finest man she had ever known. But if some day it became necessary, she would claim that Daddy and Uncle Peter and Gordon had all sexually abused her, and everyone would believe her and excuse her, a small, frightened woman nervously knitting. It was her ultimate fall-back position, and although she knew she would never need it, she also knew it would work.

People were so hopelessly gullible. The Bissettes had wanted to meet a nice young couple with whom they could become friends, because, like most people living together on yachts, eventually they had become desperately sick of each other. Once you knew what people wanted and expected—and it was usually obvious—they could be made to respond any way you wished.

She admitted to herself that the hunt was no less about domination for her than it was for Gordon. For him it was domination through force, while for her it was domination through guile.

After her parents were gone—she always phrased it that way, "after they were gone"—her aunt and uncle grudgingly took her in because her grandfather told them to, and he was enough of a Teutonic patriarch to have his orders obeyed. Their house was on about three acres of some of the most expensive residential real estate in America. It had a living room so large that two baby grand pianos did not come close to cluttering it. Each of her dear cousins had her own piano, although neither of them had the musical talent of a crow.

The Spanish revival house on the end of Shippan Point in Stamford, Connecticut had three bedroom suites on the second floor. Originally only the master bedroom had had its own sitting room, but doors had been cut and doors had been sealed to make two identical suites out of the other four bedrooms: one for each of their daughters. The house had been built in the twenties, but in the ten years Alice had lived there, it had never been finished. Aunt Janet always had some project under way, mainly, Alice was sure, so that at cocktail parties she could seem to complain while really bragging about her contractors.

Her aunt had been a rail-thin chain smoker who sucked on a cigarette with the intensity with which someone who could not swim would bail a leaky boat. She usually wore her hair in a snood, and she never let anyone finish expressing a complete thought. She either interrupted or muttered something like, "Not now, dear. I'm busy," and walked away.

Despite her construction compulsion, she hadn't built a bedroom suite for cousin Alice. Oh no. She had shown her to a room on the third floor that had probably been intended for servants, and then she had stolen the first of the many things they had taken from her: her name.

"Dear, Uncle Peter and I have discussed it, and we're afraid that having two girls whose names are so similar living under the same roof will cause endless confusion."

"I like my name, Aunt Janet. I don't . . ."

"It's all settled, dear. I'm sure you'll come to think of yourself as Louise in just a day or two. It's a lovely name."

With that, she had walked out and left her niece to unpack her few belongings in the room at the top of the house with its one dormer window. The window had looked out over Long Island Sound, though. It was a fine place to stare and to dream, even if hers were not the pink-flowered dreams of a nine-year-old girl living in a palace.

His Princess Alice, because she had been both his beloved daughter and a substitute son to her father, had been taught things that few little girls are taught: to shoot and to handle a nightstick. "The shins first, Princess. Nobody expects that, and once you rap someone hard across the shins, he's paralyzed, so you can put the second one anyplace you want."

She looked past Gordon's head at the town and realized how tired she was. It had been a tough three days. The second morning at sea, the wind had swung back into the northeast where it belonged, so they had had to beat all the way back. They had gotten into Dominica late last night, and this morning she had done her round of the banks, telling the managers that they were having major engine parts shipped down from Canada and needed cash to pay for them and get them out of Customs.

Now they would motorsail to Guadeloupe, and in the morning she would use Missy's credit cards and the same story to get whatever her maximum cash withdrawal was. The makeup job would be trickier. Missy looked about twelve years old in her passport photo. But if she wore a scanty enough bikini top, and dealt only with men, she was sure she'd get away with it. By noon tomorrow, the Bissette women's identities would join them at the bottom of the sea.

That was the lovely thing about the sea: It was the ultimate graveyard. Ashore, no matter how carefully hidden or buried things were, they might always, through some fluke, be found. But not in the sea. The sea was a conveniently located, huge, self-sealing cemetery.

In a lot of ways, the Caribbean was not much changed since the days of Blackbeard, and some things were even better for the modern members of what had once been called the Brethren of the Coast. There were no navies involved in the suppression of piracy anymore, and it was not necessary to sneak ashore on a moonlit night, like a sea turtle about to lay eggs, in order to bury the loot. It was only necessary to fly up to Florida and discreetly visit a few jewelers who were used to young women quietly disposing of grandma's jewelry, then fly over to Grand Cayman and deposit the proceeds in a numbered account.

They never touched charter boats no matter how tempting, because if one of those went missing, the charter company would know about it in a week or two at the most. But cruisers from all over the world converged on the Caribbean, and by the time anyone back home realized a boat was missing, they would have only the vaguest idea where to start looking. And if they did come looking, there was nothing for them to find. The Caribbean was still a very fine place for the Brethren.

When they got to Antigua, it would be less than a week since Gordon had had his date with the Bissette women. It should be safe to leave him alone on the boat while she flew to Florida and the Caymans. She could go see Granny, too.

If it was much more than a month or so since his last date, she couldn't leave him alone someplace where he might decide to go hunting on his own. She could remember when it had been three or four months. But his cycle was becoming shorter and shorter, and she knew that eventually she would have to do something. They had met under the most bizarre of circumstances; it would undoubtedly end that way, too.

Her two cousins had gone off to college: one to Yale and one to Sweet Briar, in Virginia. Sweet Briar: it sounded like just the place for that phony little bitch, Alicia. By the time she came home for Thanksgiving, she already had a southern accent. When Alice had started her search for a college, her aunt had ended it by saying, "I'm sorry dear, but your uncle has had some significant financial reverses lately. I'm sure you understand that with both Ali and Cari in expensive private schools, we won't be able to help you. By scrimping, though, we can afford to pay your way through an excellent secretarial school. It's in Norwalk."

"What about my . . . "

"I think I hear the painter, dear." She had turned and left.

Alice had learned to knit in a domestic arts class in high school, where she had been asked out on very few dates and never twice. The boys who asked her were never the jocks or the class officers, they were always the middle-class losers she came to despise. When they came to pick her up—her aunt and uncle always insisted they pick her up at home—they were always tongue-tied and stupid when they came up the three steps under the portico and were shown into that huge living room by the maid. They never asked her out again, to her great relief. Not like the preppy hunks that took out her cousins. They were always completely at ease in those surroundings and able to talk to her aunt and uncle like social equals, not like frightened serfs. After her sophomore year she never accepted dates and, after a while, was never asked. It was as though she were not there, as though she were not a part of the intense high-school life that went on around her as she knitted, watched it all, and seethed inside.

At twelve she had acquired her first *Cinderella*. Her uncle had bought the Blue Jay for his daughters, but they had been more involved in the tennis program at the Club. The little open daysailor had been abandoned after a few halfhearted attempts at sailing had ended with the discovery that sailing was infinitely more complex and could be a great deal more unpleasant that the worst tennis match ever played. Her cousins had never been good at complexity or unpleasantness, and she had decided after one tennis lesson at the club that it was a stupid and useless waste of time, the only sort of thing

they were good at. They had never even seen fit to name the little
boat, and when the lonely little girl put the stick-on letters on the
transom and poured a little stolen wine over the bow, no one had
cared or noticed.

She taught herself to sail. At first she had only sailed inside the
harbor; then, toward the end of the first season, she ventured outside. Eventually she even crossed the Sound. When the wind died,
as it so often did on summer afternoons, she would row the Blue Jay
home. The rowing left her with a thin, hard body, which was a great
deal stronger than it looked, but was slowly given the appearance of
softening as she matured. Ironically, she had a better amateur tennis
player's physique than either of her cousins.

She vividly remembered the night she had been told it was secretarial school or nothing and had confronted her uncle, even though
her mind had completely rewritten the scene many times over the
years. "I can remember Grandpa saying that my father had a life
insurance policy. Then there was the money from the sale of my
parents' house. I don't want to go to an Ivy League school; I just
want to go someplace that has a naval architecture program."

In the version her mind had evolved, he had replied, "Louise,
naval architecture is a very difficult course, particularly for a girl. I
think you should forget that dream right now."

"What about my money?"

"There is no money, and never was. Every penny your father
had, most of your grandfather's, and some of mine, went into legal
fees. Every penny. The insurance policy your father left has long
since been spent on your upkeep. We've given you a good life here,
Louise, and I'm really sorry to see you behave so ungratefully. Times
are tough for us right now, and we want to help you, but secretarial
school is the best we can do. I've been assured that it's a very good
one."

But then she met Gordon, and her life and the life of her uncle's
family changed radically and forever. Her uncle hadn't known what

tough times were until she met Gordon. His name had been Emil then. That had been the first of the many things about him she had changed.

One night, a month before she was to graduate from the secretarial school, he had grabbed her and tried to drag her into his van. She had struggled for a second, then gone limp, and when he tried to take advantage of her limpness to improve his grip, she had driven a knitting needle through his thigh. He had screamed and slumped against the van as she ran away.

But she hadn't called the police or told anyone about it—to this day she was not sure why. She still kept the mate to that knitting needle in the bottom of her bag, sharpened to a sewing-needle point. At first, she hadn't told anyone because she thought it was her own fault. It had only happened, like all the bad things that happened to her, because there was something wrong with her. Nobody would ever dare to drag one of her dear cousins into a van in the parking lot of the seedy strip mall that housed the secretarial school, mainly because her dear cousins would never go near a secretarial school in a seedy strip mall. All the good things happened to them, and all the bad things happened to her.

The following Saturday she discovered that her uncle had sold her boat without telling her. She found out when she went to the club and saw a ten-year-old boy and his father peeling the stick-on letters from the transom. All the bad things happened to her and all the good things happened to them because that was how her aunt, her uncle, and her dear cousins wanted it. When the man had explained that he had bought the little boat for his son, she had turned and wordlessly left the club, thinking it was time that the bad things, the really bad things, happened to her cousins for once.

Two weeks later she was walking past a fast-food shop when she saw the old gray van in the parking lot. She stayed out of sight behind the corner of the building until he came limping out carrying a food bag. When he was settled in the driver's seat with his lunch spread on the motor box beside him, she climbed into the passenger seat and asked what she still considered one of the best questions anyone had ever asked. "Tell me, do you intend to stay a two-bit rapist hanging around strip malls for the rest of your life, or do you aspire to better things?" His mouth had dropped open, and she ate one of his French fries while she waited for him to stop stuttering.

CHAPTER FIVE

Lawrence Selby was one of those big, red-faced Englishmen who always seem to be married to small, emaciated women with a permanent look of exhaustion about them. He and Agatha had a modest income that permitted them to live in a small, heavy-displacement wooden boat capable of taking them, albeit rather slowly, anyplace on earth they wished to go. They had an almost religious belief in the opinions of a British couple of a generation before who had sailed the world in small, heavy-displacement wooden boats and written a number of books about it. If everything that they suggested was no longer the easiest or the most comfortable way to cruise about the world, it had always gotten the Selbys to their destinations safely and eventually.

The boat had plow-iron rigging and galvanized steel hardware from which most of the zinc coating had been worn or had dissolved years before. No matter how carefully they scraped and primed every two years when they hauled and painted *Hidden Virtue*, within a few weeks she was again streaked with rust. But, as Lawrence was fond of saying, she was just like his Agatha—perhaps not the prettiest around, but as strong and as solid as any man could wish. Selby thought this was a compliment to both his boat and his wife. His wife never said what she thought of it.

Now he was glad of just how solid the rust-streaked boat with its unintentionally matching red sails was. The wind had been right out of the north, so they had taken the short way 'round Virgin Gorda and had left Round Rock Passage at the south end the evening before, hoping to reach St. Martin in time to have a peaceful Christmas Eve at anchor. But the wind had built and veered into the east just enough to make what should have been a fetch into a beat, and now they were close-hauled and snugged down.

It required a nice compromise to carry enough sail to push *Hidden Virtue* through the steep and confused seas caused by the rollers coming in from the Atlantic butting head-on into the current running out of the Caribbean, while the easterly wind built a chop at right angles to the whole bloody mess. Too little sail and she just bounced up and down in the same place, too much and she heeled too far, lost her grip on the sea, and slid off to leeward.

At least the complicated iron pipe contraption mounted on her stern that did the steering—that was what Agatha and he always called it: The Contraption—was holding a reasonably straight course. He watched it for a while, and then went forward to the mast to unroll the main a couple of turns by cranking the boom. Perhaps a little more sail would help. It couldn't be much, though. Perhaps just one turn.

When he had set up the halyard, he stood on the cabin top holding onto the mast for a moment and peered forward, hoping to see some trace of land. Nothing. He checked his watch and mentally updated the DR plot he maintained in his head. Almost noon. He was tempted to try for a sun sight to verify their position, although he had learned over the years that navigational fixes, no matter how frequent, did not increase the boat's rate of advance in the least. There was a lot of spray coming aboard, though, and the mirrors on the sextant were none too good as they were. There was no point in dragging it up and getting it soused with salt water yet again.

It was a clear Caribbean day—quite beautiful, really—and once they were across they would be across and he'd see the islands rise from the sea. It wouldn't happen any sooner no matter how precisely he determined their position. It would be nice to get in before dark, though, and have a nice, quiet Christmas Eve Pimms or two.

The bloody Anegada. Over the years, they had been across it five times and had gotten their guts kicked out every time.

Lydia Polizzi did a very careful preflight on the ramp in Virgin Gorda. She lifted the cover on each engine in turn, checked the oil, and then inspected, pulled, and shook every tube, wire, and fitting she could reach. She was normally quite careful about these things, but had become positively paranoid a week ago, after a mechanic, with typical West Indian attention to detail, had left a rusty box wrench on top of an engine. She still got alternately queasy and angry when she thought about it falling into the machinery or maybe shorting a couple of spark plugs on takeoff.

When she was done with the engines, she took hold of a wingtip and shook the aircraft as violently as she could. Then she walked to the tail and carefully inspected the empennage before grabbing the tail plane and again shaking the hell out of the airplane. Next she duck-walked under the wings and nose to inspect the tricycle landing gear and tires before grabbing the other wingtip and again bouncing the plane around, using all of her strength and weight.

Stuck into the waistband of her khaki Bermuda shorts was a laminated plastic checklist she had made and memorized; now she pulled it out and read down it line by line rather than trust her memory.

Her briefcase was lying in the shade of the left wing and she opened it, put the checklist into a pocket in its lid, and took out a glass beaker that she set on the wing next to the pilot's door where she couldn't miss it. Then she spread a chart on the wing next to it. The cockpit would be an oven; she was not about to get into it any sooner than she had to. At least out here there was a very pleasant breeze that forced her to hold the chart with both hands as she once more studied the course lines she had drawn on it the night before.

She and Stroud had spent the last five weeks searching the Virgin Islands and found nothing but false alarms. She had spotted a Grand Banks 42 at anchor off Jost Van Dyke two days after they had searched that island completely. Stroud had sailed back around Tortola all night to reach it while she fretted that the Grand Banks would leave before he could get there. She disliked just about everything about Stroud, but she had to admit, he was one thorough son-of-a-bitch. He had anchored near the Grand Banks at dawn, put on his mask and fins, and swum all around it. Then he had called her with the builder's number that was cast into the upper right-hand corner of the transom and a detailed description of the entire boat, including the bottom. It was definitely not her parent's boat.

The sailboats were even worse. There were so many of them that were similar to a Far Horizons 38. She carefully studied each potential yacht that she spotted, comparing it to photos of Stroud's daughter's boat and pictures from a manufacturer's brochure. If she could not with certainty eliminate it, then it had to be investigated. Sometimes it was easy. If the boat was anchored near an island with an airport, she would land and check it out herself.

If it wasn't, or if it was on the move, she and Stroud would work out a strategy on the cell phones—if they could get through, of course. Cell phone service was, like many things in the West Indies, diabolically undependable. She could always get through if she had nothing to report, but the more urgently she needed to talk to Stroud, the less likely it was that the damn thing would work. She wondered how they knew. She also wondered how many people had called the FAA about the nut case in the Beech who had buzzed them repeatedly and then flown away.

She folded the chart, put it onto a clipboard that also held her boat photos, then took her beaker and opened the drain in the sump of each tank to determine if any water had been supplied with the gasoline. Sometimes water could settle in the corner of a tank instead of in the sump where she could find it, and it would crouch there, waiting to first kill an engine and then kill her. That was why she always shook hell out of an airplane after it had been fueled and then gave any contaminates time to settle before checking the tank sumps.

Today they were going to search the Anegada Passage. The Anegada Passage topped the list of all the places on earth where she did not want to go missing. Even its name gave her the creeps. Anegada: if you heard the word and didn't know it was just an eighty-mile-wide body of water, you might think it was a particularly poisonous tropical snake. She certainly had reason to feel this way, but she had met a lot of others who felt the same. Sailors called it the OhmyGoda Passage.

The night before, she and Stroud had had dinner at the Virgin Gorda Marina and then planned the next phase of their search in *Lullaby's* cabin. He had been quite sure there would be few boats actually crossing the Passage on any given day, especially now that the Christmas Winds, the strong northeast trades, had begun to blow. He read her a paragraph from one of his cruising guides. It said that when the winter winds begin to blow, the eastward transit of the Anegada becomes very difficult for larger boats and almost impossible for smaller ones. Then he explained that from other comments in the book, it was obvious that the author thought anything less than about eighty feet was a smaller boat.

He had walked her to her hotel and then gone back to the boat to catch a few hours sleep before sailing north around the Island. By now he should be out through the Necker Island Passage learning if the Anegada deserved its reputation. As she stood on the wing and opened the door, the breeze, so pleasant here ashore, almost tore it out of her hand.

Stroud was sitting under *Lullaby's* dodger as she slid along on a close reach powered by her number 3 jib and a double-reefed main. The autopilot was steering, and the hinged bar on which were mounted the GPS and depthsounder was swung around from over the chart table into the hatch where he could see them from the cockpit. Using the course made good function of the GPS; he was able to compare their actual course over the bottom with the plotted one written on a piece of tape stuck to the bulkhead beneath the steering compass and feed small corrections for leeway and drift into the autopilot. Some boats had the GPS directly hooked to the autopilot, but Stroud was too good an engineer to trust two machines not to do something immensely and fatally stupid if wired so they could conspire together in secrecy.

He put in a small correction, trimmed the jib sheet a half-inch, and then studied the main for a second. It was still okay. Well, maybe not. He moved the traveler up a bit while watching the streamers on the sail's trailing edge, then eased it back down as he thought, *When in doubt, let it out.* He was damned glad he had come north around Virgin Gorda. If he had gone south through Round Rock Passage, not only would he be hard on the veering wind now, but the chop which came from the forward quarter would have been square on the bow, where *Lullaby* would have had to plow right into it.

Just visible on the horizon, ahead and to the south of him, was a boat with dark sails that was doing just that. It was the only vessel he had seen since starting across, other than a couple of cruise ships.

Then he saw a dot in the sky to the north, on a parallel course. It might be, and probably was, Polizzi. She certainly knew how to fly. He had gone up with her several times and been impressed with her thoroughness. Too bad she was such a pain in the ass. It was also too bad that she had such difficulty telling one sailboat from another. She seemed to think about a third of the boats she saw were Far Horizons 38s. If it had less than two hulls, it was a possibility. If it had less than two masts it was a probability. If it was also less than fifty feet, white, and did not have a cove stripe, it had to be checked out. But he had to give her one thing: he was now almost positive neither of the boats they sought was in the Virgins.

Too bad she was such a pain in the ass.

By four o'clock, the wind had backed into the northeast again, thank God, and Lawrence Selby was able to free things up a bit. He didn't think they were too far south of his intended track, because the current running north into the Atlantic had probably compensated for most of their leeway. The shifting wind didn't help the chop, though. The waves were just the wrong length for *Hidden Virtue*. A bit longer and she would have ridden them like a duck. A bit shorter and she would have used her heavy displacement to walk through them like a rugby player through a cobweb. But as it was, she had to bash and bounce her way through them as best she could. It certainly wasn't pleasant.

He looked below to where Agatha was lying in a bunk, reading a cookbook. A wonderful strong stomach had Agatha. Even as rough as it was, the cabin was as neat as a pin. It was tiny and it was their only home and everything in it was far cleaner and in far better condition than it had been when they bought the boat twenty years before. Then, the cabin had had the gray look and the musty smell of a small boat receiving less than superb care in a damp climate. Now everything gleamed.

"Any hot water left in the thermos, Ags? It's about brew-up time." Between four and five every afternoon, they always had tea, no matter what the conditions, and they had had their tea in far worse conditions than this.

"What little's left is probably cold b'now." She closed her book, placed it in the rack over the bunk, and sat up. "I'll make a pot. With a few biscuits, that should hold us 'til we get in."

As she went forward to the old Primus stove that had served them so well over the years, he stood up and once more looked forward for the islands. If St. Martin wasn't in sight by twilight, he'd have to get a fix.

The surface of the sea was empty except for whitecaps and a boat whose sails were just as white. It had passed them to the north and was now hull down on the horizon ahead. A less practiced eye than Lawrence Selby's probably would not have been able to distinguish it from the white wavetops all around it.

The last leg of Polizzi's search took her south almost to Saba. Except for three cruise ships and a couple of maxi motor yachts that were almost the size of small cruise ships, the Anegada had been almost deserted. The only sailing vessels heading west were Stroud and another yacht even smaller than *Lullaby*. She had seen three others running east, but none of them resembled a Far Waters 38. The lack of traffic wasn't surprising. It was Christmas Eve, after all.

She flew north until she found *Lullaby* at the point of a snow-white wake—Stroud was making good time, by the looks of it—and buzzed her before heading for Marigot Airport on the French side of St. Martin. The commercial airport was on the southern, the Dutch, side. Lydia had been flying for almost four hours now, and that was about the most either her backside or her bladder could stand. As she climbed back to three thousand feet, she again thought about how little chance they had of succeeding. Although they were conducting this search as well as they knew how, if they found either boat it would still be by blind luck.

Once she had landed, she would find a hotel, and wait for Stroud. In the morning, Christmas or no, they would continue the search. It would probably be a good day for it, because fewer boats would be on the move. It was the boats that moved that turned their determined, scientifically planned search into a crapshoot. If the boats and people they sought were on the other side of St. Martin right now, and left tonight, heading west, they would miss them and probably never find them. She decided that in the morning, before they continued to search eastward, she would backtrack over the Anegada. God, how she hated that word.

A half hour later she was still in the air, circling out over the sea, trying to raise the tower at the small, private-aircraft airport on the north end of the island. She had been advised to use it rather than the large commercial airport on the Dutch side. She wondered what the problem was. She looked around very carefully and could see no other planes in the air, nor did she get an answer when she asked on the radio for anyone flying in the vicinity to identify themselves. As she banked around to head out to sea once more, thinking that a mid-air collision would certainly ruin her Christmas, she spotted two boats rafted together at anchor in Marigot Bay: a motor yacht and a sailboat. The bay was crowded and a number of other boats were rafted together, but she noticed those two because powerboats and sailboats usually rafted with their own kind, not with each other.

Still no answer from the tower. She began to wonder if they had already gone home to begin their holiday. She changed frequencies and called the tower at the commercial airport on the Dutch side of the island. They told her that there did not appear to be any other traffic in her area and, with a polite Dutch chuckle at typical Gaelic inefficiency, suggested that the tower at the smaller airport had probably closed down for the holiday. She did not wish to land on a runway from which someone else was just about to take off, so she decided to make one more circle out to sea before buzzing the airport. If there was still no response and everything looked quiet, she'd land. She really had to find a bathroom soon.

As she banked around, she got a clearer view of the motor yacht; it was a Grand Banks 42. She completely forgot about the tower or the bathroom as she tightened the turn and dropped lower for a better look.

Agatha Selby went through the routine she always followed when lighting her stove. First she checked the kerosene—she called it paraffin—in the tank mounted on the bulkhead beside it. She thought about gas stoves as she did it. They had been guests for dinner on a boat in Tortola that had one of those propane stoves, and she had been envious. One had only to turn it on, light it, and cook. Lighting the Primus was more like lighting off the boilers on the old destroyer in which Lawrence had been an engine-room artificer. The propane stove had an honest-to-God oven, too, with a built-in thermostat. The Primus had what was actually just a metal box that sat on the burners and was usually either too hot or too cold for whatever it was she was trying to bake. On top of it all, the new stoves were made of stainless steel; she would not have to continually scour the rust off a stove which had once been galvanized, but was now mostly bare, if gleaming, pitted steel.

But Lawrence claimed that propane, because it was heavier than air, could collect in the bilges and blow them and *Hidden Virtue* to

kingdom come.   Besides, they had always used paraffin stoves.
Lawrence was a fine man, the best any woman could ever want, but,
she had to admit, he wasn't very flexible. He had his ways and that was
that.

The tank was more than half full, so she replaced the cap, took a
dozen stokes on the pump to pressurize it, then fished a circular wick out
of a can of priming alcohol—she called it meths—set it in a cup under
one of the burners, and lit it. While it warmed the burner to the point
where the kerosene would vaporize and burn, she turned to the sink
opposite and pumped fresh water into her copper teapot. The sink had
two spouts and two pumps: both cold. The other provided seawater for
washing up.

She turned back to the stove just as the alcohol flickered out, opened
the valve that allowed kerosene to flow into the burner, and lit it. It was
then that the old pressure tank, from which Agatha had been meticulously cleaning the rust and along with it the steel for many years, frac-
tured and sprayed pressurized kerosene onto both her and the stove. In
an instant, she and the galley were engulfed in flames.

Stroud had sailed all his life on the crowded waters of Long Island Sound,
with its large selection of idiots, lunatics, and devil-may-care tugboat
captains, and the survival technique of doing a 360-degree look-around
every few minutes had become a habit. As he looked aft, he saw a smudge
of black smoke just on the horizon. It could have been a ship blowing
down its boiler tubes, or a diesel engine with a bad injector, but the
bearing was just about where the boat with the red sails had disappeared
over the horizon a half hour or so ago. He climbed below and turned on
the VHF radio just as the cell phone rang. "Hello?"

"Bill. Thank God I reached you. I think I've found both of the
boats we're looking for. They're at anchor, rafted together in Marigot
Bay. How soon will you be here? I'm afraid they'll sail tonight and split
up. How soon can you get here?"

"Where are you right now?"

"Out on the end of the breakwater at the north end of the bay. Everything's closed up and I couldn't find anyone with a boat to take me out for a closer look. I almost broke my leg climbing out here over these damned rocks."

"Lydia, calm down and tell me about the boats. Can you see them from where you are?"

"I can see the Grand Banks clearly; it looks just like my parents' boat: the same maroon Bimini top and rail cloths on the flying bridge. I can't make out the name from here—they would have changed it, anyway—but it's on a varnished plank over the door to the pilothouse, just like my folk's boat."

"Tell me about the sailboat."

"I can't see it from here. It's on the other side. But from the air, there was no cove stripe and it had all its antennae and a wind-powered generator on the sternrail. Oh, and it's obviously less than forty-two feet long. It's shorter than the Grand Banks."

"What about the mast?"

At that instant the VHF radio squawked into life. "Mayday, Mayday, Mayday. This is the sailing yacht *Hidden Virtue of Hamble*. We are afire and abandoning ship in the Anegada Passage about twenty miles west of St. Martin at approximate latitude eighteen degrees, naught minutes, north. Come back, please." It was a controlled, almost laconic, British voice, but even through the lousy speaker of the VHF radio, Stroud could hear the fear and horror in it.

"Its an unpainted aluminum mast with single spreaders and the roller furling jib has what looks like a blue cover, although it's somewhat faded. Bill, it's them. It's too much of a coincidence not to be them. How soon can you get—"

"Mayday, Mayday, Mayday. This is the sailing yacht *Hidden Virtue of Hamble*. We are afire and abandoning ship in the Anegada Passage about twenty miles west of St. Martin at approximate latitude eighteen degrees, naught minutes, north. Come back, please."

"Hold on, Lydia."

"Bill, if they sail, all I'll be able to do is watch. I'm low on fuel and everything is closed up tight here. There wasn't even anyone in the tower. When are you coming?"

"Mayday, Mayday, Mayday. This is the sailing yacht *Hidden Virtue*—"

"Hold on, damn it."

"—*of Hamble* and we are afire and abandoning ship in the Anegada Passage about twenty miles west of St. Martin at approximate latitude eighteen degrees naught minutes north. Come back, please."

Then another voice came on. "*Virtue*, this is the U.S. Coast Guard Cutter *Cape Elizabeth*. Please give a description of your vessel and number of souls on board. All other stations clear this channel. Over."

"We're a sloop with red sails, and there are just Agatha and I aboard. But I can't see her and I'm—" a series of racking coughs followed, and then silence.

"Bill, what's going on? Don't you understand me? I think I've found them."

"Shut up, Lydia."

"Come in, *Virtue*. This is the cutter *Cape Elizabeth* calling the yacht *Virtue*. Come in, *Virtue*."

Silence.

"Come in, *Virtue*. This is the cutter *Cape Elizabeth*. We are approximately fifty miles from you and our helo is about twenty minutes out from us. As soon as it is recovered and refueled we will launch it to you. In the meantime we are making our best speed toward you. Over."

Silence.

"Any other vessels in the Anegada Passage near a position about twenty miles west of St. Martin at approximate latitude eighteen degrees, zero minutes north, please come in."

"This is the motor vessel *Nordic Fantasy of Bergen*. We are east-southeast of St. John and making our best speed toward the reported position and will be there in less than two hours. Hold on, *Hidden Virtue*. Over." The voice had a Scandinavian accent of the sort anyone would be glad to hear responding to a Mayday at sea.

"Bill what's the problem. Are you coming or aren't you? Do you want to find them or not, for God's sake!"

"Thank you, *Nordic Fantasy*. *Virtue*, please come in. This is the cutter *Cape Elizabeth* calling the yacht *Virtue*. Over."

Silence.

"Come in, *Virtue*. Help is on the way. Come in, please. Over."

Silence.

"Bill, are you there? What's going on? Answer me, damn it."

"This is the cutter *Cape Elizabeth* calling any vessel other than *Nordic Fantasy* in the Anegada Passage near a position about twenty miles west of St. Martin at approximate latitude eighteen degrees, zero minutes north. Over."

"This goddamned cell phone. Bill, can you hear me? If you can, say something."

"Hold on, Lydia. I'm busy." He got his position from the GPS, plotted it, stared at the chart for over a minute, and then spoke into the phone. "I'm about thirteen miles west of St. Martin. I'll be there in maybe three hours or so. Watch them. I'll anchor near them and come get you. Is there a dinghy dock?"

"Right at the head of the bay. You can't miss it. I'll watch them from here until I see you coming, then I'll come around and wait for you on the dock. Okay?"

"Yeah. I guess that's okay."

He went back on deck and looked aft, but the smoke, and probably the yacht *Hidden Virtue*, were gone.

The sun had set when Stroud entered Marigot Bay and saw the Grand Banks and the sailboat rafted together. Several inflatable dinghies and small Whalers were tied to the step on the motor yacht's transom; there was a lighted Christmas tree on her flying bridge—a party was obviously taking place in her cabin. Stroud had started the engine and gotten the sail off *Lullaby* as he approached the harbor, and now he swung across the Grand Banks' bow and studied the sailboat. It wasn't a Far Waters 38. It was another goddamned Niagara 35. Polizzi would never learn the difference.

It was probably the wrong Grand Banks, too, but he still had to check it out. He found an empty anchoring spot, put the engine in neutral at what he judged to be the right place, and went forward as *Lullaby* coasted up to where he wanted to drop the anchor. She was just about stopped when she reached it, and by then he had the hook ready to lower. Once it was in, he came aft, checked the depthsounder, gunned the engine in reverse for a few seconds until she was making stern way, then he went forward again to cleat the anchor line once the right amount of scope for the depth had been veered. One more touch of reverse to make sure the anchor was set, then he killed the engine and pumped up the dinghy.

When he came back aboard, he was in an even fouler mood. He had rowed right up to the rafted boats, ignored by the merrymakers aboard. The number on the Grand Banks stern was wrong, and the anchor winch and bowsprit setup was entirely different from the pictures of Polizzi's boat he had memorized. *Lullaby*'s cabin table had an eight-inch-wide center section to which its drop leaves were hinged, and when he came below he lifted its cover and took a bottle of bourbon from among the bottles in its rack. It was Christmas Eve, and fuck this Caribbean rum shit. He would have a proper drink that tasted like real liqour, not like a goddamned lollipop.

He should go ashore and pick up Polizzi. She was probably standing on the dinghy dock wondering what had happened to him. Good.

He put some ice cubes in his second drink and took the bottle with him as he went up on deck to look at the stars, listen to the sounds of the Christmas parties on the boats around him, and think about some poor bastard who might still be drifting around in the Anegada where Bill Stroud had left him.

For the first time in his life he had failed to do his duty. Duty—something Polizzi's generation laughed at the way people always laugh at things they either don't understand or find embarrassing. But all his life, he had put what was important to him behind his duty to other people: other people who were often strangers and usually did not care what became of Bill Stroud, his family, or anyone else, for that matter. The management and stockholders of that goddamned company, and the U.S. government, to begin with. He had spent four years going to reserve meetings after he got out of the army, while at the same time going to night school, to finish his degree. And what did it get him? The assholes who ran the company into the ground got rich while he only got half a pension, and the draft dodgers who thought those who did their duty were fools, got control of the goddamned country and were running that into the ground, too.

Maybe he was finally beginning to learn how the United States and the world worked. If some asshole set fire to his boat twenty miles from the nearest land, that was his problem, not Bill Stroud's.

But that poor bastard in *Virtue* wasn't the one who got hooked up with a half-witted bean counter from the Corn Belt who couldn't learn to tell one sailboat from another and who kept crying wolf.

It would have taken him an hour to run back, and the Coast Guard or the Norwegians would have been there a half hour or so after that. But to a badly burned person immersed in salt water, a half hour could be an eternity. *Oh, bull shit. If I had gone back, I wouldn't have been able to find anything in the sea that was running, and wouldn't have found them unless I happened to sail right over them. And if Lydia had found* Cinderella *and the* Grand Banks, *and they had sailed before I got here . . .* But they hadn't sailed, and they weren't the boats they were looking for. It was another of Lydia's goddamned false alarms. Fuck it. What was done was done. The way he felt about himself now was just one more part of the price he had to pay to find out what happened to Nell. And whatever that price, he was willing to pay it.

Stroud awoke as something hit the outside of the hull opposite his head. Before he was fully awake he heard footsteps in the cockpit and the sound of an outboard motor accelerating away. Then Polizzi appeared in the hatch and asked, "What the hell happened to you last night? I waited on that stupid dock for two hours."

He sat up and swung his feet off the bunk as she came down the hatch. They both ignored the fact that he wore only his jockey shorts. Without replying, he went forward into the head and closed the door. She eyed the empty bourbon bottle, the glass, and the remains of the can of ravioli he had obviously eaten for supper and said through the door, "By the time I gave up on you it was too late to get a hotel room; everything was either full or closed up tight. I was lucky to find a drunken cab driver who took me back to the airport."

Through the door, by way of reply, came, "Yeah. So what?" followed by the sound of his brushing his teeth.

"So I wound up trying to sleep on a wooden bench in the waiting room at the airport while I worried if the Holbrooks had made you disappear, too."

He didn't reply for a while, and then the door opened and he came out dressed in shorts and a button-down dress shirt with the sleeves none too expertly shortened. "Turn on the gas, will you? I need some coffee."

She went on deck to the anchor locker on the bow, turned on the valve at the bottle, and hung the red streamer on the hatch handle as he had shown her. When she came back below, he had a pot of water on and was measuring coffee into a filter. "Look, Bill. What happened? Those boats are still here."

"You mean the Niagara 35 and the Grand Banks with the entirely different bowsprit and anchor winch setup? Christ, lady, another wild-goose chase. But it's the last."

"What's that supposed to mean?"

He ignored her question and said, "It's almost eleven. What did you do, sleep late on your wooden bench?"

"I've already flown three hours this morning. They asked for volunteers to search for some boat that went missing in the Anegada yesterday."

"Find anything?"

"No, we didn't. A cruise ship fished a badly burned guy out of a raft last night. But there's no sign of the boat or his wife."

"I heard his Mayday."

"Is that what was going on when we were on the phone?"

"No. That was what was going on when you were completely full of shit and going nuts on the phone."

"How far away were you from them?"

"Probably too far to have done them any good; but you never know."

The pot whistled and he poured the water into the filter as she said, "That's why you're pissed off, isn't it."

"No. That's not the reason. I had to make a decision and now I have to live with it. That's the way it works in the adult world, even if you and your generation are unaware of it. I'm pissed off because, just like every other baby-boom bean counter I ever met, you don't have the foggiest notion of how to do the job you're trying to do, and you're too damned arrogant to find out.

"This is the adult world, lady, and I don't need some middle-age teenybopper who wants to fly around in her toy airplane and won't take the time to learn the details of what we are trying to do because some dull-normal B-school prof once told her to ignore the details because only the big picture is important. Things either succeed or fail because of how well people deal with the twiddly little details you think are beneath you.

"Do me a favor. Go back to Ohio and those poor bastards who work for you in the bank and, at the moment, are probably damned glad to have you out of their hair."

"I honestly thought there was a good chance those were the boats."

"That's just what I mean. Grand Banks changed to a three-station windlass system four years ago, before they built your parents' boat; they changed the bowsprit and the rail around it at the same time. If you had carefully read and compared all the brochures, you would have known that. Anyone could see that this boat was an older model.

"Go back to Ohio. You're obviously too damned lazy or too damn stupid to understand that at sea, and particularly if we find the Holbrooks, the details are what will keep us alive or kill us. That guy yesterday, he was more alone out there than he would have been on a flight to the moon. There was no Mission Control checking and double-checking all the thousands of details for him, and ready, at the first hint of trouble, to tell him what to do."

"I am damned careful about the details of my flying."

"Yes, you are. It's the details of everything else in life that you don't give a shit about."

"God damn you, Stroud. The details of my life are my business. You sound just like . . . " She bit off the sentence and her eyes filled with tears.

"Who do I sound like, Lydia? Your own father?"

"Yes. You do. Damn you. No matter how many things I did right, he would never let me forget any mistake I made. I suppose that was the way you were with your daughter, too."

He thought about it as he poured out two cups of coffee and handed her one. "Watch it. It's hot. No. I never had to. Sure, Nell was a pain in the ass when she was in high school—all teen-aged girls are monumental pains in the ass to their fathers at that age; we had our share of arguments. God, they were awful. No matter how carefully I phrased something, I got hysterical screams or hysterical tears, and usually both. But we always sailed together in the summer, went skiing together in the winter, and we had an unspoken agreement that those were neutral times when we only talked about things we both wanted to talk about. We came out of that period of her life with an even better relationship than we had when we entered it. I know a lot of fathers who can't say that. I don't know what we would have done without her when Dwight died."

She studied the coffee in her cup, and then said, "From the time I was about twelve it just got worse and worse. Then, when I was in college in the sixties, things happened, and no matter how well I did after that, he never forgot them. I could see it on his face every time he looked at me." She stared down into the cup for a long moment before she looked up and continued. "My parents were the World War Two generation, and they really only cared about their family, their religion, and their country. I'm pretty sure that when my father died he still thought of me as a whore and a traitor to my family and my country. The worst part of it is, back then, when I was a kid, he was right. But no matter how hard I tried in all the years since then, he never let me live it down.

"My niece Lydi and I were quite close. My father didn't approve of it and found all sorts of small ways to let me know. I think he was afraid I would infect her with the disease I had when I was twenty." Again she wiped her eyes with the back of her fingers. "It's Christmas. You know, I was planning on coming down here and spending Christmas on the boat with them. I was hoping that after he had been living down here for a while he would have mellowed out, and maybe . . .

"Well, it didn't work out, did it? Like you told me once, unless you're a sociopath, there is no such thing as closure, and life is filled with things you can never get behind you." Then she looked up from her coffee cup and smiled a sad smile at him. "Well, at least you know now why you piss me off so much, Stroud. Merry Christmas. It doesn't feel like Christmas, does it? Too hot. More like Memorial Day or the Fourth of July. I need to use the head."

She was in there for quite a while, and when she came out her makeup was repaired but her eyes were still red. He had set the table and was standing at the stove. "How do you want your eggs? Scrambled okay?"

"Fine. What happens now? If you won't work with me, I'll keep searching on my own. I mean it."

He thought about it for a minute. "Let's have breakfast, then you probably want to take a nap."

"I'm okay if I don't have to sleep on that damn bench again to-night."

"You're welcome to the forecabin if you want it."

"Bill. I'm sorry about that false alarm yesterday. I don't blame you for getting pissed off."

"Look. Have you read much naval history?"

"No. I hate war. I don't read that stuff."

"In the Pacific. At Midway, for instance."

"That was in the Second World War, right?"

He let that one go. "Yeah. That's right. Anyway, the Japanese had hundreds of ships spread over thousands of miles of water and the U.S. navy had three carrier groups, and each side had dozens of planes searching for the other, and they still had a hell of time finding each other. And when they finally did find each other, the ship identifications were all screwed up; destroyers were mistaken for battleships, tankers for aircraft carriers. And the pilots on both sides reported about ten times as many hits as they actually scored."

"So?"

"So I shouldn't get upset with you for misidentification. You're in a long tradition of naval scout-plane pilots. The Pacific is a lot bigger than the Caribbean, but our targets are a lot smaller and our task force only has one plane and one ship."

"I was thinking the same thing yesterday, but not in those terms."

"What we need is some kind of intelligence. Something that gives us some idea where to look and when. That was the critical advantage the U.S. Navy had at Midway: intelligence."

"How'd they get it?"

As he had learned from watching *Jeopardy*, her generation's ignorance of geography and history, even twentieth-century history, was appalling. "They were reading the Jap codes and knew they were about to mount a major operation, but didn't know where. The Jap messages only referred to AF as the objective. The U.S. suspected it was Midway but weren't sure, so they had Midway radio back to Pearl Harbor in the clear that they were running out of drinking water. The Japs stupidly radioed their units that AF was running out of water, and that was the tip-off."

"Why stupidly? They were outfoxed, but that didn't mean they were stupid."

"Stupid because by encoding information that their enemy already knew, they compromised their own security system. That doesn't mean that they or any other government learned anything from it, though."

"Does that mean you don't have any more respect for the military mind than I do?"

"I have plenty of respect for the military minds who fought that war for America. It's the B-School nitwits like Robert McNamara and the apprentice Neville Chamberlains in the White House and State Department that I find contemptible—the people for whom no sacrifice is too large as long as it doesn't involve them personally."

"So tell me, Bill, how do we get the intelligence we need, since we can't crack the Holbrook's codes, not having any way to intercept their messages?"

"I only wish I knew." He split the scrambled eggs between two plates, put a piece of toast from the stove-top toaster on each, and handed one to her as he sat down opposite her.

They ate in silence for a while, and then she said, "We could fly down through the islands and systematically check Customs and Immigration at each island. That would be quicker than this harbor-by-harbor search for their boat."

He thought about it. "I guess we could, but if we ask too many questions of too many people, the Holbrooks are liable to find out someone is looking for them. They've been here for years. They're bound to have contacts. Our lack of intelligence is our biggest problem, but the fact that they don't know we're looking for them is our biggest advantage."

"So what if they find out? We have nothing to hide. What we're doing is perfectly legitimate."

"Lydia, if you stuck your head out of the hatch right now and saw them dropping their hook next to us, what would you want us to do?"

"You mean, if we checked out everything and it was your daughter's boat?"

"Exactly."

"Why, I guess we would have to go aboard and ask them for an explanation."

"All right. Now tell me what sort of innocent explanation they might offer."

"Well, maybe they bought the boat in good faith from someone else."

"And what about your parents, and niece, and their boat?"

"It could have been an accident. Maybe a fire and explosion like that boat last night."

"And all those traveler's checks that got cashed posthumously? Look, Lydia, if you just went over there and confronted them, there's a good chance you might find yourself going for a midnight swim while wearing a garbage bag and a couple of cement blocks for a bathing suit."

"Well, I suppose the smart thing to do would be to go ashore and show the gendarmes the papers from the Coast Guard hearing and let them sort it out. What would you do?"

He looked at the empty whiskey bottle on the counter and thought about tossing a Molotov cocktail down their hatch and letting St. Peter sort it out. But instead he said, "Yeah. Okay. But I want you to promise me that if you find them before I get there, you won't contact them in any way until we can agree on how to handle it. What do we do if we find them at sea or in an obscure anchorage?"

"Then we follow them until they get someplace where we can get the gendarmes to sort it out. All of which is academic if we don't come up with some better way to find them. I have to get better at identifying boats from the air, though. This is tough enough without any more false alarms than absolutely necessary."

"Did you bring your photos and brochures with you?"

"Back at the plane."

"I'll run you ashore and you can get your stuff. I think we should hang out here for a day or two while we try to get our act together."

While she went to the plane and returned, he had a long swim off the beach, and then they ate lunch in a sidewalk cafe before returning to the boat and going to work. Instead of just showing her what a Far Horizons 38 looked like, as he had done a dozen times before, he showed her similar boats in the crowded anchorage and pointed out the critical differences to her. She took detailed notes, and when he asked if she would be able to dig through them, fly the plane, and check out a boat at the same time, she answered, "No. But before I take off again, I'll have them memorized."

That night he cooked a couple of steaks on the charcoal cooker hung over the transom and served them with just a salad. He had a beer with his, but she drank only a diet soda and then retired to the forecabin with her notes. In the morning, he was up early and after wiping the dew from *Lullaby*'s brightwork with a chamois, took the dink into the beach to swim. When he returned, she was up and dressed, and while he rinsed off under the sunshower he hung from the boom, she set the table for breakfast and asked him what he wanted.

"Just cereal and toast. That's all I ever have, except on weekends or holidays."

"This is Boxing Day."

"This is an American ship in a French port. It's not a holiday here."

"Cereal it is, then."

When they had finished eating and had taken their coffee up into the cockpit, she asked, "Have you thought of any way to attack the intelligence problem?"

"No, and I've thought about little else."

"You told me that you talked to everyone you could find in St. Thomas who might know something, and you drew a complete blank. Could you have missed someone, or something?"

"Maybe. I don't know. Let me look." He set down his cup, went down the hatch, and returned a few minutes later with a thick, spiral-bound notebook. "I keep notes, too." It appeared to be a journal. He flipped through it and a few pages from the beginning found what he was looking for; he then read her each of the brief entries he had made as he had searched for someone who might know something about the Holbrooks. No one had known anything about them, or if they had, they certainly hadn't admitted it.

In silence they watched a tender full of people come through the harbor entrance from a cruise ship anchored outside and head for the dock by the brightly colored tents set up in the square next to it. He said, "Another load of tee shirts, funny hats, and cheap rum—"

She interrupted him with, "Somebody, someplace must know something about them, or at least remember them or the boat. Suppose I go back to St. Thomas and talk to all the people you talked to again, and to anyone else I can find. That was the last place we know they were for sure. It can't hurt, and we could get lucky. Do you want to come with me?"

"I don't like leaving the boat alone. We could do an air search of Anguilla, St. Bart's, and the other side of St Martin first, and then I can search any likely-looking spots while you're gone. That way we'll have them checked off the list in case you don't come up with anything better than what we're doing."

"Let's do the air search today. I want you to come with me to help me practice my boat identification."

Although she was sure she had questioned people with a good deal more subtlety and diplomacy than Stroud was capable of, after a week of trying, Lydia had had no more luck than he. The St. Thomas waterfront, like all waterfronts, was the most transient of societies; many of the people Stroud had talked to were no longer around. But she talked to a number of the people Stroud had interviewed and to quite a few he hadn't: a marine equipment repairman, the meteorologist at the airport weather station, and several others he had not thought to approach or who had not been around then.

One of the people she didn't bother to re-interview was Ruth Connelly in the marina office. She probably wouldn't be much help, anyway. Stroud was sure she had told him everything she knew and had helped him as much as she could. Besides, she was in Florida spending the holidays with her family and was due back at work, according to the woman who was subbing for her, the following Monday.

A waitress told her about a group of sailors who met informally every Sunday morning for breakfast at the marina restaurant; she decided to join them to see if they knew anything. Then if she again drew a blank, she would fly down to St. Kitts, meet Stroud, and use that as a base while they searched the next group of islands.

Although the people who sat around the long table were as pleasant a group as she had ever met, none of them had ever heard of the Holbrooks. They accepted the story she was using, that she wanted to thank them because they had made her parents' last days pleasant by the interest and the friendship they had shown to a couple of green-horns from the Midwest. She decided not to hand out the cards with her answering machine's number on it, because she had done her best to make her interest in the Holbrooks seem only casual, and that might be showing too much interest.

It was while she was walking out of the marina telling herself, *Well, Polizzi, Mata Hari you ain't,* that she saw Ruth Connelly walking toward her.

Connelly recognized her and greeted her by name. "Hello, Miss Polizzi. How are you?"

"Fine. How was Florida?"

"Oh, you know Florida. Too hot, too muggy, too many people. It's good to be back in Paradise. Are you on vacation? Mine's over in the morning, and I thought I'd come in for a couple of hours this afternoon to get caught up."

"Oh, I'm sort of on vacation, I guess. Tell me, did you ever hear from the Holbrooks again? You know, the people who were so nice to my parents. I never managed to get in touch with them to thank them."

"It's odd you should ask. Two weeks ago today, when I left for Florida, Alice Holbrook was on the same flight from here to San Juan that I was on. I don't know where she went from there, though. But I know who would know."

"You do?"

"Do you know Granfield Evans? He used to work here as a yacht broker. He was seeing her off at the airport."

As she drove through the gate and up the hill to Evans' house, Lydia thought, *The yacht broker business must be really good in St. Thomas.* It was one of those low, long, Caribbean-style houses, covered by three connected hip roofs, circled by a wide gallery, and set in about two acres of landscaped lawn. A five-year-old BMW convertible was parked in the drive, so she parked her rental behind it and yelled, "Inside" as she climbed out. This, too, is the Caribbean style.

Evans came out of the house wearing swimming trunks and sandals, looked down at her over the gallery rail, and asked, "Can I help you?"

She said, "I hope so," as she climbed the stairs with her hand held out to be shaken. "I'm Lydia Polizzi. You may remember my parents."

He took her hand but he did not meet her eyes. "Ah, no. I don't think so."

"The Grand Banks 42 that went missing in the Anegada last spring?"

"Oh. Now I remember. I may have seen them around the marina, but I don't think I ever met them. I was sorry to hear about it, though. You have my sympathy. Is there something I can do for you? I was just about to have a beer. Would you like one? Or a soft drink, perhaps."

"A beer would be fine."

There was a bar refrigerator in the furniture arrangement at the corner of the gallery; he waved her into a wicker easy-chair as he opened two beers and pointed at the rack of glassware above the fridge. "A glass?"

"Please. I'm sorry to bother you on a Sunday, Mr. Evans, but your office was closed and I'm leaving this afternoon. I understand you've been in touch with Alice Holbrook recently, and I was hoping you could tell me how I could reach her."

"Why would you want to reach her?"

"She and her husband were very kind to my parents in the last weeks of their lives. My mother repeatedly mentioned them whenever we spoke on the phone. I've never thanked them and I'd like to."

"I'm sorry. I'd like to help you, but I haven't seen either of the Holbrooks since they left here back before the hurricane season."

"That's funny. I was told you were seen at the airport with Alice Holbrook two weeks ago."

"No. That's not true. Oh, wait a minute. I know what happened. I had a couple come down from the States to look at a boat, and the wife did look a lot like the Holbrook woman, now that you mention it. It was an honest mistake." He smiled and then took a long pull off his bottle.

"My source knew Alice Holbrook quite well. I don't think she would have made that sort of mistake."

"Well, I'm afraid your source, whoever it was, was mistaken."

"She said Holbrook flew over to San Juan on an American Eagle with her."

"I sincerely wish I could help you, but I have no idea what you're talking about. Now, when you arrived I was just about to go for a swim..." He stood up.

"I thought you said you were about to have a beer when I arrived. Which was it?" She made no move to leave but let him stand over her awkwardly for a few seconds, then asked, "How's your geography, Mr. Evans? Do you know where Cervione is?" She pronounced it with a heavy accent on the second syllable, in Italian.

"Should I?"

She reached into her handbag, took out a Leatherman ten-in-one tool, removed it from its case, and began to play with it. "Sit down, Mr. Evans. We're not done yet. Cervione is on the east coast of Corsica; my grandparents were all born within ten miles of there. What do you know about Corsicans, Mr. Evans?" She opened the pliers and studied them while she waited for an answer.

"Other than that Napoleon was born there, nothing. Now, this is all very enlightening, but . . . "

"I said, sit down. I'm not leaving until we're through."

He asked, "And when, pray, will that be?" But he did sit down.

"Why just as soon as you understand about Corsicans, of course." She opened something that looked like an awl or a short, fat icepick from one of the handles of the pliers. "Corsicans like hard, shiny things with sharp edges, Mr. Evans, and they have two overriding interests: family, and revenge. Everything else is secondary to those two things. Corsicans always get a lot more than even. When it comes to vendettas, Mr. Evans, Corsicans make Sicilians look like Quakers. Are you beginning to get some idea of what I'm getting at?"

"To tell the truth, I don't have the foggiest idea what you're getting at."

"Let me go on, then. The Polizzi are a very large family. I have about thirty cousins in the U.S. and probably several hundred back in the old country. Mr. Evans, you've been lying to me from the minute I got here: first about whether you were going to have a swim or a beer, and then about seeing Alice Holbrook. I can't help but wonder why. My reason for wanting to contact her was perfectly innocent, even benevolent, and yet you're lying to me. The only reason I can think of is that you and the Holbrooks had something to do with the disappearance of my parents and niece.

"I hope that's not why you're lying to me, because if it were, it would become a Polizzi family matter. I'd have to call my brothers—I have three brothers—and a cousin who lives in New York who is in almost daily touch with the cousins in Corsica. I'm sure, Mr. Evans, that a nice white Anglo-Saxon like yourself certainly doesn't want to get involved in matters as socially unacceptable and potentially uncouth as those of a Corsican family. Believe me, it would be best for everyone if you just told me how to reach the Holbrooks and why it is you don't want to tell me."

"And if I don't, I'm liable to wake up with a horse's head next to me in bed, right? I don't own any horses, honey, so why don't take your bullshit and your other paraphernalia and get off my property." She looked at him from under those big black eyebrows, and he had to admit that she was one ugly, scary broad; but she wasn't the scariest broad he knew.

"You know, the idea that you and the Holbrooks might have had something to do with my parent's disappearance never occurred to me until you started lying just now. All right, if that's the way you want it. Thanks for the beer." She stood up. "Someone will be around to talk to you in a day or two: someone far more persuasive than I am. This is not the end of this, Mr. Evans. It's only the beginning, because you obviously have no innocent and plausible reason for lying to me."

He thought about it for a minute, and then said, "Okay. I had seen Alice Holbrook around the marina when they were here last spring and we'd talked a few times. You know. Then a couple of weeks ago on a Saturday afternoon I ran into her on Bay Street, and we got to talking. She was here alone, she never said why, and well, one thing led to another and we had a drink, then dinner, and then wound up here. That's all it was: a one-night stand, and not a very memorable one at that, to tell the truth. I didn't want to talk about it because she is, after all, a married lady. The next morning I ran her out to the airport. That's it."

"She must have said where she was going."

"To Jamaica. Kingston. Her husband was there waiting for her on the boat. They were afraid that if they left it alone, the Jamaicans would steal everything, including the varnish off the teak."

"And?"

"And what?"

"And if they're not in Jamaica, you are in very deep shit, Mr. Evans."

"Look. I've told you all I know."

"Where in Jamaica? Where do they usually tie up?"

He thought for a minute. "If I had to guess, I'd say the yacht club, the Royal Jamaican. I've seen her wearing a shirt with their logo on the pocket."

She put the ten-in-one tool back in its case, dropped it in her bag, and stood up. "Thank you very much, Mr. Evans. You've been a big help. Of course, if you're still lying to me, you can expect another visit."

"I wouldn't lie to you. The Royal Jamaica. That's all I know."

As Polizzi went down the stairs, she fished her cell phone out of her bag and as soon as she was in the car called first information and then an airline to inquire about connections to Jamaica.

Evans went into the house thinking, "That's why she was so thick with that bastard, Stroud. They're in this together." Then he, too, made a phone call. He did not, however, need to call information. He had the number memorized.

CHAPTER SIX

Getting bounced out of the Ginger Bay Marina had made no difference in either Granfield Evans' business or personal life; they both continued to cruise along nicely with very little effort on his part. He had opened a small office on Bay Street in Charlotte Amalie and, working mostly through the Internet, managed to make enough to give him, along with his other income, a decent living.

His personal life continued as it had for most of the twelve years since he had discovered that being a world-class Star Boat sailor and getting a college degree had one thing in common: they both required a great deal more work than he was willing to expend at anything.

He sat at his computer the day after Polizzi's visit, scrolling through listings of yachts wanted, hoping to find someone who might be interested in one of the half dozen or so boats he had for sale. His clients could have done the same thing and saved his commission, and eventually everyone would, but there were still enough computer-ignorant people so he was not yet completely obsolete. But that didn't worry him any more than Polizzi's threats had. Something would come along. Something good had always come along, and it always would.

He finished his search, sent an e-mail to a listing that might be interested in the old Phil Rhodes ketch he had been trying to peddle for months, and then brought up his financial program and checked on his current net worth. Comfortable. His mother owned the house where he lived, so his living expenses were minimal. There was the income from the trust fund his grandparents had left him—his mother still con-

trolled the principal—and the money he had made over the years selling boats legitimately and from what he called windfalls. Like that deal
on the 42 last summer. Every once in a while Alice and Gordon would
come up with a great boat at a fabulous price, and all he had to do was
find a buyer who would pay cash and ask no questions. It wasn't difficult, because the world was full of people who would pay cash for a great
boat and ask no questions if the price was right.

He swiveled his chair around, leaned back, and gazed at the enlarged photo of a Star Boat that hung on the wall behind his desk. Its
crew, a blond boy steering and a teenaged girl with her dark hair blown
around her face, were hiked far out over the rail, oblivious to the photo
boat that must have been just ahead and to weather of them. Maggie
had been the best crew he had ever had: she was as big as he was, even
stronger, and had loved him madly. A week after the picture had been
taken they had hit a buoy, lost a race, and had such a bad fight on the
way in that they had nearly piled the boat on the breakwater. He had
ended it by telling her she was a stupid cow and a lousy lay whose only
use was crewing for him and sucking him and she could do neither worth
a shit. Maggie had neither crewed for him nor spoken to him again.

The summer after he graduated from prep school, he went to the
Eastern and then the North American Championships, at great expense
to his doting parents. But without Maggie, he hadn't done better than
the bottom third of the fleet. So instead of going south to sail all winter
and get ready for the Olympic tryouts, as he and his parents had planned,
he had gone to college.

He hadn't been any great shakes at college either, and had dropped
out after a year and come to the Caribbean.

But St. Thomas had been good to him. He lived in a house on a hill
overlooking the sea, there was plenty of attractive female company, and
here, where many of the ancient trade routes for both legitimate goods
and contraband met, there were plenty of windfalls.

And there was Alice. Two weeks before, he had been about to close
the office for the day when the phone rang and a female voice asked,

"Hey, baby, how'd you like to haul the ashes of a sailor who's been at sea much too long?"

"Where are you?"

"Sitting on your gallery, looking at the ocean, rubbing my thighs together and wondering when you're coming home."

"Right now. I'm leaving right now."

"I thought that's what you'd say."

Somewhere he had read that you should never go to bed with some-one crazier than you. Whoever had written it had no idea just what going to bed with Alice Holbrook was like. It wasn't her body: it was smooth, round, strong, and suntanned, like many of the female bodies in St. Thomas, but it certainly wasn't spectacular, as many of them were. But she was the most aggressively submissive woman he had ever met. She would do literally anything to please him. Given only the slightest hint, she would become whatever he wanted, from cowering child slave to brutal dominatrix. This compulsion to gratify him, and her utter lack of inhibitions, made her far and away the best sexual partner he had ever found. The brutal candor with which she discussed her need to satisfy his needs made her a little scary, but it added to the eroticism that made him start to stiffen the second he heard her voice on the phone.

She would just show up to get her ashes hauled, as she called it, never on any schedule and always without warning. Once, she had appeared in his bedroom and calmly told the lady who was with him at the moment, "Granny and I have business. If you'd like to stay and join us, that's fine. I'm sure we'll find something interesting to do with you. Or you can leave right now." She had then calmly begun to undress. The lady had fled the house and never come near Granville Evans again.

He had no idea what her relationship with Gordon was when they were alone on that boat, but he was almost sure there was nothing physi-cally sexual between them. She had once told him, "Gordon and I have a completely symbiotic relationship." He had looked at her blankly, so she had explained, "That's when two dissimilar organisms live together in close union for their mutual benefit."

Last spring he had come upon them at the Ginger Bay Marina, standing at the head of the dock studying the Grand Banks 42 as the Polizzi girl washed the decks. Gordon Holbrook had neither taken his eyes off her nor even noticed Evans' presence as Evans and Alice talked. To make conversation, he had told her that he had a client who wanted to buy a boat like that: a Cuban government official who wanted to use it as a rumpus room now, and later, when Castro died, as an escape vessel.

The Holbrooks and the Polizzis had become friends soon after that, and both boats had sailed a couple of weeks later. Then Alice had flown back from Tortola and offered him the Grand Banks for half its market value if the deal could be done at sea, in the Anegada Passage, for cash. He had asked, "What about the Polizzis?"

"The old man says the two women are seasick all the time, and he just wants to get shut of it. But I don't think that's the truth. If I had to guess, I'd say he didn't acquire the boat or the money he bought it with in any way he wants anybody to look at too closely. And, from the way he keeps looking around, I think someone may be after him. His name is Polizzi, after all. It's either the mob or the Feds. I think that's why he asked me to set it up this way. If I had to guess, I'd say the Feds are going to move them into witness protection. There's plenty of money in this deal for both of us, Granny."

"What about Gordon?"

"Oh, there'll be a little something in it for Gordon, too. Don't worry about him. It won't be part of your share."

It had been pretty thin, but afterwards he had realized that it was supposed to be thin. Just thick enough to give him the rationalization he needed to agree, but afterwards, once the Polizzis had disappeared, so thin that he neither wanted to ask questions nor wanted anyone else to ask any.

It had been a lot of money, though. It was amazing how much money could be made selling luxury yachts that way.

Lullaby **rounded the northeast corner of Saba** driven by the trade wind, the swell, and her spinnaker. Stroud was hand steering because the autopilot could not anticipate the power and the precise direction of each wave as it rose under her counter, and anticipation was what kept any particular wave from spinning her around onto her beams end in what was technically called a broach, but which the guys he had once raced with called the banana surprise. Anticipation developed over years of practice had kept her under control as she surfed down one perfect wave after another all the way from Gustavia on St. Barts.

The trip had only taken—he checked his watch—just over two and a half hours. That meant she had averaged about nine knots: not bad for a boat just under twenty-four feet on the water line. But they had had the wind over the quarter and the seas from behind all the way, and the speedo had touched ten knots often and gone over eleven a half dozen times as they slid down the largest waves in a welter of foam.

Maybe she didn't have a shower and a hot-water heater and a refrigeration system and air conditioning and an auxiliary generator, but at times like this, the couple of thousand pounds saved made all the difference. He would gladly pass up a hot shower and ice in his drink in order to do this kind of sailing.

Downhill skiing may be the closest a human being can come to feeling like a bird in flight, but this was as close to it as you could come with nine thousand pounds of boat under you. But it was over already. The truly great sails were never long enough, but the lousy one always took forever.

Stroud loved to go to weather. He loved the feeling of harnessed power of a perfectly trimmed boat as it knifed through the seas. But sometimes, like now, it was fun to put up the kite and just go like hell downwind. Especially in these surroundings. Saba, a volcanic cone only two and a half miles in diameter, rises just over 3,000 feet straight out of the sea. Despite its small size, it is so high that it produces plenty of rain and is therefore a lush green. With the blues of the sea and the sky and the white of the surf and of the cloud around its crest, Stroud was sure Saba was one of the most beautiful landfalls on earth.

Once they were clear of Torren's Point and the Diamond Rocks offshore of it, and had begun to get a lee from the island, he dropped the autopilot onto the tiller, punched in the course, and stood watching it for a minute before punching in another fifteen degrees of left rudder. As the boat came up toward the wind and the spinnaker collapsed, he eased the sheet, then the halyard, and began to pull the spinnaker under the boom into the cockpit.

He really needed four hands for the job: two for the halyard and at least two more to drag in seven hundred square feet of wildly flapping nylon. If he released the halyard too fast, the sail would drop into the sea and fill with water. If he eased it too slowly, the sail would tighten, fill with wind, and try to lift him right out of the boat. He was in the middle of this pickle, while noticing over his shoulder how quickly the island was sliding by—if he didn't get the hell-machine down pretty quick, he'd have to turn around, put up the jib and beat back—when the damned phone rang, of course. Why else would anyone have a telephone on a boat except so it could ring while he was doing a single-handed spinnaker takedown with twenty knots of wind over the deck.

He ignored it. He knew who it had to be and he knew that she would call back. When he finally had the sail aboard, he dumped it down the hatch in a heap, where it pretty much filled the cabin. Then he rounded up and dropped the anchor in eight fathoms in Ladder Bay, a couple of hundred feet off a thousand-foot cliff that rose straight from the sea with only a few feet of rocky beach at its foot. A steel ladder set into the cliff's face gave the place its name. It went up a hundred feet to where perched a tiny building that, according to the cruising guide, was a Customs house.

He dropped the mainsail and began to fold it on the boom as he looked in awe at the absolute magnificence of the place and said aloud, "You ain't on Long Island Sound now, Toto." It was then that he was reminded that everything, no matter how seemingly perfect or spectacularly beautiful, has its price. The current flowing around the island slowly carried *Lullaby* forward so her anchor line went slack and she turned sideways to the swell and began to roll.

Stroud had been in rolling anchorages before—Stonington at the eastern end of the Sound is famous for its rolls—but nothing like this. He hung onto the boom, wondering how many more rolls it would be before she dug her deck edges under. He knew that a boat with her rig intact and over forty percent of her displacement in ballast could not be rolled over in an anchorage by anything but a tsunami, but it sure didn't feel like it.

He staggered aft like a drunk and played with the tiller for a while, hoping the current on the rudder would hold her at some angle to the seas so that the rolling would be at least moderated, but it didn't help. She would sit in a calm spot for a moment and almost come to rest, then another big sea would drop the water from under one side and then the other, flinging him and anything else that was loose in the boat from side to side. Not that there was much loose gear aboard—he was very careful about that. But nonetheless, the stuff in the lockers made a racket like a pail half filled with bolts being shaken.

After he finished doing a none-too-neat job of folding the main, a maneuver akin to trying to fold a sail atop a trapeze bar from which he was swinging, he went below, pushed the piles of nylon out of his way, wedged himself in the corner of a settee, and repacked the spinnaker. He had just decided that dinner would have to be PB and Js, the modern sailor's replacement for salt horse and weevil-laden biscuits, when the phone rang again.

"Bill, it's Lydia." He was holding the phone with one hand and the handrail by the hatch with the other when a particularly violent roll swung him against the edge of the chart table, so his reply was a pained, "Oh shit."

"That's a hell of a greeting."

"Not you. The boat just rolled and bounced me off the furniture."

"You're at sea? I called you a while ago and couldn't get an answer."

"I'm at anchor in Ladder Bay in Saba, and the boat is rolling her and my guts out."

"Bill, I think I found out where AF is. It's Jamaica. I got it out of Evans. You remember Evans the yacht broker?"

She told him what had happened with Evans, and when she was finished he asked, "Do you really have a bunch of homicidal Corsican cousins?"

"Probably. My grandparents were so sick of them and their vendettas that they emigrated to the U.S. and never looked back.

"Do you think he finally told you the truth?"

"I'll find out tomorrow. I'm on the morning commercial flight to Kingston. It'll get me there a lot faster than the Beech. Do you want to meet me there?"

He thought about it for a minute. "I can't leave the boat here, that's for sure." Another pause, then, "I'll sail down to St. Kitts tonight and wait to hear from you. If *Cinderella* is in Kingston, call me and I'll fly over and we'll go to the cops and the U.S. Embassy together. But be discreet, Lydia. Don't spook them and don't do anything until I get there. If it is them, I have a right to be there, and besides, two of us will have more weight with the authorities than either of us alone. Jamaica. Old Port Royal. I suppose that's where you'd expect them to be. What are you going to do if Evans was lying and this is another wild-goose chase?"

"I guess you'll have to talk to him."

"I thought that was what you've been afraid of all along, that I might behave like one of your hypothetical Corsican relatives. Did the bastard tell you I got him fired?"

"I don't think he even knows that we're associated. Your name never came up."

"Good." *Lullaby* took a particularly violent roll as he said it. "I've got to hang up and get the hell out of this place. It's like being inside a paint shaker. Call me as soon as you find out anything."

She should have flown the Beech, or perhaps rented a boat and rowed to Jamaica. Almost anything was better than trying to get any place on Liat, the Caribbean's own airline, as it billed itself. Instead of arriving in Kingston at eleven-thirty, it was after five when the taxi dropped her at the Royal Jamaica Yacht Club. The early morning flight from St. Thomas to San Juan had only been an hour late getting in; something the passengers who were used to flying the airline considered amazingly early. Liat was supposedly an acronym for Leeward Islands Air Transport, but the waiting passengers passed the time swapping other explanations such as Leaves Island Any Time, Look Immediately for Alternate Transportation, and Lost In A Tizzy.

Then, when they were finally in the air, the pilot calmly announced that they weren't going directly to San Juan as scheduled, but would make a little side trip to St. Croix to drop off a part for one of their aircraft that was on the ground there. He was sure the passengers wouldn't mind. By the time they got to Puerto Rico, she had missed her connection to Kingston.

When the cell phone rang, Stroud was cooking the last of the steaks he had bought in St. Martin on the charcoal grill that hung over *Lullaby's* stern as she swung at anchor off Basseterre, the capitol of St. Kitts. He lifted the almost-cooked piece of meat off the fire with a fork and stood for a second wondering what to do with it before carrying it below as he scrambled for the insistently squawking phone that lay on the chart table.

"Hello?"

"Bill, it's Lydia. I'm in Kingston. Either Evans was lying or honestly mistaken. They belong to the Royal Jamaica, all right, but they haven't been here in a year."

"Shit. What do we do now?" He paused in thought for a minute and then said, "Maybe I'd better talk to Evans. Explain the seriousness of the matter. I could be the good cop, I suppose. Tell him that crazy Corsican broad is about to have her relatives set his balls on fire, and I don't want to be a party to that, so if he could help us . . . You know."

"Might work. Here's his phone number. Office first, then home." She read them off and then continued, "I'm going back to St. Thomas in the morning, or at least I'm going to try to go back if the damn airline lets me. What are you going to do?"

"I'm at Basseterre on St. Kitts. In the morning, I'm going to sail over to Nevis and look for *Cinderella* there, in case this whole Evans deal turns out to be complete bullshit. Call me when you get to Charlotte Amalie."

He turned off the phone, studied the half-cooked steak, and said aloud, "Christ, they could be through the Panama Canal and long gone by now."

When she called the next afternoon, he was at anchor in Mosquito Bay on Nevis, sheltering from the rising trade winds and the procession of squalls they brought, each more violent than its predecessor.

"Bill, I'm back in St. Thomas. Did you talk to Evans?"

"Yeah. He was terribly sorry for sending you all the way to Jamaica, and he wanted me to convey his apologies."

"Do you believe him?"

"I honestly don't know, and I don't know if it matters. He said he was about to call you, anyway. He claims he just received a Christmas card the Holbrooks mailed from Antigua the week before Christmas."

"They could still be there."

"If they were ever there. This could be just another of Evan's wild-goose chases."

"We have to follow up on it, though." Then after a pause, she asked, "Did he say where on Antigua?"

"No, but I'd start to look in English Harbor, I guess."

Then another squall came down and he was glad he was anchored behind Hurricane Hill. The wind rose to a screaming howl and the nearly horizontal rain pounded against the cabin and the topsides. He didn't know if she had heard his last words before the signal was blocked out by the almost solid mass of falling, wind-driven, water. It reminded him of the old sailor's joke: *I'll bet it's pure hell ashore on a night like this.*

She called back about half an hour later. "What happened, Bill?"

"Squall. Very bad, very loud squall. But it's gone now and the wind has settled down to a nice solid force-seven or so, blowing straight out of the east."

She obviously didn't understand the implications of this, because she replied, "I'm going to fly the Beech over early in the morning. It's only fifty miles or so from Nevis to Antigua. If you left now, you could meet me." Stinkpotters.

"Look, Lydia. It's a night like they used to have at the beginning of those old Hammer horror flicks, and the wind is dead foul from Antigua to Nevis. If I left now, I'd be lucky to be ten miles out of the Narrows by morning."

"I thought you liked to go to weather."

"I like Jack Daniels, too. But that doesn't mean I want to drown in a vat of it. I'll see what it looks like in the morning, although if you believe the people who live here, this could go on for weeks. They call it the Christmas Wind and seem to be quite surprised that it's over a week late."

"I'll call you when I get to Antigua."

Just after dawn, Stroud stood on the dock in front of the Oualie Beach Hotel studying *Lullaby* as she rode to her 35-pound CQR, forty feet of chain, and eighty feet of half-inch nylon, out in the bay. She was slewing and dancing like a nervous stallion waiting for the Dalton boys to emerge from a bank as the gusts swirled around Hurricane hill and hit her first at one angle and then at another. But the anchor was holding fine.

The inflatable dink, tied to the dock at his feet, was another story. Stroud was glad he had rowed in and left the outboard safely on the mount on the big boat's sternrail. The dink was tied to the lee side of the dock; half the time it stood straight out at the end of its painter, suspended a couple of feet above the water on a cushion of wind. A minute ago it had been turned upside down and then righted by two successive gusts. At times like these, he missed the old fiberglass Dyer Dhow that had been *Terrible Twosome's* tender and now hung from the rafters of the garage in Connecticut. But the Caribbean was no place for a towed dinghy. He silently debated dragging the inflatable up the beach into the shelter of one of the buildings, but decided against it.

The only safe place for the damn thing was rolled up in the box abaft *Lullaby's* mast, where it lived at sea.

He had come ashore to check on the weather forecast that one of the charter captains who worked out of here regularly picked off the Internet and posted on the bulletin board in the bar. He was out of range of the NOAA weather station on St. Thomas.

The forecast was not encouraging. Most of the U.S. was blanketed by snow, rain, and low pressure, while a high out over the Atlantic was trying to fill this meteorological hole any way it could. At least it told him where all this air was going in such a damned hurry.

The report was from the night before, and he wanted to stay ashore until this morning's was posted, but with the dink behaving as it was . . . He stood watching it lift off and settle back a few more times before finally climbing down into it and spending the next half hour rowing this thing that was half boat and half blimp the two hundred yards out to the anchored yacht. From there he could see around Hurricane Point to where the breaking seas rolled into the Narrows and smashed themselves against Booby Island in deluges of snow-white foam.

Maybe it was just here where the bottom shoaled and the waves were squeezed between the islands, that the seas were so insanely steep and breaking. Maybe if he could claw his way a mile or two to sea, they would be longer and *Lullaby* would be better able to ride them as she worked to weather.

Damn it. It might be more of Evans' bullshit, but *Cinderella* could be in Antigua, and he could miss her if he didn't get his ass in gear and get over there.

As he deflated the dink and rolled it up he kept looking for any sign that the wind was moderating. He had just finished stuffing it into the deck box when the next squall hit, and he had to duck below to keep from getting soaked. He stood in the hatch, under the dodger, for a minute or two, looking out at the solid gray wall of the squall, then turned to the chart table and pulled *Street's Cruising Guide to the Eastern Caribbean* from the rack, opened it to the section on the approaches to Antigua, and found that it said, "The beat from

Nevis or St. Kitts may be one of the longest forty miles you have ever done." And that was in normal conditions. "Shit."

Ten minutes later the squall was past, the sun was shining intermittently between rapidly scudding clouds, and the trade winds had not abated one whit, as far as he could tell. He stood in the cockpit studying the seas out in the Narrows for a while, thinking, "The wind only scares you; it's the seas that kill you." Then his thoughts returned to *Cinderella* being in Antigua and he said aloud, "Screw it. God hates a coward," and dragged the bulletproof storm jib out from under the other sails in the cockpit locker and went forward to hank it onto the forestay. It was brand new and he had never hoisted it in anger before; at least now he'd find out how it worked in a real breeze.

The jib seemed anxious to start. As soon as he had the bronze hanks clipped onto the stay and pulled the bag off, it blew up the stay and he had to drag it back down and kneel on it as he tied it to the pulpit. He knotted the sheets into it and then took the cover off the mainsail and tied in the third and deepest reef, wondering if this small area of sail would be enough to push her through those seas.

He had just about ready to hoist the main when another particularly vicious squall came over the hill and assaulted the anchorage. In an instant, the shore and the boats moored around him disappeared in a welter of wind-driven rain that was impossible to face. It stung like hail through his shirt as he kept his back to it and once more roped the wildly blowing main to the boom.

"Shit."

He ducked under the dodger, stripped off his soaked shirt, shorts, and underwear, and left them on the cabin top by the hatch while he went below to dry off and get dressed. When it cleared half an hour later, the seas looked even more violent.

"Shit."

It was almost noon when Lydia called and asked "Bill, where are you?"

"I am, as they used to say in the age of sail, embayed by the wind.

I'm in Nevis and there's no way I can get out of here until this moderates, and it shows absolutely no sign of moderating. There's one squall after another, and every time, the trades seem to blow harder once they pass. It's about force seven or eight now."

"I could see the squalls as I flew over. I had to snake my way among them. How hard is force seven or eight?"

"Thirty to forty knots. According to the book, between a moderate gale and a fresh gale. How did the seas look?"

"Awful. Why don't you fly over? You can always get a charter if there's nothing scheduled."

"I thought about it, but I hate to leave the boat here unattended in this. There really isn't a decent harbor here, and if the wind backs, it's wide open to the northwest. Where are you?"

"I'm at the airport. It's directly across the island from English Harbor and Falmouth. From the air, it looks like there are about a hundred harbors and thousands of boats."

They were both silent for a moment and then he asked, "Well, what do you want to do?"

"Rent a car and start looking, I guess."

"Why don't you go to the port of entry and see if they're there, were ever there, or left recently. They should be able to tell you. Give them some story about how you were supposed to meet them but were delayed. You know."

"Okay. I'll call you if I find out anything."

Like everything else on a Caribbean Island, it proved to be a great deal more difficult than expected. When she asked at the car rental counter for directions to Customs and Immigration, the attendant looked at her as if she were an idiot and pointed at the door from which she had just emerged.

"No. I mean where do yachts check in and out?"

Still with the same look, the attendant replied, "Wherever it is dey sails into. Dey certainly can't sail in here, though. We be only for airplanes."

"Thanks, anyway."

As she drove around to the capital at St. Johns, she became even more impressed with how many boats were in how many inlets and how few of them were accessible from the shore. Oddly, though, there were few yachts in St. Johns harbor. It appeared to be primarily a commercial port.

On many of the islands there was only one, or at most two, points of entry, but at the Customs house she learned that there were four points of entry on Antigua, though there was no central clearing house for the information they collected. It appeared that the idea had never occurred to anyone before she asked about it. In any case, no one had heard of *Cinderella* in St. Johns. The attendant at the Immigration counter seemed to have little interest in being helpful. He made only a cursory flip through his large, old-fashioned ledger before saying, "Dey's no *Cinderella* here," and rudely turned away to say something to the woman at a desk behind him in a language which, if it was a dialect of English, was completely unintelligible to Lydia.

Afterwards, she stood outside in the afternoon sun, studying the rental car map for a while, and decided there was nothing else she could do. She would just have to go around the island from port of entry to port of entry until she had either visited them all or found out something. The trouble was, if they all behaved the way these people had, when she was done, she still wouldn't be sure of anything.

Customs and Immigration in English Harbor was closed when she got there, so she found a room in a hotel, had dinner, and then wandered around the dockyard hoping to stumble upon something. She didn't.

The next morning she was at the Immigration office when it opened, but if anything, these people were even less interested in helping her than those in St. Johns had been. To begin with, the counter window had a piece of Plexiglas with about four quarter-inch holes drilled in it down near the slot through which papers and money were passed, and the woman behind it spoke so quietly that Lydia could only hear her by crouching with her ear near the slot and the holes. Once the woman learned that she was not there to pay any fees, she lapsed into what may have been the same patois the man had used the previous day, and what little communication there had been through the Plexiglas ended completely.

This was hopeless. She could spend the rest of her life going from Customs house to Customs house without ever learning anything. She had been in the West Indies long enough to know that a more aggressive attitude would get her either giggled at, turned away from, or the deer-in-the-headlights look.

The counter woman's crisply pressed uniform shirt had only one chevron sewed on upside down—*Couldn't these damn people get anything right?*—but at that moment a very tall, very black man came in wearing a shirt with some sort of brass insignia on his collar. Before he could get through the door at the end of the counter, Lydia stopped him by saying, "Excuse me, sir. But perhaps you could help me."

He looked her up and down as though he were considering purchasing her. He must have decided that he might be interested, because he finally smiled and said, "And how might I do that, pretty lady?"

Lydia gave him a look that she hoped said, "I may not be young, but I'm big, strong, built, and would be the best damn lay you've ever had," as she said, "I'm looking for some friends I was supposed to meet here two weeks ago. But I got tied up, we lost touch, and I don't know if they're still here or not. They're in the yacht *Cinderella*."

"Why don't we go into my office where we can be more comfortable?" He held the door open for her, and she wondered if her look had conveyed more of a message than she intended. She was genuinely relieved when he said to the inverted PFC or whatever she was, "Lucinda, please bring in the log for the last month."

"Bill, they were here."

Stroud was just about to make a sandwich for lunch. "When?"

"They left ten days ago. At least, the boat did. There was a couple aboard, but their name wasn't Holbrook, it was Hathaway: Shirley and George Hathaway."

"When did they arrive?"

"I don't know. They must have come in through another port of entry. But when they left, they gave their destination as St. James."

"Hold on." He had a 1-to-4.5 million scale chart of the entire Caribbean taped to the chart table under the 1-to-80,000 one of St. Kitts and Nevis which he pushed aside. He measured the distance with dividers. "Christ, that's only about seventy miles or so from where I am now."

"How's the weather there?"

"Still blowing like stink, but they expect it to moderate in the next day or so. But St James is an easy broad reach from here if the trades keep blowing in the direction they're supposed to."

"Good. I'll meet you in Jamestown. That's the capital, isn't it?"

"The capital and the only town, by the looks of it. But I don't know if I want to go roaring down there and give up the weather gauge. I don't know why they call St. Kitts, Nevis, and Antigua the leeward islands when they're to windward of everything else in the Caribbean. If I go down there and the trail leads back this way, it will be one bitch of a beat with the trades blowing like they are. The consensus seems to be that the wind will either moderate in the next few days or keep blowing like this 'till spring. Nobody knows which it will be, but they're all sure it will be one or the other." Then he paused for a second before he asked, "They changed their names, you think? Why would they do that and not change the name of the boat? This might not even be the same *Cinderella*. There must be plenty of boats with that name."

"It's a Far Horizons 38 and it was built the same year as the boat we're looking for, and Alice and Gordon Holbrook have almost the same initials as Shirley and George Hathaway."

"Three out of four. It's odd, though. You didn't find out the hull number, did you?"

"I've got a copy of the clearance papers right here. Let me look."

"How did you get that?"

"Don't ever ask. Let's just say I have a dinner date tonight that I have no intention of keeping. Here it is." She read off the number.

He was silent for so long that if it hadn't been for the background noise of the phone, she would have thought they had been cut off. Finally she asked, "Bill? Are you still there?"

"Yeah. I'm here." Then he said, "That's the hull number of *Brownian Movement,* my daughter's boat."

Again he was silent for a long time, so she asked, "How do we do this, Bill? We don't want to screw this up."

"No. We don't want to screw this up. But we can't really be sure they went to St. James, can we? Why don't you fly over there and quietly look around."

"How many harbors are there on St. James? It's not like Antigua, is it?"

"Hold on." He fumbled through the stack of charts stored flat under a bunk cushion until he found one that showed St. James and Montserrat in detail. "It looks like there's only Jamestown, and that's just an open roadstead on the leeward side of the island. I don't think anybody in his right mind would anchor on the weather side with the wind blowing the way it is."

"I'll fly over this afternoon and make sure they're there. If they are, then what should I do?"

"If they are, don't do anything; just call me and find some place where you can keep that damn boat in sight. I'll get down there as fast as I can."

"Shouldn't I go to the authorities right away? Before they disappear again?"

"I'm only about twelve hours or so away. If you tip our hand before I put the stopper in the bottle, they'll probably sail. Then I'll have to run them down at sea, and that's bound to be a great deal messier than if we catch them where we can get the authorities to impound the boat and hold them while it gets sorted out."

She thought about it for a moment, then said, "It's, ah, 12:18 right now. By the time I drive halfway around the island to the airport and get out of here, it will be, oh, about 2 or 2:30. Then the flight over to St. James—how far is that from here?"

"Fifty miles or so. If you hold on, I can give you the exact distance."

"That's close enough. Half-hour flight. Is the airport close to Jamestown?"

"Of course not. It's right around the island. Maybe twelve or fifteen road miles."

"Hmm. Yeah, that works. I should be there with plenty of daylight left. I'll check out the harbor before I land and call you."

"I'll be ready."

"Talk to you later."

As Stroud closed the phone, he realized that he had a good feeling about this. They were getting close. When it started he had been three years behind *Cinderella.* Now, at most, he was ten days behind, and maybe only twelve hours.

He put away the bread and sandwich meat; he'd eat a full meal when he was ready to sail. Pasta. Marathoner's pasta to carbo-load. After he laid out the course from the southwest corner of Nevis to St. James on the large-scale chart, he wrote it on a piece of adhesive tape with a marking pen and, leaning out of the hatch, stuck it to the bulkhead above the steering compass. He next removed the companionway ladder and the panel that gave access to the engine, checked the oil, gave the drive belts a tug, and looked for any signs of leaks or other problems. Everything was fine, so he put the panel and ladder back in place, started the engine, and then went forward to get the anchor up. He'd motor down to Charlestown charging the ship's batteries, clear Customs and Immigration, and then eat an early dinner while he waited for her call.

It was still blowing hard, but at least the procession of violent squalls seemed to have passed. It should be a very fast reach to St. James. If Lydia called and confirmed that *Cinderella* was there, he would sail late this afternoon and time it so he'd get there at about four in the morning.

That was the hour Sir Edward Pellew or Steven Decatur would have chosen to arrive.

The trades went puffy after midnight and then dropped to a gentle breeze as he passed into the lee of the St. James; it was the darkest hour of the night when *Lullaby* slipped into the roadstead of Jamestown. The moon had set a half hour before, and only a few stars were visible through the predawn haze; it would be an hour or so before this blackness became the darkest of grays. There were two small freighters and about eight yachts in the roadstead, each just a riding light and a dark blob against the lights of the town behind it.

Stroud went forward, pulled down the jib, and tied it to the pulpit. In the light breeze blowing off the land, *Lullaby* was perfectly maneuverable under her main alone—no submarine rigged for silent running was ever more quiet. Absolutely nothing was stirring in the anchorage, and he thought, "Perfect conditions for a cutting-out party. If it is *Brownian Movement*, I could cut their anchor line and drag them right out of here before the Holbrooks knew what was happening."

There it was: the Far Horizons 38. There was just enough light from the town to distinguish one boat from another. Or was it a Niagara 35? Nope. It was a Far Horizons, all right. *Lullaby* was sailing as close to the breeze as she could without a jib, but it was close enough. She would pass right under the stern of the anchored boat where an inflatable was tied. It was a red, ten-foot Achilles with a four-horse Johnson tilted up on the transom: just like the one Nell had bought Steve that last Christmas. His heart was starting to pound and it was getting harder to breathe fast enough. He prayed, "Dear God, if my heart is going to crap out on me today, please let it last just another half hour."

It had rained in the night, and the water droplets that beaded on *Cinderella's* waxed gel coat and varnished brightwork glistened like rhinestones. Whatever else the Holbrooks had done, they had certainly kept her in superb condition.

Lullaby passed the dinghy outboard's propeller with a foot to spare, and he thought, "That's the boat—my poor Nell's boat. Pull that hokey teak nameboard off, and you'll find *Brownian Movement* painted on the transom beneath it."

He kept *Lullaby* close-hauled toward the town dock, snaking through the small local fishing boats moored just off it as he waited for his heartbeat to slow. He hadn't had the fibs in weeks, damn it, but of course his heart had to act up now.

He put the helm up and jibed when the breeze brought the soapy smell of wet acacia to him off the land, and he said very quietly, "Fuck it. The damn thing can do whatever it wants—it can stop completely, for that matter—and I'll still do what has to be done today." He completed the jibe, eased the main, and headed back toward the anchored yachts.

He decided not to anchor. The proper way to conduct a blockade was to sail back and forth just outside the port, particularly if it was an open roadstead like this one, from which the enemy could sail in almost any direction. He passed *Cinderella's* bow this time, just far enough off to clear the anchor rode. Yup. That was the foredeck hatch grating he and Steve had made. No doubt about it.

When he was perhaps a quarter of a mile off the land, he brought the boat onto a reach across the wind, dropped the autopilot onto the tiller, and went below to plot his position from the GPS. He had misjudged the distance; he was almost half a mile off. He went back on deck, tacked, and as he worked in closer to where the outline of his daughter's boat was visible against the shore lights and the faintest of brightening in the eastern sky, tried to decide what to do next. He would never have found them without Lydia. She was in a hotel overlooking the harbor waiting for him to call her, to verify absolutely that it was *Brownian Movement* and say the stopper was in the bottle. Then she would go to the cops. Okay. He had made a deal. He'd live up to it. He flipped open the cell phone and called her.

The sky over the island was brightening quickly now. It wouldn't be long before full daylight. The breeze was picking up and starting to back into the north. He was just beginning to wonder what the holdup was, when the phone rang.

"Bill. It's me. The constable on duty got the police superintendent on the phone, and he's coming in. He wants to see all the proof we have, and then he'll have to talk to the Premier before he'll do anything. I need your stuff. And he needs something in writing that attests that it's your daughter's boat."

"Okay. Go out to the end of the dock. I'll hand it to you."

"Why don't you anchor and bring the stuff ashore in the dink?"

"No. They're not going to sail off while we're entangled with West Indian bureaucracy. You deal with the cops. I'll keep them under close blockade." He came about and put the boat on the reciprocal course back across the mouth of the bay, then ducked below, wrote and signed the required note, and put all the papers in a garbage bag before putting the boat on the wind and heading for the dock.

Stroud would remember the scene for the rest of his life. The sun was just coming over the blue-green hills behind Jamestown, and looking over *Cinderella's* deck he could see the ferry from St. Kitts approaching the battered concrete dock where a crowd waited for it. Lydia and two men in uniform were walking toward the end of the dock, and he was just bearing off to go around *Cinderella*—at that instant he was wondering why he could not bring himself to call her *Brownian Movement*—when the stolen yacht, peacefully at anchor the second before, suddenly erupted in a ball of orange-yellow fire and a shock wave filled with debris hurtled past *Lullaby*, shredding her mainsail and knocking her aback. It was accompanied by the loudest sound Stroud had ever heard.

CHAPTER SEVEN

Lydia, Superintendent Sandburn, and almost everyone else on the dock stood in horrified silence as the noise and shock wave of the explosion passed and pieces of the demolished yacht rained down into the sea for what seemed like ten minutes. The burning remains of the hull had been blown off in a jagged line from just above the waterline at the transom almost to the shearline forward. The wreck drifted in the freshening breeze toward the south end of the harbor with the remains of its rig, attached only by the headstay, dragging behind it.

Lullaby, her mainsail holed in a dozen places, emerged from the cloud of smoke that enveloped the wreck as the police superintendent and Lydia ran toward the end of the dock. Lydia whispered, "Thank God" when she saw Stroud stand up in the cockpit and raise a hand in a feeble wave. If *Lullaby* had been as close to *Cinderella* as it had looked, she would also be a smoldering wreck now.

As Lydia stood watching, Stroud went to the mast and dropped the sail in a heap, then, rather than carefully folding it as he usually did, he roped it to the boom in sloppy bundles to keep it from dragging overboard when he started the engine. She expected him to come into the dock, but instead he crisscrossed the area looking for survivors as he followed *Cinderella*'s remains toward the beach. There were none, so as the wreck struck in the shallows, he turned back, rigged his dock lines and fenders, and came into the dock where Lydia and Sandburn waited for him.

"Bill, are you all right?"

"Grab the bowline."

She snatched it from where he had hung it on the pulpit as he gave the engine a quick shot of reverse. Then he put it in neutral and tossed the stern line to the superintendent, who caught it reluctantly and immediately handed it to the constable standing beside him. When *Lullaby* was tied up, Stroud went onto the foredeck and picked up a large piece of fiberglass with a stainless steel cleat still attached to it. It had put a substantial gouge in the teak deck. Stroud studied the cleat and the gouge, then looked aloft and said, "This hit the headstay or the masthead on the way down. I'll have to get someone to hoist me aloft and make sure everything is okay."

Lydia again asked, "Are you all right?"

"You'll have to speak up, Lydia. You wouldn't believe how my ears are ringing. It's so loud I'm surprised you can't hear it."

This time she almost shouted, "Are you sure you're all right?"

"No, I'm not completely sure, but that's a hell of an improvement. A few minutes ago I was sure I was dead."

The superintendent said, "We thought so, too. If you had been any closer…" Then he introduced himself. "I'm Superintendent Sandburn." He was a heavy-set, completely bald, and very black man in a spotless tan uniform as precisely pressed as a U.S. Marine's.

Stroud tossed the hunk of fiberglass onto the dock and said, "Bill Stroud."

A crowd of locals was beginning to gather at the edge of the dock, so the superintendent said, "Shall we go up to my office and talk?" He told the constable to guard the boat, then turned back to Stroud, "Miss Polizzi tells me you have some papers you think I should see." He had a deep voice and the perfect Oxford accent that Americans are always surprised to hear from a black man. The accent exactly fitted what Stroud took to be a patronizing manner. He got his manila envelope and they walked in silence to the head of the dock where a Land Rover was waiting.

As he climbed into the passenger seat, Sandburn said, "Constable Shippen here will show you the way to my office. I'll join you shortly."

Stroud replied, "If you're going to look at the wreck, I'd like to go with you." He was still speaking unusually loudly.

"I think it would be better if you waited in my office; I shan't be but a moment."

He was over an hour. Stroud and Polizzi spent it sitting on a bench in the squad room of police headquarters while being pointedly ignored by the staff. The room looked like the set for a Caribbean version of *Detective Story*, only grubbier. A large framed photo of a young Queen Elizabeth, faded almost yellow, was just visible through the dirt and dead bugs that covered its glass. The room looked as if it had been neither painted nor cleaned since the Brits left twenty years before—or, Stroud thought, perhaps not since the French left two hundred years before. Yet the uniforms of every one of the cops, with their polished buttons and sharp creases, looked as if they expected to be inspected by the bloody queen herself at any moment.

When he finally arrived, Sandburn motioned them into his office, and when they were settled began it by asking, "Could I see your passports, please?" He studied their photos and faces carefully, then placed the passports directly in the center of his desk blotter. Next he stared from one to the other while tapping his lip with his forefinger for almost a full minute before he asked, "Now what precisely is, or should I say was, your interest in the yacht *Cinderella*?"

Stroud took a deep breath and rather than say what he thought of this act, made a speech he had rehearsed in his mind many times. "I have reason to believe it is the boat belonging to my daughter and son-in-law that was supposedly lost with all hands in the Atlantic almost four years ago."

"And your daughter and son-in-law, why would they stage their own disappearance? Were they wanted by the police?"

Stroud, trying not to let his irritation show, again chose his words carefully. "No, they weren't wanted by the police. He was a Yale University professor on sabbatical and she was a research biochemist. I believe they were the victims of foul play and the boat was stolen from them."

"Do you have any proof of this?"

Stroud pulled a stack of papers from his envelope, leafed through it, and none too gently tossed two documents onto the superintendent's desk. "Here's a copy of *Cinderella's* clearance from Antigua two weeks ago; the other is the U.S. Coast Guard document for my daughter's boat, *Brownian Movement*. The boats they describe are identical right down to the builder's hull number and U.S. Coast Guard registration number. You went to the wreck; are any of the numbers still legible?"

Sandburn took a small notebook from his shirt pocket, flipped through it until he found what he was looking for, then placed the notebook on top of the passports before asking, "Could you give me a physical description of your daughter and her husband, please?"

"Of course I could, but what's the purpose?"

"Mr. Stroud, it will not go well with you if you impede my investigation."

Stroud didn't get a chance to answer, because Lydia said, "I just thought of something, Superintendent. Right after the pieces stopped coming down, when you were running toward the end of the dock, there was a woman coming the other way, hurrying off the dock. A white woman."

Stroud said, "Maybe she was scared. I sure as hell was."

"She certainly didn't look scared. She looked angry. She looked right at me and she looked angry. Do you remember her, Superintendent?"

"Perhaps." He appeared bored in the way only someone with an Oxford accent can appear bored. "Actually, I find this all terribly interesting, Miss Polizzi, but if we could get back to my questions, please, Mr. Stroud. Describe your son and daughter-in-law, please."

"Daughter and son-in-law." Stroud had stopped trying to keep his irritation from showing. "They were both in their late thirties, she was five foot four inches tall and he was exactly one foot taller. Both were slim. She had long blond hair and his was brown but receding. They were pronounced legally dead by a U.S. court last spring. I have those documents here, too. In case you're terribly interested in them, ectually. Now will you tell me what the hell is going on here?"

"No. I don't think I shall, until you adopt a more civil manner. You're not in the United States now, Mr. Stroud."

"Christ, don't I know it."

Before he could go on, Lydia silenced him by saying, "Bill, for God's sake." Then she turned to Sandburn. "You'll have to forgive him. After all, he was almost killed less than two hours ago. Was there anyone on that boat? I think we have a right to know."

Sandburn thought about it, again tapping his lower lip, then said, "There were two bodies in the wreck, a man and a woman. They appear to have been in bed when the explosion occurred. They were both badly burned, but they do not fit the descriptions you just gave me. They were much older: late fifties, early sixties. Do you have any idea who they might be?"

Up until that instant, Stroud had been sure who they might be, but now he didn't know. His confusion showed as he shook his head no.

"You, Miss Polizzi? Do you have any idea who these people might be and how they fit into this mystery of yours?"

"No. No, I don't."

"What is your interest in this matter, Miss Polizzi."

Lydia thought about how to phrase it for a second and then said, "My parents, my niece, and their yacht disappeared after becoming involved with the people who owned *Cinderella.*"

"I don't understand. If what Mr. Stroud just said is true, his family owned the yacht. Mr. Stroud, why didn't you tell me that Miss Polizzi's family was with your son and daughter-in-law when they disappeared?"

Stroud turned to Lydia and said, "Shit, this is hopeless."

Before Stroud could go on, or Sandburn could react, Lydia jumped in. "Mr. Stroud's people disappeared in the Atlantic three or four years ago, and their boat was declared lost with all hands. Last spring it appeared in St. Thomas, now called *Cinderella*, and supposedly owned by a couple named Holbrook: Alice and Gordon. My family was there at the same time onboard my father's Grand Banks 42. That's a different boat entirely: a motor yacht. As far as I can find out, the two boats cruised through the Virgins Islands in company. Then my folks started across the Anegada Passage with Gordon Holbrook aboard their boat, the Grand Banks 42, while Alice Holbrooks stayed aboard *Cinderella*. My relatives and the Grand Banks were never heard from again, but Gordon Holbrook seems to have miraculously survived."

"These Holbrooks, they were West Indian? Black? White? What?"

"As best we can find out, they are white Americans."

"Well, there you have it, don't you."

"Now I don't understand."

"Miss Polizzi, I have no delicate way to explain this to you, but everyone knows of the North American's proclivities for crime and violence. This whole complicated," he paused while pretending to search for a word, "shall we say story of yours is probably involved with drug smuggling."

Stroud said, "Drug smuggling? Who said anything about drug smuggling?"

"Well, it certainly wouldn't be the first time that some American college professor decided he could either augment his income or obtain a lifetime supply for his own use by smuggling a few kilos of cocaine."

"My son-in-law was not a drug smuggler, and if he were, he would have been heading north toward the United States, not south away from it." As Stroud said it, he stood up. "Come on Lydia. This is hopeless." He reached over, shoved the notebook out of the way, and picked up the passports. Sandburn half stood and caught his wrist, but fortunately at that moment someone knocked at the door, and they froze in that position for a second before Stroud dropped the passports and Sandburn let go of his wrist simultaneously. Lydia never did discover who had caved in first.

Sandburn sat back down and said, "Come." A constable entered and whispered something in the superintendent's ear that caused him to say, "If you would excuse me for just a few moments, there is someone else I must talk to. If you would wait outside."

Lydia said, "Okay. We'll wait," before Stroud could respond. Fortunately, this time Sandburn didn't resist as Stroud reached for the passports and his other papers.

As they left, a white couple in their seventies entered the office.

Lydia leaned close to Stroud's ear when they were again seated on the bench and asked, "Bill, can you hear me? How's the ringing?"

"Better."

"There was something I didn't tell him about that woman. Maybe I should have, but he didn't seem very interested. She tossed something off the dock after she passed me. I looked back and saw her do it. It could have been a cell phone."

"Huh. Where was she when she tossed whatever it was overboard?"

She closed her eyes, trying to visualize the scene. "I think it was just about where *Lullaby* is tied up now. Right along there."

He thought for a moment, then said, "Lydia, why don't you go out to the airport and check on your airplane."

"Do you want to get me tossed in the local hoosegow?"

"You've been through Customs and Immigration, you're on the island legally, and he gave you your passport and didn't say you couldn't leave."

"What about you?"

"I haven't cleared in yet. I either have to sit here waiting for that limey asshole, or sail out a couple of miles to where the good old U.S.A. begins, and I'm not ready to sail yet. And while you're at the airport. why don't you to nose around and see if that woman left the island?"

"You got it."

She got up and strolled out of the police station.

Stroud sat on the bench for perhaps twenty minutes before the door to Sandburn's office opened and the elderly couple emerged, the woman clutching a handkerchief to her reddened eyes and the man looking grim. They hurried out of the police station, and it was another ten minutes before the superintendent came out carrying his hat and said, "Where's Miss Polizzi?"

"She went out to the airport. Something about her airplane. It's okay, isn't it?"

Sandburn thought about it, but because he was holding his uniform cap with both hands, he couldn't tap his lip. "Yes. I suppose so. You'll have to excuse me, but there are several matters I have to attend to. There's no point in your waiting here; I have no idea how long it will take. I'll have a constable show you to your boat. I'll probably have a few more questions for you later, so I'd appreciate it if you didn't sail until we can talk again."

"Should I clear in through Customs and Immigration? Would I be welcome?"

Sandburn smiled. "Not terribly, but you probably should."

The constable waited for him as he cleared, then as they walked back to the boat together Stroud asked, "Who was that nice-looking old couple who came out of the Superintendent's office looking so sad? I was sorry to see that."

"Dey's de Hathaway dat lives over in Evening Star. It be Mr. Hathaway's brother dat own de blow-up boat."

As Stroud went aboard, the cop spoke quietly to the officer who had been guarding the boat and they took positions on the dock, one near *Lullaby's* bow and the other at the stern.

An hour later, as Bill Stroud was standing on the dock with the 7x50s trying to see if he could spot any damage near the masthead, a taxi pulled up and Lydia climbed out. As soon as they were below, she said, "She's gone. She just missed the six-thirty shuttle flight to St. Kitts but managed to charter over, probably in time to catch the eight o'clock American Eagle to San Juan. I talked to the charter pilot. At least she told him she wanted to catch the San Juan plane."

"What name did she use?"

"Alice Holbrook, and that was her on the dock. Same dress, same hat. It was her, all right."

"What about him?"

"No sign of him. She was alone."

Stroud got up and went into the head, but before he closed the door, he said, "Why don't you get that mainsail off? I'll give you a hand bending on the spare later."

"What are you going to do now?"

"I'm going to put on my swim gear and go check the bottom for damage. I would appreciate it if you kept those two cops interested in what you're doing with the mainsail."

"Got ya."

She did better than that. She got them to help her fold the main and wrestle it into its bag. They hardly noticed Stroud as he climbed up the stern ladder with his mask on his forehead, proclaimed the bottom intact, and disappeared below. A few minutes later he poked his head out of the hatch and asked if anyone wanted something to drink. In unison they answered, "A soft drink only, sar," as they had obviously been trained to do.

Stroud served Cokes all around, then got them to crank the winch that lifted him aloft while Lydia tailed the line onto a cleat. After what he had seen of the St. James Police Department, he wasn't about to go up the mast with one of them tailing the line. By the time he came back down, the four of them were becoming friends. "Everything is fine up there. I was really lucky." He pointed at the piece of fiberglass still lying on the dock. "Imagine getting that on the conk." The constables laughed considerably more than seemed justified, so he went on, "I'm going to the barbecue cart at the head of the dock; can I bring you guys back something? You haven't had lunch yet either, have you?"

When the superintendent came down the dock an hour later, the four of them were sitting in the cockpit eating chicken and rice and beans. He glowered at the constables as he climbed aboard. They sheepishly excused themselves and scurried back onto the dock.

"Good afternoon. Well, we have begun to get this sorted out. The unfortunate couple on the boat was related to some American people who are permanent residents here. They bought the boat last month in

Antigua from another American couple. So it is obvious that this can have had nothing to do with the disappearance of your daughter and son-in-law four years ago, Mr. Stroud. We have established that the yacht had a propane stove and carried gasoline for an outboard motor. Fumes from either could have accumulated in the bilge and caused the explosion."

He had finally gotten daughter and son-in-law right, but his reasoning was as obscure as ever. Stroud ducked below and came right back up holding a plastic sandwich bag. "Miss Polizzi is sure she saw the woman she mentioned toss this into the harbor right after the explosion." He handed him the bag. "It's a garage-door opener control."

Sandburn held the bag out at arm's length and stared at its contents. "Very few people on St James have garage doors, Mr. Stroud, and none of them have automatic openers. It is a small island, and if anyone had such a thing I would surely know about it."

As if he were explaining to a moron, Stroud said, "Forget the garage door application. This is simply a device that will make an electrical contact close from several hundred yards away. It could be used for any number of applications that require an electrical contact to be operated from a distance—like detonating a bomb, for example. I found it on the bottom of the harbor right where Miss Polizzi said it would be, only she thought it was a cell phone."

Sandburn peered into the bag again, then said, "If this is evidence of some sort, you should have left it where it was and reported it."

"Probably. But I didn't want it to wash away or get covered up." Stroud handed him a white business envelope. "Here's a signed statement that details where I found it and why I looked there. I didn't touch it; I just swept it into the bag. Perhaps Miss Polizzi should give you a statement about what she saw the woman do."

"I do not need you to tell me how to conduct my investigation. If it is determined that this thing is important, I will see that it is examined properly."

"If you looked, you might get lucky and find bits of the receiver on the wreck." He pointed across the harbor to where *Cinderella* sat abandoned and awash. "And wouldn't it be a good idea to drag it up on the beach before anything more washes away?"

"Mr. Stroud. As I just said, I do not need your advice on how to conduct this investigation. You have no idea who this woman was, and no proof that she actually threw this thing into the harbor, or that she has anything to do with any of this, do you?"

"Just suspicions. Her name might be Alice Holbrook."

"I too have my suspicions." Sandburn said it darkly, as though the statement was loaded with implications and should give them pause.

All it accomplished was to make Stroud think of Inspector Clouseau. He looked over at Polizzi, who wiggled her eyebrows at him; he was sure she was thinking the same thing. "What about us? Can we go? Can we stay? What?"

"I'd prefer you to stay until this is cleared up, but of course, I have no grounds for holding you here. Did you ever clear in?"

"Yes."

"Well, then, you're free to enjoy our beautiful island, aren't you? I think you'll have to move off the dock, though. The Minister of Trade doesn't like private yachts tied up here for more than a few minutes."

Sandburn took the garage door controller with him, but left Stroud's statement, still in its envelope, on the cockpit seat.

It took them the rest of the afternoon to move the boat out into the harbor, pump up the dinghy, and then bend on the old mainsail Stroud carried as a spare. When they were finished, he got into the dink alone, left the outboard hanging on its rack on the sternrail, and slowly rowed over to the wreck. When he got too close, a constable on the beach yelled at him and motioned him away.

He rowed back, climbed aboard, sat down in the cockpit across from Lydia, and said, "I'll call the sailmaker in the U.S. in the morning and have him make up a new main on a rush basis."

He obviously did not want to talk about the wreck, so she answered, "This one doesn't look that bad, and what about the one I took off? Can't you get it fixed?"

"This one is pretty well blown. I think it came original with the boat. I'll get the holes in the other one repaired and make it the new spare. But this one is just about to the painting dropcloth point."

"Does it matter that much?"

"Maybe a knot or so on some points of sail. Not much until you consider that can be a twenty-five percent difference in speed. Didn't John Paul Jones say something about speed and harm's way and all that?"

"I guess you have been in harm's way today."

The sun was getting close to the horizon as they watched it, their backs toward the wreck. "Was that only this morning? You know, if I had been going any faster, I'd have been even more directly in harm's way. I guess even old John Paul can't be right all the time."

"From the dock, it looked like you were almost alongside *Cinderella*. It's difficult to judge the distance between two objects when you're looking at them over water, isn't it?"

"Good thing for me you weren't the only one to misjudge the distance."

"You think she set off a bomb with that door clicker, don't you?"

"I don't know. Like the man said, I have no proof, just suspicions. You want a drink?"

"A weak gin and tonic might be nice."

"I'll get them. Sit still."

They sipped their drinks in silence and watched the sun disappear into a cloud bank that hung just above the horizon. It lit the clouds a brilliant yellow that segued to orange, then pink, and finally faded into night. When all the light was gone from the western sky he asked, "Do you want to go ashore and eat?"

"It seems like a lot of work. I don't know about you, but I'm tired."

"How about we split a can of ravioli?"

"It just dawns on me that I still have a hotel room ashore and my stuff is there."

"What do you want to do? I'll take you ashore if you like."

"Let's split the can of ravioli and then you'd better take me ashore. There's a constable sitting on the end of the dock watching us, and I suppose if I stay aboard, it will only add to Superintendent Sandburn's many suspicions."

"That limey asshole."

Stroud awoke in the night and, as he always did, went on deck to urinate over the stern and take a couple of eyeball bearings to make sure the anchor wasn't dragging. There was little chance it would drag; it was a calm, clear tropic night, and now that the moon had set, every star in the sky was visible. He could just make out the wreck of *Brownian Movement* against the lights of the town behind it. It did not seem possible that just twenty-four hours before, he had thought that his quest was about to end.

There was a lot he didn't know. Hell, he had thought that the Holbrooks hadn't even known he was on their trail, and they had very nearly managed to ambush him. It took him a very long time to get to sleep.

When he next awoke, it was to the sound of heavy equipment. He pulled on shorts and a shirt and went on deck. As he watched, a backhoe dragged the wreck ashore and then, as a crew with chain saws cut it up, loaded the pieces into a dump truck. His first reaction was to row over and try to find out what was going on, but he decided that even if anyone knew, there was small chance they would tell him.

He was pouring cereal into a bowl when the cell phone rang. "Bill, it's Lydia. Do you see what they're doing?"

"Yes."

"What do you think it means?"

"I don't know. I can understand them wanting to get it out of there, but I'd expect them to be a little gentler about it. But you know how West Indians are with backhoes."

"Their favorite precision tool. They're probably going to send samples away for forensic examination. At least I hope they are. I don't suppose there's any point in leaving the wreck there as an eyesore. Are you coming ashore, or should I come out there? You haven't heard from Sandburn this morning, have you?"

"No. Thank God. Where are you?"

"At the hotel."

"How about I meet you there in an hour and we'll prowl around town and see what's happening?"

The town was abuzz with all sorts of rumors, each nuttier than the other. The explosion seemed to be the most exciting event to happen on St. James since the last time the French had shelled the place in seventeen something. From among all the stories, they were able to learn that the Hathaway children were due to arrive that afternoon and their funeral was to take place the next morning.

After lunch, Stroud bundled up the torn mainsail, packed it, then took it to the FedEx office and shipped it to Connecticut. He didn't feel like dealing with a strange sailmaker. Dealing with sailmakers he knew was usually bad enough.

After he shipped it, he went by police headquarters but was told that Superintendent Sandburn was in conference and no, he hadn't left any messages for Stroud.

The next morning they went to the funeral in an ancient gray field-stone Anglican Church on a promontory above the sea. The church had no windows, just white painted wooden shutters cut to the shape of the arched portals spaced around its walls. They were open now to let the fresh breeze and the magnificent view of the sea pour in. The two plain coffins of native mahogany stood at the head of a main aisle into which were set worn, flat tombstones with carved dates from the 1600s. The church was filled with whites, blacks, and a few East Indians. Stroud and Polizzi found seats in the back row as the prelude was played on a battered piano desperately in need of tuning. When it ended, the priest stood and led them in a prayer and then in a hymn.

Then the old man they had seen in the police station stood and turned toward them. "My kid brother, George, and his wife Shirley, loved St. James. They loved all of the West Indies, and they loved to sail. Many of you knew them, because they have been coming down here every winter since my wife and I retired fifteen years ago and moved here to live on this wonderful island among all of you fine people. And then this fall George and Shirley finally retired, themselves. They were planning to wander through the West Indies for a year or two before finally settling on a place. That place would probably have been here on St. . . . " He was unable to go on for a moment, but then he blew his nose loudly, dabbed at his eyes, and continued. "But it was not to be, because of this terrible accident. So George and Shirley will stay here now, on St. James . . ." He broke down again and the priest helped him to his seat. Then a younger man stood and delivered a eulogy to his parents.

The church emptied from the front as the two coffins were carried out into the sunlight for the last time toward the freshly dug double grave in the churchyard. The view of the sea was breathtaking, with a cruise ship visible in the distance and two sailing yachts obviously having an impromptu race half a mile or so offshore.

They lowered the two coffins side by side into the ground as Stroud, Polizzi, and the others from the rear rows joined those around the grave. Across the grave from them, a distinguished-looking black couple sat on folding chairs in the first row of mourners. She was light colored—Stroud knew the West Indians called it "high"—quite beautiful, and elegantly dressed in a flowered frock. He wore what used to be called a leisure suit, in contrast to most of the white men, who wore blue blazers, a few even wearing neckties. When Sandburn noticed Polizzi and Stroud, he leaned down and said something to the man in the leisure suit who glanced over at them and then looked away as the priest began to speak.

Stroud didn't listen. He never listened to the blah blah that was said at funerals, but he noticed that the coffins were positioned so they faced away from the sea. They were on the west side of the island, and he realized it made religious sense—if such a thing existed—for the dead to be buried facing east, toward the rising sun, so they would be ready at the dawn of the judgment day. But he knew that if he were being buried here, he'd want to be facing the sea and would worry about Judgment Day later—much later.

As the priest went on, Stroud watched the two sailing yachts. French built forty-footers, he guessed, sparkling white in the sun and both hard on the breeze, heading just west of north. As he watched, the one behind—it must have been taking bad air off the leader—tacked, and the other boat almost immediately tacked to cover. Here, two people were being buried and the grief was so thick you could have loaded it, like their boat, into a dump truck with a backhoe. But just out there, all unaware, those people were having the time of their lives.

They sang another hymn, and then the mourners did something seldom done at funerals in the United States any more: They watched until the grave was completely filled in and the flowers had been piled on the fresh earth. Watching two men shovel a grave full and neatly bank and pat the earth atop it, gave a sense of finality which walking away from a still-open grave, its piled dirt discreetly covered by a rug of phony grass, did not give. When the job was done, the priest gave the benediction and then said, "Mr. and Mrs. Hathaway have asked me to invite you all to their house in Evening Star for a luncheon reception at one o'clock."

As Polizzi and Stroud walked down the hill from the churchyard, Superintendent Sandburn stopped them. "I hope you weren't thinking about going to the Hathaway's reception. Those poor people have enough to deal with without your adding to their sorrows."

Stroud answered him, "Why, Inspector Lastrard, how nice to see you."

Sandburn pretended he did not hear him and said, "The Premier and I suggest that you go out to your boat and wait there for me." He turned and walked away.

When he was out of earshot, Lydia said, "I guess that's what we should do. You know, I wouldn't be surprised if we're about to get booted off of this tropical paradise."

"You can go out to the boat if you want, but I'm going to that reception in Evening Star. I was invited."

"The premier and Sandburn will probably be there. I don't know if you should go out of your way to piss them off."

"Yeah. But they're West Indians. They're sure to be at least two hours late. I'm going early. Let's walk back into town and get a cab."

It was twenty to one when the cab dropped them off at the Hathaway home. Lydia was carrying a huge tray of freshly baked cookies they had bought at a bakery in Jamestown, and as they walked across the lawn toward the long, low, white-painted house, two other white couples, both bearing gifts of food, were just entering.

At the door they were greeted by the son, who held out his hand, introduced himself as Herb Hathaway, and said, "Thank you for coming." Then he told Lydia, "The kitchen is right through there."

As Lydia headed toward the kitchen, Stroud said, "I was on the boat closest to *Cinderella*."

"Oh yes. I'm glad you weren't injured. I understand that you immediately started to search for survivors. Thank you."

"Mr. Hathaway, I hate to bother you at a time like this, but we have to talk. There is more to this, this accident, than I think you know."

"Superintendent Sandburn told me it was either a leak in the propane stove line or gasoline spilled in the bilges."

"Were your parents the sort who would ignore the smell of propane or be sloppy with gasoline?"

Hathaway thought about it for only a second. "No, they definitely were not. What are you getting at?"

"Is there some place we could talk?"

"Could this wait until after the reception or perhaps tomorrow?"

"No. I expect that the minute Sandburn sees me talking to you, Lydia and I will be kicked off the island. He isn't here yet, is he?"

"No, not yet. Can you give me some idea what this is about?"

"Well, to begin with, the boat did not belong to the couple who sold it to your parents; it belonged to my daughter and son-in-law and was supposedly lost with all hands almost four years ago. They were declared legally dead last spring. I have documentation to prove all this."

"Have you showed it to Sandburn?"

"Yes, it and more. But it had no effect. Sandburn is either an idiot or worse."

Lydia rejoined them as Hathaway replied, "Go out on the gallery and turn left. The first door is my uncle's study. If you wait for me there, I'll be right along."

They waited only a few minutes before he came in accompanied by his uncle and closed the door. "Now, Mr. Stroud . . ."

"Bill."

"Bill, then. What's this about?"

"Lydia and I have been chasing the Holbrooks for three months." He opened his manila envelope. "Here's my daughter's certificate of ownership and here's your parents' clearance from Antigua last month. Same boat." As Hathaway and his uncle studied the papers, Stroud continued, "I have reason to believe that Alice and Gordon Holbrook are the Alice and John Perkins who sailed with my son-in-law and daughter from South Carolina just before they disappeared. Gordon Holbrook sailed with Lydia's parents and niece from Virgin Gorda just before they and their boat disappeared. Alice Holbrook left this island less than an hour after the explosion, and we have no idea where to start looking again. Any information you could give us . . ."

The elder Hathaway said, "You must have the wrong people. They were here, but they both left almost a week ago. Besides, they're such a nice young couple."

Lydia said, "Perhaps they are the wrong people. They could have bought the boat in good faith from the Perkins. If we could get in touch with the Holbrooks, we might be able to sort out this whole mess. That's why we've been trying to catch up with them. But I don't understand what they were doing here if they sold the boat to your brother in Antigua."

The elder Hathaway took a deep breath and then said, "Last week the Holbrooks arrived here and told my brother that something on the engine had been giving them problems for quite a while—the heat exchanger, they called it—and they had had a conscience attack about not mentioning it at the time of the sale. They brought a new heat exchanger with them and Gordon Holbrook installed it. They said it was their penance for not mentioning the problem in the first place. They were quite charming, and after it was installed, they took us all out to dinner. You have the wrong people, I'm sure."

"Are you sure it was a heat exchanger?"

"Of course it was a heat exchanger. I saw it. It was a foot and a half or so long, maybe four inches in diameter, looked like a piece of pipe."

"Or a pipe bomb."

"Don't be silly. And besides, the engine worked fine after it was installed. If it wasn't a heat exchanger, the engine would have overheated, wouldn't it?"

"It wouldn't be hard to install it so it was bypassed and the engine was being cooled by raw salt water."

"I'm not a mechanic, Mr. Stroud, and neither was my brother, but I cannot believe that people as nice as the Holbrooks would be involved in anything like what you are accusing them of."

"We have witnesses. Alice Holbrook was on the pier when the boat exploded and tossed the detonator into the harbor as she scurried off. Lydia saw her."

Herb asked, "Has it been recovered?"

"Yes. I dove down and got it and gave it to Sandburn. He wasn't much interested. It was a garage door opener."

"A garage door opener?" The elder Hathaway said. "You're hanging this whole story of yours, and all the trouble it can cause, on a garage door opener you happened to find at the bottom of the harbor?"

"It's just a device for closing an electric circuit. It's—"

"The superintendent and the premier warned me about you. Where are you from, Mr. Stroud?"

"Beards Corners, Connecticut. What does that have to do with two murders?"

"Your little Connecticut town is probably five times the size of this island and I dare say, it probably has an economy that could swallow this one and not even burp. And that's just one town out of what, several hundred in Connecticut alone. These people have one town, six small hotels, a steady stream of cruising boats that go through here in a good season, and an expatriate community of a few hundred Americans, Canadians, and Europeans who own homes here and pump a substantial amount of what revenues the island has into its economy."

"And you don't want to upset the economic apple cart, is that it?"

"I don't want the eight thousand people who live on this island to suffer because of your delusions. Accidents happen to people on boats all the time. They're to be expected. I think you ought to consider the damage this fantasy about two Americans being murdered could do to this island if it got out."

Stroud was about to reply when Lydia interrupted him. "Mr. Hathaway, I'm sorry we bothered you on a day as trying as this one. Believe me, you have our deepest sympathy. Both Bill and I know what it is like to lose loved ones suddenly. We'll let you get back to your guests now. Come on, Bill."

Stroud said, "Yeah, I guess Lydia's right. Thank you for your time and your help, and you have my deepest sympathy." Then he thought of something. "Does either of you know if the Hathaways bought *Cinderella* directly from the Holbrooks, or was there a broker involved?"

The older man said, "I have no idea."

"Well, thank you, anyway."

As they left, the younger Hathaway followed them onto the gallery. "My uncle is seventy-five and he's not dealing with this very well. I think he feels guilty about bringing his brother down here in the first place. And yes, my dad used a broker in St. Thomas who found the boat for him."

"Was his name Evans?"

"Yes. I think it was. Is there some way I could reach you if I find out anything else?"

"Anything." Stroud jotted down their phone numbers, gave it to him, and turned to see Sandburn coming across the lawn. "Oh shit."

As they went down the stairs, the superintendent stood in their path, but before he could say anything, Stroud asked him, "Say, buddy, you don't know where I can get a cab around here, do you?"

"That won't be necessary. My driver will take you back to town and make sure you go out to your vessel and stay there until I join you. Do you understand?"

"Gee, that's a pretty fancy uniform for a cab dispatcher, isn't it?"

Sandburn pushed past them. "Now. Leave now."

The constable said not one word on the ride into town and sat in the car at the head of the dock watching them as they took the dink out to *Lullaby*. As they climbed aboard, Stroud said, "I think we are going to get booted off the island of St. James momentarily. Do you get that feeling, too?"

"You know, you didn't have to go out of your way to piss the man off." Then she laughed. "Cab dispatcher."

"How about I make some lunch while we wait for Clouseau to pass sentence. Do you feel like creamed tuna on toast?"

"What's that?"

"One of the great culinary delights of our time. I'll show you." They went below, where he mixed a can of tuna and a can of mushroom soup with some canned milk in a saucepan. While it warmed, he made four slices of white toast on the toaster frame that fitted on one of the stove burners. When everything was ready, he put the toast onto dinner plates and poured the mixture over it. Lydia looked at the plate he put in front of her with obvious distaste and asked, "What do you call this stuff, again?" It was a dull, light-gray color.

"Creamed tuna on toast. It's an old family recipe. Try it and you'll like it."

She tasted a fork full. "I guess it's not bad. It's pretty bland, though."

"It is the ultimate example of white, middle-class, protestant American cuisine, absolutely untainted by any ethnic seasonings whatsoever."

She dug in. "It's pretty hard to find fault with something like that." Then she turned serious. "George and Shirley Hathaway must have been pretty decent people."

"It's a shame they wound up that way. And what pisses me off is that limey asshole isn't going to do a damn thing about it."

When they finished eating, he said, "I'd better run the engine and put a charge on the batteries." As he removed the stairs to check the oil and belts, he continued. "I think I'll go and see that son of a bitch, Evans. Alice Holbrook tried to get rid of me and *Cinderella* and the poor Hathaways, all at the same time, and he helped her set it up. We wouldn't be here if it weren't for that Christmas card he supposedly got. Yup, I'm going to have to do something about Granville Evans."

"What?"

"I don't know yet."

He went up into the cockpit and started the engine while she filled the sink. When he came back down, she said, "I'll wash; you dry. So you're going to head for St. Thomas?"

He turned to the chart table, pushed the things that had accumulated there aside, and studied the chart for a moment. "I think I'll leave the boat in a marina in St. Martin and fly over. It's not as far down to leeward as St. Thomas, and I hate to give up the weather gauge, especially when I have no idea where I'm going next. Besides, I'll be a lot less conspicuous arriving on a plane with a bunch of tourists than I would be sailing in. I'll probably overnight in St. Kitts on the way to St. Martin. What are you going to do?"

"I have to take the plane back to San Juan; it's due for an inspection. I'll meet you in Charlotte Amalie."

They were just finishing the dishes when they heard a launch come alongside and a voice called, "Inside." Through the hatch, Stroud saw Sanford's mirror-shined shoes and razor-creased trousers appear in the cockpit as he asked, "May I come aboard?"

Stroud climbed into the cockpit and said, "You are aboard," as he none too gently pushed him aside to reach a couple of fenders in the lazarette locker. The launch was rubbing against *Lullaby*'s topsides.

Sandburn pulled back. "Be careful." He obviously did not like to be touched.

Stroud pointed at the ensign staff on the transom. "You noticed the Stars and Stripes as you came aboard, didn't you? You are now a guest on United States property, on a United States ship of which I am owner and master. You're the one who had better be careful. Otherwise, I hope you can swim."

"I think that as long as you are inside the territorial waters of St. James, you are still the guest, Mr. Stroud."

Lydia intervened. "Look. You didn't come out here to argue about this, Superintendent, so can we get on with whatever it is you want?"

He took two white envelopes from his upper shirt pocket and handed one to Stroud. After he had once more carefully buttoned the pocket he said, "Those are your clearances from this country, Mr. Stroud. I think you'll find everything in order. I expect you to be gone by six o'clock this evening. I believe the American phrase is, don't let the sun set on your sorry ass in this town again."

"I think in this case it's, 'Don't let the sun set on your ass in this sorry town again,' Superintendent."

He ignored Stroud's comment and handed the other envelope to Lydia. She said, "I have a plane at the airport and my things are still in my hotel room."

"Your things are in the trunk of my car, and you are already checked out of the hotel. I shall be pleased to have you come ashore with me so one of my constables can drive you to the airport."

As Lydia went below for her purse, Stroud looked Sandburn up and down and said, "Talk about a sorry ass. You have a double murder on your hands, and the best you can do is chase away anyone who might mention it."

"You have no proof that any crimes have been committed here, and I frankly couldn't care less how many Americans choose to kill each other in other jurisdictions."

Lydia came back on deck and said, "Keep your phone turned on, Bill. I'll call you," as she climbed down into the launch.

The St. James Police Department had packed her things about the way she expected. When they got to the airport, the constable popped the trunk without getting out of the car, and when Lydia raised the lid, she found her bag only partially closed, with a jumble of clothes hanging out of the jammed zipper. The rest of her stuff had been dumped in a plastic laundry bag. Thank God she had left her pilot's brainbag in the plane. She hitched her purse strap onto her shoulder and with a bag in each hand struggled into the dilapidated little airport of this dilapidated little island. The police car didn't move. The constable shut off the engine and sat there watching her, obviously posted to be sure she did not sneak back into this tropical paradise.

She hefted her bags onto a wooden bench next to the door and proceeded to unpack, fold, and repack everything. She was about to walk over to Immigration to clear and then file her flight plan to Puerto Rico, when the charter pilot she had talked to the other day stopped her. He was an older man who she suspected was an American commercial pilot who had been forced to retire at sixty and had come down here so he could keep flying.

"Miss Polizzi. How are you? Did you ever hook up with that woman I flew over to St. Kitts?"

"No. I haven't."

"Too bad. You wouldn't be heading for the States, would you?"

"San Juan."

"Could you do me a favor? I'm stuck here waiting for a pitot tube from the U.S. Would you believe some meathead put a ladder against it and broke it off? Anyway, this is my granddaughter's birthday present." He held out a wrapped package. "If I mail it here, it will never arrive in time for her birthday, if it arrives at all. If you could just drop it in the U.S. Mail . . ."

"Sure. No problem." She held out the now-empty plastic laundry bag for him to drop it into.

As she took care of the paperwork and paid her exit tax—she found it interesting that they made you pay to get off the island, not to get on— she had an idea. She went over to the small duty-free shop and from among the dusty bottles of rum and the tee shirts selected a locally made doll. As much as she hated to spend another penny in this country, she bought the doll and had it placed in a large padded mailing envelope. She copied the charter pilot's return address in the *From* space, but left the *To* space blank, and then put it with the other package in her plastic bag. Then she filed a flight plan—not to San Juan, but to St. Kitts.

CHAPTER EIGHT

It wasn't much of an apartment, but if you didn't want to be found, it was better to sublet a condo than to stay in a hotel. It was cheaper, too. And the apartment wasn't that bad, really—two bedrooms, one at either end, each with its own bath. The space between was a living-dining area, with a modern kitchen in an alcove and glass doors that opened onto a small balcony. The furniture was Florida functional: loud fabrics and rattan and Winslow Homer prints in bamboo frames. The building even had a swimming pool. After she unpacked her suitcase, Alice went out onto the balcony and looked down five stories to where Gordon was swimming laps.

Jerk. He couldn't do anything right any more. There must have been something wrong with that stupid detonator, otherwise the damn thing wouldn't have gone off prematurely. She was going to have to do something about him. That thought popped into her head more and more often lately.

She looked over the tops of the buildings to the Intercoastal Waterway beyond. Salt water. She remembered once when she had been rigging her Blue Jay on the dinghy dock at the club. An old man—at least he had seemed old then—had rowed in from one of the anchored boats and as he climbed onto the dock, asked, "Going sailing?" It was the sort of stupid question adults always ask children.

She had answered, "Just around the harbor."

"Perhaps. But you always have to remember, even when you're just going for a sail around the harbor, from here," and he had pointed down at the murky water beside the dinghy dock, "you can go practically any-where on earth. If you remember that, even a little sail around the harbor will be more of an adventure."

Now, as she looked out at the Intercoastal, she said aloud, "From here you can go practically anywhere on earth. But only if you have a boat."

She had no doubt that Stroud was still looking for them, and prob-ably the Polizzi woman that Granny had told her about, too. Let them look. They probably thought they were beginning to see some pattern, but it wouldn't help them, because she was shattering all the patterns. No more Caribbean; when she found a boat here in Florida, she'd buy it, all neat, legitimate, and clean. Then it would be the Canal and the Pacific. In the bottom of her knitting bag were new passports for Peter and Alicia Lowell of Wellesley, Massachusetts. They did not have the magnetic identification code strip necessary to get into the U.S. or other first-world countries—the artist in Miami who produced whatever docu-mentation she needed had not been able to duplicate those —but they would work most places on earth. She had rented this place as Alice Perkins, but it was the last time she would use her own first name. No more Holbrooks, either. The Holbrooks had worn out their welcome. Alicia Lowell. She smiled at the irony.

Lydia was in luck. The afternoon Eagle flight to San Juan had just left St. Kitts, so there was no one at the counter where two attractive black ladies in American Airlines blue stood talking. One of them turned when she approached and said, "Can I help you? I'm afraid you've missed the afternoon flight, but we've got space on the nine o'clock."

"No. That's all right. I don't need a flight. I need a little informa-tion. Dick Ashcroft, the charter pilot, asked me to do him a favor. He flew a woman over on Tuesday who he thinks just caught your morning flight to San Juan. Anyway, he's stuck on St. James waiting for a part, or he would have done this himself. The woman left this package on his plane and he'd send it to her if he could find her name and address."

She let the agent see the padded envelope with Ashcroft's return address. "He said she was about five-six or so, medium build, wearing a bright flowered dress and a big straw hat."

"That describes half the women who come through here. Captain Ashcroft flew for us for thirty years. Did you know that? Let me see what I can do."

As she started to tickle the computer, the other agent said, "I remember her. Came running in at the last minute and insisted that we had to get her on the flight, even though she didn't have a reservation. Keller, no, Kepler: something like that, anyway."

"Here it is. Kettner. Alice L. Kettner of 3075 Ocean Drive West, Stamford, Connecticut."

Polizzi said, "You're sure that's the correct name and address?" as she wrote it down. "It wasn't Kepler?"

"No. Kettner's correct. We always copy it right off the passport so there can't be any mistake, you know, if there was an accident or something. The airline is very strict about that. Kettner with two tees."

"That's odd. Captain Ashcroft wasn't sure, but he thought her name was Holbrook, or something like that."

The agent tapped a key several times and then said, "No. No Holbrook. No names that begin with an H at all."

"Bill, it's Lydia. Where are you?"

"Bombing along west of Montserrat, watching the sunset and giving thanks that my sorry ass is no longer on St. James. Where are you?"

"At the airport in St. Kitts."

"What happened to San Juan?"

"Tomorrow. I had an idea, so I stopped off here, and it seems to have worked. What time do you expect to get here?"

"Give me a second." After a pause he said, "I should make Basseterre sometime between maybe midnight and one if the breeze holds and doesn't back into the north. Otherwise, who knows? That's why sailboats go toward, not to."

"I'll get a room and see you in the morning."

"I was planning on grabbing a couple of hours sleep and then getting under way again very early. It's about sixty miles to St. Martin, and I want to make it in daylight."

"Okay. I'll be waiting for you on the end of the dock in Basseterre when you get in—under the street light."

"Like Lilly Marlene."

"Like who?"

"Forget it. It's an old folks' joke."

It was almost three when *Lullaby* slid alongside the pier under power and Lydia jumped aboard. As he steered out into the anchorage she asked, "What kept you?"

"Wind backed, and this main isn't much good close-hauled. Besides, everything with sailboats always takes longer than planned." He swung the boat into the wind, said, "Dis be de place," put the engine in neutral, and went forward to get the anchor down. He let fall just as the boat stopped and then veered line, as she drifted backwards, before coming aft and gunning the engine in reverse to set it.

As he shut the engine down, Lydia said, "Herb Hathaway left a message on the machine and I called him back."

"What did he want? Come talk to me while I bag the jib."

"You want me to put the cover on the main?"

"Nah." He pulled the bag out of the sail locker.

"Why bag the jib if you're not going to cover the main?"

"The cover on the main protects it from ultraviolet. Not a big problem between three and six in the morning. But if a squall comes through in the night, I don't want to be staggering around on a wet jib while I try to reset the anchor. What did Hathaway want?"

"He confronted our buddy Superintendent Sandburn after we left."

She followed him forward and watched as he left the jib clipped to the headstay and pulled all the folds between the hanks to the starboard side. "And?"

"And he didn't get anyplace, of course."

He untied the jib sheets from the clew ring and stretched the sail along the deck so it fell into natural folds from each of the hanks. Then he rolled it toward the headstay as she said, "But Clouseau showed him something interesting. In order to convince him that sailing in the Caribbean is so dangerous that accidents happen all the time, he showed him a letter from some guy in Montreal named Bissette." The sail was neatly folded in a pile against the headstay by now; she stopped talking while he wrestled it into the bag. Only then did he unclip it from the stay as she continued, "Seems a boat with this guy's father, mother, and sister went missing a month or so ago on their way to the Panama Canal, and he sent this letter to the cops on all the islands. Sandburn said it showed how common accidents were down here in these dangerous waters."

Stroud ran the bag's drawstring through the tack grommet of the sail, then pulled it tight and tied it through a strap sewn to the bottom of the bag. Lydia was amazed at what a small, neat package it made. Every time she bagged a sail, it looked as if she had stuffed a circus tent into a mattress cover.

After he had tied the jib sheet ends to the pulpit, they came back to the cockpit, where he dropped the sail into the locker as she went below. When he joined her, she took a scratch pad from her bag and said, "Somebody ought to go and see Jean-Claude Bissette in Montreal. This is his address and phone number."

"Why don't we just phone him?"

"The disappearance of his people may have nothing to do with the Holbrooks, but if it does, I don't want to tell someone on the phone that his family has all been murdered."

"Yeah. That makes sense. What are you doing here, anyway? You said you had an idea that paid off."

"I managed to find out that Alice Holbrook flew into St. Kitts on a charter flight right after the explosion and left less than an hour later on American Eagle—only now she was Alice L. Kettner of Stamford, Connecticut."

"How'd you find that out? You're sure it was the same person?"

"Nobody named Alice Holbrook left on the Eagle that morning, but an Alice Kettner did. And the gate agent remembers that she just made the flight and that she fitted the description of Alice Holbrook to a T."

"You mean you can enter a country on one passport and then leave on another an hour later?"

"I don't see why not. Most countries don't have the computer resources to spot such things, even if they tried."

"So this Kettner identity might be just one of a suitcase full of passports she has."

"It could be. But while I was sitting on the dock waiting for you, I thought about it. It may be easy to switch identities inside a country, but the one place you would not want to get caught using a phony passport is entering the United States in Puerto Rico. You've gone through there. You know how they run your passport through the computer and check it and you very carefully. What with all the illegal aliens and drug mules that must try to come in through San Juan, it's no wonder. I certainly wouldn't want to try to get into the U.S. at San Juan on a phony passport. This Kettner identity could be genuine."

"It could be somebody's genuine identity. Not necessarily hers."

"One of us ought to check it out, though."

"First I have to find Evans and follow up on anything I get out of him. But I have to go to Connecticut eventually, to check on the house and pay bills. Alice Kettner? One or two tees?

"Two. Alice L. Kettner of," she tore the page out of her notebook and handed it to him, "3075 Ocean Drive West, Stamford, Connecticut."

Evans was no longer there, of course. Stroud was not surprised. The house was closed and shuttered, and when Stroud went to his office in Charlotte Amalie, it was empty except for, of all people, Wes Lundy, the little Englishman from the used-boat junk store. He was kneeling in the middle of the floor painting a For Rent sign on a piece of used plywood.

"Hello there."

He gave a start and said, "You gave me a froight."

"Sorry. What happened to Evans?"

"'E run off owing me two months rent, 'e did."

"You don't know where to, do you?"

"I wish I did. 'Ere, I know you. You bought some gear from me a whoyle back, didn't you? Back from the cruisin' life already? A lot of people find it's not all they expected."

"Still cruising. I only came back here because I had some business with Evans. But you don't know where he went?"

Lundy stood, picked up the sign, and held it at arm's length to admire it. The other side, the side toward Stroud, said, "Granville Evans––Broker in Fine Yachts" and at the bottom were the crossed bungees of the St. Thomas and another yacht club. "I wish I could help you, but I 'ave no idea where the bastard went."

Stroud smiled and said, "That's all right. I know where to look for him. All roads seem to lead to Connecticut."

Bill Stroud drove his own eight-year-old Ford into Lockford and then turned down Harbor Avenue toward the harbor. It was a cold, drizzly, Connecticut January morning, and he had forgotten just how depressing such a day could be. He passed the old houses on the high ground above the harbor, then the new condos on what had been a swamp beside the harbor, and then a boatyard, before turning into a driveway marked with a sign saying, "Lockford Yacht Club—Members Only." The same burgee he had spotted on Wes Lundy's scrap plywood in Charlotte Amalie was painted above the lettering. As he drove into the parking lot, empty except for a dozen covered, stored boats and an old pickup truck, he looked out through his intermittently flicking windshield wipers at the gray river winding through the gray landscape beneath the gray sky, and realized just how far away Charlotte Amalie was.

He parked beside the truck. There were more covered boats wet-stored in the slips that branched off the main docks, their canvas and plastic tarps glistening with rain. Two men were kneeling out near the end of a dock working on one of the bubblers that stirred warm water up from the bottom to keep ice from freezing around the boats. When one of them looked up and saw him, Stroud gave him a friendly wave and the man returned his wave and went back to his bubbler. Stroud was not a member here; but he belonged to the Ansantawae Yacht Club in the next town, knew this place well, and knew the self-confident behavior that was expected.

The unlocked dock office was obviously being used as a spillover area for the workshop located behind it. Tools and parts for the bubbler system covered by dried marine growth were strewn about. A soldering iron, a stack of three-quarter-inch galvanized thimbles, a roll of friction tape, a rigger's knife, a fid, and dozens of burned bits of nylon rope littered the desk. On a shelf behind it, Stroud found what he was looking for: the club's yearbook for the previous summer. Only one Evans was listed: Helen G. Her address was on Bayside Avenue right across the harbor from the club.

Stroud did not drive directly there. First he went to a Home Depot out on the Post Road where he bought a large plastic work apron, a pair of gardening gloves, a roll of duct tape, and a cheap, three-pound sledgehammer that had been made in China, even though he normally avoided the trash tools the Chinese made. He paid cash and tore up the register receipt as soon as he had dumped his purchases in the trunk of his car. Then he drove down the Post Road to Paul's, the last place left on earth that made real hamburgers and milk shakes, and got one of each for lunch.

He parked the car down the block from the Evans house while he ate. It was a large brick colonial on a landscaped lot, and although he knew the bricks were red and the hemlocks planted around the foundation were deep green, it all looked gray in the drizzle. If it was going to rain, why didn't it rain and get it over with? In the Caribbean, it rained as if it were coming out of a fire hose for a few minutes, then the sun came out again and the colors were even richer than before, and even out in a harbor you could smell the wet acacia. Here it could drizzle gray for days and the only smell was diesel exhaust.

He was beginning to wonder how much longer he could sit here before some neighbor called the cops, when a Mercedes came barreling down the street toward him, made a squealing turn, and slid to a stop in the Evans' driveway. He had just decided that he had hit pay dirt when, instead of Granville Evans, a little old lady with blue hair hopped out of the driver's seat and in the same motion, popped open an oversized golf umbrella. Another lady, her blue hair covered by a clear plastic rain hat, climbed slowly and stiffly out of the passenger's seat and hurried as best she could after the driver to the front door. A few minutes later, a Buick pulled more sedately into the driveway beside the Mercedes and another blue-haired lady climbed awkwardly from it and went into the house. Whoever was peddling blue rinse in Lockford must be making a fortune.

He had come here looking for Granville Evans and had obviously discovered the Blue-Haired Ladies' Saturday Afternoon Booze and Bridge or Bingo Club instead. What the hell? He opened his cell phone and called the number. A deep rasping voice whose sex he could not guess answered it almost immediately. "Hello. This is the Evans residence."

"Is Granville Evans there, please?"

"I'm sorry, he's not here at this time."

Stroud was tempted to ask her if she was a recording. Instead he asked, "Who am I speaking to, please?"

"This is Mrs. Evans' companion."

"Could I speak to Mrs. Evans, please?"

"Mrs. Evans is engaged with guests at the moment. Call back some other time." He felt as if he had stumbled into some thirties comedy movie by mistake. He looked out at the bleak Connecticut winter and decided it was even in black and white. He was sure that Josephine Hull would be playing Mrs. Evans. "Let me be sure I have the right place. Does Granville Evans live there?"

"He hasn't lived here in some time."

"Let me speak to Mrs. Evans, please. It is a matter of some urgency about her son."

"I'll take a message."

"This doesn't concern you. It directly concerns Granville Evans and may indirectly concern his mother. Now let me talk to her."

"If you won't give me a message, you'll have to call sometime when Mrs. Evans is not entertaining guests."

"Look, lady, let me talk to her, damnit."

"Rudeness deserves only rudeness in return." And with that she hung up on him.

"Shit."

He sat there in the rain for most of the afternoon until the lady with the golf umbrella and her companion came out, climbed into the Mercedes, and backed, tires squealing, out of the driveway and roared off down the street. A few minutes later the other old lady left, as well.

Now what? If he went to the door looking for Evans, and later something bad happened to the bastard, the cops would come looking for him right away. If he didn't, there was no chance he'd ever find him, and Stroud really wanted to find him. But he remembered what had happened when he blithely sailed into the Harbor at St. James, so he went home to think about it.

"Hi, Bill. It's Lydia. I'm still in Montreal."

"How'd you make out with Bissette?"

"I haven't talked to him yet. He works for the Canadian Pacific Railroad and he took his family to Bamff, skiing. He's due back in his office Monday morning. I'll get him then. Did you find Evans?"

"No. But I think I found his mother. I haven't talked to her yet."

"Why not?"

"Well, I don't think I want anyone to know I'm looking for him."

"Because of what you plan to do to him when you find him?"

"You aren't going to give me any of your 1960s pacifist bullshit, are you?"

"Go talk to her, Bill. Or I'll come down there and do it when I'm through here. Evans may be with the Holbrooks, and they may all be in the U.S. someplace. If we can find them, and they're here, we certainly have enough to get the authorities to investigate."

"But we have to find them first and establish that it's really them."

"Yes, and Evans' mother may know where."

"I just had a thought. Maybe Evans is swimming with the fishes, as you Italians say."

"You could tell her you're trying to keep him from swimming with the fishes. That might get her to tell you where he is, if she knows."

"I don't think I want to get into any of this with Evans' mother, and I certainly don't want to discuss it with her companion. I didn't tell you about the companion, did I?"

"What about the companion?"

"Don't worry about it. I'll think of something."

The next morning, Sunday, because he didn't know what else to do, Stroud was parked in the still-falling raw drizzle down the block from Evans' mother's house, when, at a quarter to ten, the garage door opened and an old Honda backed out. The woman who was driving was obviously not old enough to be Evans' mother—she didn't look as if she'd ever be anyone's mother—so Stroud assumed she was the companion.

He sat contemplating his next miscalculation, as he called it in his mind, and then said, "Oh shit," aloud before walking up the block and ringing the doorbell.

To his surprise, the lady who answered did not have blue hair: It was thick, wide, hung below her shoulders, and was dyed a bright yellow blond. The teenager's big hair and the little old lady's tiny wrinkled face that looked out from it was so discordant that she had to ask, "Yes?" twice before he answered.

"Hello, Mrs. Evans. My name is Stroud, and I'm trying to get in touch with your son, Granville."

"Are you the rude person who called yesterday? Annie told me about you."

"I'm sorry if Annie thought I was rude."

"Annie is very sensitive to rudeness in others, but doesn't know it is often caused by her own inadvertent rudeness. You were probably wise to wait down the block until you saw her leave for church before ringing my doorbell." She was wearing a tweed skirt, a cashmere turtleneck, high heels, and a single strand of perfect pearls. The outfit looked expensive, elegant, and about forty years too young for her. "Why are you looking for my son?"

"I bought a boat through him last fall, and he did really well by me. Now I'm thinking about a bigger one, and I'd like to have him represent me again."

"Do you expect me to believe that, Mr. Stroud? Granville never did really well by anyone in his whole life. Except for that offshore tan, you look rather like a bill collector to me. Are you a bill collector, Mr. Stroud?"

Stroud had just about decided that there must be some other way to find Evans, but he said, "No, I'm not a bill collector, although if I locate your son I'll probably tell his landlord where he went. He ran out on a couple of months' rent."

"That's sounds more like Granville. But why are you looking for him?"

"Could I come in? It's wet out here."

"Only if you agree to tell me two things."

"What two things?"

"The truth and something interesting. And if it's very interesting, it doesn't have to be completely true. You have no idea how deadly boring it is to live with Annie and then have to listen to the conversation of my bridge club every Wednesday and Saturday."

He smiled. "Okay, it's a deal."

When they were seated in the living room on the sofas that faced each other in front of the cold fireplace, he still didn't know what to tell her, so he said, "Mrs. Evans, I don't know what to tell you. You are a lot better off not knowing most of it." He paused for a moment, and then plowed on, "Your son has gotten tangled up with some very bad people. I don't think he has any idea just how bad. They seem to have used him, perhaps without his realizing it, in one of their schemes. I'm trying to locate him before he gets further involved, or gets hurt."

"Well. I don't know if that's the truth or not, but it's certainly interesting. It does sound like Granville, though. Isn't that a terrible name for a boy? Imagine going through school with everyone calling you Granny. But my husband insisted. Why do Wasps always stick their kids with two last names and no first name? My maiden name was Granville, but there was nothing distinguished about my family except the sound of the name. My father was a Bridgeport cop and was not much good as either a cop or a father. I suppose if his name had been Mulligan my husband would have let the family name die with him. But then again, if my name had been Mulligan, he probably wouldn't have married me in the first place. He was a terrible snob."

Stroud felt way over his head by now. "Do you know how I can reach your son, Mrs. Evans?"

"I only hear from him at Christmas, my birthday, or when he needs money, or claims to. That reminds me—what is his landlord's name and how much does he owe him? I'll send a check."

"I don't know how much. But the landlord's name is Wes Lundy and I'm sure he's in the Charlotte Amalie phone book."

"Charlotte Amalie. Rhymes with family. Did you go by our house? I hope Granville had the decency to close it up properly before he blew town."

"It seemed to be. All the storm shutters were closed."

"It's really not a bad house. You wouldn't be interested in buying it, would you? My husband insisted that we had to have a winter home in the Caribbean so he could put two addresses on his calling card. I think he hoped that would make people forget that his money came from his grandfather's plumbing supply business. When I really wanted to get his goat, " she said it rather wistfully, "I used to call him the toilet bowl tycoon."

"But you don't know where your son is now?"

"He's drifting. Granville is just like his father: a drifter. Oh, not from place to place. He's too lazy to move from place to place unless something forces him to. He drifts from situation to situation as circumstances push him. It's a good thing Grandpa Evans made so much money in the toilet bowl business; my poor husband never initiated a single action on his own in his whole life. A drifter in the most profound sense; just like his son."

She was silent for a moment, but Stroud didn't interrupt her thoughts. If he had wanted to, he wouldn't have known how.

"Granville was our third child, Mr. Stroud. He has two older sisters, Emmy—Emerson actually, the maiden name of one of my husband's grandmothers—and Loridson, the maiden name of his other grandmother. She goes by Lori. Three kids and not a single first name among them. Emmy is a criminal defense attorney. She selected Annie for me from the steady stream of axe murderers that seems to flow through her office. Lori married a guy named Muldoon: six kids and no end in sight. They have to be the last couple in America that's still getting fan mail from the Vatican. Lori never grew out of playing with dolls. That was probably my mistake with Granville. I really didn't want another baby, but his sisters sure did. They were nine and eleven when he was born, and he was just the ultimate in dolls to them. So I lived my life and let them pretty much raise him. Now that I look back on it, it was a terrible mistake. Have you ever watched little girls playing with dolls, Mr. Stroud?"

"No. Not really. I had a daughter, but she was never much interested in dolls."

"They spoil them rotten. Little girls treat their dolls the way they wish their parents would treat them, and little girls, just like everyone else, want to be spoiled rotten. What was your daughter interested in, Mr. Stroud?"

"Oh, school, and science and boats—and Shakespeare, she was always reading Shakespeare—but not necessarily in that order."

"Granville was interested in boats, too. He was the terror of the Star Class at the club when he was in prep school, he and the Dawson girl from Devon who was his crew. Actually she was the terror. Everyone thought he was the skipper because we bought him the boat and she let him steer it, but then they had a dreadful fight one day. I must admit he behaved very badly. The things he said to that poor girl. She wouldn't sail with him any more, and without her, he fell right down to the bottom of the class. She's done very well: crewed on an America's Cup boat, although it got eliminated early. The owner was more interested in social engineering than in marine engineering, from what I could see. Now she's involved in some sort of round the world racing. Sounds dreadfully wet and uncomfortable."

Again she paused, and then she said, "These bad people that you say Granville is involved with, I'll bet one of them is a very assertive woman. Granville needs an assertive woman to tell him what a wonderful man he is and how dependent she is on him, while she tells him exactly what to do. And since neither his sister Emmy nor the Dawson girl are around ... I can tell by your face that I'm right, aren't I?"

"Yes. One of these people is an assertive woman. You called that right. Do you have any idea where they might be?"

"None. He called me Christmas Eve from St. Thomas. He could call me tonight, or it might not be for three months. I have no way to tell. If he calls, I'll tell him you're looking for him. Is there some way he could reach you?"

Stroud had to think about that one for a minute. Finally he said, "It might not be such a good idea to tell him I was here, if he is under the thumb of that woman." It sounded lame even to Stroud.

"I assume these people are involved with drugs?"

"I have no reason to think that at all."

"What, then?"

"It involves a boat that was stolen from the family of a friend. Quite an expensive boat. It appears your son might have been involved in its resale."

"And you don't want me to tell him that you're looking for him?"

"I think he knows I'm looking for him. I'd just prefer that you didn't... Oh, that's all right. Yes, if he calls, tell him I was here and ask him to call me. I'll give you some numbers where I can be reached."

When he walked back to his car it had actually stopped raining, and by the time he had driven through town and gotten onto I-95, the sun was glaring on the wet pavement so badly that he had to put on his sunglasses for the first time since leaving St. Thomas. He didn't have anything better to do, so he drove past his exit and went on to Stamford.

The city had grown immensely. The grubby industrial sections had been rebuilt into office buildings and condos, and the traffic circle at the base of Shippan Point that had once been a swamp, had long ago been filled and landscaped as a park. Stroud remembered driving past here with his father when he was a boy and seeing the carcass of *Ranger*, the last and the greatest J-Boat to defend the America's Cup, irreverently dumped here. During World War II they had stripped her of her lead and anything else of use and eventually buried the rest of Olin Stevens' most perfect design here, without even a gravestone to mark the place.

The yacht club was a few blocks off to his right; he knew it well from any number of yacht races that had started here. But he stayed on Shippan Avenue to its end and then turned right, onto Ocean Drive West, looking for 3075. There were houses in sight to his right, the shore side of the road: large houses behind wide, landscaped lawns, most of them dating from the early days of the twentieth century. The left side of the road was lined with high walls of brick and hemlock, with the occasional gate set between imposing posts. 3075 was one of those with a brick wall, but fortunately the wrought-iron gate was open.

He didn't know whether to drive in or not. It looked like the sort of place that would have security guards who would instantly have him arrested, or worse. But parking on the street, especially since there was a No Parking sign every ten feet, would probably bring down the Stamford cops in about two minutes. He drove through the gate and pulled up the drive to a four-car garage with a Lexus parked in front of it. The house, with a portico covering the circular drive where it passed the front door, was another fifty yards of lawns, shrubs, and flowerbeds away. Beyond the house he could see Long Island Sound. He parked beside the Lexus; his Ford was not the sort of vehicle one parked under a portico.

He got out of the car and was about to approach the house when he heard the sound of racquets and tennis balls from the other side of the ten-foot hedge behind the garage. He followed the sound to a court where two pretty, oriental young women in identical sweatsuits were playing a very serious game. It wasn't until one of them called, "Great shot, Mom," that he realized their relationship.

He waited until they had finished a game before calling, "Excuse me." They had been so intent that neither had noticed him.

The mother came over to him as the daughter walked to the opposite court. "Can I help you?"

"I don't know. I'm looking for the Kettner family. Do they live here?"

"No. We live here. We're the Woos." She had no trace of any accent. "They lived here once, but we bought the house from them five, almost six, years ago."

"I'm looking for their daughter. Alice. She was a friend of my daughter."

She wiped her face with a towel and then asked, "How long ago was she a friend of your daughter?" She had suddenly grown guarded.

"Years ago. In college. Then they met again in North Carolina about three years ago."

"That is not possible. When we bought this house, both their daughters were dead. It was very tragic."

"Maybe I have the wrong Kettner. But I'm sure her name was Alice L. and she lived on Shippan Point."

"One of the daughters' name was Ali, as I remember. But if your daughter had known her in college, you wouldn't be looking for her now. If you will excuse me . . . " She turned and walked to the side of the court opposite where her daughter was ready to serve, nervously bouncing the ball.

"Thank you for your help. I'm sorry I bothered you."

The late afternoon Florida sun was pouring through the windows of Granville Evans' hotel room when Alice arrived. He let her in and went back to the easy chair where the *Miami Herald* he had been reading lay open to the classified section on the footstool. She put her purse and the knitting bag she carried everywhere on the table by the window and then walked toward him, thinking, *God, he's handsome. Six one, 190 pounds, blond hair, great features, wide shoulders, narrow hips, and all of it in proportion. Not like Gordon. Gordon looks like Al Falfa on steroids: as if he had been assembled out of spare parts bought at garage sales.* Evans was just the sort of preppie hunk who had lived on Shippan Point or up in Darien or down in Greenwich: the kind who had always dated her cousins, the kind who had never given her a second look.

He noticed her studying him. "What are you looking at?"

"A hunk. Has anyone ever told you that you're gorgeous, Granny?"

He obviously enjoyed the compliment. "All the time."

Then she changed the subject. "Did you find anything?"

"A Hinckley Bermuda 40. I called. It's an old one, and they want two bucks fifty for it. That's high. No Swans, except that 38 on the Internet, and you already told me you didn't want to pay anywhere near what they're asking. But there's a Sweden Yachts 38 in the paper that might be worth a look."

"I really want a Hinckley or a Swan, Granny. That Swan 38 would be perfect, but I'm not used to paying anywhere near that much for a boat. That's why I need you to help me." She was standing in front of him now, and she lifted her arms over her head and stretched onto her toes. Her light summer blouse pulled tight across her chest and her short skirt rode up her thighs. "I know I'm not as gorgeous as you are, darling, but do you think I might be worth a Hinckley or a Swan? Would I bring enough at auction to buy one, do you think?"

He felt himself instantly stiffen. "Everybody wants to own a Hinckley or a Swan, Alice, and yes, I'd certainly pay a bundle to own you."

She pushed the newspaper onto the floor and knelt on the footstool at his feet, her eyes downcast. "But you already own me, don't you, Granny? And you can order me to do anything you want. And if I displease you, you can punish me, can't you?"

"Or send you back to the market to be sold to someone else."

"Would you do that? Would you want to see me standing on a block, defenseless and completely submissive, while I'm forced to strip myself nude so I can be appraised?"

He smiled at her and with some difficulty managed to get the words out, "That certainly has potential."

Without another word she went to the windows and closed the drapes, then pulled the footstool into the center of the room. She adjusted the two floor lamps so the stool was the only thing lit in the darkened room, and, her expression a perfect mixture of fear and resignation, stepped up onto it, her wrists crossed in front of her.

He studied her for a full minute before saying, "Raise your arms." Another minute passed, then, "Turn around." She stood perfectly still for several more minutes while she felt his eyes studying her back. She was glad he obviously didn't want to rush this, but on the other hand, her arms were getting tired. Then, when he could wait no longer, "Face me and remove your outer garments." He was unaware how much this sounded like a line from an old B movie, and of the difficulty she had staying in character as she turned to obey.

As he watched her undress, he said, "Oh yes, you might be worth a Hinckley or a Swan. But we'll have to see, won't we."

They finally fell asleep after midnight, and then slept the sleep of the sated. It was midmorning when Granny watched as Alice, wearing his shirt and nothing else, put the handcuffs she had used as a prop in their little passion play back into her knitting bag. He wondered what else, besides her knitting, she carried around in it. After she had gathered her clothes and gone into the bathroom, he rolled over, picked up the phone, and called his mother.

When Alice emerged fully dressed and with her hair still damp from the shower, he said, "I just called my mother; Stroud was in Lockford looking for me on Saturday."

"You called your mother from that phone?"

"Sure, why not?"

"Because Stroud is looking for you, and he might have some way to get the phone records. That's why." Her manner was about as submissive as a drill sergeant's.

"How would he do that?"

"I don't know how he would do it, but I know it's possible, and that's enough. He has no idea where to start looking for you, and I'd just as soon it stayed that way. You've got to get out of here."

He sat up on the edge of the bed. "I don't know why, but if you insist, I'll move to another hotel."

"No. You'll move to another state."

"Why would I do that? I'm not afraid of old man Stroud. Even if he finds me, what difference does that make? And I thought you said that if I got him to go to Antigua with that story about a Christmas card, he'd just keep going south and we wouldn't have to worry about him again. Why is he so intent on finding you, anyway?"

"I don't think he's interested in me at all. I think he's really looking for Gordon. Don't ask me why."

"You mean he's looking for me so he can find you, and he only wants to find you so he can find Gordon?"

"Seems complicated, but it's the only explanation I can think of."

"What about Polizzi? Where does she come into all this?"

"Polizzi has all those gangster relatives you told me about. God knows what they're up to." Then her voice softened. "That's another reason for you to get out of here. I certainly don't want anything to happen to you, my darling."

"Come with me."

"I can't. I have to stay with Gordon. Where are you going to go?"

"When are you going to get free of Gordon?"

"Soon. But right now he needs me and I have to stay with him a little longer. Not much longer. Where can you go?"

"I have a sister in Chicago. Is that far enough? Look, Alice, there are gazillion motels in Florida. I'll just move to another one. My mother is going to wire me some money here, and as soon as it arrives I'll move up the coast a ways."

"Well, that solves the problem of Stroud tracing the phone call, doesn't it? Now the only question is whether he, Polizzi, or the money arrives first. I can't believe you told your mother where you are."

"If I can't trust my mother, who can I trust?"

She shook her head, and then continued, "Call your mother back and tell her to forget the money. I'll loan you some if you need it. Then call the airlines. No. Forget that. Let me think." She picked up the leatherette binder with the hotel's logo on it from the dresser and flipped past the room service menu to the listing of their other locations. "Do you know anyone in San Diego? Do you have any relatives or friends there?"

"No."

"Have you ever been there?"

"No."

"Good. You're going to love it. This chain has a hotel on Shelter Island, right on the harbor. Check in there and see if you can find me a Hinckley or a Swan, but for God's sake don't call anyone until you hear from me."

"What about money? My credit card is almost maxed out and I can't find anyone who will cash a check on my bank in St. Thomas."

"Don't use a credit card. Didn't you tell me the Polizzi woman was a big wheel in some bank? She might be able to trace it. Pay cash for every-thing." She went into her knitting bag and this time came up with a roll of bills in an argyle sock. She peeled off a stack of hundreds. "Here's three cents. That should do it. Fly coach, and you don't need to rent a car. There are plenty of marinas within walking distance of the hotel to keep you amused." She noticed him looking at the roll. "My mad money. Every girl needs some mad money. Now call your mother back, and for God's sake, don't tell her where you're going. And tell her not to tell Stroud anything. Tell her he's a dissatisfied customer, a violent one with a grudge." Then she paused in thought. "Did your mother say the Polizzi woman was with him?"

"She didn't mention her."

"What does she look like?"

"She's almost eighty, but she has the most beautiful head of hair you've ever seen."

"Not your mother, Granny. Lydia Polizzi."

"Oh, her." He thought about it for a second. "Like somebody whose name ends in a vowel. Big, with thick gray-streaked black hair and bushy eyebrows. You remember that Italian movie actress, Anna Magnani? Like her, only bigger, hairier, and uglier."

Alice mused, "She was the one on the dock with the cop."

"What dock? What cop?"

"Don't worry about it. Call your mother while I get your stuff together. I'll walk out with you." She wanted to be sure he left.

"What dock? What cop?" he repeated. "And why the hell do I have to go to San Diego. I want to know what's going on."

"No, you don't. What you want is another one of the best rolls in the hay you've ever had, and so do I." She nuzzled him, and he reached for her but she twisted away. "But not now, my darling. Call your mother and get dressed. Go to San Diego and see if you can find me a Swan 38 in good shape, really cheap."

"Or a Hinckley?"

"Or a Hinckley."

Late that same afternoon, Stroud was in his basement garage wondering what to do about supper and going through his collection of miscellaneous boat hardware looking for stainless steel thimbles, shackles, and blocks. *Lullaby's* spare parts inventory was inadequate. But of course no ship's inventory in the history of the sea had ever been adequate. He had just dumped another shoebox of parts onto the workbench when a car horn blew in the driveway, and through a window in the door, he saw Polizzi getting out of a new Chevrolet. He hit the button that lifted the door and as it rolled up said, "Hi. What are you doing here? How did you make out with Bissette?"

"Hello." She came in and he hit the door switch again. It was starting to get cold as the sun went down. "I talked to him this morning. It sounds like his father, his stepmother, and his half-sister were victims of the Holbrooks, too. They called him in November to say they were sailing the next morning from Port de France on Martinique for the Panama Canal, but a couple of days later they drew a bundle of money out of their credit cards in Dominica and then did it again the next day on Guadeloupe. He expected them to call from Colon in ten days or so, but he never heard from them again. He is very unhappy about it, because the credit card companies say that since the cards were never reported lost or stolen, his father's estate is liable for it. Only he can't get at his father's estate because as far as the Canadians are concerned, his father is still alive."

"What did you tell him?"

"About us, about our people."

"And?"

"He was very French. Mon dieu and zut and we must get zee gendarmes on this right away. Weird guy. I got the distinct impression that he was more interested in proving something had happened to his people than in finding out what had happened to them."

"Huh? Start at the beginning, will you?"

"Yeah. Okay. Let me start at the beginning. He's a financial executive with the railroad. Big flashy office. Very sharp dresser. In his forties, but desperately trying to look younger. As I said, weird guy. To begin with, he insisted that we speak French. Said that when he comes to the U.S. he is forced to speak English, so in Quebec I should speak French."

"How is your French?"

"Pretty good, actually, but rusty, and my accent is a lot better than that foghorn one they have in Canada. I spent my junior year abroad in Paris."

"I spent my junior year abroad with the Fifteen Armored Cav on the Czech border. Anyway . . . "

"Anyway, when I asked him about his people, he was totally uncommunicative until I mentioned that your daughter and son-in-law had been lost at sea and declared dead three years later. Then he perked up and even began speaking English. It seems that the Canadians say he has to wait seven years to get at his father's estate. He handled his father's affairs, paid his bills and such while he was away, but I suspect the old man had him locked out of the serious money."

"What about the women?"

"Oh yes, the women. He obviously did not approve of his stepmother at all. From what I could gather, she was considerably younger than his father. But while not approving of her, it was pretty obvious that he has been nursing the hots for her for quite a while. When I asked for a description, he gave me one that Freud would have loved."

"Gee. This guy really is French, isn't he?"

"The daughter was sixteen and his description of her was a lot more detailed as to zee length of zee leg and zee shape of zee bodice than most brothers could give, too."

Stroud turned off the light over the workbench. "Let's go upstairs." As they entered the kitchen he asked, "Have you eaten yet?"

"A box lunch on the plane."

"I don't have much in the house. I didn't want to buy a lot of groceries and have to dump them when I took off on the next leg of our great adventure. Now it looks like I should have bought groceries. You didn't tell me what you're doing here."

"I didn't know where else to go. And to be honest, I thought if you found Evans, it would be a good thing if I were here to keep you from doing something dumb."

"You mean like believing anything the bastard told me. You've got it backwards, anyway. I'm the good cop, remember; you and your Corsican relatives are the bad cops. You want a drink?"

"The sun is below the yardarm, isn't it?"

He opened a kitchen cabinet. "Bourbon okay?"

"Fine."

He got out a couple of glasses. "Rocks, water, up?"

"Rocks is fine."

While he wrestled the four-months-old cubes out of the freezer he said, "Go on about Jean-Claude Libido."

"Not much more to tell. I started out afraid that I'd have to tell him his family might have been murdered. It turned out to be the best news he'd ever heard. If we can prove it, he won't have to wait seven years for his father's money."

"Yes, but he won't be able to get into his stepmother's or his half-sister's pants, either."

In a heavy French accent she replied, "Life is never perfect." Then she dropped the accent and said, "It took me a while to get through to him that other than a fleeting glance at her, we really don't even know what these people look like, let alone what their real names are, or where on earth, literally, they are. He definitely wants to help any way he can, but he knows a lot less than we do. On his lawyer's advice, he sent letters to the cops on every island in the Caribbean, but I'm the only response he's gotten. So, other than establishing that there are now ten potential victims, it was another deadend. What about Evans?"

"His mother doesn't know where he is."

"You believe her?"

"I don't know. Maybe. She's pretty ditsy. She gave me brutally frank character sketches of everyone in her family for the last couple of generations without my asking. If she knew where Evans is, she'd probably have told me. I checked out the Kettners of Shippan Point, too. Another deadend. The people who own the house bought it from the Kettner girl's parents five or six years ago. She and a sister, from what the woman who owns the house now said, were both dead by then. She also said the girl's name was Alicia, not Alice."

"American Airlines was sure the name on the passport was Alice."

"The woman must have had it wrong."

"They died as infants?"

He thought about it for a moment, trying to remember exactly what the Woo woman had said. "I don't think so. She said they were dead when they bought the house, and it was tragic. Hmm . . . When I told her she was a college friend of my daughter's, she accepted it. It was only when I said my daughter had run into her three years ago . . . No. She must have died as an adult, but more than five years ago. She said if my daughter had gone to college with her, I wouldn't be looking for her. Maybe she meant she died in college. Anyway, it was a deadend. Holbrook obviously used her name to set up a phony identity." He thought for a moment as he sipped his drink. "You know, you're right. We've been chasing these people for four months now and we don't even know their real names—if they have real names."

He noticed her glass was empty and without being asked, tossed in a couple more cubes and refilled it. She took a small sip and said, "My Dad always drank Jack Daniel's."

"I don't think too many people do, anymore. White wine and Perrier, maybe a little vodka to keep the breath smelling sweet. Bourbon is too American to be politically correct, I guess. Were you and your dad close?"

She thought about it for a second, and then gave a bitter little laugh. "Until I was fifteen or sixteen. Then . . . No, as an adult, the last thing I was, was close to my father."

They were sitting opposite each other at the white Formica-topped kitchen table, and he leaned his elbows on it as he said, "Being the father of a teenaged girl isn't easy. Nell and I had our problems, like everyone, I guess. She wanted to be too free too early, and I wanted to hold on too tightly, and for too long. But deep down we liked each other. I think at that point liking each other is probably more important than loving each other. Everybody loves everybody else in this wonderful, loving society of ours, but it doesn't help much if they don't like each other, does it? But no matter how much Nell and I disagreed, we liked to sail and ski together and to tease each other. Although there was a period of, oh I guess, maybe six or seven years, when I had to be damned careful how I teased her. You were close to your mother, then?"

She took a pull of her drink and rolled it around in her mouth before swallowing. "No. Neither of my parents. The only one I was close to was my niece, and my father didn't like that at all. He was sure I'd be a bad influence. She wasn't really my namesake. My mother's name was Lydia, too." Again the bitter little laugh. "I was the last one anyone in my family would name a daughter after."

"You're smart and successful and, I guess, decent is as good a word as any. Why would they feel like that toward you?"

"The last thing my father thought I was, was decent."

"He couldn't have been that mad at you if he paid for a junior year abroad—in Paris, yet."

"He sent me to France to get me away from the unsuitable people I had associated with my freshman and sophomore years, and, he hoped, to stop my unsuitable behavior." She finished off her drink, then chewed an ice cube before continuing. "Then again, I suppose he knew my unsuitable friends and behavior would continue, but if I were in France he wouldn't have to watch it. You don't suppose I could have another drink?"

He built them both another one. "Did it continue?"

"My unsuitable behavior? Of course."

"You must have had a hell of a good time, though."

"The odd part is that at the time I thought it was having a great time, but when I look back at it now, it was the most miserable period of my life. God, I was dumb. I was busted about a half dozen times at protests and sit-ins. We said they were about politics and the war, but they really didn't have anything to do with politics or the war. They were really the social events of the day; like fraternity parties and J-hop in the forties and fifties. Only we wouldn't be caught dead at fraternity parties or J-hop. Twice they found drugs on me. Twice. Can you imagine anyone so dumb as to go out knowing she'd be arrested—hell, planning to get arrested—with marijuana in her jeans. My father got me out of it both times. Then he sent me to France."

"But it didn't work?"

"Hardly. Two weeks after I got home, I found out I was pregnant."

"What did your father say to that?"

"I didn't tell him. I kept quiet about it and eventually went to Planned Parenthood."

"You mean Unplanned Parenthood."

"That's right. It should be called Unplanned Parenthood, shouldn't it? If it were planned, you wouldn't need them." She took a long pull of her drink. "Anyway, I had an abortion."

"And he found out?"

"Oh yeah. Those wonderful people botched the job and sent me home bleeding. I damn near died. You know the irony of it, Bill? That was a turning point for both my father and me. For him it was the last straw. He just wrote me off. But it convinced me that if I didn't straighten out, I was going to either wind up dead, or on the run from the FBI. That was what happened to the girl who was my roommate my freshman year. She got involved with the Weathermen and hasn't been heard from since, as far as I know."

They both silently finished their drinks, and then he said, "You want some supper? I'd suggest a restaurant, but I don't think either of us should be driving. Pizza or Chinese?"

"What kind of question is that to ask a Polizzi?"

"Pizza it is."

After he had called and placed the order, he asked, "You have brothers?"

"Three of them. One older and two younger."

"Why isn't one of them sitting here?"

"They're all too busy making money, although God knows there's plenty of money. We all have trust funds and income from the company—Pop took it public before he retired—and good jobs we don't really need. I guess it's pretty obvious that I'm the one sitting here because I'm the one with the most guilt about my parents."

"If your father were in my shoes, what would he be doing now?"

"You mean if I had been the sort of daughter to him that Nell was to you? He'd be doing just what you're doing, and he'd be just as relentless. Corsican blood, remember."

"Maybe the reason you're sitting here and none of your brothers are, is because you're the one most like your father. Maybe that's the root cause of everything that happened, and is still happening, between you and him. You want another?"

"I think I've had enough. Where's the girl's room?"

He showed her the lavatory, then rinsed the glasses and set the table. She was a long time in the bathroom, and when she came out her eyes were redder than the bourbon alone would explain. "I'm going to have a beer with the pizza. What would you like?"

"A beer would be fine."

The doorbell rang then, and he went to answer it. When he came back, she said, "It sure looks like we're at a deadend, though. We don't even have any loose ends to pull on, do we?"

"This Kettner thing might have some loose ends. When the bad guys set up a phony identity, they're supposed to use the name of someone who died as an infant, not an adult."

"A loose end?"

"I don't know. Let's go pull on it in the morning."

"We don't have much else to do."

CHAPTER NINE

When Alice returned to the apartment in Jupiter, John wasn't there. First she looked into his meticulously neat bedroom and then into her own sloppy one before going out on the balcony to check the pool area where he spent much of his time. She had not intended to leave him alone for almost eighteen hours, but one thing had led to another. That was the great thing about Granny, one thing always led to another. Stamina. There was no substitute for stamina. Brains were unimportant in a consort. Neither Prince Albert nor Prince Philip had ever been accused of being very bright; but she was sure they both had had stamina.

She forced herself to stop thinking about Evans and start worrying about Gordon, now named John and perhaps soon to be Peter. Forget Gordon. They were through with Gordon.

But Emil—that had been his name when she met him—gave her more to worry about than just keeping his names straight. It was almost two months since he'd had a date. They always called them dates, but more and more she thought of it as her need to feed the beast. She wondered for the thousandth time if pornography relieved or increased his hunger. Ted Bundy had blamed pornography for his behavior, but who in his right mind would believe anything Bundy said. She had once spent a day in a university library trying to learn the truth. It was, after all, a matter of great practical importance to her. But all she had learned was that the authorities were split right down the middle on the question. For every expert, there was an equal and opposite expert. She suspected some of them spent significant amounts of their research time drooling over pornography themselves, while those holding opposing views were probably driven by guilt about secretly wanting to drool over it. The TV in Emil's room was on at all hours of the night, and she knew that when he got his hands on a few bucks he usually spent it on skin magazines. But she had always been intentionally neglectful on the subject, because she hoped pornography helped him control his tensions rather than aggravating them, and because she did not know what else to do.

He was really a total mystery to her. He had appeared in the parking lot of the secretarial school, and for all she knew he had been born, full-grown, a minute before. Oh, she knew he had probably been abused as a child, and had started fires and tortured small animals; that was the standard profile, after all. But he and his predilections, as the psychologists called them, had come to her as a convenient tool for a job she wanted done, and she had used him without any more curiosity about his origins than she would have had about any tool that suited her needs at the moment. That moment was just about over.

She heard the apartment door open, and he came in carrying a K-Mart bag. She asked, "Where the hell have you been?"

"I got sick of hanging around waiting for you to come home, so I hiked up to the mall and bought some underwear." He waved the bag at her.

"Where'd you get the money?" She kept him on a very short leash. The last thing she wanted was for him to accumulate enough cash so he could rent a car. Her worst fear was that he would rent one or steal one and get caught with one of his dates in the trunk.

"It was left over from the groceries you sent me out for yesterday."

"Okay. But I don't want you doing anything stupid. We have to lay low until we can get another boat."

"Yeah. You're laying low, all right. Laying low under Evans while I hang around here doing nothing. You know, Alice, there are a lot of good-looking women wandering around that mall."

"Don't even think about it." When she said it, she realized how dumb it was to tell him not to think about it. It was all he ever thought about. "Look, I've got a line on a boat. It will only be a little while longer. When we're ready to sail, I'll get you a date."

When Lydia came downstairs after sleeping in Stroud's guest room, she was more than a little hung over, and from the slow, stiff way he moved as he poured orange juice and made coffee, she was pretty sure her host was, too. Neither said much until they were on their second cup, then she asked, "Any ideas?"

"The more I think about why she would take the identity of someone who died so recently, the more it looks like a loose end. Okay, I agree she probably needed a 100 percent genuine passport to come into the U.S., something she wouldn't need going in and out of Caribbean islands. But taking the identity of someone who died as an adult would be pretty risky."

"I suppose she could run into someone who knew the real Alice Kettner, but what are the chances of that?"

"A lot less than the chances that the Feds would have put the news that Alice Kettner of 3075 Ocean Drive West was dead into their computer. No, the one thing we know about this woman is that she is very careful and very crafty. She must have had a reason. If so, I want to know what that reason was."

"So what do we do?"

"I think we go to Stamford and try to find out everything we can about the Kettners. That may tell us why Holbrook chose that particular identity."

"And?"

"And knowledge is power. Besides, it's either that or give up. Are you ready to give up, Lydia?"

"Let's go to Stamford."

As Alice and John Perkins came down the floating dock where the Swede 38 was tied, another couple was just climbing off the boat. He was tall, gray haired, handsome, and dressed in a sport shirt, pressed chinos, and the mandatory leather deck shoes. She wore designer linen slacks and a silk blouse and was too old to be his daughter but was probably too young to be a first wife. After they were off the boat, the woman leaned one hand on his shoulder to steady herself as she took off her deck shoes and replaced them with the low-heeled sandals she carried by the heel straps. As they approached, Alice saw that she wore a diamond solitaire far larger than most first wives ever wore.

The two couples smiled at each other as they passed, and the broker standing in the cockpit greeted them with, "You must be the Perkins. Or is it Perkinses. What's the proper plural, I wonder?" She was an overweight woman in her late thirties who was not carrying her middle-aged fat very well; it was all settling into her hips and legs.

Alice thought that she should definitely not wear Bermuda shorts, but she smiled and said, "I've never found out. This is my husband, John. I'm Alice."

"And this is *Rumpelstiltskin.* Gorgeous, isn't she?"

She had been gorgeous, and could be gorgeous again, but her teak decks needed work, and the gel coat along her topsides was badly scratched and scuffed. Whoever owned her had obviously not been very good at estimating distances when approaching docks. Her dodger, mainsail cover, and the sun strip on her roller-furling jib were all badly worn and faded. The broker said, "She was built in ninety, but a boat like this will quite literally last forever."

Alice asked, "Who made the sails?"

The broker consulted her clipboard. "The main, number one, and number three were made by the North loft in Stockholm. There's a spinnaker from Bethman, and they made the storm jib, too."

Alice said, "So all the sails are original except for a spinnaker and storm jib made in Hong Kong?"·

"Is Bethman a Hong Kong outfit? It doesn't sound Chinese. That's the punch line from an old joke, isn't it?"

"Something like that. So she needs a suit of sails," Alice bent and studied the topsides, "as well as an Imron job."

"It's all cosmetic. She'll pass the most rigorous of structural surveys. Do you guys have a boat now?"

"We sold it last month and now we're looking for something bigger."

It seemed to sharpen the broker's interest. "Well, I'm sure the sails and the gel coat problem could be a negotiating point. Would you like to go below?"

They weren't interested. The batteries were flat, so they couldn't start the engine, and when John looked at them he found that they too were Swedish and obviously original. Alice wondered how they had gotten them to last this long. She also wondered why people would put a boat on the market that was not really for sale. If it were, all this obvious stuff would have been taken care of for a tiny percentage of the over-inflated asking price.

As they walked toward their rental car, Alice looked through the window of the marine supply store and saw the couple they had passed on the dock standing by the paints. She said, "Come on." And then as they entered the store, "Go look at electronics." The electronics were in the next aisle to the paints where the couple was shopping.

He was wearing half-framed reading glasses and holding a quart can while they both read the label. Alice interrupted by asking, "Well, what did you think of *Rumpelstiltskin?* She certainly could use some paint. Are you thinking of buying her?"

He smiled, put his glasses in his shirt pocket, and said, "Oh yes, she needs paint and a lot of other things. But this is varnish for our present boat. Funny how seeing that boat, and hearing that price, makes you think about upgrading the boat you own now." Then he said, "I take it you didn't put down a deposit."

Alice laughed, "No. Not much chance of that. What is your present boat?"

"A Cape Dory 36. Pretty good boat really, and it only draws five feet. That Swede draws seven-four. If I'd known that, we wouldn't have even looked at it." His wife added, "We live on the St. Lucie River, and we'd don't have seven feet at our dock most of the time. Do you have a boat?"

"We sold ours last month in Guadeloupe. It was a Cape Dory 32. We loved it. Carl Alberg really was a fine designer, wasn't he? The same boat in whatever size you wanted, from eighteen to fifty feet. But they're all good boats."

"Most of those late CCA Rule boats were good ones. A lot better sea boats than these glorified lake scows they race offshore now under the new handicapping rules. Do you know that a ninety-knotter went through the 1960 Bermuda Race, and of the 175 boats in its path not one was lost and not one person was injured. That's why no one remembers it. Now, if anything over about fity knots catches a racing fleet offshore, they have a national disaster on their hands."

"They are wonderful sea boats. But ours just got too small for the sort of extended cruising we do. The first year or so it was okay, but then you start accumulating stuff, and eventually you either have to move up to something bigger, or use the boat for cargo and live in the dink."

"How long were you in the Caribbean?"

"Three years. We're looking forward to getting back. We have a house on Nevis that we use as a base camp."

He realized he was still holding the can of varnish and asked, "How did you take care of your teak? Ours is raw, but as you scrub it, it gets rougher and rougher. Then if you sand it, you start wearing through the fastening plugs. I'm thinking about varnishing ours, but everyone says it's a bitch to keep up."

"We had the same problems, so we varnished it. Actually Peter, my husband, did it. I think he put on about eight coats to begin with, then he'd sand it and put on another coat every few months. It always looked grand."

"Do you know what kind of varnish he used? This Epiphanes stuff is supposed to be really good, but it sure isn't cheap."

She looked up at the shelves. "I think he used that Pettit Easypoxy; the can looks familiar, but I'm not sure. Here he is. You can ask him yourself." Then she turned to Emil as he joined them and said, "These are the . . . I'm sorry . . . "

"Belnap, Seth Belnap." He held out his hand. "And this is my wife, Maureen, but everybody calls her Mo."

As the men shook hands, Alice said, "We're Peter and Alicia Lowell, but most people call me Alice. Dear, I was just telling Seth and Mo how well you kept up the teak on our Cape Dory 32. Seth wanted to know which varnish you used."

"Oh, whatever I could get in the Caribbean. Pettit's mostly, though. But any good polyurethane will do; the preparation is much more important than the brand."

"That's what we were just comparing: the instructions for surface preparation. Every one of them tells you to use a different grade of sandpaper, anywhere from 80 to 220."

"It really depends on the condition of the wood. But there's more to preparation than just sandpaper."

Belnap looked at his watch. "Mo and I are going to have lunch in a great place just across the street. That's the main reason we came down here, but don't tell the broker. Why don't you join us so I can pick your brain, Peter."

Afterwards, when they were driving back to the apartment, he asked, "What the hell was that all about, Alice? I thought you were going to buy a boat. Besides, a Cape Dory 36? I thought you wanted something bigger and faster than a Cape Dory 36. And at the apartment I'm John, but around them I'm Peter. I hope we can keep it straight."

"We'll just have to concentrate a bit, won't we, dear? And it always pays to have a Plan B ready in case you need it. The Belnaps are Plan B. What do you think of the lovely Mo?"

Because they had no idea what else to do, they went to the Stamford Public Library and started through the microfiches of the local newspaper. Stroud took the rolls beginning four years before, sat down at one machine, and searched the obituaries while Lydia started the same search eight years back at the machine next to him. They worked in silence, the only sound the intermittent whirring of the motors that turned the spools. Then after an hour she said, "Here it is . . . No, it isn't." Then, "Maybe it is." He rolled his chair over so he could read over her shoulder.

Alicia Kettner

Private funeral services were held this morning at the Bennington Brothers Funeral Home on Atlantic Avenue for Alicia Margaret Kettner, twenty, daughter of Peter and Janet Kettner of 3075 Ocean Drive West, Stamford. Miss Kettner, a junior at Sweet Briar College in Virginia, was found dead in a wooded area outside of Fredericksburg last Tuesday. She was a graduate of the Darien Country Day School and was majoring in classics at the time of her tragic death. She is survived by her parents and a sister Consuela. Internment was in Long Ridge Cemetery.

They both read it twice, and then Lydia said, "Right address. So it was Alicia, not Alice."

"Have you ever read a newspaper article about something you had first-hand knowledge of, and not found mistakes?"

"True."

"But either could be Ali. The Woo woman said she was called Ali."

"But she wouldn't have been called Ali on her passport, driver's license, or birth certificate or in her obituary."

"Keep scanning back. There has to be more."

The motor whirred, stopped, whirred again, and then she said, "Here it is." The picture had obviously been taken for her high school yearbook—one of those eerie photos of the pretty victim who, on the day it was taken, had no idea of the headline that would one day appear beneath it.

Stamford Girl Found Murdered in Virginia

Police are investigating the death of Alicia Kettner of 3075 Ocean Drive West, whose nude body was found in a wooded area outside of Fredericksburg, Virginia yesterday. Miss Kettner was a student at Sweet Briar College at the time of her death and disappeared from the campus late last week.

There were several paragraphs of the quasi-information and biography with which such stories are padded. From it they learned that the victim's father, Peter, was a senior partner at the Wall Street Law firm of McNeil, Benchley, and Brotherton. Lydia recognized the firm. The bank had used it several times. She tapped the screen and said, "Big firm, big job, big bucks. Very big bucks."

Stroud replied, "3075 Ocean Drive West" as they read on.

Near the end there was one other interesting item:

Last year Miss Kettner's sister, Consuela, then a senior pre-law student at Yale, disappeared from her dormitory room in New Haven and has not been heard from or seen since. Police are investigating if there is any connection between these two occurrences.

Stroud said, "My God. They lost both daughters."

"We don't know that yet. I wonder if they ever caught whoever killed Alicia."

"If they did, it will be in the paper, probably on the front page. Did you check the front pages?"

"Just the indexes down the bottom to find the obituaries."

"Me too. But it could be on the second page . . . or the front page of the second section."

She started the machine rewinding. "Okay. Let's go through them again. Everything except the sports, the comics, and the classifieds."

They found two other brief stories about Alicia's murder, both within a week of the obituary and both saying that the investigation was continuing. After that there was nothing, but it took them the rest of the morning to verify it.

As they walked out of the library she said, "What now? Go see the father?"

"Let's call his office first before we traipse all the way into Manhattan."

The switchboard operator at McNiel, Benchley, and Brotherton said that Peter Kettner had retired from the firm four years before. So Lydia said, "My name is Lydia Polizzi; I'm a senior VP at First National Midwestern Bank, and I need to talk to him. Is there someone there who would know how I can reach him?"

"I'll put you through to Ms. Davenport."

When Ms. Davenport came on the line Lydia introduced herself again and added, "I really have to speak to Mr. Kettner about a personal matter."

"Are you in Columbus?"

"No. At the moment I'm in Stamford, but I've learned that he no longer lives here. I really need to talk to him."

"Is this about his family?"

"Yes, it is."

"Mr. Kettner took early retirement because of what happened to his family, and I doubt that he wants to talk to anyone about it. I was his private secretary for nine years, so I'm quite sure of it. Successful lawyers practically never retire, Ms. Polizzi."

"I know that, Ms. Davenport. And I know first-hand how awful it is to lose loved ones under suspicious circumstances. Was Consuela ever found?"

"Why do you ask?"

"Because I lost my niece in a similar way, and with me is a man whose daughter also disappeared."

There was silence for a moment, and then Ms. Davenport said, "Give me your phone number. I'll get back to you."

As soon as she hung up, Lydia hit speed dial and called her own secretary in Columbus. "Meg. In about two minutes you're going to get a call from a Ms. Davenport at McNiel, Benchley, and Brotherton in New York wanting to verify my existence. Tell her that I'm on leave of absence, but I just called from Connecticut and told you to expect her call. Thanks. Oh, and tell her anything else she wants to know."

Twenty minutes later Davenport called back and gave them Peter Kettner's address.

The house was a small Cape Cod in Shelton, very different from 3075 Ocean Drive West. It was on a large lot, though, and behind the detached garage the Far Mill River ran along the back of the property. The river was swollen almost onto the lawn by the recent rain and the snowmelt. Kettner answered the door wearing a CPO shirt and corduroys. He was a large man a few years younger than Stroud, with a shock of silver-gray hair and two very pronounced vertical wrinkles that went from the corners of his mouth down to his chin, making him look like an old Charlie McCarthy. But when he spoke, his manner and his deep, pleasant voice completely wiped away any impressions the wrinkles might cause.

"Come in. I'm Peter Kettner. Madge Davenport told me a little about—well, what we seem to have in common." The front door opened onto a narrow central hallway that ended with the stairs leading to the second floor. A dining room and kitchen were to the right, and he motioned them to the left into the small but comfortable living room. There was a fireplace at one end, cold now, with studio photos of his two daughters on the mantle. By the fireplace, two leather-covered barrel-backed chairs flanked a coffee table; a swivel chair rested between a desk and the workbench that filled the opposite end of the room. He motioned them to the easy chairs and sat down in the chair by the bench. It had a tiny vice attached to one edge and was strewn with scissors, tweezers, and knives, as well as bits of hair and feathers and spools of thread. He noticed their curiosity and said, "I tie trout flies. Are you a fisherman, Mr. Stroud?"

"No, I'm a sailor. Once in a while I'll troll a line, but the trouble with fishing is that you might catch something, and then you have to deal with the mess."

"I only fish for trout and salmon and I always release them alive, so I don't have those problems. Now, what did you want to see me about?"

"I don't know quite where to start. Your younger daughter, was her name Alicia, or was it Alice? I know that newspapers seldom get everything right."

"Newspapers seldom get anything right. Her name was Alicia, but everyone called her Ali. I have a niece named Alice, but we called her by her middle name, Louise, to avoid confusion while she lived with us."

Lydia said, "Alice L. Kettner of 3075 Ocean Drive West, Stamford, Connecticut."

"Yes. That's my niece."

"She, or someone using her passport, came into the U.S. through San Juan a week or so ago. Do you have any idea where she is now?"

"No. I haven't seen her or heard from her in years, not since my daughter Ali's funeral. She had graduated from secretarial school the June before, and supposedly gone back to Michigan to get a job, but she never told us where. But she came back for the funeral."

"Do you have a picture of her?" Lydia asked.

He thought about it for a second. "No. I don't think so. When I moved up here from Stamford I got rid of several tons of stuff. Why do you want it?"

"It would verify that she's the person we're looking for. Could you describe her?"

"About five-six, slim but well proportioned. Medium brown hair. The last time we saw her, at the funeral, she said she had met a young man and they were going to live on his yacht in the Caribbean. My wife and I were both surprised at how attractive she had become. While she was growing up she was always a mousy little thing, but she seemed to have grown about six inches in the year since we'd last seen her. The last I knew she was in the Caribbean, so she might very well have come in through San Juan recently. What is this about, and what does it have to do with my daughters?"

Lydia said, "It could be her, Bill."

Stroud replied, "I frankly don't know what it has to do with your daughters, but I do know that my daughter and son-in-law disappeared after becoming involved with a woman who fits your niece's description, and the same thing happened to Miss Polizzi's father, mother, and niece."

Kettner thought about it for a second before asking, "Do you have proof of any of this?"

As he opened his manila envelope, Stroud said, "I'm not sure it will constitute proof to a lawyer, but I'll show you what we have. Why don't you pull your chair over here while we take you through this stuff?"

It took half an hour or so, and when they finished Kettner sat in silence for a while and then asked, "Would you like a drink, or a cup of coffee, or something? I usually have a cup of tea about this time every day."

"Tea sounds good."

"Excuse me, then."

Stroud didn't speak as he gathered up his papers from the coffee table and put them back in the battered envelope. But Lydia said, "You really ought to get a briefcase for that stuff, Bill."

"I've got a briefcase; my wife gave me a really good leather one when I made department manager. I lugged it around for years while I thought I was getting someplace. Now just the sight of it makes me feel like an asshole."

When Kettner returned, he put the tray with the tea things and a small plate of chocolate chip cookies on the table between them, resumed his seat, and as he poured said, "First I should tell you how sorry I am to hear about your families. Was your daughter an only child, Bill?

You don't mind if I call you Bill, do you? And please call me Peter. We seem to have a lot in common."

"No. She had a brother who was killed in the Marine Corps years ago."

"But the years don't help, do they? It never gets any easier, does it? I find myself looking at the calendar and wondering what one or the other of my daughters would be doing on this day if . . . Anyway, I'm sorry to hear . . . Oh hell, you know. We've all heard the same things a million times. And I heard you say the sight of your briefcase makes you feel like an asshole. I know exactly what you mean by that, too. That's why I retired early, sold that monstrosity on Shippan Point, and moved up here. My wife is in a home in Middlebury. Janet was a very intense person, always with a project. Something always needed to be built or improved or repainted. But she loved those girls, all three of them, although Louise was certainly not an easy child to love. Janet never recovered from what happened to Ali and Connie, and now, on top of it, she has Alzheimer's."

Lydia said, "I'm sorry," and then, "Oh Lord. Aren't we a bunch." Stroud nodded in agreement as Kettner once more paused in thought.

Then he said, "Where should I start? I think that deep down I've always suspected something about Louise without ever letting myself admit it. At Ali's funeral, I clearly remember the last thing she ever said to Janet and me. As we were walking away from the grave, I said, 'Thank you for coming, Louise.' And she said, 'I'm Alice again, Uncle Peter. I've taken my name back, because now my dear cousin won't need it anymore, will she?' Then she just walked away and we never saw her or heard from her again."

He took a sip of tea and then continued, "I don't know, that may have been a subconscious factor in my deciding to retire. Ever since that day, I've felt that—other than my wife, who isn't really alive—I don't have a single living relative. But that's not technically true, because there is Louise. But I've never really felt like we're related. We tried to make her our third daughter, but . . . " He paused again. This was obviously a man who considered his words carefully. "The good thing about trout fishing and tying flies and planning fishing trips is that it fills your mind. I occasionally lecture at Yale, and I write journal articles when something comes along that interests me. It's not a bad life, considering what a lousy life it is. I suppose sailing does the same thing for you, Bill. As Janet always said, you have to have a project."

Stroud replied, "Yes, I guess it does. I hadn't thought about it that way, but you're right. Anyway, you said Alice was difficult. How long did she live with you?"

"Let me start at the beginning, because it really doesn't start when she moved in with us. Actually, now that I think about it, everything was probably decided by the time we took her in. My father was an immigrant German toolmaker who worked for Ford. We lived in Dearborn. I was the eldest, and went through Michigan and Michigan Law. My brother, Alice's father, Dieter, was four years younger and the jock in the family. He went off to State on a football scholarship. Nobody called him Dieter, though, except my parents. From the time he was in junior high everyone called him Duke, but it had nothing to do with John Wayne or with having any charm or any class. It referred to his fists. My brother was a violent and brutal man, and now when I think about it, I suspect he passed it on to his daughter."

Kettner was speaking in a rush now; he seemed to want to get it all out. "When she first came to live with us, we really tried to make a third daughter of her. Both my girls, Ali and Connie, were involved in the tennis program at the Stamford Yacht Club, so we arranged for her to have lessons. The first time the pro pointed out what she was doing wrong, she grew silent; the second time she called him a foul name. When he tried to kid her out of it, she walked over to him, dropped to one knee, and hit him across the shins with her racquet frame. This was a nine-year-old girl, remember. It dropped him, and if Connie hadn't caught her arm she'd have brained him with her second shot."

Lydia said, "Nice kid."

"We got her some counseling, I got the club and the pro to keep it quiet, and needless to say, we took her out of the tennis program. She could not take any form of criticism. Any form. Just like her father. His first semester at State, he slugged a teaching assistant. The Athletic Department did not think this serious enough to warrant disciplinary action, so he was reprimanded and warned. During his second semester, he slugged an assistant coach; that was another thing entirely, as far as the Athletic Department was concerned. They tossed him out of school, and had him arrested for assault.

"The judge, when confronted with a reasonably intelligent and promising eighteen-year-old obviously in need of discipline, did what she thought was the rational and humane thing. She adjourned the trial for three years and told him that if he then came back with an honorable discharge from the U.S. Army, she would quash the charges entirely.

He went into the army, and when he came home on leave after basic training he had calmed down a lot. I suspect that some sergeant had taken him behind the barracks and administered the sort of lesson my brother had needed for a very long time. Not surprisingly, I suppose, he applied for, and was assigned to the military police. After school in Texas they sent him to Frankfurt, Germany where he spent the next two years as a guard at the Gutleut Kaserne, the central prison for the U.S. Army in Germany."

Stroud said, "I spent my Army time at Graffenwoehr. I know about Gutleut. We'd send really tough incorrigibles up there for sixty or ninety days and they'd come back Little Lord Fauntleroys. That place made Fatso Judson's Stockade look like a Girl Scout camp."

"Yes, but while it was tenderizing the prisoners, it brutalized the guards. That's always the problem, isn't it? It was exactly the wrong job for someone like my brother, although I'm sure he was very good at it; it was right up his alley. Anyway, when he returned, he brought the judge his honorable discharge, thanked her profusely for the chance she had afforded him, and flattered her shamelessly about her foresight, intelligence, and mercy and told her she had been the single most positive force in his entire life. She not only quashed the old charges but also recommended him for a job on the Detroit Police Force. A year later he married Sofi Soroski from Hamtramck, and seven months later Louise was born."

Lydia asked, "Did he abuse her?"

"Sofi? Oh yeah. But never Louise. He did something that may have been even worse to Louise. I have never seen a child more badly spoiled. We were at my parents' house for a family Christmas when she was five—she had just started school—and when she opened one of her presents it was a book bag, the kind kids wear on their backs. But it was not exactly the one she had asked Santa for, so she started to scream and carry on. We all expected Duke to give her a shake or send her out of the room, or something. Instead he gave her a hug and said that her mother would get her exactly the one she wanted first thing in the morning. When poor Sofi said, 'The one she wants costs three times what that one did, Duke. We have to draw a line somewhere,' he reached over and, in my parent's living room and in front of the entire family, slapped her. Hard. It was the last family Christmas we ever had, but the next morning little Louise got the book bag she wanted."

"How much longer did Sofi put up with it?"

"Another three years or so. Then one day while he was at work and Louise was in school, she just packed her clothes and left. When he found out, my brother went roaring over to her father's house and demanded to know where she was. Her old man met him at the door with a shotgun and told him he didn't know where she was. To tell the truth, I don't think he did. I tried to contact her through him after we took Louise in, but he was no help."

"What did your brother do?"

"He never looked for Sofi again, although he probably would have if things had turned out differently." Without asking, he refilled their cups, holding the pot's top in place with his left hand as he poured the last of the tea into his own.

Lydia picked up her cup and saucer as she said, "Your brother didn't try to find her? That doesn't fit the pattern for wife beaters. What stopped him?"

"He never got the chance. Three days after Sofi left, he was notified that he had once more failed to make sergeant. His test scores had not been good enough to overcome the point handicap they were giving white males because the Detroit Police Force was in so much trouble with the EEOC. That night he stopped a Cadillac with four black kids in it. It turned out they were on their way to their senior prom. But one thing led to another, and my brother threw the driver onto the hood of the car with such force that he went completely over it and landed on his head on the curb. The kid's father was a prominent civil rights lawyer and Democratic politician, and Duke, on advice of council, pleaded guilty to manslaughter. He died not long after in a prison yard at the hands of person or persons unknown, who were probably not unknown to him."

Then he said, "He was a really nice kid when he was small. My old man was always working. I don't think he turned down a minute of overtime in his entire life. And he was pretty German too, you know, reserved. I taught Dieter how to tie his shoes and ride a bicycle and how to swim. It was easy. He was a natural athlete. Maybe if he'd played baseball . . . But he loved football because he loved the contact. He was always saying how much he loved the contact."

He slowly ate a cookie and they waited for him to go on. "Janet and I didn't do Louise any good, either. We didn't know anything about raising a difficult child like her. From the time they were born, Ali and Connie had always been delights. Good in school, very considerate. I guess easy to civilize is the best way to describe it. Poor Louise was not easy to civilize, although eventually it became possible to live with her if you didn't mind the surly silence she maintained most of the time."

"The counseling didn't help?" Lydia asked.

"Counseling only helps if the counselor can get at the truth. When Louise discovered that tantrums or violence weren't going to get her what she wanted, she proved to be the most gifted and compulsive liar I have ever seen. I ran into my share of liars when I was practicing law, believe me, and the worst ones were those who could convince themselves they were telling you the God's honest truth. That was Louise."

"She barely got through high school, and maybe that was our fault, too. I don't know. Our girls went to Darien Country Day School, an excellent prep school, and we would have sent her there too, but her grades were never very good, even though once in a while she'd ace some standardized test. She's not dumb. So we sent her to the public high school." Then he said. "Her only interest was in sailing a little boat I bought for my girls and they never used. I only kept it because it gave her something she liked to do. I gave it away when she was about to graduate from secretarial school and obviously wouldn't have any more use for it."

"Did she sail with anyone?"

"No. Not that I know of. She dated a couple of times in high school, but never the same boy twice. She really had practically no social life in high school, and that may have been my fault, too."

"How so?"

"Well, there was a boy kidnapped from one of the homes on Tokenecka Road at about that time, and the Moxley girl had been murdered down in Bell Haven a few years before. Everybody in our circle was nervous about their kid's security. A limousine service would pick us up every morning. First he'd drop me at the station, then he'd drop off Louise, and then he'd take Ali and Connie up to Darien. In the evening he'd do the route in reverse. It didn't make any difference to my daughters; many of the kids at their school came in limos. But it may have helped to make Louise even more of an outcast than she made herself in the public school." He finished with a shrug. "I don't know."

The three of them thought about it for a few minutes while they sipped their tea and finished the cookies, then Stroud asked, "Do you feel up to talking about Connie's disappearance?"

"There's not much to talk about. One night she walked out of her residential college in New Haven, that's what Yale calls a dorm, and was never heard from again. If anything, that was even harder for my wife to deal with than what happened to Ali, and God knows, that was damn near impossible to deal with."

"Just walked out?"

"Her roommate said she heard her talking to someone on the phone. She didn't know who it was. She was in bed, half asleep, in the other room. Then she heard Connie leave."

Stroud said, "Hmm. What about Ali? Did she get a phone call and then run out?"

"I don't suppose anyone ever checked. She lived in a single room. She was on her way to the library when she disappeared."

"In the evening?"

"No. Midafternoon."

"Could someone have just grabbed her off the campus in midafternoon?"

"That was one of the questions that was never answered." Then he paused and said, "Oh, my God. You don't think she just went with . . . ? No. That's not possible"

"Was there anything else in common between the two cases?"

"Nothing the cops or the FBI could find. And they really looked. Two sisters within a year. They couldn't believe it was a coincidence, even if they did happen five hundred miles apart. But eventually they had to admit it probably was. But you don't think it was, do you? And, after what you've told me, I'm beginning to doubt it, too. My God, and she lived under our roof, and ate at our table for all those years. And you think she lured . . . that she and this mystery man of hers . . . "

Lydia said, "We don't know anything for certain. But it begins to look more and more like it. Something Bill didn't tell you. She blew up a boat in St. James two weeks ago, killed two people and only just missed getting him, too. That's where I saw her. We've never seen her mystery man and have no idea who he is, other than he's using the name of Gordon Holbrook."

Kettner was staring into the cold fireplace as though he were watching a fire, and they were silent for quite a while until he finally fished out his handkerchief and blew his nose. Then he said, "You have no hard evidence of any of this, do you?"

"No. None. Just a long trail of coincidence, but no hard evidence at all."

"I suppose as a lawyer I should be demanding that you present some hard evidence or stop making these accusations, but all I can do is keep asking myself how my brother and I, without intending it at all, turned this thing loose on the world?"

As they walked out to the car, Lydia said, "Chalk up four more victims for Alice Louise."

"Yeah, and we still have no idea where on earth she is, and no more hard evidence that she had anything to do with what happened to her cousins than we have about any of the others."

"She was originally from Michigan. Should we look for her there?"

Stroud thought about it as they got into the car and he drove to the end of Kettner's street. Then as he pulled up at the stop sign, he turned to her and said, "Other than the general understanding of Alice Louise that he gave us, the only bit of hard information was that even as a kid she was only interested in sailing. She won't be in the middle west."

"They sail in the middle west."

"Only in the summer and only on lakes. To someone who was raised here, that doesn't count. Only salt water counts. A short season on a lake, no matter how big . . . No. I don't think so. But if you want to look for her there, go ahead."

"If not the middle west, then where?"

"Christ, I don't know. Either coast."

"Do you think Evans is the mystery man?"

"Something else I don't know, but somehow I doubt it. He was in St. Thomas about the time the Canadians went missing, wasn't he?"

A car behind them blew its horn, so he said, "Blow it out your ass" and turned onto Route 110 headed toward the Merritt Parkway.

They were silent until he drove over the Housatonic River Bridge and took the exit toward Lockford, and then she asked, "Are you sure Evans' mother doesn't know where he is?"

"I don't know. She's as sharp as a tack, even if she does look like Ophelia long after she drowned." He shrugged. "I honestly don't know."

"Maybe I should talk to her."

"She doesn't look like she'd be afraid of the Corsicans, or anything else for that matter. But okay. You talk to her. You'll have to get past her companion first, though."

Instead of turning down the Post Road toward Beards Corners, he headed for Bayside Avenue, as Lydia asked, "Is there a florist around here?"

When Annie opened the front door, she was confronted by a woman six inches taller than herself, who handed her a business card and a bouquet of baby's breath and yellow roses and said, "Please give these to Mrs. Evans and tell her I'd like to speak to her."

Annie looked at the flowers as though they might conceal a tarantula but took them nonetheless, said, "Wait," and closed the door in Lydia's face.

Two minutes later, she opened the door, said, "Come," and showed her into the living room where the very little old lady with the very big young hair was arranging the flowers in a Waterford vase.

With no preliminaries, she asked, "So Miss—" she held the card at arm's length and squinted at it, "—Polizzi, is that right? I suppose you're looking for my son, too. What interest would the First National Midwestern Bank have in him? I don't think he has an account there. If he did, I'd already be covering checks for him."

"No. This is a personal matter, Mrs. Evans."

"That's what that fellow who was here last week said. Are you in cahoots with him?"

"What fellow?"

"Oh, come on. Nobody has come looking for Granville in twenty years, and suddenly two of you show up in three days. Don't try and tell me there's no connection."

"Do you know where your son is, Mrs. Evans?"

"I can honestly say, no."

"Have you heard from your son recently?"

"If I had, why should I tell you?"

"Because I suspect your son may be getting into something . . . "

"Oh yes. That guy Stroud had the same story, but it turns out he's just an unhappy customer with a grudge."

"Your son told you that?"

"Never mind who told me that."

"Has Granville always told you the absolute truth, Mrs. Evans?"

"Of course not. What child ever has?"

"Mr. Stroud is not a customer with a grudge. He never bought anything from your son. Just the opposite. He refused to do business with him and got him fired from his job at the Ginger Bay Marina. Did your son tell you he had been fired from the Ginger Bay Marina for trying to cheat them out of a commission?"

"No. Of course not. But I'm not surprised. Granville has been fired from just about every job he ever had. I even fired him from cutting the lawn and hired someone else to do it when he was a kid. When your own mother cans you . . . "

"Where is he, Mrs. Evans? Believe me when I say I don't want anything to happen to him any more than you do."

She thought about it as she put the flowers on the mantle, stood back and looked at them, then moved them to the coffee table. "I think I like them here better, don't you? He called me twice within an hour from a hotel in Vero Beach, Florida. First he wanted me to send money, and then he didn't want me to send money. That was a first. When you see Stroud, tell him the woman he talked about—the domineering one—I could hear her telling Granville exactly what to say during the second call. I don't think she knew I could hear her."

She went over to a mahogany breakfront desk, opened it, and handed Lydia a piece of paper. "Here's the address and phone number. But I don't think he's there any longer. And Miss," again she squinted at the business card, "Polizzi, is it? Remember one thing when you deal with Granville. Although I am completely aware of his faults, well, to me he's like the only poker game in town. I'm only giving you this because I'm worried about him. That woman sounded like a perfect bitch."

As she came down the walk toward Stroud, Lydia was talking on her cell phone. When she finished, she closed it, and as she got into the car said, "He was at the Hilton in Vero Beach but checked out yesterday."

"Was there anyone with him?"

"I asked, but they would only say he was registered alone and had checked outyesterday. His mother said that when he called her she could hear a woman in the background."

"I guess we head for Florida."

"Yes, before the trail gets any colder."

"I really have to get to the bank, pay a bunch of bills, and arrange for someone to come in and make sure the furnace doesn't quit during a cold snap. I don't think the neighbor I had doing it is very dependable. The mailbox was overflowing when I got here."

"How long will that take?"

"Tomorrow and maybe the next day. I might get to Florida tomorrow night if I'm lucky."

She opened her phone again. "Let me see if I can get a flight tonight." She could, but she'd have to hurry to get to LaGuardia. Then she said, "Let me check my machine," and punched the speed dial. She listened for a minute or so, then dialed another number and said, "This is Lydia Polizzi. Is he there, please?" A pause and then, "Mr. Bissette, either slow down or speak English. You've lost me." A long pause this time. "Where was this book store?" And then, "Yes. That fits. Look. Can You fax . . . No, that won't work. I'll tell you what. Call the credit card company and have them e-mail or fax you copies of the actual receipts. The receipts will have more information than the bill. Make them do it today. Then FedEx me copies of everything. I'll be at the Hilton in Vero Beach, Florida. I'm on my way there right now . . . Yes. Of course. I'll certainly inform you of anything I find out."

She closed the phone and said to Stroud, "Would you believe that Bissette's father charged some stuff two weeks ago in a store in Titusville, Florida. At least, his credit card did."

"Now all roads lead to Florida."

CHAPTER TEN

Lydia had assumed that the Adventurer's Book Store specialized in marine literature, although it was odd that the receipts Bissette sent listed the items purchased by stock number only. But when she drove her rental car down the street in a seedier section of Titusville and saw the sign giving the store's complete name, she realized how wrong she had been. "Adventurer's Books, Videos, and Much, Much, More" was painted across the single blacked-out display window. Beneath it in smaller print was "Adult Literature and Supplies for the Truly Adventurous." Centered beneath that in still smaller print was "Ladies Welcome." As Lydia got out of the car she said to herself, "Oh Lord, how do I do this?"

The place was narrow but surprisingly deep, like an old-fashioned railroad flat, one room opening through an archway into another behind it, each lit by spots aimed at the merchandise while leaving the aisles between them in semidarkness. The better, she supposed, to provide some privacy and anonymity for the customers while they browsed. There was a checkout counter across the front with an entrance turnstile at one end and an exit framed by some sort of detector at the other. Behind it, perched on a stool, a small Cuban man, with a small Cuban mustache, was smoking a small cigar she assumed was also Cuban, and reading a magazine. The seediness of the place was made more intense by its permeating smell of mildew, disinfectant, and old cigar smoke. When he saw her, he placed his cigar in an ashtray on a shelf behind him with one hand, and closed and covered his magazine with the other.

But she could see the title above his tobacco-stained fingertips: *Big Bad Babes*.

She smiled at him. "Hi. I thought that if you worked in a candy factory, you were supposed to lose your sweet tooth."

He slowly looked her up and down before he said, "I shall never lose my sweet tooth, my sweet."

She flashed one of her business cards at him but didn't let him have it. He was not the kind she wanted to have one of her cards. "I'm investigating a case of credit card fraud for my bank." He moved his hand away as she put the receipt down on top of *Big Bad Babes*. "Is this yours?"

"Yup. And it's completely legitimate. Your bank better damn well pay it."

"I'm sure it is, and that you've done absolutely nothing wrong, Mr. . . . ?"

"Sanchez. And your name, my sweet? I didn't get it when you whipped that card past me."

She ignored the question and asked, "Could you tell me what these charges are for? Your receipt only gives the stock numbers."

"Sure. But I always like to know who I'm talking to, Miss . . . ? It is Miss, isn't it?"

"Holbrook." He was really giving her the creeps.

"Miss Holbrook, then. Although I would have guessed something more Mediterranean, more fiery. Oh well, now you've given me something, so I'll give you something in return. That's the way the world works, isn't it?" With surprising dexterity he entered the numbers into the computer on the counter. "Mr. Bissette bought, on the sixteenth, two videos, one entitled *Pain*, and the other, interestingly enough, called *Anguish*. Total price $319.95. He also bought four magazines at $9.95 each for a total of $381.34 with tax."

"Three hundred and twenty bucks for two videos?"

"He bought the set. If purchased separately, they go for $179.95 each. Satisfaction never comes cheap, does it?"

"I guess not."

"Take this little number." He pointed to a dusty torso mannequin on the shelf behind him. It was wearing what could be described as either a very porous black vinyl bikini or a collection of straps. "It doesn't look like much, but it sells for $199.95. That's about seventy-five bucks an ounce. Of course if you were interested, I could make you a special deal."

"No. I don't think so. Did you check this Bissette person's I.D.?"

"Always." Again he tickled the computer. "He had a Canadian driver's license. Do you want the number?"

"Yes. Do you remember him? Did he match the photo on his driver's license?"

"I copied down the number and made sure the name was the same as the one on the credit card. As for the photo, license pictures are usually useless. You want the number?"

"Yes." He read it off and she copied it down. Then she asked, "Do you remember him? Could you give me a description?"

"I could maybe do a lot better than that."

"Oh. How?"

"I think it's time for you to give me a little something again. I think you'd look just wonderful in this little number. A big strong girl like you." He nodded toward the mannequin.

She laughed, "Forget it."

"Think about it."

"I don't think you have it in my size."

"One size fits all. That's part of its charm. We have a fitting room, if you'd like to try one on."

"I'd never get into that thing. It's way too small."

"Way too small is not all too bad."

"Talk to me about Bissette."

"Not until we finish our present negotiation."

"Okay. How much do you want for it?"

"For you, I'll knock off fifty bucks. $149.95. Of course I'll do even better if you'll model it for me."

She reached into her purse, pulled out three fifties, and dropped them beside *Big Bad Babes*. He reached under the counter and came up with a box only slightly larger than one she had once received from her staff. That one had contained a pen and pencil set. "The fitting room is right through there to your right."

"I'll take your word that it fits. Now, about that description..."

He pointed over his shoulder. "We have a security system. You'll probably find it hard to believe, but we occasionally get some unsavory characters in here. That's a video camera up there; I have a little foot switch here that turns it on and off."

She asked, "Is it on now?"

"I turn it on for both the unsavory and the very interesting."

"Did you tape him?"

"As a matter of fact, I did. I tape any credit card transaction over a hundred bucks."

"Do you still have the tape?"

"Probably. We keep them for a month or two, then record over them again."

"Okay. I want to buy that tape. How much." Then as an afterthought she said, "I want copies of the two videos he bought, too."

"No, you don't. I can tell you aren't that kind of lady."

"Why not?"

"Because *Pain* and *Anguish* are two very bad videos. I don't mean badly produced or badly photographed. I mean bad. Rotten bad. They're what used to be called snuff flicks, and I don't think anyone really knows if they're authentic or not. Take it from me, if this Bissette guy bought those two videos, he's one sick cookie."

"But you sell them, don't you?"

"That's business. He bought them for pleasure."

"I may need them for evidence. How much for them and the tape that shows him?"

"I think maybe it's time for you to do a little something for me again." He pushed the fountain-pen box toward her. "The fitting room is right through there to your left."

"Forget that noise. But I'll pay you . . . " She opened her purse and counted her cash. "I'll give you a thousand bucks for the three tapes."

"That's a lot of money for a picture of a guy who only committed three hundred and eighty bucks worth of credit card fraud. Fifteen hundred."

"Twelve hundred and fifty bucks cash for the three tapes. I only have twelve eighty on me."

"Okay, twelve fifty. But it seems like a lot of money to avoid a few minutes of modeling that might even turn out to be fun."

She counted out the money while he went in the back and came back with the three tapes. She held onto the cash and asked, "How do I know this isn't *Debby Does Dallas?*"

"There's a viewing room through there to your right."

A few minutes later she returned to the counter and put the twelve fifty on it. He grabbed it, then put the three tapes into an unmarked bag and dropped the fountain-pen box in on top of them. "We almost forgot your other purchase." Then he looked her up and down again and said, "Ah, the stuff that dreams are made of."

Lydia came into her hotel room followed by a bellboy carrying a cardboard box containing a small TV set with a built-in tape player. She had bought the unit because she was afraid if she fooled with the hookup of the hotel's TV, within minutes law enforcement would come crashing through the door. After the bellboy left, she unpacked it and crawled around under the furniture until she found an outlet. When she turned it on, it worked; something she found amazing whenever she tried a new piece of electronic equipment. After inserting the security tape, she ran it forward to the date and time on the credit card receipt and cycled it back and forth several times, studying the very ordinary man buying *Pain* and *Anguish*. He was far more appetizing-looking than the little man in the porno shop who had turned out to be almost charming, in a creepy sort of way. But this well-groomed, unremarkable man, in his sport shirt and slacks, with his neatly trimmed hair, big shoulders and narrow head, so intent on the simple, mundane task of making a credit card purchase, could be the worst kind of creep there was.

She finally turned off the TV and sat staring into space for a long time before she went into the bathroom and took the long, hot shower she had felt she needed ever since leaving the Adventurer's Book Store. As she was drying off, the phone rang; she answered it with the towel wrapped around her.

"Hi. It's me. I'm at La Guardia."

"I found out what the mystery man looks like, Bill, and I have a video tape of him."

"Great. Tell me about it when I get there. I don't have much time. Do you want to meet me at the airport?"

"I think you'd better rent your own car. We may want to go in different directions."

"Okay. I'll see you at the hotel in four or five hours, if all goes well. If not, and I get in late, I'll see you first thing in the morning."

As she hung up, she noticed the fountain-pen box tossed in with the wrappings from the TV set. She picked it up and stood tapping it in the palm of her hand until she finally smiled, and said, "What the hell."

He had been right about it being tight, but not so tight she couldn't get into it. It had all sorts of buckles and adjustments. When she finally had it on, she looked in the mirror and said, "I really have to go on a diet." But as she studied herself, she remembered a comment she had once heard a boy make about her. "She may have a face like a pan of worms, but that's one great body."

"Well, it's gotten to be far too great a body, especially for a rig like this." Then she remembered something her father used to say, "All that meat and no potatoes," and started to giggle. She kept giggling as she struggled out of it—it was almost as hard to get off as it was to get on—then she stopped giggling as her mood changed, and she quickly dressed in the most conservative outfit she had with her. She stuffed the rig, as she now thought of it, into the center of the TV wrappings and, in turn, stuffed those into the TV's box. Then she took a newspaper she had not yet read, crumpled it, and pushed that into the box, too.

She turned on the TV and tuned it to a news channel, but found herself looking at the box and wrappings by the door instead. She really didn't want anyone to find it and know it was hers. So she fished out the kinky outfit and the box it had come in and put them into the plain brown bag, along with the crumpled newspaper. Then she went outside and walked down the street until she found a Keep Vero Beach Clean receptacle, and dropped the bag in.

As she walked back to the hotel she realized what a prude she had become. If she had had an outfit like that when she was twenty, she would have danced on tables in it. But now she was a staid, middle-aged lady who really needed to go on a diet. She knew her father would be surprised, but she also knew he would be pleased.

The Lowells had invited the Belnaps out to dinner, and had been invited, in turn, to have drinks at their home in Port St. Lucy before going to the restaurant. Seth Belnap had said, "Come about five or so, while it's still light. I want Peter to see how my teak looks. Hell, I want the whole world to see how my teak looks."

The house was hidden from the street behind a high, white-painted wall with bougainvillea planted along its base. When they pulled up to the ornate wrought-iron gate, a video camera scanned the Lexus Alice had rented that afternoon, and then the gate silently slid open. The house was white, too: large and with a portico over the driveway at the front door like the house on Shippan Point. The leaf-and-flower pattern carved into the mahogany front doors was the same one that was worked in iron on the front gate.

When they pulled up, Mo came running down the steps in a flowing silk pants suit that only seemed to touch her body at her ankles and where a belt of gold chain circled her waist. She opened the car door for Alice, and as she climbed out, kissed her just shy of one ear and then just shy of the other. "Alice. Seth and I are so glad you called." Peter was coming around the car, so she turned to meet him, gave him his two near-miss kisses, and said, "Come in, please. Seth is down at the boat. We thought it would be fun to have our drinks in the cockpit, where he can stare at his varnish."

She led them through the entry hall, down two steps, across forty feet of living room, and out through the French doors centered in its glass rear wall. The view of the river was quite good. Not as good as the view of the Sound from 3075, but quite good. The dock was across a hundred feet of manicured lawn with an elliptical swimming pool centered in it. Seth waved at them from the cockpit of the Cape Dory 36 tied to one side of the dock. A twenty-six-foot runabout with *Couponclipper* on its transom was tied opposite it. The Cape Dory's name was *Coteme*.

He welcomed them aboard and asked, "Well, what do you think? It only has four coats so far."

Emil-Gordon-John-Peter answered, "It's coming great, but don't stop too early. Give it the full eight coats. You'll be glad of it later on."

Mo had climbed below and handed up cheese, crackers, and a bowl of cashews, which Seth put on the folding table attached to the wheel pedestal. Then he, too, went below, asking, "What would you like to drink?"

Peter, as Alice had taught him long before, asked, "What are you having?" It did not do to ask your host for something he might not have in the limited bar selection of most cruising boats.

"Mo and I usually have a gin and tonic about this time."

Alice said, "That's what Peter and I drink, too. Tell me, how do you pronounce your boat's name?"

Mo smiled. "Coe-tea-me. Shall I tell them what it means, dear?"

Seth reached two tall glasses up to Alice and Mo as he said, "You will anyhow."

"When I met Seth I was flying for Delta. It's a contraction of coffee, tea, or me. Isn't that awful?"

He handed up two more drinks and climbed into the cockpit. "Yes, but she got even with me. When I bought that little stinkpot, I said she could call it whatever she wanted, so she said she was going to name it after me."

They all laughed, then Alice asked, "Where do you sail from here?"

"Mostly here on the river. But I know what you're thinking. This is a lot of boat to sail a few miles up and down a river. But it's quite a ways down to the Waterway, then you have to go south to the St. Lucy Inlet or north to Sebastian to get outside. And if you get outside and it blows up, you may not be able to get back in for a week. That's why I bought *Couponclipper*, so we can run outside once in a while. This is a great place to live, but it's not much of a place to own a sailboat."

Alice took a sip of her drink and then said, "Like a frigate bird in a cage. Our house on Nevis is at the other extreme. We're on the lee side of the island facing St. Kitts, so we're protected from the northeast trades, but it's completely open from the southwest. Fortunately, it doesn't blow from there very often. But the good part is, we can sail off the mooring and be in the open sea in either the Atlantic or the Caribbean within fifteen minutes. It blows hard just about all winter, so we have at least one reef in most of the time. But no place is perfect, is it? Do you ever take any longer trips? Over to the Bahamas or down into the Keys?"

"We've talked about it for years, but all of our friends are either stinkpotters, or happy sailing back and forth on the river and racing against the same people, over the same course, every Saturday. Most of them have gone back north in the last few weeks. Then too, Mo and I agree that getting across the Gulf Stream, after some of the horror stories we've heard, is a bit more than we want to try on our own."

"The Bahamas are a fabulous cruising ground, well worth the trip to get there. Peter and I did it—when was it, dear? About five years ago? We just loved it."

"Would you be interested in going back?"

"Oh yes. If we find a boat on the east coast, we plan to cruise down through the Bahamas on our way home. If we ever find a boat on the east coast, that is. We're going up to Savannah to look at a Bermuda 40 tomorrow."

Stroud's plane was late, and there was a far longer line at the rental car desk than the single, confused clerk on duty could handle, so it was very late when he got to the hotel. He and Lydia met for breakfast and then went back up to her room and looked at the security videotape. While it was rewinding, Stroud said, "So that's him? He doesn't look like much, does he?"

"We'll have to get some still photos made, then start asking for him in every marina and yacht club we can find. Somebody must have seen him." Then she had a thought. "At least it's not Evans. His mother will be relieved."

"And motels, and porno shops, too. We know he frequents sex shops."

"You can do that part of the search. Those are no place for a nice girl." As Lydia said it, she changed the tape. "I got copies of the tapes he bought with Bissette's credit card. The guy in the porno shop said they're so bad he didn't want to sell them to me. I haven't looked at them yet. To tell the truth, I've been a bit afraid to. But I suppose it's necessary."

"It might give us a better idea what we're dealing with?"

"Your interest is purely academic, right?" She laughed, and to cover her own nervousness and embarrassment said, "Now try to control yourself, Bill. I've heard how this stuff affects men."

"Not men at my age. Nothing affects men my age. But I understand that many recent studies have found that younger women are sometimes turned on by it. Should I have a cold towel ready for you? Or maybe a bucket of ice water?"

"Here goes." And she punched the remote.

There was no chance of either of them getting turned on by it. After the first few minutes, they watched what was being done to a succession of girls and women in fast forward, hoping each was the last. By the time it ended, her head was buried in his chest and she was sobbing.

She finally pulled away and went into the bathroom, where she stayed for a very long time, while Stroud, his jaw set, sat perfectly still, staring at the blank TV screen.   Then he put the security tape back in and cycled it back and forth again and again, burning the image of the man buying that other tape into his mind. Watch, rewind, watch, rewind, watch, rewind . . .

When Lydia finally emerged, he stopped the tape as she said, "I'm sorry I lost it, Bill. But all I could think of was my niece . . . " Her reddened eyes again filled with tears, but she wiped them with the back of her hand, sniffled loudly, and fought for control.

"I know. I know exactly what you were thinking."

The Hinckley Bermuda 40 was exactly the boat Alice wanted, the one she had wanted for as long as she could remember. It was a centerboard yawl like those that had been owned by the old-money people at the club, most of whom only belonged to the Stamford Yacht Club so they'd have someplace on Long Island Sound to keep their boats. Their real allegiance was to the New York Yacht Club that the new-money people, like her uncle, not only could not join, but could not even enter unless specifically invited by a member. Such invitations were rare. Even thought her uncle had worked in New York all his life, was very successful, and was keenly interested in the America's Cup, he had only actually seen the thing when it had finally been won by the San Diego Yacht Club. San Diego not only allowed members of other clubs to drink at its bar and made them welcome in its restaurant, but it even let their bourgeois eyes gaze upon that holiest of prizes, something New York had never condescended to do.

The Hinckley was in beautiful shape; its fiberglass hull and its varnished cherrywood interior still glistened as it had ten years before when it left the plant in Southwest Harbor.

But it was a lot of money. Almost twice what she had planned to spend. If she bought it, she would have to go to Grand Cayman and get the funds. But it wouldn't clean her out. Not by a long shot. The odd part of the comfortable lifestyle they lived was that it didn't cost all that much—at least, the way they did it.

And the money would be well invested in the Hinckley; she could always get it back if Emil didn't pile it on the rocks someplace. She wondered why she thought of him more and more as Emil when she hadn't thought of him by that name in years.

Once they had recovered from watching *Pain* as much as they ever would, Lydia searched the Yellow Pages and found a photo shop that advertised it could transfer films to videotape. She called them and learned that they could also do the opposite. The shop was only a mile away, next door to a Kinko's.

After Bill had explained what was wanted to the woman behind the counter, Lydia asked, "Do you take passport photos, and how long do they take for you to develop?"

"Yes, we do, and it's almost instantaneous."

"Let's get our pictures taken, Bill."

"Why? My passport is good for another nine years or so."

"Humor me."

When she had the passport photos, she left him waiting for the stills from the security tape and went next door.

A few minutes later, the woman came out of the back and put the tape and a half dozen photos on the counter. "These are the best frames I could find. It's only thirty-eight seconds of tape, and although they show him quite clearly, the camera was above his head so there's a lot of distortion, and most of the time he was looking down at the counter. Fortunately he glanced up once; that's where I took these from."

He looked at them one at a time, selected the two best, and said, "Could you make, oh, a dozen of each of these, please?"

"Sure. It'll take a few minutes."

While he waited, he went next door to see what Lydia was up to. She was just leaving a copy machine with a stack of papers in her hand. "Hi. How did you make out?"

"Pretty good, considering that most of the time he was looking down, away from the camera. I'm having twelve copies of the two best printed up. What are you doing?"

They were at a laminating machine now, and she fed a stiff sheet into it that had both their pictures on it, one above the other. When it came out, she cut it into two wallet-sized cards and handed him his. At the top she had duplicated her bank's logo from one of her business cards, and beneath it, using a different font, she had printed, "Department of Bank Fraud Investigations." Beside his photo it said, "William T. Stroud. Inspector."

He studied it for a second, then said, "Aren't computers great, especially for forgers. Does your bank have a Department of Bank Fraud Investigations?"

"It does now. If we're going to go around showing people pictures and asking questions, we ought to have some sort of authority."

"Hmm. Something's missing, though. You should have left a space for me to sign my name before you laminated it."

"Oh, shoot. I'll have to make them again."

"I'll go see if the pictures are ready."

The next morning they started in Titusville and he worked his way north as she headed south, stopping at every marina, marine supply store, yacht broker, motel, and adult book store along the way. There were thousands of them, and when they returned to the hotel that evening, they were both intimidated by the size of the task they had undertaken. No one they had questioned had seen the mystery man; that did not make it any better.

She said, "Bill, this could take forever."

"You want to stop?"

"Hell, no."

Ten days later, she had reached Melbourne and he was slowly approaching the outskirts of Daytona Beach. Neither had had any luck, other than a few of the accommodating types in yacht broker's offices who, if asked if they had seen King Kong around here, would say, "Gee, you just missed him. He went down the street carrying Fay Wray just a minute ago. But he's due back any time. In the meantime, I have this wonderful boat I'd like to show you."

Alice made an offer on the Hinckley and then flew down to Grand Cayman to visit her bank. She brought the money through U.S. Customs as two certified checks that she declared and then justified by showing the Customs inspector a phony bill of sale for a nonexistent house on the island, a bill of sale that her forger in Miami had made for her. The Customs inspector made her fill out and sign a form and then said, "Miss Kettner, you know you'll have to declare any capital gains on the sale of this house if you don't reinvest in another residence within a year. We report this to the IRS."

She said, "Oh, yes. My accountant takes care of all that. Thank you for your help."

She had left John with a stack of groceries, no car, and practically no money, after telling him that if he did anything stupid while she was gone, she would turn him in herself.

He had replied, "Bullshit. You squeal on me and I squeal on you. You know how dedicated I am to women's lib; what's sauce for the gander is sauce for the goose."

But he had lapsed into silence when she told him, "When I get done telling them about how you've abused poor little me all these years, they'll not only let me testify against you in the penalty phase, they'll let me come up to Stark and throw the switch. And I don't want you going anywhere near Mary Beth Bradley, either."

Nevertheless, when she came back from the Caymans, she was relieved to find him sitting by the pool, flexing his muscles and girl-watching.

He followed her into the apartment and she asked, "Did Bradley call about the offer?" Bradley was the yacht broker who ran the Stuart office of the brokerage firm that was handling the Bermuda 40.

"Nope."

"That airhead. I called her three times from Grand Cayman and got her machine every time. I'm going to change and run up there right now."

"You want me to come?"

"I don't think so."

"If we get the Hinckley, could we invite her out for a sail?"

"Maybe."

Mary Beth Bradley really was an airhead, but she was the youngest daughter of a family that owned boatyards and brokerage offices all along the coasts of the Carolinas and Virginia. Alice suspected they had sent her down here to open a one-woman office just to get her out of their hair. She had a round, pretty face that usually wore a vague smile and was framed by a bush of curly honey-blond hair. Every time Alice saw her, she was reminded of Harpo Marx. Not that she had a body like Harpo Marx. She was small and had one of those pneumatic Gibson girl figures that had been popular at the end of the nineteenth century. The combination of the vacuous smile and the lush body made her the girl of Emil's dreams. Buying this boat was proving to be complicated enough, without having to worry about his abducting the broker in midnegotiation.

When Alice walked into the little office, Bradley was sitting behind her desk with her tongue sticking out of the corner of her mouth trying to type something into her computer. When she heard the door close she pulled her tongue back into her mouth, and smiled her Harpo smile. "Hello, Mrs. Lowell. I was just going to call you."

"I'll bet you were. Have you gotten a reply to my offer yet?"

"Oh no. I don't expect to hear anything about that for at least another couple of weeks. Didn't I tell you?"

"No. You didn't tell me anything."

"Oh. Maybe I didn't. Mrs. Leland is traveling in Europe until the end of the month: some sort of wine-tasting tour. We won't hear anything until she gets back. I was sure I told you."

"You mean she just went off for a month in the middle of negotiations?"

"I don't think Mrs. Leland is exactly desperate for the money." Then she had an idea. "To expedite things, in the meantime, we could begin to line up any financing you might need."

"I'm not desperate for the money either, lady. I told you this was going to be a cash deal. Did you tell Mrs. Leland that?"

"Oh gracious. I'm sorry. You wanted me to tell her that, didn't you? I don't know how I could have forgotten it. I had no idea you were in a hurry, though."

"The end of the month?"

"Oh yes. As soon as she gets back, our Savannah office will be right on it for me."

"Well, okay, I guess."

"How is Mr. Lowell?"

"He's fine."

"Such a charming man. You're a lucky woman, Mrs. Lowell."

"I count my blessings daily."

"A funny thing happened this morning, though." Again the Harpo smile.

"Oh, what?" Alice decided that as soon as this deal was completed, she was certainly going to get this dippy broad a date with Emil.

"Oh, a lady was in here. Some sort of investigator or inspector or something. And she had pictures of a man who could be Mr. Lowell's brother. She said he was wanted for credit card fraud. Isn't that funny? Some guy who is wanted for some minor credit card fraud that looks like a charming man who is about to buy a Bermuda 40 for cash. How's that for a coincidence?"

Alice hesitated for only a second before she said, "Mr. Lowell doesn't have a brother, and if he did, I doubt if he would be involved in credit card fraud. The Cabots and the Lodges would never forgive him." This caused Bradley's face to light up with a particularly confused smile. "I certainly hope you didn't mention him to this lady cop, or whatever she was."

"Oh, of course not. I knew it couldn't be him. But I don't think she was a cop. She didn't have a badge, just a little card with her picture on it that said she works for some bank."

Emil was down at the pool when Alice stormed into the apartment, tore his room apart, and found Charles Bissette's driver's license and Master Card under the VCR after she had thrown both it and the TV crashing to the floor.

But when he came into the apartment an hour later, she was sitting in an easy chair in the living room, calmly knitting, her packed bags next to the door and her knitting bag in her lap. She had obviously emptied the refrigerator, because the counter that separated the kitchen area from the living room was stacked with food, and the shelves from the fridge were stacked on top of it. "What's going on, Alice?" Then he glanced through the door into his demolished bedroom and said, "Jesus, Alice, what did you do that for?" He was a compulsive neatnick, something else she hated about him.

She tossed the credit card and license at him and said, "I've always known you were stupid, Emil, but I never guessed you were this stupid. You must have used this someplace where they took a picture of you, and now the Polizzi woman is running up and down the coast showing it to people. And if she's here, Stroud must be here, too. And after all I did to get rid of them."

"Okay. I made a mistake. I admit it. But sooner or later they would have shown up. We've just been here too long, Alice. People in our line of work can't stay in the same place this long." He was tempted to say, "If you hadn't insisted on a Hinckley or Swan we would have been long gone by now." But he knew better than to even imply that she had made a mistake. Instead he asked, "What's with the refrigerator?"

"I've just about concluded that my best course of action is to put you in the fridge and beat it out of here. It will be a couple of weeks before anyone finds you, and I'll be long gone by then."

"I might not be so easy to put in the fridge."

Her hand came out of her knitting bag with a .380 automatic. "If I decide you should be in the fridge, asshole, you're in the fridge. You've been just dying to do something stupid ever since we got here, and you finally managed it."

"You know as well as I do that we have to get moving, and we both know how we have to do it. And you can't do that alone, can you, Alice?"

As she moved farther south, Lydia began to have better luck. She found two yacht brokers who were both quite sure that the man in the photos had been shopping for a luxury sailboat with his wife. But neither of the brokers had had anything listed that the couple wanted or had gotten so much as a telephone number. It wasn't much, but it was enough to restore her faith that her next stop might be the one that paid off. The same faith is indispensable to slot-machine players and door-to-door salesmen.

Stroud had had no luck at all, so they decided he would join her and they would work their way south playing leapfrog.

"Hi Mo, It's Alice. First, I want to thank you for that lovely dinner the other night. Tell Marzina that if she ever gets tired of working for you, she has a job in Nevis any time she wants it."

She paused while Mo made the telephone equivalent of the kisses beside the ears, then she continued, "Peter and I have moved out of that apartment we were staying in. It belongs to his family's trust, and they have a long-term renter lined up who wants to move in on the first, so it has to be painted. Just as well. It was a dreary little place. Anyway, we're moved into a suite at the Hilton in Vero Beach. Much better. What are you and Seth

doing tomorrow night? Would you like to join us for dinner at the hotel?"
Polizzi and Stroud were convinced that they were on the verge of finding the Holbrooks, because Bill had found another yacht broker who recognized the man in the photo. Their search was almost down to Jupiter now, and the fifty-mile drive each way to the hotel in Vero Beach seemed a waste of time. So forty-five minutes before their quarry checked into the Hilton, they moved out.

Seth Belnap walked around the suite with a gin and tonic in his hand, looking in at the elegantly furnished bedrooms and going out on the balcony to check out the view. Then he pronounced judgment. "Not too shoddy."

Gordon answered him, "And I don't have to eat Alice's cooking. That makes it even better," as he finished making his own drink.

"How are you making out on the Bermuda 40?"

Alice answered, "We've made an offer, but the woman who owns it is off in France tasting wines until sometime next month, would you believe?"

"She doesn't seem too anxious to sell."

"It was her husband's boat and I'm sure she wants to get rid of it, but she wants to play the merry widow, too. It is a truly lovely boat in cream-puff condition, so we'll just have to hang out and wait for a couple or three weeks. We're hoping she'll call the broker if they have a sobering-up day on her tour, but there doesn't seem to be much chance of that."

"We don't have much going on, either. Why don't the four of us pop over to the Bahamas for a week or so?"

They finally found a broker in Jupiter who recognized the picture and had a phone number and address for John and Alice Perkins, as they were then calling themselves. Lydia was driving, and as she pulled to the curb across the street from the apartment building she asked, "How do you want to handle this, Bill?"

"I don't know. I feel like a dog that's been chasing cars all his life and has finally caught one."

"Should we call the police?"

"And tell them what? That we've tracked down a guy who we're pretty sure committed a three hundred dollar credit card fraud?"

"We've got a lot more than that we could tell them."

"Yeah. But how do we link it to these people?"

"Wasn't John and Alice Perkins the name they were using when they sailed with your daughter?"

"Pretty common names. Besides, that broker hadn't talked to them in over a month. We don't even know if they're still here."

They sat in silence for a while until he finally said, "She saw you close up, but I don't think she knows what I look like. Wait here while I nose around."

He came back twenty minutes later, climbed into the car, and said, "I talked to the super. He said he hasn't seen either of them in almost two weeks. For a twenty, he let me into the apartment. They're long gone and the place looks like a Swiss dairy plant. They cleaned it from top to bottom before they left, probably to make sure they left absolutely nothing: no fingerprints, nothing. The super was happy, though. He said that when people skip they usually leave a mess."

"Now what?"

"I wish I knew." Then he said, "When you can't go forward any farther, there's only one thing to do."

"I know. Back up."

"We might as well go to the hotel while we contemplate our next miscalculation."

"You drive. I want to go through my notes."

As he drove back to the hotel, she looked up from her notebook and said, "It seems to me that they must have had a reason for bugging out like that, and the most likely reason is that somehow they found out we were looking for them. Watch out!" A huge Lincoln, its driver so small that only the top of his gray head was visible, pulled unconcernedly out in front of them. Stroud hit the horn and the brakes together and swerved into the fortunately empty oncoming lane. The Lincoln rolled on with no sign that anything out of the ordinary had happened.

They were both silent while the adrenaline burned off, then she asked, "When exactly did the super say they left?"

"He didn't know. He just said he hadn't seen them in maybe a week and a half or so. I showed him the picture and he verified it was our guy. He said he hung around the pool a lot when they were here. Usually saw him every day."

"A week and a half ago." She went back into her notes and finally said, "About that time I talked to a yacht broker up in Stuart. A woman, kind of spacey. I made a note that when she first looked at the picture I thought she recognized him, but then she was adamant that she had no idea who the guy was."

He started the car. "It's only two o'clock. Let's go to Stuart."

By the time they introduced themselves and exchanged greetings with Mary Beth Bradley, Stroud knew what Lydia meant by spacey. She asked her, "Miss Bradley, when I was here last week I showed you this picture and you said you had never seen this man before. Was that the truth?"

"What, that I had never seen the man in the picture before? Of course it was the truth? I always tell the truth." She gave them a wonderful, heartwarming, and completely inappropriate smile.

"Is that still the truth? You've never seen this man before?"

"No, of course not. I saw him the last time you showed me the picture."

"No. I don't mean the picture itself. I mean the man in the picture. Do you know who he is?"

"No. I don't know who the man in that picture is."

Again she smiled, and Stroud was afraid Lydia was going to hit her if she kept smiling. This woman did the best inadvertent Gracie Allen impression he had ever seen. So he asked, "Miss Bradley, do you know anyone who looks like the man in the picture?"

She answered brightly, "Oh, yes." And then said to Lydia, "If that's what you wanted to know, that's what you should have asked."

Spacey—not dumb, but spacey. Stroud now asked her, "Who do you know who looks like the man in the picture, Miss Bradley?" He almost called her Gracie.

"Why, Mr. Lowell. Mr. Peter Lowell. He's a client of mine. At least I think he's a client. I'm beginning to wonder."

"Why do you wonder if he's a client, Miss Bradley?"

"Well, he and Mrs. Lowell made an offer on a yacht and I about killed myself chasing down the owner in France. You wouldn't believe my phone bill. She made a counteroffer—the owner, Mrs. Leland, that is—but I haven't been able to reach the Lowells to tell them about it. The offers aren't that far apart, and I was sure they really wanted that boat, but I haven't been able to reach them since she was in here a week or so ago complaining that she hadn't heard from me."

"Is Mrs. Lowell's name Alice?"

"Why, yes. How did you know that?"

"What made you so sure Mr. Lowell wasn't the man in the picture?"

"A petty credit-card cheat? People who offer to buy a Bermuda 40 for cash cannot be petty credit-card cheats. Besides, Mr. Lowell is very kind and very charming." The way she said it strongly implied that Stroud was neither.

Now Lydia asked her, "When Mrs. Lowell was in here last week, did you tell her about my visit?"

"I think I did. Oh yes, I did. We both thought it was just an amusing coincidence."

"Do you have a phone number and address for the Lowells?"

"Yes, but I can't give them to you. That wouldn't be ethical." The dizzy smile was back.

"Is this them?" Lydia read off the address and phone number of the apartment.

"If you know all this stuff, why are you asking me?"

"Where is the Bermuda 40?"

"Why? Are you interested in buying it if the Lowells don't take it?"

"We'd like to see it first."

Now they really got a wonderful smile. "It's up in Savannah in my daddy's boatyard. Tell my brother I sent you." She scribbled the address.

When they were outside, Lydia said, "How far is Savannah? About 400 miles or so? If we drive straight through, we can be there in the morning when they open."

"Sounds good to me."

She was just pulling onto I-95 when he said, " You know, she's a flake, but that's one damned attractive woman. I don't know why."

"You want me to go back and drop you off? She doesn't have a brain in her head, Bill."

"You're right. I knew there was a reason she was so attractive."

"Men."

CHAPTER ELEVEN

The sailing yacht *Coteme* lay at anchor in Cross Bay, the open anchorage between Settlement Point on the western tip of Grand Bahama and the entrance to Freeport's commercial harbor. But she would be *Coteme* for only a few minutes longer. Alice was sitting crosswise on the center seat of the inflatable, alternately softening the letters of the name on the transom with a rag soaked in thinner and scraping at the paint with a razor blade. She worked carefully so she wouldn't scratch or dull the gel coat. A radio on the cockpit seat was playing reggae a bit louder than necessary, but it didn't matter. It was a quiet, velvety Bahamas night, and the only other boat was anchored at the far end of the bay, out of earshot.

She hummed along with the music as she worked by the light of a battery lantern held between her thighs, and completely ignored the muffled sounds that occasionally escaped from the closed cabin. When the name and homeport had been removed, she carefully inspected her work, shining the light on the fiberglass from various angles to be sure the job met her standards. Finally she was satisfied, so she carefully measured and marked two light pencil reference lines across the transom, then stood up in the dink, put the batten, pencil, and rule she had used into the cockpit, and sitting back down, opened the envelope containing the adhesive-backed vinyl letters of the new name and hailing port. When they were in place, she applied two coats of boat wax to the entire transom, then untied the dink and let it drift away as she leaned on the oars and admired her handiwork. The Cape Dory 36 was now *Noriecka, Stamford, Ct.*

An hour later she had changed the tan dodger cover, the mainsail cover, and the staysail's sausage bag for the new blue ones she had brought with her. The old ones were heaped on top of a fifteen-foot piece of anchor chain in one wing of the T-shaped cockpit. Peter had hacksawed two pieces from an anchor rode that afternoon; the other was already doing its job in a thousand feet of water. She banged on the hatch boards. "Are you done in there yet?" She hadn't heard a sound in quite a while.

"Just cleaning up."

"Well, hurry it up. I want to be out in deep water before the sun comes up, and I need a hand getting the inflatable aboard and stowed."

At dawn she went below and made fried egg sandwiches and coffee for breakfast. By then the old dodger and mainsail cover, and the bundle he had dragged up from the cabin wrapped in the plastic painter's cloth he had used to protect the upholstery, had been dropped over the side. Neither of them had forgotten the chain-wrapped bundle, but it had been stored in their memories differently from the way normal humans store such things. Their brains stored the memory of the bundle in the place that kept things they knew about but which had no personal significance. It is the place where most people store the plots of old movies and novels and of fairy tales heard in childhood, not things they have actually done in the last thirty-six hours.

They ate in the cockpit and like any couple with a new boat in a light breeze on a perfect morning, enjoyed how well she stepped along on a reach with a gentle easterly and the Gulf Stream pushing her northward. When they had finished eating, he said, "I don't know why we don't just go out through the Providence Channel into the Atlantic and get as far away from here as we can."

"First, because *Noriecka* never cleared out of the United States. *Coteme* did, but *Noriecka* didn't. Remember? And second, because I have a little more business to do in the States."

"Why that name, anyway? It sounds like that Panamanian dictator."

"He was Noriega."

"I hope you aren't going to try and milk their credit cards. I've had enough of credit cards."

"No. No credit cards." She gathered up the plates and cups. "Just keep her going about 310. I want to go into Jacksonville, but I'd just as soon get across the stream before a norther blows in. I'm going to catch some zees."

She went below, rinsed the dishes and put them away, then took off her shirt and shorts, kicked off her shoes, and, wrapping a sheet around herself, lay down on the lee bunk. In two minutes she was asleep, completely oblivious to what had happened in this cabin just a few hours ago and with absolutely no thought of the last woman who had lain on that bunk. It was the dreamless sleep of the totally innocent, known only to small children, saints, and psychopaths.

Stroud and Polizzi were waiting the next morning when Bernard Bradley came to work at the full service boatyard he managed. It took only a few minutes to establish that other than a short visit a couple of weeks before, he had neither seen nor heard from the Lowells since.

"She certainly seemed to want that boat, although he seemed sort of apathetic. That's directly the opposite of most couples that look at a boat. I didn't think anything of it at the time. I was sure we had the boat sold. They made an offer, Mrs. Leland made a counteroffer, and then they just disappeared. At least, that's what my sister said happened. You've met my sister?"

Stroud said, "Yes. A lovely lady."

"I suppose she is, but . . . "

He let the sentence hang so Lydia said, "But you have no idea what became of the Lowells."

"No. None. I sure hope nothing happened to them. They certainly seemed like nice people. You know, when you deal in boats like these—we don't broker anything less than thirty-eight feet or less than top quality: Hinckleys, Swans, Aldens, Little Harbors; no bourgeois boats—well, to be honest, you meet some very obnoxious people. You wouldn't expect it, but I suppose if a lot of them weren't overly aggressive, they wouldn't have that kind of money. And some of them aren't very comfortable with their money either, and this kind of boat is a way to—I guess legitimize it is a good a way to say it. But the Lowells—her, at least; he didn't say much—were quite nice and quite knowledgeable, too. Some of those others have no idea what they're looking at. The Lowells were first quality, too. I sure hope nothing happened to them."

When they were back in the car, Lydia said, "Nice guy, but although I'm sure he doesn't realize it, he is his sister's brother, isn't he?"

"Blood will tell. What now?"

"Well, our clothes and your rental car are at a hotel in Jupiter. You feel up to driving back? Or do you want to find someplace to sleep?"

"Nah." They had taken turns sleeping and driving on the way up. "There's a Denny's. Let's get some breakfast and head back."

As they were eating, she said, "Poof. Gone again." Then after a pause, "I suppose they abandoned buying the Hinckley because they were afraid we'd trace them to it."

"Well, we did, didn't we?"

"So where would they have gone?"

"That's pretty obvious, isn't it? Having hunted all up and down the tickytacky delights of Florida's east coast searching for the boat of her dreams, they probably scooted over to the west coast where she can find more boatyards and he can find more porno shops, wonderful, charming people that they are. You know, I'm really coming to hate Florida. Even St. James doesn't look so bad after you've been here awhile. It's relentlessly flat, ugly, and overrun by crazy old folks driving tanks. Even in a swanky neighborhood, you're only about a quarter mile tops from a tacky commercial mess."

"Up near Ocala, in the horse country, it's pretty nice. At least it used to be. Where on the west coast?"

"You pick it. Let's go back to Jupiter, spend the night, and get started early in the morning."

"God, I'm sick of going door to door like a Bible salesman."

It would be a night of firsts in their relationship. Just before sunset Gordon slipped quietly below, fished two frozen chicken pies out of the refrigerator, and put them into the oven of the propane stove. That was not a first, though; he often prepared the meal at the change of watch. What was new was that he could watch Alice sleep as he did it. All their previous boats had had aft cabins that she had appropriated for herself and where he was never permitted to enter. This boat had only a quarter berth back under the cockpit, its head protruding into the main cabin to form a seat for the chart table. Like all quarter berths, in calm weather no one could sleep in it because there was no ventilation, and in rough weather it was too wet, even if the sails, life jackets, duffel bags, and whatever else always accumulated there, were piled somewhere else. The forepeak was no place to sleep, now that the boat had entered the Stream and was beginning to bounce around. Whether she liked it or not, they were going to have to share the main cabin when they were at sea. The sheet had slipped down, exposing one breast. That was a first, too. He had never, in all their years together, caught more than a fleeting glimpse of her body. Maybe this boat wouldn't be so bad, after all.

She opened her eyes then, saw him, pulled the sheet around her shoulders, and smiled. "Hello there. What's for supper?"

He wondered how long she had been awake. "Chicken pie, and there's some of that salad Mo made the other night." He mentioned Mo as if she were asleep in the forecabin or safely ashore.

"Oh good." Her legs came out from under the sheet as she sat up. "Now get out of here so I can get dressed. How's the weather? Do you want to eat in the cockpit?"

"It's a bit wet for that. You eat and then relieve me. There's a lot of steamer traffic passing us heading north. We must be just about in the middle of the Stream. Somebody better be on lookout all the time."

When he relieved her at one o'clock—they always split nights at sea in two this way—Alice came below and marked the position from the Global Positioning System on the chart. They were still in the Stream, well past Cape Canaveral now. The Cape Dory, despite its full keel, was not the total dog she had feared. She was no clipper ship either, but Alice had to admit that the no-longer-fashionable steep deadrise of her hull gave her a wonderfully soft motion in a seaway. On the way over from Florida, Emil had noted how comfortable it was working on the foredeck, even with the club for the staysail in the way.

When she had drawn and labeled the little mark on the chart that showed their precise location, she noticed two notations printed either side of it. One of them was 571 and the other was 637. It was the depth in meters. She took her knitting bag and went into the head, and when she came out she was wearing only her bikini briefs. Rather than wrap herself in a sheet and lie down, she left her knitting on the chart table and went back up into the cockpit. It was to be a night of firsts.

There was a half moon still well above the horizon, and although there is no place darker than out at sea at one in the morning, he could see her quite clearly by its light and the red glow of the compass and instrument lights. It was the first time he had ever seen her without clothes. "Peter, I think we're going to have to change the basis of our relationship if we're going to live together in this boat." She smiled, "It's a much more sociable layout than we're used to, isn't it."

He was sitting in the windward T of the cockpit, and she stepped over the bridge deck and stood facing him over the wheel, bracing herself with both hands on the pedestal stand. "God, you're beautiful, Alice. But I don't know if I can . . . "

"You can do anything, if I help you do it. After all these years together, you should know that. Once I get my business done in Jacksonville, we're going to be a long time together at sea, sharing that cabin . . . " She moved around the wheel through the other wing of the tee, sat, and pushed in behind him. He started to turn toward her but she reached her left hand over his shoulder, inside his shirt, and as she stroked his chest, said, "Eyes front, darling. Watch the compass. I know what you need. Let me give it to you."

With her right hand she reached around and pulled the little .380 automatic from where she had taped it to the small of her back, flicked off the safety, and shot him in the right ear, twice.

It was another first in their relationship; in all the years they had been together, it was the first time she had ever personally killed anyone up close. As she watched him slumped over the combing in his final convulsions, a sensual thrill made her shiver, and she realized how much she had been missing.

They decided to renew their search in the Tampa /St. Petersburg area, because the Yellow Pages showed the shores of Tampa Bay to have the most pages of yachting businesses on the west coast of Florida. Using what they had learned, they concentrated on brokers and boatyards that specialized in high-priced boats. There were many, but none of them seemed to have ever heard of the Perkins or the Lowells or ever seen anyone resembling the man in the picture. Stroud worked north and west around the bay toward Clearwater, while Polizzi went south toward Baedenton.

Nothing.

"Alice. Thank God you called. I've been frantic. Where've you been?"

"At sea single-handed. I needed to get away to clear my mind. Did you get the money I sent you, Granny?"

"Yes, thanks. You were at sea single-handed? Where's Gordon?"

"Oh Lord, so much has happened since the last time I talked to you that I don't know where to start. Well, to begin with, Gordon left me. We had rather a bad argument that brought everything that's been going on between us to a head—his behavior toward me, his other women, and, I have to admit, his suspicions about you and me. I was afraid he was going to beat me again—he has gotten violent with me before. I never told you because I was afraid of how you would react. Anyway, he was carrying on like a madman, and he frightened me so badly I called 911, and he just ran out of the apartment. When the cops got there, he was gone. I had to go out a while later to look at a boat—I bought it, as it turned out—and when I came back, he had taken his stuff and decamped. You have no idea how relieved I was."

"Are you going to get a divorce?"

"That's something I have to admit to you, my darling. Oh Lord, this is just so difficult. I feel so cheap for having deceived you. I hope you can forgive me, Granny. Your forgiveness is the only thing on earth I truly need or want. Gordon and I were never married. We met when we were working for a charter outfit in the Grenadines, and when we came across a couple who wanted to sell a good boat cheap, we pooled our resources, bought it together, and went cruising."

"That was *Cinderella?*"

"The first *Cinderella*. Gordon wrecked her on those rocks in the middle of the channel between Nevis and St. Kitts."

"But you stayed with him."

"I realize now that I was a classic case of battered woman's syndrome. I don't think I would ever have broken free of him, would ever have had the courage to call 911 that day, if it weren't for all you've given me. There. It's all in the open. If you don't ever want to see me again, I'll understand. I know that I'm damaged goods."

He thought about it for a full minute before he said, "You're like a *Bermuda* 40 that's been through a hurricane. A little polishing, a few new sails, and you'll be like new again."

"What a wonderful thing to say. You have no idea how I've dreaded telling you the truth, and how much I hoped you would say something like that. You don't know someone who might want to take over a battered Bermuda 40 and make a project of her, do you?"

"Oh, yes. I know someone. How soon can I see you?"

"How soon can you get here, my darling?"

"Where are you?"

"I'm at a marina in Jacksonville." She gave him the address.

"You bought that Hinckley?"

"No. The deal fell through. Some nephew wanted it, so the lady gave it to him. Just gave it to him, as if it were one of her husband's old suits. I bought a boat, though. An absolutely cream puff Cape Dory 36. How would you like to sail off into the sunset with me, Granny?"

"I don't think I can make it by sunset today, though. Can you wait until tomorrow?"

"No, but I suppose I'll have to.

Another ten days of fruitless searching.

Stroud and Polizzi sat at a tiny table in the back corner of the hotel's bar sipping bourbon. "They've never been here, Bill. Let's face it. There comes a point where we have to admit this is hopeless. We've searched from Clearwater almost to Fort Myers."

"If you want to quit, go ahead. It's just that I don't know what else to do. They're out there somewhere and eventually I'll find them."

"What about Evans? His mother might have heard something by now.

"The other day you said you were going to call her."

"I did. I tried her three or four times. No answer."

"That's odd. I didn't get the impression she and Annie were frequent flyers. Maybe she's sick."

"I'll try her again." She pulled her cell phone out of her bag, saw the battery-low light, and held it up so he could see it. "I'll try her from my room. When do you want to eat?"

"I want to take a walk first. This restaurant food is piling it on me. Six o'clock in the lobby?"

"Fine."

But when he came back from his walk at five-thirty, she was waiting in the lobby with her bags at her feet. "I'm going to Connecticut on a seven-thirty flight, Bill. I tried to call Mrs. Evans, but Annie wouldn't let me talk to her. She said Mrs. Evans was exhausted from a trip they just returned from. A trip to Florida."

"Go."

"What are you going to do?"

"Keeping working south, I guess."

"Look, I won't get to see her until tomorrow morning, then I'll get past Annie no matter what it takes.   Don't go banging on doors in the morning.   Hang around here and I'll call you as soon as I know anything."

Annie was not going to be easy. Lydia knew it as soon as she opened the door and said, "Mrs. Evans is not receiving guests, least of all your sort."

"Then she'll have to tell me that herself.   Now get out of the way. I'm not in the habit of taking crap from servants."   She put as much disdain into "servants" as Annie had put into "your sort."

"Who is it, Annie?" came from the living room as the sound of the TV was muted.

"That big Italian person. I forget her name."

"Miss Polizzi. Let her in, Annie. I have to talk to her."

Lydia found Mrs. Evans sitting in front of the TV she had just turned off, a cup and a china coffeepot on the table beside her. "Sit down, Miss Polizzi. Annie, don't stand there scowling. Get Miss Polizzi a cup." As Annie skulked out, the old lady with the strange hair said, "Annie is not easy, and I'm afraid you and she did not hit it off well, but she has a good heart."

"What did you want to talk to me about?"

"Miss Polizzi, the fact that you are here tells me you are still looking for Granville. I want to tell you that you can stop. Whatever you think he was involved in, he's completely clear of it now. And those people you and that Mr. Stroud thought he was associated with, well, he'll have nothing more to do with them ever again, I'm sure. So I want you people to leave my son alone."

"He told you this? Is that why you're so sure of it?"

"Miss Polizzi, I'm sure of it because my son, at long last, has grown up. He has finally met a wonderful girl from a fine family and married her. That's where Annie and I were, at the wedding. As a matter of fact, I am so convinced of it that as soon as you leave, I'm going to call my lawyer and tell him to draw up the papers turning Granville's trust fund over to him. I've controlled it until now."

"They were married in Florida?"

"Jacksonville. It was beautiful wedding at the yacht club.

"I don't suppose you'll tell me where Granville and his bride are honeymooning."

"They're someplace you couldn't bother them even if you wanted to. But I'm hoping that I can make you stop wanting to bother them."

"How do you propose to do that?"

"By reasoning with you. You seem like a decent and reasonable person, Miss Polizzi. Once you understand that Granville has turned his life around, as they say, I think you'll be more than willing to leave him alone."

"Turned his life around?"

"Granville has never been attracted to the sort of woman I would have chosen for him. The last even semi-presentable girl he went out with was the Dawson girl who crewed for him, and she was from Devon. Do you know what NOKD means, Miss Polizzi? It means 'Not Our Kind, Dear,' and I don't know how many times I was forced to say it to Granville. I'm sure that criminal woman you told me about was extremely NOKD. But if I had selected her myself, I could not have found a lovelier girl than the one he has just married. When I saw him row her out to their yacht, in that little boat, him in his tux and her in that beautiful gown, it was the culminating moment of my life. The yacht had been in a slip, but he had it moved out to a mooring during the ceremony, so he could surprise her, and me, by rowing her out to it. My husband did the same thing for me at our wedding. It is quite the most beautiful and symbolic beginning possible for a marriage, don't you think?" Her eyes filled with tears and she wiped them with a lace handkerchief she pulled from her sleeve. Then she said, "Excuse me. I get teary just thinking about it."

"It must have been lovely. Were any of her relatives there?"

"No. And no friends, either. She wanted her roommate from Sweet Briar College to stand up for her, but she's in Europe and couldn't make it on such short notice, so my daughter Emmy was the matron of honor, Lori was the bridesmaid, and my little granddaughter was the flower girl. For a wedding arranged on such short notice, it was truly lovely."

"I'm sure it was. They're honeymooning on the boat? It must be quite a boat."

"It's not one of these mega-yachts those dot com people buy, if that's what you mean. Those are rather NOKD too, aren't they? It's a beautiful boat for two people on a honeymoon, a Cape Dory 36 she recently bought. A friend of my husband's at the club had one just like it." She turned wistful. "He was a good friend of mine, too. They're wonderfully comfortable boats."

The line "There is nothing, absolutely nothing, so worthwhile as messing about in boats" popped into Lydia's mind, and she suspected that Mrs. Evans had done some messing about in a Cape Dory 36 in her time. But she asked, "Is the boat's name *Cinderella?*"

"No, but it would be better if it were. It's *Noriecka*. Sounds like that Panamanian dictator, doesn't it? But he's Noriega. My new daughter-in-law said it was the boat's name when she bought it, and it's bad luck to change a boat's name, especially at the beginning of a very long voyage. It's some Indian word."

"Mrs. Evans, you have no idea how relieved I am to hear this. Mr. Stroud and I were terribly worried about your son. You can rest assured we won't do anything to bother him again, especially on his honeymoon. They're cruising the west coast of Florida and the Keys? What an idyllic trip."

"Oh no. Nothing so mundane. Granville's bride is an accomplished sailor, just as he is. They have so much in common."

"So they're going to do the Bahamas, too. I really envy them, now."

"Well, that's what they told everyone else, Miss Polizzi. That they were going to cruise down through the Bahamas and then move into our house in St. Thomas. But they changed their minds just before the wedding. I had told Granville that if he didn't want the house, I was going to put it on the market and rent it until I found a buyer. As they were leaving the reception, he told me that he really didn't expect they would need it. Both he and his bride have always wanted to sail in the South Pacific, and they had decided to head straight for the Panama Canal. I don't suppose there's any harm in telling you, now that Granville has gotten himself free of whatever it was you were investigating. They left yesterday morning. Annie and I had a suite in a hotel overlooking the harbor, and when I got up at dawn as I always do, they came motoring past my balcony with Granny hoisting the main and his lovely bride steering. Miss Polizzi, that's another picture I will never forget. A picture I've dreamed of seeing for years, and will never forget."

"They left yesterday, the morning after the wedding, headed for Panama?"

"Yes. They want to get through the Canal before the hurricane season starts."

"It's April, Mrs. Evans. The hurricane season starts in August."

"That's what I thought. But Granville said the farther south you go, the sooner it starts. They want to be through the canal and down to the Galapagos before then."

"I didn't know that, but I grew up in Ohio, where we don't have hurricanes." She supposed that made her NOKD, too. "It must have been a lovely wedding. Do you have any pictures? I'd love to see them."

"Annie took scores of them, but they aren't developed yet."

Lydia stood up. Annie never had brought her a coffee cup. It was now time to get one thing verified, and she took a second to consider exactly how she would do it. "Well, Mrs. Evans, I'm so glad you shared your good news about Granville with me. It's quite a relief. Tell me, is his bride from Connecticut?"

"Oh yes. She grew up on Shippan Point in Stamford. A very fine family."

"How interesting. Her uncle may be an old friend of my family. I was talking to him the other day and he mentioned that he had a niece getting married in Jacksonville this week and I know she grew up on Shippan Point. His name is Peter Kettner."

"How very odd. I didn't know Alice had any living relatives."

"Bill. I've got it sorted out. Would you believe that Alice Kettner and Granville Evans were married two days ago at a yacht club in Jacksonville? A lovely wedding with the bride in white and the groom in his tux. His mother is still shedding tears of joy."

"His mother told you this?"

"Oh, yes. She's sure it's a match made in heaven."

"Did she tell you where they're honeymooning?"

"At sea. They sailed from Jacksonville headed for the Panama Canal yesterday morning. They're in a rush because they want to get there before the hurricane season starts."

"They've got three months. What are they sailing, a hollowed-out log?"

"A Cape Dory 36. It's hers, but God knows where she got it."

"Did Mrs. Evans say what their first stop will be? The Bahamas, the Virgins, what?"

"He told his mother they were heading straight for the Canal."

Stroud was silent for a minute, then he said, "I need a chart. Call me back in a half hour. I'm going to run out to that chandlery down the block. Make it an hour."

When she called back, she was sitting in her car in the parking lot of a Barnes and Noble on the Post Road, a brand-new atlas open on her knees.

"Bill, It's me. I bought an atlas. What route do you think they'll take?"

"If they're in a hurry, there's only one way to go: head southeast from Jacksonville, staying north and then east of the Bahamas until they turn south through either the Mayaguana or the Caicos Passage, depending on the winds. But everything depends on the winds, doesn't it? From there it's a straight shot through the Windward Passage and across the Caribbean to the Canal. Cutting the corner around the Bahamas as close as possible, it plots out at about 900 miles from Jacksonville to the Windward Passage, but in reality it's probably more like eleven or twelve hundred. If they get across the stream without getting clobbered and then get a norther that carries them through the variables down to the trades, they might get to the Windward Passage in ten days or so. But if they don't get a norther, they could have slow going down to about 23 north where the trade-wind belt begins. In that case, it could take two or three weeks, unless they have enough fuel to motor through the variables."

"So we've got plenty of time to get to Panama and be waiting for them."

"If that's where they're going. I forgot to ask you before: Mrs. Evans didn't mention the mystery man, did she?"

"No. She said Alice didn't have any friends or relatives at the wedding."

"Hmm. I wonder what became of him."

They were both silent for a while, then she said, "She did say she was going to sign over Granny's trust fund to him. You don't suppose that's what this is all about, do you?"

"Christ, who knows? The new Mrs. Evans and her mystery man belonged to a yacht club in Jamaica, didn't they?"

"Yeah. That's right. So he could be waiting for her there."

"That's what I've been thinking—unless he's swimming with fishes, of course."

"That's where we thought Evans was." Now there was a long silence before Stroud made a decision. "Lydia, thanks for all your help. When I first met you, I never dreamed we would ever become friends, but we have, haven't we. Really good friends. I'll get in touch with you as soon as I get back."

"What, get back? You aren't going to go to Jamaica or Colon without me. Forget that noise."

"I'm not going to Colon or Jamaica."

"Where then? Damnit, I don't deserve to get dumped now, when after months of chasing these people, we finally have a chance to get in front of them for once. Where, Bill? Where should I meet you?"

He started to say something, stopped, thought for a moment, and then said, "Yeah, well, I guess you're right. Meet me in St. Martin just as soon as you can get there."

You think they're heading for the Virgins or the Leewards? Why?"

"No. I don't think they're heading for the Virgins, and I don't know if they're heading for Jamaica or the Canal. But I suspect that we've made the Caribbean too constricting for Alice L. and her friends. My best guess, and it's not a very solid one, is that they're heading for the Windward Passage; then it's either meet the mystery man in Jamaica and head for the Pacific, or if he's no longer a factor, Mr. and Mrs. Evans go right through to Panama. But even if they are going out east to St. Thomas, a Cape Dory 36 isn't exactly a twelve-meter to weather in heavy air. They might very well want to go south of Hispaniola rather than have a 700-mile beat into the trades in the Atlantic to get to the Virgins. They don't call the route north of the Greater Antilles the Thorny Path for nothing.

"My best guess, and it's not a very solid one, is that the most likely place to find them is the Windward Passage, no matter which of those three options—Jamaica, Panama, or the Virgins—they pick. And when they get there, if they get there, I want to be waiting for them. But it's going to be a near thing if they get good air and push it. So you better be in St. Martin when the bus is ready to leave if you want to come along."

"How far is it from St Martin to the Windward Passage?"

"About 600 mileson the rhumb line, but they'll have more than a three-day headstart. I've got a seat on a plane that leaves Tampa at two, so I'll be in St. Martin tonight. I want to get under way tomorrow, but there's a lot to do first. At best, it will be afternoon before I get it all done. I won't wait for you. When I'm ready, I'm gone."

"I'll be there if I have to swim."

It was not yet noon when Lydia lugged her bag down the dock to where *Lullaby* was tied off in the center of her slip with a line draped along each of her sides hanging within a foot of the waterline. As she came closer, she could see Stroud holding onto one of those lines as he tried to regain his breath through the snorkel tube attached to his facemask. "Bill. What are you doing?"

He lifted his head out of the water, spat out the snorkel's mouth-piece, and gasped for a minute before saying, "Scrubbing the bottom. Never start a boat race without scrubbing the bottom. She looks like the bearded lady down there."

"Can't you hire someone to do that?" He was obviously having trouble catching his breath.

"Not today. Busy taking tourists snorkeling. Not much left to do. List of grub on the chart table. Run into town and get it." He put the snorkel back into his mouth, took two or three breaths, and disappeared under the boat.

She tossed her sea bag aboard and then, after waiting for him to come up for air, pulled the boat as close to the dock as the lines allowed and leaped aboard. When she came out of the cabin with the list, he was under the boat again, so she once more waited for him to surface before pulling the boat over and jumping onto the dock. She wondered if he would still be alive when she came back from the store.

He was still alive. As she unloaded the food from the trunk of the taxi into a dock cart, she saw him dressed and with a bath towel over his shoulder, pushing another cart down the dock. When she got to the slip where *Lullaby* was now tied close to one finger pier, he was wrestling a block of ice down the hatch into the sink.

She lifted a cardboard box of food out of her cart, and he poked his head out of the hatch and said, "No cardboard boxes. Unpack the boxes on the dock." He handed her a large plastic dishpan with a piece of ice in it. "Use this. Corrugated paper is full of pregnant cockroaches. Put the ice in the drink cooler in the cockpit locker first." As he went back to chopping the rest of the ice into pieces just small enough to fit through the opening of the galley icebox, he continued, "You're early. I didn't think I'd see you until late this afternoon."

"I took Delta to Jacksonville last night, then a chartered Lear Jet over here this morning."

"Jesus, what does that cost?"

"You don't want to know." She stacked canned goods and boxes in the dishpan as she continued, "I found the yacht club where they were married and got a description of the boat from a guy who works on the dock: white with Cape Dory tan decks. Long, low deckhouse with five elliptical bronze opening ports to the side. A cutter with a club-footed staysail. The name is Noriecka - not Noriega - Noriecka. Mrs. E. said it was an Indian word."

"I've heard it someplace before—Noriecka, I mean. Sounds like your standard Cape Dory 36. Did the guy on the dock mention any distinguishing marks?"

"The only one he could remember was that although the dodger, mainsail cover, and the bag for the staysail on the foredeck were blue, the strip up along the jib that protects it from sunlight when it's furled was tan or brown. He wasn't sure which, but he knew it wasn't blue like the rest of the canvas work."

"On the flight down here you didn't happen to see them, did you?"

"I think so. After we took off, I had the pilot fly quite low —at least, low for a Lear Jet—for the first couple of hundred miles right down the rhumb line east of the Bahamas. There was only one sailboat out there, but it was quite a ways north of where I expected them to be."

He leaned down into the box and placed the last piece of ice, then went over to the chart table where he had already taped a chart showing Florida, the Bahamas, and the Northern Antilles. "Can you show me about where they were?"

She handed him the pan of groceries and a bag from a delicatessen. "This stuff should go on ice." Then she came below and reached into her purse. "I had the pilot get a GPS fix. We were at," she read from her notebook, "28.6 North, and 77.4 West. That was at 0725 this morning. The boat was a couple of miles north of us."

He plotted the position, measured the distance, and said, "They can't have much for wind; they've only made good 245 miles in . . . When did they leave?"

"Mrs. E. said she saw them motoring out of the harbor at six on Sunday morning. Where do you want this stuff?" She pointed at the groceries.

"Everything goes in plastic bags. The boxes go in the locker under the sink, the cans under the port bunk." Then he picked up his calculator. "Call it seventy-two hours. 3.4 knots average, point to point. Of course the Stream set them north. When you took off from JAX, which way did you head?"

"West, then we did a 180 and headed out to sea. The wind was west-southwest, light and variable."

"So the current . . . Ah, who the hell knows? Tell me, was the boat you saw flying a spinnaker?"

"No, just a main and big jib."

"Well, that's good news: down wind in light air and no kite."

"If it was them, of course. But we didn't see any other sailboats. A lot of freighters, though. And it fit the description."

He stared at the chart for a minute more, then straightened up and said, "Give me your passport and I'll clear us out of here while you get the rest of the groceries aboard, then we'll fill with fuel and water and get going."

As she started up into the cockpit for another load, she paused on the ladder. "So you think we can beat them to the Windward Passage?"

"I honestly don't know, but I don't think just beating them there is going to be good enough. We have to beat them by so much that we know we've beaten them. Otherwise, we won't know if we've locked the barn door too late and rather than hang around waiting for them, we should right away head for Jamaica, or the Canal, or the Virgins, or Trinidad, maybe. Once they're through the Windward into the open sea, the chances of finding them drop way off." He thought for a moment and then added, "Of course, we don't know if the horse has already climbed out the side window of the barn and headed for the Azores."

Now that they were finally across the Stream, Alice was hoping for a norther. The Gulf Stream was no place to be when a cold front swept down through the Carolinas bringing a stiff northerly wind that blew right into the teeth of the current and produced seas the approximate size, shape, and distance apart as the houses in a low-income development. But there had been no norther, and it had seemed that they would never get across the Stream, which had been as placid as Granny's soft blue eyes. But they were finally free of it, and now most of what they were making through the water, they were also making in the same direction over the bottom.

Despite Granny's constant trimming, with her full main and her biggest jib—the 150 percent number one—fully unfurled, *Noriecka* was still doing less than four knots in the fluky southwesterly that had been blowing since they left Jacksonville. If Alice hadn't been in a hurry, it would have been a perfect honeymoon cruise: gentle breezes, blue skies, a few puffy white Gulf Stream clouds, the indigo waters of the Stream itself—and Granny with his stamina. They made love all over the boat playing what he called, "Nymphs and Satyrs." They were going to have to wear more clothes or suntan lotion, though. Both of them were beginning to burn badly in places people don't usually have sunburns.

But she was in a hurry because, she had to admit, her beautiful Granny was not exactly a genius. They had decided they would tell everyone they were going to take a leisurely cruise through the Bahamas and then move into his mother's house in St. Thomas. She convinced him that was best, because they certainly didn't want Stroud and Polizzi to learn they were heading for the Pacific. That part had been easy because, although he would never admit it, he was afraid of Polizzi and her relatives.

But on their wedding night, he had admitted that after supposedly swearing his mother to secrecy, he had told her where they were really heading. By now, the wacky old bat had probably told her bridge club and half of Lockford. Alice admitted that her new mother-in-law was more than a bit hard to comprehend. But every new bride probably thought the same thing.

She was standing at the chart table when he came below after trimming the sails and adjusting the autopilot for the thousandth time in the last three days. He was everything a woman wanted in a husband: an excellent sail trimmer, one hell of a lover, and he always believed everything she told him. He kissed her on the ear as he reached inside her string bikini and fondled her buttock. Then he looked over her shoulder at the chart and asked, "How're we doing, Captain? I don't know why you don't let me help with the navigation."

"You're a Star Boat sailor, darling. If you get more than three miles offshore, the committee boat has to come out and lead you home. Trim the sails; that's what you're good at."

"So how are we doing?"

"Not well. I wish we'd get a norther. The radio is predicting one for this area."

He moved his hand around into the front of her briefs. "What do you want a norther for? This weather is ideal for my purposes."

"Oh, yes." She turned toward him. "I'm well aware of your purposes, my good sir."

He pushed her down onto the head of the quarter berth, and she smiled up at him, one arm resting on the chart table and the other against the sail bags stacked in the berth. "Are you? Do you have any idea what my purposes are as far as you're concerned, young lady?"

"I'll have to do some investigation before I'm sure." She reached up and with some difficulty pulled down his swimming trunks. "I'm sure now, sir. Oh yes, I'm quite sure."

Lullaby **motored out of the harbor,** and as soon as they were clear of
a cruise ship lying just outside, Lydia steered her into the wind as Stroud
hoisted the new main and the heavy number-three jib that was his working headsail in the Caribbean. He climbed back into the cockpit as she
bore off onto the course written on a piece of adhesive tape stuck beneath the compass: 307 magnetic. It would take them across the Anegada
toward the Necker Island Passage through the Virgins. The northeast
trade wind was blowing a moderate Force-5 here in the lee of the island,
and with it over her quarter *Lullaby* was soon stepping along at five and
a half knots or so. Stroud put the autopilot onto the tiller, fooled with
the buttons until it was on the course he wanted—he'd fine-tune it once
he could determine the set and drift of the current—and stood with his
chin resting on his folded arms on the aft edge of the dodger. After a
minute or two he said, "She'll carry the kite." He dragged it out of the
cockpit sail locker and then took it forward, dropped the pole from where
it was stored on the front of the mast, and rigged the lines.

Once the spinnaker was up and drawing and the autopilot was
once more on course, he sat down in the cockpit next to Lydia and
said, "That's better." *Lullaby* was doing a steady six and a half now.
"I feel like I'm coming down with something, though. Just what I
need."

"Maybe you're seasick. It's nothing to be ashamed of. Nelson
was always sick when he went to sea after a while ashore." They
were getting out into the Anegada now, and its famous short, steep
seas coupled with the spinnaker, were making the boat roll.

"I've never been seasick in my life. And wasn't Nelson the guy
who chased the French fleet all over the Mediterranean and the Atlantic for nine months before he finally caught them?"

"He finally caught them, though, didn't he? Oh, I meant to tell
you, I hired a lawyer in Jacksonville last night. I just kept calling
down the list of single-lawyer offices in the yellow pages until a real
person answered the phone."

"What for?"

"The short answer is, for 500 bucks. That's what she wanted for a retainer. But I know what you mean. I told her to find out if any Cape Dory 36s were sold on the west coast of Florida in the last month, and if not, had any gone missing. I thought if we tracked them somewhere and could prove they were in a stolen boat . . . I didn't tell her why I wanted to know."

"Isn't that more a job for a private detective?"

"With a detective you don't get client-attorney confidentiality. Who knows? Someday we might need it."

"When is she going to start looking?"

"As soon as she gets the check, I imagine. I mailed it on the way to the airport this morning. Bill, you don't look well. Why don't you lie down for a while if you think that will help?

He stood up. "Maybe I will. Call me if the wind rises, or the kite starts to act funny, or there's traffic. Keep a sharp lookout for traffic; check all around every few minutes. A lot of these freighters operate on the Playboy and autopilot system: the autopilot runs the ship and the crew reads Playboy. In any case, call me in two hours so I can get a fix and do a course correction."

"I can log a fix and calculate the drift."

"That's right, you do find your way around in airplanes, don't you. Four hours, then. Then we'll have supper and I'll take over."

He didn't get four hours. The wind started to rise as the afternoon wore on and they drew out into the Anegada. Only an hour and a half later, the boat started to heel sharply and grip up to windward as the autopilot beeped to signal that it could no longer hold the designated course. The first time it happened, the chute collapsed and the pilot stopped beeping as the boat swung back on course downwind. Then the sail filled with a bang and the cycle began again. She didn't have to call him. He appeared in the hatch almost immediately. But as he said, "Time to hand the kite" and stepped over the bridge deck, a harder puff hit, and this time *Lullaby* kept swinging and rolling until she was broadside to the wind with solid water flooding the deck beside the cabin and splashing over the cockpit coaming.

Lydia screamed, "Oh my God," but Stroud calmly reached down and freed the spinnaker sheet from its cleat. The line ran out through the turning block, and the boat immediately righted herself as he unhooked the autopilot from the tiller and swung the boat even closer to the wind. Then he hardened the mainsail and said, "Keep her going like this and ease the spinnaker halyard once I catch the sheet, and I'll get it down." When he looked at Lydia for a response, she was holding onto a weather lifeline stanchion with both hands, her knuckles and her face both white with fear.

Stroud said, "Jeez, don't tell me that was your first banana surprise. We used to say that the mark of a good racing crew is that when the boat broaches like that, they nonchalantly pile over the lifelines with brushes and scrub the bottom while it's exposed."

"I thought we were going to roll over."

"Not with almost four thousand pounds of ballast. Here." He handed her the tiller. "Ease the halyard when I wave at you."

When the jib was up, the pole was again stowed on the front of the mast, and Lydia had put the boat back on course and was herself back to normal, he came into the cockpit, dropped the spinnaker below, and said, "I just stuffed it in the bag. I don't think there's any rush to repack it ready to hoist; the wind still seems to be rising." Then he checked the speedometer and said, "I guess I should have warned you, but I didn't know you were a banana virgin."

She laughed, then said, "That sounds particularly obscene."

"I guess it does. Anyway, she's doing a nice steady six and a bit with the main and number three, I think . . . " Then he scuttled down to leeward and threw up over the side. When he finally stopped heaving, he turned toward her and asked, "Nelson?"

She answered, "Hornblower, too."

"I can't believe I'm seasick. I've got a sore throat, too. God, I hope it's not the flu."

She thought, but didn't say, *Or something you caught swimming in that marina water.* Instead she said, "Drink something, Bill." She stood up and took a quart bottle of Gatorade from the cooler in the locker under her seat and handed it to him. "You don't want to get dehydrated. And go back to bed. I've got her."

He took a small swallow, then a larger one. "I'll work up a position and hit the sack. Call me if . . . You know."

She heard the radio giving the weather report as he worked at the chart table, but could not hear the words. Finally he stuck his head up through the hatch and said, "Good news and bad news. Good news first. In the four hours we've been at sea, we've made good just over twenty-six miles. But punch in five degrees less on the autopilot. We're being set north."

As she did it, she asked, "What's the bad news?"

"There's a strong norther approaching the west coast of Florida and the Bahamas in the next twelve to twenty-four hours. They'll be running before it."

"Is a Cape Dory 36 fast downwind?"

"Even a haystack is fast downwind."

CHAPTER TWELVE

When Lydia came below at 2200 after four hours on watch, the wind was still steady from the east-nor'east and she couldn't tell if Stroud was awake or not. He muttered, "Wha. . . . ?" as she touched his forehead to check for fever—he was quite hot—but other than that, showed no sign of life at all. He looked awful, even in the glow of the red light over the chart table; his skin looked old, sagging and gray.

She pulled a blanket over him, then turned to the chart table and plotted their position. The Anegada's current was still setting them north of the course line. The autopilot would need another five degrees of correction, maybe three degrees. The light on Pajaros Point at the northeast end of Virgin Gorda should be visible in an hour or so. It was supposed to have a range of sixteen miles. Three degrees for now, until she saw the light. Then it should be a straight shot through the Necker Island Passage into the Atlantic.

She turned and looked at Stroud for a minute, then fished one of the deli sandwiches she had bought in St Martin out of the icebox and went back up on deck.   Let him sleep, or whatever it was he was doing.

At two in the morning, *Lullaby* was in the middle of the Necker Island Passage with the light on Pajaros Point abeam to port. But it was another hour before Lydia felt they were far enough clear of the islands for her to go below, log their position, and check on Stroud. When she put her hand on his forehead this time, he opened his eyes and said, "Get up, Nell, Dwight's already up and I want to get out to the starting line a couple of hours early and practice spinnaker sets and takedowns." His eyes closed then, and he drifted back to wherever he had been.

The fever was definitely worse, so she got his medical book out of the rack and studied it. In a way, it was good news. If the harbor's waters had given him cholera or dysentery, the first two diseases she looked up and the two she was most worried about, he would have had diarrhea. This could just be some terrible strain of flu, or it could be almost anything except cholera or dysentery.

Then she thought about all the years of expensive education she had had, and that the higher up the educational tree she had climbed, the more useless the courses had become. Her last year in graduate school had taught her nothing except the half-baked theories of a bunch of business profs whom no one with an ounce of sense would let run a lemonade stand. Every useful thing she knew about business she had learned from watching her father—a man every bit as contemptuous of business-school grads as Stroud was—run his business. All of that education, and not one course that taught the symptoms of the most common fatal diseases, and what to do if you encountered them. But of course, knowledge like that could only save your life; it wouldn't help you acquire money.

She got another half sandwich from the icebox and went back up into the cockpit.

It was coming dawn when she noticed that as they drew away from the Virgin Islands, the wind was rising. She was below, plotting their position, when she heard the autopilot begin to beep, and she hurried on deck to find it holding the tiller far up to weather as the boat tried to round up into the wind. The mainsheet traveler was already all the way down to leeward, so she eased the sheet and the boat came upright as the beeping stopped, but now the mainsail was flogging. She took in the mainsheet until the sail partially filled, then stood wondering what she should do next. Then she heard his voice say, "Needs a reef" and saw Stroud coming out of the cabin. "I'll do it. Ease the mainsheet."

He went forward to the mast in his bare feet—he never went barefoot on deck and would not let her do it—and dropped the halyard to the first mark, winched in the reef lines, coiled and stowed them, and then without another word, went below and fell into his bunk.

By the time she had trimmed the mainsail and gone back to the nav station to plot a course that would take them safely north of Puerto Rico and Hispaniola, he was already asleep. She decided if he wasn't better by the time they were off San Juan in about seventy more miles, she'd give up the chase and get him to a hospital.

This time she made a thermos of coffee to go with the half of a deli sandwich she ate for breakfast in the cockpit. There was a lot of steamer traffic now, and she didn't want to let *Lullaby* sail blind for very long.

At midmorning, when she came below to plot their position, he stirred when she touched his forehead, said "Whaa?" again, and staggered into the head. She heard him dry-heaving in there, and when he finally came out she said, "Bill, I'm going to land in San Juan. You should see a doctor."

"Like hell. And how did we get to San Juan?" He sat down on the edge of his bunk and stared at his feet. "I'll be okay. Awful thirsty, though."

She went up into the cockpit locker for another bottle of Gatorade, but when she returned, he was asleep again. His fever might have been a little better. She wasn't sure.

All that day, *Lullaby* reached westward toward Great Inagua Island with the trade winds and the long seas they had built over the winter driving her so fast that the wind appeared to be blowing from ahead of the beam, although it was actually on her starboard quarter. Lydia had not slept for almost two days now, and she sat in the cockpit willing herself to stay awake, as the steamer traffic to and from the Mona Passage between Puerto Rico and Hispaniola grew heavier.

Every two hours she went below, plotted their position, and searched for something to eat that would not involve cooking. When she had eaten the last of the now-soggy deli sandwiches, she switched to peanut butter and jelly, and when she could stand that no longer, she ate an entire package of Oreo cookies and two apples for supper.

There didn't seem to be much change in Stroud's condition. She kept telling herself that if it was the flu, it should break soon.

By five o'clock, the line of fixes had marched across the chart to a position northeast of San Juan, but when she went below, his fever seemed to be down and he was sleeping quietly, so she decided to press on. Although she did not realize it then, after two days without sleep, she was incapable of making any new decisions. She could only acquiesce with decisions already made.

When Alice came on deck just before sunset, there seemed to be a line of dark clouds right at the edge of the horizon behind them. Granny was sitting in the T behind the wheel, but the autopilot was steering. She sat down opposite him and looked aft as she said, "I think it's finally going to get here. I wonder if we should change down to the smaller jib."

"You're supposed to do it the first time it crosses your mind, aren't you? And changing these roller furling things is no picnic."

"I know. But in the breeze we have now, she needs that big jib. I want to hang on to it as long as I can. If it comes on to blow tonight, we'll either partially roll it up or roll it up all the way and set the staysail."

"How does she go under a reefed main and the staysail?"

"I don't know; I haven't tried it yet."

"Alice, why are we in such a hurry to get south through the Caribbean? I thought we were going to have a leisurely cruise down through the Bahamas."

"I want to get well south of the hurricane belt before the middle of July. I told you that. The storms have been coming sooner, more frequently, and farther south in the last few years."

"That's what I told my mother. But you act like you're in a race or something."

At midnight, the norther hit them like a bucket of ice water. One moment Alice was knitting in the cockpit on a warm, hazy, pleasant night while *Noriecka* sailed herself in the light southwesterly breeze. The next moment the boat was thrown onto the other tack as the wind came roaring out of the northwest, the mainsail crashed across, and the jib was forced against the mast and stays, pushing the boat over on her side. Alice let the jib sheet run and tossed her knitting up under the dodger as the boat came up on her feet and Evans came up the companionway. "What happened?"

"The norther is here." It was already appreciably colder. "Help me get the jib rolled up. Free the sheet." The flogging sails were making so much noise that in order to be heard, she had to shout into his ear. He freed the windward sheet, and as the sail blew across the boat, she got two turns of the leeward sheet onto the winch and tried to minimize the flogging. He crossed the cockpit, knelt on the seat beside her, and hauled on the furler line that turned the drum at the base of the headstay to roll the sail around it.

He could barely move it, so he put the line on the other winch and began to laboriously crank it in. The sail was furled about a third of the way when he stopped cranking, afraid that he would break the line. "Something's jammed."

"Maybe that's enough." She cranked the sheet winch backwards, in the low-speed direction, until the sail filled, but the boat immediately heeled over in the rising wind and buried the lee side deck. Alice eased the sheet and yelled, "Go clear it" as the jib started to flog again, adding its racket to the noise the mainsail was making.

He turned on the spreader lights and went forward, clinging with one hand to the rail that ran along the leeward deckhouse roof while trying to find a knot or kink in the furler line with the other. He wasn't even to the mast when he had to crouch low on hands and knees to keep from being brained by the wildly swinging corner of the jib, or from having his head pulled off like the stem from a cherry by the flailing sheets. Finally he got to the bow, and having found nothing wrong with the furler line, sat facing aft on the pulpit that surrounded the short, plank bowsprit, studying the drum. After a few seconds he kicked it fiercely several times, then motioned for her to try it. She tried it and shook her head in an exaggerated "No" motion. Then she motioned him to come back to the cockpit.

This time he came along the weather side so he didn't have to dodge that homicidal jib, and when he got to the cockpit she gave him a handful of sail ties and said, "Get the main down. I know what we have to do." With the wind trying to blow both him and the sail off the boat, it took him what seemed like hours to tie it in messy bundles on the boom. But when it was done, at least the noise was a little less. "Look, Granny. I'm going to start the engine, but before I put it in gear, you have to get hold of the sheets as close to the jib as you can and cut them, then pull them aboard. Make absolutely sure we don't have any lines in the water that can foul the prop. You got that?"

She only hoped the engine had enough guts to push the boat repeatedly through the eye of the rising wind. It was all right for maneuvering the boat in and out of harbors in flat water, but it did not develop the power to push the boat anywhere near as fast as it should have. Emil suspected that the folding propeller was not the right one for the boat. She had wanted to have something done about it in Jacksonville, but just hadn't been able to find time. Now she wished with all her heart that she had made the time.

As he started to climb out of the cockpit Evans yelled, "Okay. I don't know why you want me to do it, but okay."

That part of it went amazingly well; when he cut the second sheet, the sail flew straight out in front of the boat and she put the engine in gear and proceeded to motor in circles, each circle unwinding one turn of the jib from around the headstay. The wind was already beginning to build up a sea, so each of the dozen or so circles it took was more difficult as it became harder and harder for the engine to push the boat's head up through the eye of the wind.

By the time the sail was fully unwound, it was in shreds from flogging against the shrouds and the inner forestay each time they turned through the wind. A half-dozen seams had been torn apart and the canvas suncover along the leach was separated for its entire length, held only by the headboard and the grommet at its clew. With the engine wide open, she set the autopilot to steer the boat into the howling wind and stinging drops of cold water that might be spray or rain and were probably both, as he went forward to the bow to pull the sail down. When she was sure the autopilot and engine could just hold the boat's head into the wind, she went to the mast to ease the halyard. As the sail came out of the track that ran up the stay, there was nothing to hold it, so it immediately slithered under the lifelines into the sea like some flat, white reptile intent on devouring the propeller. Alice let the halyard run and rushed forward to help him drag the damn thing back on deck before it reached the prop.

When the remains of the thoroughly evil jib were finally captured in a bag and tossed below where they could do no more harm, Alice and Granny hoisted the double-reefed main and the staysail, shut down the engine, and bore off to the southeast. Finally.

Once the boat had been trimmed and the autopilot was holding it on course, they went below, where he stuffed the remains of the jib into the quarter berth. Then they stripped off their wet clothes and toweled themselves dry, because they were even too tired to dry each other. When he had pulled on a dry sweatsuit, Evans slumped into the corner of a bunk and said, "I wonder who the bastard was who invented the roller furling jib. What a labor-saving device that fucking thing is. You've been through that drill before. I could tell."

"Three or four years ago. I should have learned my lesson then. They always crap out at the worst possible moment. As soon as we get somewhere where there's a sailmaker, I'm going to get piston hanks put on all the headsails and heave that fucking roller thing overboard."

"We're going to need a new number one, anyway."

She didn't answer him because she was plotting their position from the GPS. Then she said, "That labor-saving device up on the bow that makes sail handling so easy, helped us to make good five miles in the last three hours, mostly in the wrong direction."

"I suppose one of us ought to be on deck. Whose watch is it, anyway?"

"I'm too tired to remember."

At two in the morning, Lydia had now been forty-three hours without sleep; she sat under the dodger facing aft and fighting to stay awake by standing up every few minutes and searching all around. They were almost due north of the Mona Passage now, and the lights of ships were all around them. She must have dozed off for a minute or an hour—she had no way of knowing—but when she awoke, a teenaged girl was steering the boat. "Hi. I'm Nell—Eleanor really, but everyone calls me Nell. Not Nellie. I hate being called Nellie. I think you're going to have to do something about the sails, Lydia. The poor boat's on her ear and I'm having a devil of a time keeping her on course. She has a terrible hard mouth."

The odd part of it was, that although Lydia knew she was hallucinating, she also knew that the wind really had risen and the boat really was hard-pressed.

She asked the girl, "What should I do?"

"Get Daddy. My daddy always knows what to do. Just like your daddy."

"Your daddy's sick, and I don't think I should disturb him. Can't we just go on like this until he gets better?"

"You could drop the main."

"Won't that slow her down a lot? We're in an awful hurry."

"Oh, I know that. Daddy and Dwight and I are always in a hurry whenever we go anyplace in a boat."

Lydia must have dozed off again, because when she looked up, the girl was gone, a lot of banging and slatting was going on, and the autopilot was beeping because it could no longer hold the course. Nell had been right; Lydia had to do something about the sails. She just wished she knew what. Maybe if she took just a little nap it would clear her mind enough so she could figure out what to do.

Then she came fully awake with a start. They were head to wind with the sails flogging wildly and the boat bouncing up and down in the same spot, and she knew that if she didn't do something right then, any minute something was going to shake loose or break. She freed the tiller from the autopilot and forced it over until the boat fell off, fortunately onto the proper tack. Then, as *Lullaby* began to make headway, she put the autopilot back onto the tiller. When it began to beep again, she let the mainsheet traveler down to the stop, and when that didn't help, she slacked the mainsheet until the sail was again flogging but the beeping stopped.

When she looked forward, Nell was standing with her back to the mast and said, "You'd better not let that brand-new sail flog like that for long or Daddy will be awful mad."

Lydia was almost in tears. "I don't know what to do. Please tell me what to do."

"Get Daddy." Then the girl was gone again.

"Bill, can you hear me? Wake up."

"What? What's the matter? What?"

"The wind is still rising and I don't know what to do. Bill, can you understand me? Are you all right?"

"Yes. Yes. I understand you. What time is it? Am I due to relieve you on watch?"

"You were due to relieve me twenty-eight hours ago. I wouldn't disturb you, Bill, but I don't know what to do and I have to get some sleep. I've started to hallucinate."

He slowly moved to a sitting position on the edge of the bunk and stared at the cabin sole between his feet. "Give me a minute." Then more to himself than to her he said, "I can do this." He pulled on a pair of trousers and his foul-weather jacket, then labored to a standing position, bracing himself against the motion of the boat by holding with both hands to the grab rails bolted to the overhead.

She asked, "Do you want something to eat?"

"Don't know if I could hold it down. Better not chance it. Just some water, I guess." She handed him the bottle of Gatorade that stood in the galley sink and he drank thirstily as the boat rolled, sloshing it on the front of his tee shirt through the unfastened jacket. He didn't seem to notice. "Get some shut-eye, Lydia. I've got her."

"Will you need help changing sails?"

"No. I'm all right. You get some sleep."

She awoke when the rising sun shone down the hatch into her face, feeling more refreshed than she could ever remember feeling in her life. The boat seemed to be sailing quite well, except that there was an odd clicking sound that she could not place. When she climbed into the cockpit, he was sitting huddled in the corner of the cockpit with his knees drawn up to his chest and a sail bag wrapped around his shoulders. He was soaking wet; the clicking noise was his teeth chattering. He had changed down to the Number 4 jib and put the third reef in the main, and *Lullaby* was showing her gratitude by reaching along like an express train with only a moderate degree of heel. It was still blowing hard.

"Bill, I'll take over now. Get below into some dry clothes. You're freezing."

Noriecka was finally beginning to make some miles down toward 24 North, where she should find the trade winds. Maybe it would be at 25 if they were lucky, or closer to 23 if they weren't. But if this norther would just hold till then . . . It certainly showed no signs of weakening. With the double-reefed main and the staysail, she was doing a steady seven and a half. This boat wasn't the total dog Alice had feared. *Cinderella,* with her more modern underbody but wider beam, wouldn't have been doing any better. Maybe old Carl Alberg who had designed her and given her a full keel underbody and moderate beam knew what he was doing, after all. She had done 161 miles in the twenty-four hours since they had gotten the number one off her at dawn yesterday and started to ride the norther southeastward.

Granny was out at the end of the short plank bowsprit, wedged backwards between the headstay and the pulpit, in the absolutely worst place on the boat to work on a piece of machinery, trying to free the roller furler drum by forcing it back and forth and spraying it with penetrating oil. Every time *Noriecka* stuck her nose into the back of a sea, he and the drum would get dowsed. He finally came aft and told Alice, "It's stuck solid. I'll need some tools to take it apart."

"Forget it. Don't even try; that thing connects the headstay to the bowsprit, and that's what supports the top of the mast. Besides, it's full of little pieces, and your chance of not dropping at least some of them overboard is about zero."

He seemed greatly relieved, but now whenever they wanted to hoist a jib, they'd both have to be on the foredeck, one feeding its leading edge into the slot in the track that ran up the headstay, while the other was at the mast, hoisting it. Getting it down in a rising wind would be the same, only worse, because then someone would have to lie on the damn thing to keep it from sliding overboard as it was freed.

By noon, *Lullaby* was across the Mona Passage, roaring along the north coast of Hispaniola, although it was out of sight over the horizon to the south. When Stroud came up to relieve Lydia, it was a beautiful Caribbean day: blue water, blue sky, whitecaps, and white clouds. "Hi. I made some sandwiches." He handed them to her. "Hold these while I shake a reef. I think she needs more sail."

When it was done, she handed him his sandwich and said, "It's good to see you up and taking nourishment. How do you feel?"

"Better. Pretty fragile, like I'm made out of glass, but much better. I'm out of that twilight zone where you don't know if you're awake or asleep. It's nice to be back among the living."

"Bill, I feel bad about rousting you out the way I did. But I'd reached the end of my rope. I was hallucinating, and I really couldn't trust my own judgment about what to do about the boat."

"Tell me about your hallucinations. Anything specific?"

She debated whether to tell him about Nell or not, then thought *What the hell* and said, "Your daughter Nell was steering, not the autopilot, and she was complaining that she couldn't control the boat any longer. Too hard-mouthed, she said."

"How old was she?"

"Oh, about thirteen or fourteen, I'd guess. She had blond hair in braids and looked a lot like you. Funny how detailed it was. I can even remember that she was wearing a sort of baseball cap with horns like those on a Viking helmet."

He thought about it for quite a while before he said, "She was thirty-eight when she died, but at fourteen she was, pound for pound, the best sailboat steerer on Long Island Sound."

"Oh, she knew what she was doing, all right. She insisted on my getting you up to change sails. Funny the tricks an over-tired mind plays."

He took a bite of his sandwich and slowly chewed it as he stared at the horizon. Then he said, "It was a fourteen-year-old Nell who helped me change down the jib and tie in the third reef when all I wanted to do was lie down on the cockpit sole and lapse back into the twilight zone. And she was wearing that wacky cap with the Viking horns she always wore when we sailed together back then."

They were silent for a long time, and then he went forward to change up to the number three. They never mentioned that night again.

Noriecka found the trades before midnight. The norther had started to die out in midafternoon, growing puffier and flukier as the day wore on and they crossed 25 north. By sunset, what wind was left had backed into the southwest again, and the boat was bouncing around awkwardly and barely making any headway through the leftover seas. If they had

had a number one, they might have set it, but instead they pulled down the staysail, sheeted the main amidships to damp the rolling, and ran on the engine. By 2000 they began to feel a few puffs from the northeast, and by midnight, they were steering due south for the Ciacos Passage with the northeast trades abeam and the main, the staysail, and a jib topsail all pulling like mules.

By 1400 on Saturday afternoon, *Lullaby* had passed Cape Isabella, the most northerly point of Hispaniola, although they couldn't see it because it was twenty miles beyond their southern horizon. They altered course to due west and had 120 miles to go before they could turn south into the Windward Passage. The course change brought the wind almost astern and knocked the speed down to barely five knots for the first time since they had started across the Anegada.

Stroud said, "Time for the hell machine again." He looked for it in the cockpit sail locker, and then remembered that he had put it below but never repacked it. He found it where it had been tossed into the V-berth forward, and dumped it out of its bag in the center of the main cabin. They had originally been called parachute spinnakers, and packing one so it could be hoisted untwisted was a lot like packing a parachute, except the seven-hundred-square-foot sail had to be sorted and packed in a space not much bigger than the interior of a luxury car.

When he was done, he lugged it up into the cockpit, and just as every other man about to set a spinnaker at sea has done, he asked himself if the boat wouldn't go just as well with a jib set out on the pole. And, just as every honest man who had asked himself that question has done, he set the spinnaker. But he was damn glad *Lullaby*'s fractional rig gave her a kite of manageable size. He wasn't sure he'd have nerve enough to set a masthead spinnaker in these conditions.

Lydia had come on deck to help him get it up and drawing, and now with the boat again averaging better than six knots, they settled down to watch *Lullaby* slow as she climbed each of the long rollers the trade wind had built as it blew in the same direction for months, and then accelerate as she slid down the other side.

Without any prologue he said, "I remembered where I heard the word *Noriecka* before, and it has me more than a little worried."

"Oh? Why?"

"Do you remember an old John Wayne movie called *The Searchers?*"

"I think so. It had Ward Bond in it. I always liked Ward Bond. They were chasing some Indians who had kidnapped Natalie Wood. Is that the one? Why would that worry you?"

"Yeah. That one. Anyway, somebody in it says the tribe they're looking for is the Noriecka Comanche, and Wayne says something like, 'It means wanders like the wind. Man says he's going one place and goes another.'"

"You mean they might not be headed for Panama or the Windward Passage at all?"

"Alice Kettner—Alice Evans, at the moment—is one cagey lady, and I can't believe she'd tell her mother-in-law where they were going."

"But Evans would. Evans is not all that cagey." Then she had another idea. "Maybe she knew you'd know what Noriecka meant, and named the boat that so . . . You know, fake and double-fake."

"And triple-fake. That's why I'm worried. They could be headed east across the pond toward the Mediterranean, for all we know, and we've just come 500 miles downwind in the wrong direction. Not much we can do now, though. We're committed to the Windward Passage. But if I'd remembered what *Noriecka* meant back in St. Martin, it would have made deciding which way to go even tougher."

"Maybe you were supposed to remember what it meant back in St. Martin. Maybe that's what she expected."

"You mean only having about two dozen functioning brain cells left is one of the advantages of old age? Oh, another thing I forgot. Did you ever hear from your lawyer in Jacksonville?"

"I called her, I think it was two days ago, when we were close to Puerto Rico. I'll tell you, my mind is more than a little fuzzy, too. She could find no record of any Cape Dory 36s being sold on the east coast of Florida or Georgia in the last month, so she was starting to see if any were missing."

"I suppose there's no point in trying to call her now."

"There's no cell-phone coverage in this part of the world."

The sun was just setting when Alice came up into the cockpit and said to Granny, "Only another twenty-five miles or so to the entrance of the Caicos Passage."

"Are you sure you want to run it in the dark? I was reading the cruising guide, and Caicos Island is ringed with reefs. It said you should use extreme caution when approaching it. Maybe we should wait for dawn."

"The reefs are all close to the northwest side of the island and on the bank that runs south and east of it. We'll get a GPS position every fifteen minutes to be sure we aren't getting set down on them. It's a straight shot through: no turns or doglegs. The only thing we have to worry about is Hog Sty Reef northwest of Inagua Island, and we won't be there until well after dawn."

"I just don't know why you're in such a hurry."

"Come on. Don't be such a sissy. You aren't a sissy, are you, Granny?" She reached into his shorts. "You don't look like a sissy, a big strong man like you." A few seconds later she continued, "And you certainly don't feel like one."

Afterwards, they ran the Caicos Passage in the dark.

By Sunday morning, the wooded mountains of Tortuga were visible on the southern horizon, so they jibed *Lullaby*'s spinnaker and headed southwest into the Windward Passage. After the jibe and a late breakfast, Stroud spent an hour at the chart table, then stood in the hatch and said to Lydia, "I think we may have set some kind of record for a passage from St. Martin to Tortuga for boats less than twenty-four feet on the waterline. About 540 miles over the ground in under four days. The log says we had to go 602 miles through the water to do it. We were lucky with the winds, though, and we've had a favorable current pushing us for most of the way, as well. But the old girl likes to pick up her skirts and run, doesn't she? You did one hell of a job of sailing her, too, Lydia."

"What do we do now, Bill? Or are we like the dog that finally catches a car?"

"I was just working on that. To begin with, even giving them the most favorable conditions once they caught that norther the radio talked about, working from where you saw them on Wednesday morning— God, was that only Wednesday? It seems like a month ago. Anyway, I don't see how *Noriecka* could have gotten here yet. So now the problem becomes, how do we patrol the passage. It's just under fifty miles wide. They won't want to go into Cuban territorial waters, and neither do we, so that means staying fifteen miles or so off to have a three-mile margin. Same for Haiti. I don't think anyone wants to get boarded by one of their patrol boats, either. If it happens to us, we could raise the Stars and Stripes and scream for the U.S. Navy. Guantanamo Bay is only seventy miles away. But I don't think the Evans family wants to get tangled up with any kind of authority, since it looks as if they didn't buy the boat. So that leaves about twenty miles down the middle, about as wide as Long Island Sound between Milford and Port Jefferson—nothing Nelson couldn't patrol with three frigates. The passage is about twenty-five miles long."

"Okay. How far away do you think we can see them, if it stays clear like this?"

He pointed at the heavy volume of *The American Practical Navigator* lying on the chart table. "According to my trusty *Bowditch*, about eight miles. If you're standing on top of the cabin at the mast, most of *Noriecka's* rig should be visible over your horizon at that distance. I only wish we had radar, although that would only tell us there was a boat, not if it was them. There are northbound and southbound ship traffic lanes, each about five miles wide with a five-mile-wide separation zone between them. To avoid getting run down, any yacht rounding Great Inagua

Island to port and then Punta Maisi on the tip of Cuba to starboard and headed for either Jamaica or the Canal, would stay over on the western side of the passage, outside of the southbound steamship lane. That's probably what they'll do. But they may not. If I were them, trying to dodge me, I'd go across to the other side and run down the edge of Haitian waters, beyond the northbound lane. We should cover both sides, but Frederick the Great said that to defend everything is to defend nothing. I don't know."

"What about at night? Especially with all this traffic." There were four steamships in sight at the moment.

"That's worse. I think we should work our way across the passage this afternoon until we're fifteen miles or so off Point Miasi on Cuba. Then at dusk we'll jibe and sail southwest during the night, diagonally back across. That should put us at the south end of the passage on the Haitian side around dawn. Then we'll come about and head back toward Cuba during the day, aiming to be off Cape Miasi again at sunset."

There were now five steamers in sight: two containerships and three tankers. "Bill, isn't that like strolling back and forth across I-95 at the rush hour?"

"That's why both of us will have to go on the night shift. No more six on and six off. From sunset to dawn we'll both have to be on watch, both to watch for *Noriecka* and to keep from being run down. We'll split the daylight hours right in half and sleep then. If you have any better ideas, Lydia, I'd sure like to hear them. But unless you can come up with those three frigates . . . "

By late Sunday afternoon the low-lying smudge of Great Inagua Island was visible to port as *Noriecka* ran southwest. Evans thought it looked rather like Block Island and said so to Alice as she came up after plotting yet another GPS fix. She looked over at it and agreed with him, although the truth was that she had never seen Block Island. Then she said, "I've got some stew on the stove. Let's eat and then I'll turn in. We'll hold this course until midnight. If the wind drops, and I think it might, start the engine and keep her going at about five and a half. Now that I think of it, in any case, start the engine and run it for a couple of hours. The batteries need it. At midnight, I'll relieve you and we'll turn due south for the Windward Passage. By this time tomorrow night, we should be through it and home free."

Lydia came on deck at sunset, and Stroud asked her, "Did you sleep?"

"A little, I guess. I take it you didn't see anything."

"Lots of tankers and freighters and a big ketch going north."

She handed him an odd-looking pair of binoculars. "I forgot I had these with me. I bought them when I was doing air searches in the Virgins."

He studied them and said, "12 by 36 I.S. These might work fine in an airplane, but on a boat with everything bouncing around, 7 power is about the most magnification you can see through." He had his own 7 by 50s hanging around his neck. "What does I.S. mean?"

"Image stabilized." She reached over and pushed a switch he hadn't noticed. "They have a little computer in them that automatically compensates for movement. Try them."

He lifted them to his eyes and focused on a ship a couple of miles off. "Boy, are these nice. They probably cost a bundle."

"Bill, you and I have so much money invested in this enterprise that another thousand here or there is peanuts." Then she said, "I'll be right back. I've got supper on the stove."

He called after her as he searched around the horizon with the glasses, "What's for supper?"

"Creamed tuna on toast."

"I'll make a WASP out of you yet."

They spent the night snaking their way through the ship traffic, Lydia steering most of the time while Stroud used a hand-bearing compass to determine if they were on a collision course with any of the ships. If they were, *Lullaby* did not follow the rule about steam keeping clear of sail; she followed the rule that says the greatest gross tonnage has the right of way and altered course immediately and radically. The only other pleasure craft they saw was a hundred-foot motor yacht that passed them going south just after midnight.

At dawn, he cooked a breakfast of scrambled eggs, and when he had washed the dishes, they turned *Lullaby* to windward and sheeted her in hard. The wind, which had softened during the night, filled in again from the north as the day warmed, and soon she was slicing along on the starboard tack under the full main and number three, headed north of west back across the passage. Stroud was below, trying to sleep in the port bunk.

They had decided to start back up the strait on this tack in case *Noriecka* had slipped behind them during the night, so, as they sailed across, Lydia sat on the windward side of the cockpit and concentrated her attention to the south. But every few minutes she would scan all around to see if there was any steamer traffic that needed dodging.

It was just after ten when she looked north and then used her glasses to study the boat running down toward her. She lowered the glasses, looked away for a second, then looked at it again and yelled, "Sail ho!"

It was hot in the cabin with the foredeck hatch closed to keep out the spray; Stroud had been barely dozing, although he had been up all night. When Lydia yelled, he was not quite sure if he was dreaming or not, so he stood in the companionway and asked, "Sail ho? Did you actually yell 'Sail ho'?"

"There's a boat running down toward us, Bill, and it's about the right size, I think. It's bow on."

He stepped into his deck shoes, stopped at the galley sink to splash some water on his face, and joined her in the cockpit. She handed him the glasses. He studied the oncoming yacht for a second and said, "Double-head rig, and the jib topsail seems to have a brown edge, but it's hard to tell. I can't see the dodger from here, but there's a logo on the main I can't quite make out. It could be a C." He put the glasses in the compartment cut into the lee coaming and started to uncleat the jib sheet. "Ready about."

She lifted the autopilot off the tiller bracket and said, "Helm's alee" as she pushed it over toward the boom. In twenty seconds they were on the port tack thrashing through the chop, and in two minutes it was obvious that they would pass the other boat to port within perhaps twenty yards. She asked, "Don't we want to stay ahead of them?"

"No. We want to get to weather of them. Besides, this way we're hidden by their headsails. They may not have seen us yet. I'll take her."

As he took the tiller she said, "Oh yes. The weather gauge. I've heard of that."

He snaked *Lullaby* to windward through the chop coming down the passage, steering closer to the wind in the flat spots and easing her off slightly when she needed more power to drive through the bigger waves. Lydia could do it, but not nearly so well. He anticipated in the way that a great jazz drummer always seems to be a millisecond ahead of the beat. When the boat came over a wave and entered a flat spot, he had already headed up five degrees, and he had eased her off just before any larger wave arrived, so she had the power to climb over it.

Alice had roused him at dawn as they came up on Cape Miasi saying, "Wake up, my darling; a beautiful new day is breaking, and the doorway to freedom is just ahead of us."

Now she was asleep below, and he was watching as *Noriecka* slid past Cape Caleta and the shore of Cuba started to fall away to the west. The autopilot was steering, and Granny was planning exactly how Alice and he would celebrate once they were in the open sea. The last day and a half of navigating on soundings had worn them both out, but this afternoon . . . He lost himself in fantasy for a few minutes, but was brought back to reality by a sound he had heard many times in his racing days: the flogging of sails that starts and stops almost instantaneously as another boat passes through the cone of bad air to leeward of your own boat. He looked under *Noriecka's* boom and there, just emerging from behind the headsails, was the one thing on earth he did not want to see, a Hallberg-Rassy 29. What made it even worse, Polizzi and Stroud both waved at him as they passed.

When they were fifty yards to weather of *Noriecka*'s transom, Stroud gave Lydia the tiller and said, "Ready about," then crossed the cockpit and freed the sheet. As *Lullaby*'s bow came through the eye of the wind, he hauled in the jib sheet so quickly that it took only two or three cranks on the winch to have it properly trimmed. He pulled the mainsheet traveler to weather and, as they crossed the stern of *Noriecka, Stanford, CT,* said, "I think this is when we're supposed to fire a raking broadside into them."

He seemed to be kidding, but Lydia replied, "But we won't, will we, Bill? We're going to dog them until they land someplace where we can turn them and their stolen boat over to the authorities."

"I sure would like to know where that boat came from."

A woman Stroud assumed was Alice Kettner was looking over at them, so Stroud gave her a friendly wave as he handed Lydia the binoculars and asked, "Is that the bitch that tried to blow me up?"

She studied the face glaring at her across twenty yards of water. "That's her."

"Funny. I know her so well but this is the first time I've ever seen her. She looks so ordinary." They were rapidly drawing past *Noriecka*'s wake now, and Stroud said, "Ready about," and then, "You're sure you don't want to give them a broadside?"

He still might be kidding, but Lydia wondered. "I'm sure. Helm's alee." Once they had tacked, she once more looked at *Noriecka* through the glasses. "Boy, is that woman pissed. They can't get away from us, can they? I mean, are there some conditions where they're faster than we are?"

"Nah. They've got that baggy roller-furling jib topsail, and probably an even bigger and baggier jib down below, and no spinnaker. They've got a longer waterline, so if their engine is big enough, they might be able to outrun us in a motorboat race in a flat calm, but that's not likely to happen."

"So we can just stay maybe a mile or so away and dog them wherever they go?"

"Sure. But not forever. Nothing lasts forever."

"But until we get somewhere where there's a cell-phone connection so we can verify that they stole that boat and then call the cops?"

"You think that's what the dog should do, now that he's finally caught the car?"

"What else can we do?" Then it dawned on her. "You've still got that rifle, don't you?"

"It's under a false bottom in the table pedestal, under the wine rack, just in case."

"Leave it there. They've got to make port sometime. They've been at sea over a week now."

"Just pray they don't head for St. James. I really don't want to explain this to Superintendent Sandburn."

"It looks like they're heading for Panama. And you said yourself, there's no way they can outrun us."

"I didn't say there's no way they can give us the slip, though. Okay. We'll dog them. But we cannot let that woman get away to do more harm. We cannot let that happen, Lydia."

CHAPTER THIRTEEN

That damned boat positioned itself a half a mile or so behind them, and then turned and followed in their wake. Evans started the engine and tried to motorsail away, but the breeze kept filling in, and pretty soon they could see someone working on the foredeck, and then a spinnaker blossomed, and if anything, the Hallberg seemed to be catching up as it surfed down the following seas. Then the foot of the sail was pulled narrower and the leading edge stopped fluttering as it was intentionally overtrimmed, and the Hallberg dropped back to its station a half a mile or so behind.

Evans noticed that Alice did not deal with it well. No, that wasn't right. She dealt with it strangely. When she first came up into the cockpit and saw Stroud and Polizzi she was obviously very angry, but she was also icily calm. She watched the other boat for a few moments after it tacked in their wake, and then she seemed to reach a conscious decision to emotionally collapse. She suddenly started to shake as she said, "It's them: that awful Polizzi woman you told me about and that Stroud." She hurried down into the cabin as if to flee from them, and said, more to herself than to him, " I thought I had put it all behind me, but I'll never escape from what Gordon did."

Evans checked around the horizon and *Lullaby* was the only other vessel in sight at the moment, so he turned on the autopilot and followed Alice down into the cabin. "Is that why we've been in such a rush? Will you please tell me, once and for all, what's going on? Every time I think I'm beginning to understand you, you suddenly change into someone else. It's like being married to the bride from outer space."

She looked out the hatch at *Lullaby*'s mast. "They aren't gaining on us. I wonder what they're up to?"

But Evans kept after her. "Don't worry about that. Tell me why they're here in the first place."

At least she had stopped shaking. She took a deep breath and steeled herself like a little Mother Courage. "I'm positive that Gordon robbed people and I'm pretty sure he killed people. But for a long time I couldn't admit it even to myself. He always seemed like such a sweet, 'aw shucks, ma'am' sort of guy. But I don't think Polizzi's parents and niece are in any witness protection program. He told me, and I told you, that they wanted to sell the Grand Banks because the mob was after them. Gordon went out into the Anegada with them, but when he met me in Anguilla he was alone. He told me they had sold him the boat, and the Coast Guard had picked them up and taken them someplace safe. I always suspected something was wrong with his story, but I could never admit it to myself." She started to cry and between sobs said, "He may have killed them."

Evans handed her a paper towel from the roll over the sink and asked, "And Stroud—why is he after you?"

Another mood change as she stopped crying and became almost testy. "I don't know. Maybe it's something Gordon did to him that I don't know about. Or maybe he's just Polizzi's boyfriend along for the ride."

"No. He was looking for you before . . . Wait a minute. When he showed up at the Ginger Bay Marina he wasn't looking for you and Gordon. He didn't know who you were. He was looking for *Cinderella*. Where did Gordon get her?"

"I don't know. He bought her in the States after he piled our other boat on the bricks off Nevis. At least he told me he bought her in Carolina someplace. I was in Connecticut visiting my folks when he called me, and I met him in Charleston and we brought her down here."

"Last January you told me if I sent them on a wild goose chase to Jamaica and then to Antigua they'd just keep going south until they got tired of looking and went home."

"I thought they would, too." Then she appeared to think of something. "Oh God. *Cinderella*. The people we sold her to blew her up in St. James. It was in the Florida papers. I told them the solenoid valve on the propane line to the stove was sticking and I even showed them where the spare was in the toolbox. They said they'd change it when they got around to it. I tried to tell them it was important, but they were in a rush to go cruising. I'll probably get blamed for that, too. Oh Lord, what am I going to do?"

Now she started to cry again, so he hugged her while he thought about it. "That Vindo 38 I sold for him—where did Gordon get it?"

Now she was the picture of bravery as she sniffled, wiped her eyes and nose with the soggy paper towel she had been clutching, and then said, "He lied to you. He didn't buy it cheap from some drug smuggler on the lam, like he told you. It came into a cove in Bequia one night, fresh from an Atlantic crossing with a Swedish couple on board. They were exhausted and had sailed right past Barbados. We were the only other boat in the cove, but they managed to hit us as they were trying to get the anchor down. Gordon rowed over in a rage and an hour later he came back, got his stuff, and told me to have you find a buyer for the boat and meet him in St. James."

"But he had a bill of sale."

"He has a guy in Miami who will make him any kind of phony paperwork he wants. And face it, Granny, neither you nor that buyer asked a lot of questions or looked too closely at the ship's papers."

"For that price no one was going to ask questions or look too closely at paperwork. But how did Stroud and Polizzi follow us here?"

She sat down on the head of the quarter berth. "They had a picture of Gordon; I don't know where they got it. He must have done something to Stroud that I don't know about; maybe that's where they got it. They were going all over Florida showing it to people. I found out about it and told Gordon. That's what started that last fight we had. That's probably why he took off when I called the cops. Not because he was afraid they'd arrest him for something as unimportant as abusing me." She broke down again and cried more real tears, but as he started to reach for her, she waved him away and went on, "Oh darling, we are so good together, and I thought I was finally free of him and we could have a life together . . . They say that when you find the right person it's like finding the other half of yourself, and that's how I feel with you. And I don't just mean the sex. The night the roller furler crapped out we worked so well together. But now it's all over. Even though I sensed what Gordon was, I couldn't bring myself to believe it. The whole thing was just too preposterous to be true. Things like that just don't happen to nice girls who grew up on Shippan Point and went to Sweet Briar."

This time she sobbed into her hands for a minute, then looked up and continued, "Those two are going to follow us wherever we go, and they'll have me arrested the minute we land anyplace. But I don't want you hurt by this. We'll go to Kingston and I want you to get on the first plane for the States and never look back. When you're safe, I'll give myself up and they can do whatever they want with me."

"I won't do that, Alice. You're my wife. We've got plenty of food and fuel, we're better sailors than those two, and we've got a bigger boat. Right now the weather is in their favor. But it's got to change, and when it does we'll either outrun them or give them the slip."

All that day the two boats ran south as Evans kept the deck and Alice lay in a bunk, only getting up occasionally to go into the head. Every time he looked down into the hatch and saw her come out and lie down again, she looked older. It was as if his beautiful young wife was aging into a hag as he watched.

The wind dropped as they moved into the lee of the mountains of Haiti and left the northeast trades for the different weather patterns that prevail along the southern shores of the Greater Antilles. At midafternoon, Evans started the engine and dropped his headsails and

Stroud did the same. But an hour later their headsails were up and drawing again as they reached in the southwesterly sea breeze that the warm land of Haiti drew toward itself.

When Alice came on deck at sunset, she looked terrible. Her complexion was the gray of wet cement; the only colors in her face were the puffed, reddened rims of her eyes and the blue-black shadows beneath them. "I'll take over now, darling. You get some rest. I made you a can of soup. It's on the stove. I'm sorry I don't feel up to cooking you a better meal. Get some rest."

As he went below he said, "I'll turn on the running lights."

"Yeah. It's about that time."

Stroud and Polizzi decided to stick with their system of only sleeping during the day, but it was wearing on them and they didn't say much as they motored south following *Noriecka's* stern running light after the land breeze died. Every two hours, one of them would go below, plot their position, and come back on deck with two mugs of coffee and perhaps a snack or a couple of pieces of fruit.

At two in the morning, both boats were running under power as a tanker slid by a half-mile or so to port. Lydia lost sight of *Noriecka's* stern light in the clutter of the hundreds of lights that lit the tanker's decks, but when it was past, the running light was gone. Stroud was dozing under the dodger, and he woke with a start when she said, "Bill. Wake up. Their running light disappeared."

He peered over the bow for a second, then climbed up on the cabin top and slowly searched the 180-degree sector ahead with the stabilized glasses. Then he said, "Shit. Gone." As he went below to look at the chart, he handed her the glasses and said, "Keep looking."

Two minutes later he returned to the cockpit and said, "Come right to 350" as he shoved the throttle up to 85 percent power. Any more than that just pulled down the boat's stern without pushing her any faster.

"You think they bore off to the west?"

"No. Due west there's nothing but the Caymans and then the Yucatan and when you get there every other place on earth is a long beat to weather. I don't think they just turned off their lights and high-tailed for Kingston, either. Too easy for us to catch them there."

"You think they're sneaking across the shipping channels, running dark?"

"That's what I'd do, if I wanted to get away from me."

"Then why are we going west?"

"If they see us following them, they'll turn off in some other direction and we'll lose them for sure."

"If they get run down, it will solve our problem."

"I suppose so." He reached down and turned off *Lullaby*'s running lights, then looked aft. A few minutes later he said, "Okay. That's long enough, and there's as wide a hole in traffic as we're probably going to get. Come around and head east."

As she turned the boat she said, "Of course, if we get run down, it will solve their problem, too. Are you sure you want to run without lights?"

"Don't worry about it. None of these ships has anyone on lookout, anyway."

When Alice swung toward the path of the tanker that was about to overtake them, she thought she had plenty of room to cross, but as the waterfall noise of its bow wave and its huge black side got closer, she realized it was coming much faster, and the distance they had to go to get across was much farther, than she had thought. Now Granny was screaming at her to bear off, but she kept on as the white wave and the black wall behind it bore down on them. If it hit them, so what. Getting ground to bits would be worth the exhilaration she felt right now.

Then they were across and the bow wave shoved them bodily away from the ship as its crest poured over the transom and flooded the cockpit to their knees, and he sobbed with relief while she broke into hysterical laughter.

She stayed with him as they crossed the separation zone and then the northbound ship lane without incident. Then she said, "I think we're okay now, darling. We should be off Cape Carcasse at the southwest tip of Haiti by dawn." She looked over the side into the sea and said, "You know, from here we can go practically anyplace on earth. We're free."

But at dawn they found they were not free. In its gray light they saw *Lullaby* coming up over the horizon toward them, as relentless as death's angel.

When Alice saw her, she said only, "I'm going to lie down" and went below.

Hispaniola is so large and so high that most of the time it creates its own weather on its southern and western sides. During the day, as the tropical sun heats the land, the warm air above it rises and sucks in cooler air from the sea. This causes a westerly breeze to blow at its western end and a southerly to blow along its Caribbean coast. At night, when the land cools, the pattern is reversed as the cooling air falls, often bringing rain, and the wind blows away from the land.

As the sun rose higher that morning, the sea breeze filled in again, and Evans set the jib and staysail and beam reached on a course just south of east. It was *Noriecka's* best point of sail. When he looked back, Stroud had hoisted his main and number three, and Evans was sure that *Noriecka* was slowly pulling away. He had finally found some conditions where the Cape Dory was faster.

Then *Lullaby's* jib disappeared and she fell rapidly behind for a minute or two as she sailed bald headed on her mainsail alone. But then a bigger jib blossomed and she began to inexorably creep up again, so Evans hardened *Noriecka* up as close to the wind as she could sail, heading southeast now, and said out loud, "Okay asshole, let's see if you can move a boat to weather faster than a Star sailor."

He could. In a few minutes it became obvious that *Lullaby* was not only moving through the water faster, but was probably pointing five or ten degrees higher than *Noriecka* could under her jib and staysail. Evans mumbled, "This fucking Cape Dory cow with her whore's drawers sails…" What he wouldn't have given for a decent number-one jib to replace that torn-up roller furling thing.

At noon, with *Lullaby* still hanging half a mile off their weather quarter, Evans went below to check on Alice and, he hoped, get her to eat something. When he touched her shoulder and she rolled toward him, it was obvious that she had been sobbing in her bunk all morning. Her face was bloated, pasty, and old-looking. She seemed to have aged another ten years since dawn.

"They're still there, aren't they? I heard you trying to get away from them, trying to save me. But nothing works, does it? They're going to follow us no matter where we go, and have me arrested as soon as we get there."

"Get a hold of yourself, Alice. They can't punish you for what Gordon did."

"Don't you understand—it was piracy and murder, and you could be blamed for it, too. You helped him sell those boats. Granny, Gordon isn't here. He got away, and Polizzi and her Sicilian vendettas . . . ."

That threw his mind into an entirely new track, and without thinking he corrected her. "Corsican."

"Whatever. Will you please listen to me? Polizzi and her relatives are going to make sure someone pays for what Gordon did, and they only have us. I don't know about you, but I don't want to be at the mercy of the judicial system in one of these tin-pot islands. Not with the Polizzi Clan buying and intimidating the judges and juries." Then she wrapped her arms around him. "But I won't let them get you. I'll tell them you had no idea what Gordon was doing. You were just an honest yacht broker. I won't let them get you."

"I was. I was just an honest yacht broker that didn't know what was going on. And we'll get the best lawyers. And even if you have to spend a year or two in jail, I'll be waiting for you when you get out."

"Oh Granny, you still don't get it, do you? There won't be any getting out. Not for piracy and murder. I'll be lucky if I get life, if they don't hang me. They still hang people in these islands. Hang them by the neck until dead. How can I get you to understand how frightened I am? I've been laying here all morning thinking about what it will feel like when they put that sack over my head and that rough hemp rope around my neck. And if it's like everything else the damn West Indians do, they'll probably botch the job, and I'll hang there kicking while I slowly strangle, trying to scream, but unable to scream because my throat is being crushed by the rope." She sobbed helplessly, her face against his chest.

By now Evans was crying too as they clung to each other. "There must be some way out of this. If it weren't for Stroud and Polizzi . . . . There must be some way to make them leave us alone. I could talk to them—maybe I can reason with them and convince them that they should go after Gordon and leave us alone."

"You've met them. You know you can't reason with Polizzi and her no-neck relatives. And Stroud—when you tried to make a deal with him, he got you fired, didn't he? No. Let them do whatever they want to me, just as long as they don't hurt you. That's all I care about any more."

"I'll never leave you, Alice. You're my wife. There has to be some way . . . ."

She kept sobbing; he could feel her shaking with terror as he held her. And then she gasped out in the voice of a frightened child, "I just want that boat to go away. Make it go away, please Granny."

"Don't worry, Alice, I'll make them go away." Evans' voice was filled with alpha male decisiveness. "I know what I have to do, how to get free of those people for good. Late tonight, just before dawn when they're least on guard, we'll go back and T-bone them. We'll get going just as fast as we can and ram them amidships. It happens at turning marks in Star Boat races all the time, and the boat that does the ramming almost always survives, but the one that gets rammed usually goes straight to the bottom. This Cape Dory is built like a tank. That's what we'll do. And if *Noriecka* doesn't survive, at least we'll be together."

The paper towel roll was empty, so she took the dishtowel that hung on the oven handle, wiped her eyes and blew her nose into it, then handed it to him. "Oh Granny, you'd do that for me? Maybe we won't have to risk *Noriecka* to be rid of them, my darling. If you're willing to do such a thing, maybe there's a better way." With that she turned to the quarter berth and dragged out the bag containing the ruined number one and handed it to him. "Just toss this stuff in the V-berth for now." Then she gave a sad little smile and said, "Don't worry, Granny, we'll clear it out when we're free of them." The V-berth was one of his favorite places to catch her when they played nymphs and satyrs. Next she handed him the other sails, the duffels of unused clothes, the sleeping bags they might need if they ever got to a temperate climate, the briefcase with his business records, four life jackets, and a shopping bag of wedding gifts he thought they had left in Jacksonville. Then she dragged the bunk cushion up over the chart table, and crawled head first into the space until she could open the lid of a compartment hidden back there. She wiggled out of the space dragging a worn black backpack and causing his mind, as he watched her legs and hips move, to wander momentarily from the subject.

She sat up with the bag in her lap, and said, "Gordon left this in the back of a closet. I don't know what crimes he committed with it, but I suppose he hoped the cops would find it and blame them on me. I was going to drop it overboard once we were in deep water, but I never found the time or the opportunity." She opened the bag and laid a machine pistol and three banana clips of ammunition on the chart table. He looked at it as though she had dumped a coiled cobra on the chart table, so she continued, "No. I can't ask you to commit a crime in order to cover up Gordon's crimes. That's too much to ask. No matter what they do to me, I'll find a way to deal with it as long as nothing bad happens to you. We'll throw this overboard."

"I don't know if I could . . . Other than the saluting cannon when I was on the race committee, I've never even shot a gun. That one looks awfully complicated. I'm not all that good with machinery, anyway." But then he recovered his courage. "But if that's what it takes . . . But I don't know how to work a thing like that. You'll have to show me."

"That's all right. I know how to work it. You just steer the boat. We'll come up on them under power—no, they might hear the engine— we'll come up on them under sail just before dawn and finish this once and for all."

Being hanged was not the only thing she had been thinking about that morning.

They reached toward the southwest all day—like two boats owned by friends cruising in company—as the breeze built during the afternoon and then died after sunset. The farther they came from the Windward Passage, the fewer ships they saw, until *Lullaby* and *Noriecka* were as alone on the Caribbean as Columbus' ships had been. When the sea breeze died at sunset, they motored until about eight o'clock. Then, after a few tentative puffs, the land breeze filled in, and the two yachts jibed their mains, rehoisted their headsails and continued on over a sea as flat as Long Island Sound on an August afternoon.

Just after midnight, a quarter moon rose ahead of them and they could see *Noriecka* clearly in the silver path it lit on the water, so Stroud said, "Why don't you turn in, Lydia. They aren't going to give us the slip now, even if they turn their lights off."

She stepped over the bridge deck. "Maybe I will. Thanks, Bill. I'll plot our position and then sack out. Wake me when you get tired."

As the moon rose, it was intermittently obscured by the clouds that blew out to sea from the cooling land, and as the peaceful night wore on, Stroud alternately dozed and wondered what Alice Kettner would do next.

At about four, they were moving along quite nicely, beam reaching under the full main and the number one in the land breeze that had probably reached its maximum. This was *Norieka's* best point of sail, and *Lullaby* needed the big headsail to stay with her. Stroud dozed off for a few minutes and when he woke, a cloudbank obscured the moon and *Noriecka's* masthead running light had disappeared again. He reached into the coaming compartment for the binoculars, and then the moon reappeared and he saw the Cape Dory perhaps a hundred yards away. It was close-hauled and beating back toward them with someone standing on its plank bowsprit. He dropped the glasses, freed the tiller from the autopilot, and pushed it hard over, then turned to the engine controls. The engine started as the bow came through the eye of the wind, and as he freed one jib sheet and started to haul in the other, he heard a ripping noise and felt a sharp burning pain across his back, as if someone had hit him with a whip.

He ignored the pain as *Lullaby* came hard through the wind and he held the tiller amidships with his backside and hauled in the mainsail as the next burst stitched a line of holes across it. He was winching in the jib when he heard the next burst ricochet off the water and hit the transom.

But *Lullaby* was beginning to move now; she heeled down onto her lines and started to go to weather as if her life depended on it. It was then that he noticed Lydia standing with her head out of the hatch yelling something at him and he shouted, "Get down!" When he looked back toward the other boat, another burst of fire came from the person standing on *Noriecka's* bow, and the teak caprail on *Lullaby's* transom erupted in a cloud of splinters and his face felt as if it had been pepper sprayed.

Lydia thought Stroud would be dead in minutes. The back of his shirt and his shorts were soaked in blood. As she yelled at him, the gun fired again, and a line of holes stitched diagonally across the back of the cockpit from the lower corner to the rail above the tiller and she heard the scream of the ricocheting bullets. Then blessedly, the shooting stopped as the person on *Noriecka's* bow reloaded.

When Stroud turned back toward her, his face was covered with blood and he said, "Can't see." He pulled off his glasses, "Towel." He used it to wipe the blood out of his eyes. Then he said, "Thank God. My glasses saved my eyes."

"Are you hit?"

"By splinters. The worst wounds were always caused by splinters."

Alice wasn't going to waste this clip the way she had wasted the first one. If the fucking moon had only stayed behind the clouds for a minute or two longer, she would have been close enough to do the business with that first clip. But she must have hurt them badly. *Lullaby* was beating toward the beach, her tail between her legs, leaving the way open for her and Granny to run off into the sea where no one could find them again.

But she wasn't going to run off. She was going to stop that damn boat with this clip and then go aboard and finish it once and for all with the last one. But she wanted to be close enough this time so she could fire it into them and then board them through the smoke. She liked the sound of that. If they fucked with the Brethren of the Coast, then they should expect to be fired into and boarded through the smoke.

She needed to be closer, but that damned Hallberg under her engine and full sail was slicing to weather like a knife. She turned and yelled at Granny, "Get the engine started and pour it to her. All ahead flank. Get us close, damn it! I want to finish this before it gets light."

His back was really stinging now and he could feel his shirt, shorts, and the backs of his legs wet with blood. He was sitting on the cockpit sole facing aft, steering *Lullaby* as fast and as close to the wind as she would go while with his other hand he held a dishtowel to his forehead to keep the blood from running down into his eyes and blinding him. He had to lengthen the distance between the boats. He risked a peek over the stern and saw that *Lullaby* was working out to weather of the other boat as they both motorsailed as fast and as close to the wind as they could.

Noriecka was definitely not pointing as high as *Lullaby* and didn't appear to be going through the water any faster, even though the size of her bow wave gleaming white in the moonlight showed she was being pushed as fast as she could go. Thank God she couldn't point with *Lullaby*. They might escape yet another of the Holbrook woman's ambushes.

He risked another quick look. Yes, *Lullaby* was definitely pointing higher and going faster and had opened up a lead of several hundred yards.

Then the engine coughed once and stopped.

Even with the engine helping Noriecka's full main, jib, and staysail push her through the water, that damn Hallberg was still getting away. In order to keep the sails drawing, Granny had to steer a course farther off the wind than the other boat with her newer, flatter, and perfectly trimmed main and number one jib.

Then she noticed that *Noriecka* was suddenly footing faster than *Lullaby*—noticeably faster.

Stroud twisted the key and the engine cranked, but it did not even try to start; Lydia said, "It reeks of diesel fuel down here, Bill." She lifted the hatch in the cabin sole under the stairs. "The sump is full of it."

"Must have hit the tank. It's right behind the engine."

She stood on the ladder with the first-aid kit and all the dishtowels from the drawer under the sink. "You're bleeding to death. Take off your shirt." There was a ten-inch gash across the muscles of his back; an inch deeper and it would have hit his spine and paralyzed him. She said, "Bend forward" as she poured a bottle of hydrogen peroxide along the wound, then used a clean towel to wipe away the blood. There was something hard at one end, and when she squeezed it, a lead slug popped out and fell to the sole. Stroud asked, "What's that?" She was greatly relieved. She had been afraid the pain of what she had done would send him into shock.

"Bullet." She handed it to him. "Sit still while I bandage this. At least it's not bleeding quite as much."

"Good. Don't worry about it, then. Bandage my head so the damned blood will stop running down into my eyes. I have to be able to see. And what happened to my glasses?"

"They're here. They're covered with blood, too. You look redder than the first time I saw you. Hold still. There's a big splinter in your eyebrow." She yanked it out and then wrapped gauze around his head so he looked like the fifer in the *Spirit of 76*. As she rinsed his glasses in the sink, she continued, "That was the biggest one. I'll dig out the others later."

All this time he had been steering *Lullaby* as fast and as close to the wind as she could go while he sat on the cockpit sole. She wondered how he could do it. *Noriecka's* sails were visible on the starboard quarter as she slowly worked even with them, while sailing at a larger angle to the wind than they were.

"What happens now, Bill?"

"They're going to get past us, so they'll be sure they can head us off, then turn toward us and motor up close enough to finish us off. That looks like a nine-millimeter bullet: a pistol round. Not much stopping power at anything over fifty yards, and not very accurate at half that. That's why the kiddies all need guns that go ratatatat in order to hit anything. We'll tack when they turn. A stern chase is a long chase, but eventually they'll get close enough for that thing to be effective."

"Can't we get away?"

"Not in these conditions. Not while they've got an engine and we don't."

"What about the radio?"

"Even if we can raise someone, it will be all over by the time they get here."

She thought about it for a few seconds before she said, "We're going to have to kill them, aren't we?"

"I'll settle for just getting them to stop trying to kill us. I'll try to hold them off, but yes, we'll probably have to kill them."

"I'll get it."

Oh yes, they were footing considerably faster: definitely gaining. It was glorious standing out here on the bowsprit as *Noriecka* sliced through the small chop the land breeze had kicked up. She loved to sail fast at night. It was amazing how six knots could feel like a hundred miles an hour when you were out on the bow in the dark watching the water rush by.

Not that it was really dark now, with the moon shining intermittently through the clouds and the eastern sky starting to brighten. They were close enough now so she could see why *Noriecka* was footing so much faster. She must have hit their engine, because there was no prop wash under *Lullaby's* counter.

She searched all around the horizon. Good. No other vessels in sight. She called, "Anything on the radio, Granny?"

"Nothing. Just the occasional chatter between ships."

She wondered why they weren't putting out a Mayday, not that it would help them. Another couple of minutes or so and *Noriecka* would be far enough ahead to overcome *Lullaby's* advantage in weatherliness. Then they would turn, and in another twenty minutes it should be all over. When the new day dawned she would be free to go anywhere she chose and do anything she wanted.

Lydia put the three major subassemblies of the old M-1 on the bridge deck, and Stroud dropped the autopilot onto the tiller bracket, punched the button that told it to hold this course, and grinding his teeth to keep from screaming, twisted around so his hands, quite unaided by his mind and operating on reflexes conditioned forty years before, could put the barrel and action into the stock and then shove the trigger assembly into its cutout and snap the trigger guard in place.

He loaded one of the clips of black-tipped armor-piercing ammunition. The two clips he had used to sight the gun in were now loaded with soft-point sporting ammunition, and he pushed those to one side as Lydia asked, "Does that thing have more range than that machine gun? If you could hit their engine from here, we could outrun them under sail alone."

"Yeah. This thing has a lot more range and a lot more punch than a nine-millimeter: a whole lot more. But with both boats bouncing around, the best I'm going to be able to do is hit them and hope for the best." Then he said, "Come on and tack, you bastard. What are you waiting for?"

This should do it. Stroud would probably tack as soon as she did, but it wouldn't do him any good. *Noriecka* was far enough ahead now so they'd be able to sail a bit free for that last four or five hundred yards until they were close enough for twenty-four rounds of nine-millimeter to do the job. She yelled, "Take her about, Granny" as she ducked around the headstay to avoid the jib as it came over. As the bow came through the wind, *Lullaby* also tacked. A lot of good that would do them. Just another four or five hundred yards closer. She wanted to be within fifty feet when she gave them the next clip.

"Uh-oh. He's got a gun." She said it out loud. She could see Stroud's head over the transom as he pointed it at her. She had expected him to have a shotgun for sure, and maybe a revolver. Old guys liked shotguns and revolvers. He could shoot a shotgun at *Noriecka* all day at this range and not do any harm. By the time they got close enough for it to be effective, she would smother him with nine-millimeter.

Then all hell broke loose.

Lydia was still standing in the hatch when Stroud started to shoot—eight close-spaced but deliberate cracks followed by a *ting* as the clip was ejected. At each shot, the recoil rocked him backwards and the gash started to bleed again, so she leaned over the bridge deck and pushed a towel against his back to try to stop it. He dropped the butt, loaded another clip, and the cycle of eight closely and evenly spaced cracks followed by a *ting* was repeated. When she looked past him, the person on the bow had disappeared and *Noriecka* seemed to be slowing. She had no idea how many rounds he fired before he finally stopped, but the cockpit was littered with spent brass and clips, and she was afraid he would bleed to death if she didn't stop the flow.

When he finally put the rifle down he said, "That'll teach them to shoot at a .30-06 with a fucking pistol. I'm awful light-headed, Lydia." Then he said, "Damned blood's going to stain hell out of the teak" and toppled against the seat.

When *Noriecka*'s engine quit, she came head to wind and stopped dead in the water. Alice crawled aft dragging her right leg down the side deck opposite that madman and his cannon. Her knee had been destroyed by whatever it was that Stroud was shooting at them. Not that the deckhouse would stop the bullets from the damn thing. She could hear the rounds tearing down the length of the boat's interior an instant before the sound of the shot reached her. Raking shot. She remembered reading about raking shot in sea stories when she was a girl.

Her leg was really starting to hurt now. At first there had been a tremendous flash of pain and then it had gone numb. But now it really hurt and the pain was becoming worse every minute. But the shooting had stopped and that damned Hallberg was pulling away from them, still hard on the wind heading toward the coast of Haiti.

As she crawled around the dodger, she saw Evans lying face down across the wheel, his groin soaked in blood and a huge hole in his back. Her beautiful Granny. They had taken away her beautiful Granny.

She crawled below, dragging her ruined leg and her machine pistol, telling herself it wasn't over yet. Nobody could hurt the Princess Alice and get away with it. But it hurt so. She had never really known what pain was before, and never really believed it could happen to her. Pain had been something that only happened to things that weren't Alice Louise Kettner.

Lydia had rolled Stroud face down on the leeward cockpit seat and used butterfly bandages to pull the wound closed as well as she could, and then she had put several layers of gauze pads and bandage on it. Now she was trying to hold it all in place by wrapping adhesive tape completely around his chest. As she pushed the tape roll under him he groaned, then asked, "What hap . . . How long . . . " and started to sit up.

"Lie still or you'll start it bleeding again."

He sat up anyway. "I can't lie here for a month until I . . ." The pain stopped him.

His face was punctured in a dozen places by small wood splinters. "Jesus, Bill, your face . . . "

"It hurts worse than my back."

"Come below into the light, and I'll get them out."

"Later."

She handed him two pills. "I found these prescription codeine pills in the first-aid kit. They're long out of date, but take them anyway."

He tossed them over the side. "They'll make me sleepy. Give me four Tylenols instead."

"It will be a good thing if you sleep."

"I can't. This isn't over yet. Where's *Noriecka?* We can't just leave them drifting around."

"Bill, let's just get away from here."

"Lydia, for Christ's sake, listen to your Corsican blood for once. We have to finish this right here, or the misery and the killing will just go on and on."

They turned and ran down to where Noriecka lay with her sails listlessly flopping, looking as abandoned as the *Mary Celeste*. They crossed her stern a couple of hundred yards off, as Lydia studied her through the glasses. When Stroud tried to raise them to his eyes, the pain in his back became excruciating.

"She looks abandoned, Bill. I don't think either of them is still alive. You fired a lot of shots into them. My God, there are holes in the transom. The bullets from that thing must have come down the whole length of the boat and out the back." Then she said, "I never wanted it to come to this."

"Neither did I, Lydia. You have to believe that. But once the shooting starts . . ."

"Should we go alongside?"

"I don't know." Then he said, "Drop the jib. It'll make her a lot easier to maneuver and we don't need speed anymore. Just bunch it up and tie it to the lifelines. Then I think we should work our way in slowly. Dear Alice is really good at ambushes, remember." With his jaws locked, he slowly picked up the M-1 and loaded a clip of soft-nosed sporting ammunition. "If we don't draw fire, I'll go aboard forward of the mast." He put a couple of spare clips in his pocket.

When she came back into the cockpit she said, "I'll go aboard. I can shoot that thing if I have to."

"No. If it comes to that, you'll hesitate and Alice Kettner certainly won't." Then he forced himself to stand and said, as much to himself as to her, "I can do this, damn it."

Lydia tacked and then jibed *Lullaby* and then tacked again, as they spiraled in toward the other boat. This time they crossed close under *Noriecka*'s stern, and although it was rapidly getting lighter as the short tropical dawn broke, the light was wrong, so they could not see into her cabin. They tacked once more and came up on her forward quarter. As Stroud forced himself to climb over *Lullaby*'s lifelines and get ready to board, he thought that it was appropriate that this odyssey too should end in the rosy-fingered dawn. Thank God no other vessels were in sight.

When the boats touched none too gently he stepped across as Lydia bore off, and holding onto a shroud stood perfectly still, listening for as long as he dared. He wanted to give anyone who was lying in ambush time to panic and make a move, but even more, he wanted this business finished while the two boats were alone. When, after a few minutes, he had heard nothing other than the sounds of the boat drifting with its sails slatting in the light breeze, he worked his way aft to the mast, expecting a burst of fire through one of the deckhouse ports he had to pass. He lowered himself awkwardly to his knees on top of the deckhouse, and fighting the pain that flashed through his back from his heels to his scalp, looked through the partially open main cabin deck hatch into the darkened cabin and wished he had a grenade. He took the winch handle from its sock at the base of the mast and thought about dropping it through the hatch to see if it would draw fire, but discarded the idea when he realized that if it did, the shots would probably come up through the deck where he was kneeling.

He slipped the winch handle into his belt and crawled on elbows and knees aft to the life raft container bolted to the deck just forward of the dodger, then popped his head up and looked over it through the salt-encrusted plastic dodger window. He could just make out someone, a figure, sprawled over the wheel. He slowly lifted himself until he could see over the dodger and saw it was Evans sprawled there, literally shot to hell. A round must have ricocheted off the engine and come up through the cockpit sole spinning like a saw blade. Stroud thought, *Poor dumb bastard* and dropped back down behind the doubtful protection of the life-raft container.

Then he heard the slightest of sounds. He waited for what seemed a very long time before he heard it again. It sounded like someone shifting slightly somewhere below, aft of the companionway.

He studied the cockpit seats. The one to port had a locker hatch let into it, but the starboard side was solid. Then he said, "Mrs. Evans, Alice, it's over. I know you're down there. Toss out the gun and come out. I won't hurt you."

She answered in a little girl's voice. "I don't have any gun. Granny dropped it overboard when you shot him, and I can't come out. You hit me too; I think I'm paralyzed. Something hit me in the neck. I can't feel or move my arms or legs. I begged him not to shoot at you. I knew it was over. I wanted to go to Jamaica and give myself up. I'm so scared. Help me, please."

"What happened to the other guy, Gordon Holbrook or John Perkins? I can't come down there until I know where he is."

"He's dead. Granny came into that apartment we had in Florida and caught him hurting me, and making me do ugly, dirty things. Gordon loved to hurt me. Granny went crazy and hit him with a big old cast-iron frying pan again, and again, and again. I couldn't make him stop. Oh God, I caused so many people so much misery. Help me, Mr. Stroud. Please help me. I can't move and I'm so scared." It was heart-wrenching to hear her.

He said, "Lie still. I'm coming." But instead he leaned over the life-raft container and shook the dodger, then tossed the winch handle into the cockpit. A burst of fire came up through the companionway and riddled the back edge of the dodger.

He froze while the sound died away and a whiff of gunsmoke rose out of the hatch, then he said, "Damn it, stop this. It doesn't have to end with one or both of us dead. This can be straightened out." Although for the life of him he could not see how.

In a voice totally different from the scared child of a few seconds ago she said, "I don't know why I did that. What's wrong with me? How can we ever straighten this out? Too much has happened to me for it ever to be straightened out."

"Toss out the gun and we'll find some way. I promise you."

"Oh God, I want this straightened out so badly, Mr. Stroud. But I've helped to cause so much misery. All I want is to put it all behind me, pay for what I was forced to do, and then move on. Maybe we can straighten this out. Maybe we all—me, you, Miss Polizzi—maybe we can all find closure somehow. I think I know a way. There's a lot of money in Gordon's accounts in the Caymans and I have the numbers. All I need is enough so I can get a start somewhere: Africa, maybe. I take responsibility for what I did, even though I didn't want to do any of it. You have you believe me."

She paused to let that sink in, and then continued, "I want to finish my nursing degree. I was in my junior year when I met Gordon. That's all I want. Enough to finish my nursing degree so I can make up for at least some of the misery I've helped cause. You and Miss Polizzi can have the rest. It won't compensate for what Gordon did to your families, but believe me when I say I really didn't want to help him. There was just nothing else I could do. When Granny killed him, it was the first time in years I wasn't totally terrified every moment of every day. And now poor Granny is dead, too. I could work for a million years and not make up for the misery I helped cause. But give me a chance to try, please, Mr. Stroud."

"Alice, that's complete bullshit and you know it. You were never anywhere near any nursing school. You were in secretarial school when you recruited Gordon to kill your cousins. I talked to your Uncle Peter. Now toss out the goddamn gun."

She was silent for a moment, then became yet another person. "Oh yes. Uncle Peter, who used to come sneaking into my bedroom when I was a little girl." Then another burst erupted through the deck and the life-raft container a foot in front of his face. When he reflexively pulled back, he dropped the butt of the ten-pound rifle to the deck and the pain of the sudden movement made him grunt. She called, "Hey Stroud, you still with us?"

He crawled back to the mast, stood, and locked the butt of the rifle against his hip with his elbow—the close-assault position, they had called it in basic training all those years ago—and pointed it down into the cockpit. It was not hard to fill his voice full of pain as he said, "Oh God, it hurts . . . You hurt me. Why did you . . ."

"You sound like your daughter, Stroud. I only wish Gordon was here so I could feed Polizzi to him the way I fed your Nellie to him. Now there was a moaner. He had her in the forecabin and with the boat totally closed up, even sitting in the back of the cockpit with a radio playing, I could hear her moaning while he played with her. She had all those college degrees, but to Gordon she was just another toy. Smart-assed bitch."

A series of pictures flashed through his mind then, infinitely faster than he had originally seen them on the VCR's fast-forward, and he fired all eight rounds through the cockpit seat and bulkhead into the quarter berth. The spring clip and most of the brass were still in the air when the bolt slammed closed on the next clip. Totally ignoring his pain and his age, and moving like a twenty-year-old infantryman, he jumped around the dodger onto the bridge deck and then leaped down the hatch, the rifle ready to kill anything that moved. Afterwards he could not believe he had done it and wondered if it was adrenaline, or if perhaps a twenty-year-old marine had helped him to do it.

He found her body where he expected, crumpled under the gear piled in the quarter berth. Even though she had not been hit in the head, her face had been pushed grotesquely out of shape by the shock waves generated by the bullets plowing through her body with almost three thousand foot-pounds of energy.

He laid the rifle on the galley counter and stood with his back to the stove, looking across the boat at her while tears streamed down his cheeks. Finally, moving like a very old man, he shuffled across the cabin, gently closed her eyes, and said, "Another father's beloved daughter . . . This defective, accursed species of ours . . ."

Polizzi and Stroud were silent for a long time after *Noriecka*—or whatever her real name was—began her 2,300-fathom fall to the bottom of the Colombian Basin, a Lockford Yacht Club burgee still flying from her masthead.

"Bill, are you going to be able to deal with this?"

"I tried to talk her out of it, Lydia. But I couldn't communicate with her. It was like talking back at a TV screen, like there was really no one there. I don't think there really was an Alice Kettner. Does that make sense? She was just a collection of roles she played to get people to do what she wanted, and at the end, when she was desperate, she just kept trying different roles on me, one after the other, hoping to find something that would make me move into a position where she could kill me. I'll never get over it, but yes, I can deal with it. What about you? Can you deal with it?"

"I watched you crouching on that cabin top talking for what seemed like hours while she periodically shot at you. When you finally opened up on her, I didn't feel anything but relief. I feel a lot worse about Evans. He was dead when you went aboard? You couldn't help him?"

"I must have hit him from here."

"Do you think he really understood any of this?"

"No. I think he understood whatever she wanted him to understand. Stupidity may not be a capital crime ashore, but it almost always is at sea."

After a pause, she said, "I'd better get those splinters out of your face before they get infected. Thank God they're small."

"Thank God she was shooting that kiddy cannon from too far away. It only threw small splinters."

When she had finished, his face was covered with spots of disinfectant as though he had some awful disease. She said, "I guess I'd better get us under way. Which way, Bill?"

"Our best course is probably to beat up through the Windward Passage again, and then bear off toward Miami. It's only a little over 600 miles, and even if we don't push as hard as we did getting here, it should only be a week at most. But I'm afraid you'll have to do most of the heaving and hauling—for the first few days, at least."

"That's fine. That's what I want to do. Just don't start your back bleeding again. What about the mainsail?"

He looked up at the two lines of holes running across it and said, "Tear along dotted lines. We'll have to change it. Alice Kettner was sure hard on poor *Lullaby*'s mainsails, wasn't she?" He kicked the two Jerry cans of diesel fuel standing in the back of the cockpit under the tiller that he had salvaged from *Noriecka*. "We'll have to rig up some way to pipe this directly from the cans to the engine. Shouldn't be all that hard. We'll use the fuel hose from the dink's outboard. This should be enough to keep the batteries up until we get to Miami."

"What about the fuel in the sump? The cabin stinks from it."

"Pump it overboard."

"Isn't that illegal?"

"Still the politically correct, environmentally aware baby boomer. Like we haven't broken any other laws this morning."

When *Lullaby* was broad-reaching back toward the Windward Passage in the rising sea breeze under her spare main and number three, Lydia put two oversized mugs of soup, a package of crackers, and a couple of spoons on the bridge deck, climbed into the cockpit, and said, "When we finish eating, you ought to get some rest before we get back onto I-95." She handed him a mug, took the other herself, and sat down beside him on the weather side of the cockpit.

"As long as it stays like this, I'd rather rest here than have to climb up and down that ladder."

"Just so you rest. Can you handle that cup?"

"I'll manage."

"Bill, what about the mystery man? Do you have any idea what became of him?"

"She said Evans killed him."

"Do you believe her?"

"I don't think so. She called him Gordon, but who knows what his name really was. He wasn't aboard, but I searched the boat pretty thoroughly before I cut the raw water and scupper hoses, and up in the forepeak, stuck in the corner of the chain locker, I found a Ziploc bag with some jewelry, some dirty pictures, and an old wallet. The wallet had an expired driver's license for an Emil Slack, a couple of hundred bucks, a picture of a woman and a young boy obviously taken years ago, and a rosary. There was a gold waist chain with some other jewelry: bracelets, anklets, things like that. None of it looked like anything the woman in the picture would have owned. The buckle on the waist chain was engraved 'to Mo from Seth' with last Christmas' date. Probably souvenirs."

"Do you think Mo and Seth were *Noriecka's* real owners?"

"Probably. There's nothing we can do to help them now, though, except let them eventually be declared lost at sea. The picture of Emil Slack on the license was our mystery man: same big sloping shoulders and narrow head. The boy in the picture with the woman could have been him, too. Alice said Evans beat him to death with a frying pan in the apartment in Jupiter. But that can't be true. Emil was on that boat, hid all his little personal treasures, and left without taking them with him."

"You think he's with the fishes, too?"

"Yeah. She probably killed him. Evans didn't have the balls to kill someone at long range with an automatic weapon. That's why he was steering and she was doing the shooting. He could never kill someone up close—with a frying pan, yet. There was quite a roll of cash in a bag with some knitting stuff, too."

"What did you do with it?"

"It's below. I left everything else. You can have it. With the planes and all, you had more expenses than I did."

"No. I don't want it either. Not that money."

"How about an anonymous gift to the hospice?"

"Fine with me. Have you thought about what we're going to tell them in Miami when they see the bullet holes in the boat and in you?"

"One more lie, then we can go back to telling the truth for the rest of our lives. A rusty trawler came up on us when we were in the Old Bahamas Channel a couple of days from now, and when we refused to heave to, they shot at us with a machine gun. But when I gave them a clip from my trusty old M-1, they turned away and were not seen again."

"Wouldn't we have tried to call someone on the radio?"

"We did, but the antenna jack at the base of the mast was busted.

I'll break it in the morning. I'll dummy up the log, too. We never went into the Windward Passage, Lydia. We sailed directly from St. Martin to Miami."

"Bill, should we have tried to radio for help?"

"Help wouldn't have gotten here in time, even if we had called. I don't think it was much over fifteen minutes from the time they first shot at us until I had to shoot at them." Then he was silent for a moment before he said, "But we'll never really know if that's the real reason, will we?"

She thought about it as she stirred the vegetables in the bottom of her cup, then she changed the subject.

"What are you going to do after Miami, Bill? Have you thought about it?"

"Yeah. You know, I've thought about Peter Kettner a lot. He's doing a lot better job of playing the cards he's been dealt than I was doing, playing mine. This is a really good boat, Lydia. The best one I've ever owned, and I'm not old enough to give her up yet. It says Beards Corners, Connecticut on her transom; I think I'll take her home. Then I'll sail her in the summer and work on her in the winter—unless I take her south again. And I'll never watch a minute of daytime TV again. What are you going to do?"

"I don't know. They've probably filled my job at the bank by now. Their human resource policies are not very compassionate." She gave a little laugh. "I ought to know: I wrote most of them. I've got plenty of money. I don't really have to work."

"How old are you?"

She laughed again, "You really are a smoothie, Stroud. What a question to ask a lady who is, as the French say, of a certain age. I'll be forty-nine on the eleventh of September."

"Nell would have been forty-two next month." He ate a spoonful of soup and then said, "You ought to get a job, Lydia. Anyone who's forty-nine and doesn't have a job is a bum, no matter how much money they have. And bums always find ways to make themselves and everyone around them miserable. Especially bums with lots of money."

"You sound exactly like my father."

"I suppose I do. Somebody should."

They both stared off at the horizon in silence for a quite a while, watching the first of what they knew would be a steady stream of ships cross their path. Then she put her hand on top of his on the seat and gently squeezed it just once. "Okay, I'll get a job, if it will make you happy. But be warned. I'm going to check on you and make sure you're eating right, staying active, and not watching daytime TV. And if the job goes well, I'll probably call you up and brag about it."

"Once in a while, if you can get a few days off, I might even take you sailing. Do you ski?"

She stood up, picked up the cups, spoons, and the wrapper from the crackers, and then said, "There's another steamer. One of us better catch a couple of hours sleep if we're both going to have to be on watch all night."

"Catch some zees, Lydia. I'll take the first watch. I'd rather sit here than climb up and down that ladder."

"Are you sure you're all right?"

"It may seem strange, but I think I'm better than I've been in a very long time."

NEVIS, 20 March 2003